Your David, My Dave

The Sunshine in our Lives

By Antonia K. Lewis

"Absence makes the heart grow fonder."

"No, no, no! In my experience, absence weakens the bond until it eventually severs and leaves you slowly withering and dying inside."

Suzanne White – 2014

"If you love something, set it free. If it comes back, it's yours. If it doesn't, it never was."

"What an absolute crock."

Louise Stewart – 2014

"You couldn't make this s**t up."

Kirsty Noble - 2014

Chapter 1

LOUISE

Saturday, 18th October 2014

"Three, two, one….SURPRISE!"

The sizeable group of gathered family and friends erupted into raucous cheers and simultaneously clapped their hands - like a herd of manic seals, noisily flapping their flippers together - as we entered the crowded bar area and a startled David took stock of the assembled motley crew of relatives and pals brought together to celebrate his birthday in style.

"Oh my good god! I thought we were having a sedate, quiet drink to celebrate; just the two of us!" David's eyes darted around the room, taking in the 'Birthday Boy' banners and multi-coloured balloons, whilst registering the party food laid out on foil-covered platters on the side table.

"Did you organise all of this, you wonderful, crazy woman?"

"Of course I did, you wonderful, crazy man. With the help of the multi-talented Kirsty Noble of course, who made every one of those cheese and ham sandwiches by the way, so I would probably avoid them like the plague, if I were you."

Kirsty may be my lovely, faithful bestest friend in the whole wide world…but Masterchef she was not.

"Happy birthday son! Twenty-one again eh?" David's mum, a vision in cerise pink, appeared right in front of him and leant in to envelop him in a massive mum-entitled bear hug, while he laughed loudly and reciprocated by squeezing her back. "Now, isn't this a fabulous surprise? So thoughtful of Louise when she has so much on her plate anyway. I hope you enjoy this little shindig that's been organised son. And it's the perfect time for me to let you know Dave - because I know I don't tell you enough - you make me so, so very proud every single day, and you deserve this night more than anyone, you really do."

"Oh come on Barb you big softy, out of the way! Let someone else get a look in!" David's amiable dad gave his wife a gentle nudge and eased her slightly to one side, although she seemed reluctant to let go of her grip on her number one son.

"Happy birthday lad, many happy returns and all that!" Not so sentimental, but said with genuine feeling.

"Thanks mum, thanks dad. I'm totally and utterly gobsmacked that Lou has managed to arrange all of this on the sly…I really had no idea! But I'm so glad you're all here; I've not seen much of you lately, with everything that's been happening, and I'm conscious that I've been a bit of a stranger…"

"Dave, or should we call you David now? No? That name still only reserved for Louise, is it? Oh, okay, okay, message received - over and out. Your father and I completely understand your situation and are just so relieved to finally see you as happy and settled as you are with this lovely young lady here." Barbara turned to hug me tightly then, squashing me into her more than ample boobs, whilst stage-whispering into my ear, "Thank you for looking after him and putting that radiant smile back on his face. I'm so pleased you teenage sweethearts finally got together again."

Oh lord, it wasn't yet eight o'clock, I'd not even had one single drop of alcohol, and I could already feel myself becoming all misty-eyed and emotional. God help me when I was three-sheets-to-the-wind in a couple of hours. They really were a lovely couple, David's parents, and in a fairly short space of time I had become unbelievably fond of them. I sensed the feeling was entirely mutual and was beyond grateful that they had welcomed me into their tight family unit with open arms; not just me, but my daughter and my mother and my best friend – despite her potty mouth, and the drinking and smoking.

Next in line was the said best friend, Kirsty, with her adorable boyfriend Nathan tagging along behind her, precariously carrying a tray of drinks, doing as he was told, as always.

"Congratulations Dishy David! Come here and give me a big fat snog!" At a guess, I would say that Kirsty was probably on about her fifth or sixth alcoholic drink of the evening and had probably knocked a couple of those back whilst slapping on her warpaint at home earlier. Nathan, having finished work only an hour ago and dashed straight here from Bolton, was some way behind Kirsty in the drinking stakes…but my experience of a tanked up Kirsty meant that I *really* hoped he had a bucket and some super-strength headache pills ready for the next morning, when Kirsty would be dying a painful death, probably face down on the settee, cursing everyone who had let her knock back the vodka shots the night before.

"Put him down Kirsty, you don't know where he's been!" A relaxed Nathan was shaking his head and laughing at his very merry girlfriend; he was used to her by now and they were supremely confident in their relationship – each knew how the other felt and there was no jealousy festering away and no doubts there at all. He had also got on like a house on fire with David on the few occasions we had managed to go out as a foursome and they had exchanged stories about nightmare customers they had experienced and troublesome cars they had owned.

"All the best mate, cheers pal!" said Nathan as he handed David a pint of dry cider and even managed to avoid spilling a single drop down David's best Next shirt as Kirsty went over on her heels and wobbled into him, none too steady on those trotters of hers encased in my best diamante shoes.

David turned to me, smiling his still-as-sexy-as-when-he-was-seventeen-smile. The novelty hadn't yet worn off; I fully expected it to never wear off. When you've been separated from the love of your life for thirty years it really makes you appreciate them that bit more.

"You do realise this isn't a big celebration birthday for me, don't you? You haven't miscalculated, have you? I mean, I may look fifty these days, possibly sixty, but I have actually only turned forty-eight today!"

He curled his free hand around my waist and drew me closer to his body and I basked in his warmth; so proud that this magnificent man was finally all mine.

"I know, I know…but it's the first ever birthday of yours when I have been by your side and I wanted to make 'a thing' of it for you; to somehow mark the occasion – to do something special for you, to show you how much I love you, Mr David White, boy of my erotic teenage dreams; man of the rest of my wonderful life."

"Ah you're just amazing, you are. It's a wonderful surprise to have everybody here with us tonight…everyone who's important to us…although I *do* know how much you love me, because it's nearly as much as I love you."

"More than lager?"

"Of course. More than chocolate?"

"Of course. More than cider?"

"Of course. More than George Michael?"

"Aw now you know that one's not fair - that's just playing dirty!" I jokingly prodded him in his taut stomach and he clutched it, staggering backwards slightly and pretending to be in agony.

He took my hand in his then and squeezed it tightly and we had a moment; a few seconds when the whole room, the whole world was excluded and we were as one. A look passed between us, of all-encompassing love, of pure pleasure, of the promise of what was to come later when we were alone.

Eventually the moment was broken by the sound of Kirsty's cackling laughter in the small but loud group that had formed next to us - friends of ours who were chatting, drinking and enjoying the evening and the company.

I breathed in the hint of David's aftershave that was in the air as he moved closer still and took me into his arms.

"Now about that 'playing dirty' you mentioned...can I book you in for a slot later this evening – say, half an hour after Last Orders - as I really, REALLY fancy a stab at this dirty play you speak of..."

God, he made my heart race and bits of me pounded that I didn't know were even capable of pounding.

"I'm available whenever you want me...as long as you do that flicking thing with your tongue again..."

"Oy, oy, what's going on here then?" A familiar voice interrupted our rapidly heating up conversation.

"Billy! I can't believe you and Jenny are here as well! I never thought I'd see the day when the pair of you made it out of deepest darkest Cornwall..." I could tell David was chuffed to bits to see that his best buddy had made the hellish journey from Newquay to join us, accompanied by his fun-loving wife.

"Dickhead! I feel like I need my passport stamping coming up here, it's like entering a different world. Had to ask the woman in the pie shop to repeat herself three times before I could understand a bleedin' word yesterday."

"She probably said we don't accept weird little plonkers in this shop, you knob!"

"Ah, you two have such a lovely way of addressing each other, don't you?" I intercepted and then was almost knocked flat on my arse on the floor as Jenny descended upon me, throwing her arms around me as if she'd not seen me for twenty years or more.

"LOUISE! It's been far too long! At least a fortnight! Come here you gorgeous girly and tell me exactly what you're doing that puts a smile like that on that handsome face of Dave's? You're clearly doing something right, he's like a dog with two dicks these days!"

"JENNY! Meet Kirsty! You two are like twins separated at birth I'm telling you, definitely on the same wavelength; same taste in humour, same sweary vocabulary..."

The two ladies happily exchanged slurred greetings and almost immediately launched into an x-rated conversation about the failings of men and the joys of sex, so I knew I could leave them to it.

I glanced around the room, searching for my elusive daughter – aah, there Chloe was in a tight, black, cropped top and the shortest tartan skirt I'd ever laid eyes on – not an ounce of fat on her flawless, lean body, and yet propping up the buffet table eating all of the ready-salted crisps before anyone else could get their mitts on them. She was still only fifteen though. Wait till she got to almost fifty and couldn't even sniff a crisp without putting on a pound.

I gave her a cheery wave and she responded with a silly pulled goon face just as she was joined by her lovely, still-on-the-scene boyfriend, Josh. It's a good job I liked him because he appeared to have become a permanent fixture around the house and their relationship seemed relatively serious. On the one hand I was glad there wasn't a steady stream of unsuitable boyfriends trailing through our home, but on the other hand I was slightly concerned that she was too young to be settling down, if that's what this was. We would see.

David's parents had now eased themselves back down onto the slightly torn, dubiously stained, velour corner seating, and were chatting away to my mum, who was thoroughly enjoying their company, but who was probably cheerily relaying such classic embarrassing tales as me wetting my voluminous orange knickers on my first day at nursery but refusing to take them off. Eugh. I shuddered to think what shameful secrets she was divulging to all and sundry.

Over by the window was David's younger brother Mark, who had matured nicely into a slightly less good-looking version of David and was now a really lovely man – not the little bastard he once was, likely to stick a crab in your beachbag or jump out from behind bushes to pretend to shoot you dead with a plastic toy gun – and thereby scare the living crap out of you. No, now he was a decent guy with a good job and he was accompanied tonight by his pretty girlfriend Amelia, who was a receptionist at the Ocean Bay Hotel in St Ives, where Mark had recently achieved head-chef status and was apparently earning mega-bucks. He always looked a teensy bit pale-skinned – I don't think he escaped from that chaotic kitchen very often and saw daylight, but he thoroughly loved his job and I was looking forward to him cooking a promised meal for our little family…although I would have to start hinting about how much I adored fish and chips or a really cheesy lasagne…I didn't want to risk him whipping up a risotto (yack) or, god forbid, something really nutritious and healthy.

Installed at the next table along were my older sister Sarah, in her one sparkly, clingy black dress that she dug out year after year for every night out, and her quiet but pleasant husband Justin who, I predicted, would only be staying for "an hour" as he was always "mad busy" with work. Wherever he went, whatever the occasion, he only stayed for "an hour". That was his thing. Bloody good escape plan if you ask me, having suffered some of our long drawn-out family celebrations when it seemed like the world would end before the frigging party would. They were accompanied by their daughter, Rachel, but not by their son, Thomas, who had supplied well-thought-through excuses practically before the invitation had even been issued – like father, like son me thinks.

Sarah actually quite liked it when Justin disappeared – he wasn't exactly a raving party animal so people tended not to notice that he was even missing from the proceedings. He didn't mingle much and I've never, ever seen him dance – not even at their wedding. Whereas Sarah was always the first one up on the dancefloor and I was quietly confident that in a couple of hours time she would be dancing 'Gangham Style' to every single tune that came on – her dress having ridden up to provide everyone with a clear view of her arse in her black tights every time she bent over…boobs jiggling, thighs wiggling, hair swinging about. Those alcopops she knocked back had a lot to answer for, but, god love her, she didn't get out much, so I just let her be.

To my surprise my brother Neil had turned up, dragged along, I suspect, by his ever-loving girlfriend Clare. I still couldn't believe he hadn't made an honest woman of her yet after all their years together but, there you go, marriage isn't for everyone and my own views were probably outdated. To be fair, I'd done the whole marriage shebang and look how it had worked out for me! I'd picked a bloody corker! I was much happier, divorced, in control and with the love of a good man - no, the *best* man- rather than married to a dickhead like my ex, Richard, who couldn't keep *it* in his skin tight jeans.

Neil was casually hovering near the door, itching to escape, but I didn't think that was truthfully an option for him. Clare definitely wore the trousers in that relationship - in fact she was wearing a very fetching, most likely from Debenhams, navy blue trouser suit tonight that looked fantastic on her but would have shown off my every bump and bulge. And she had forced Neil into a shirt and his best jeans so I think she was planning on staying for the whole evening, whether he liked it or not. I wouldn't bother attempting to speak to Neil until he had a few more sherberts down him. Trying to make conversation with him was like drawing teeth...slow and painful. He mellowed a little with a few pints of alcohol sloshing around inside of him so I would try my luck then.

Ali, Mikita, Dawn and Ashanti – friends of Kirsty's who had become equally firm friends of mine after we'd shared stories of dubious parenting and poor, inadequate sex over a week's worth of alcohol units in one messy night, some years earlier – were, of course, propping up the bar. They had already started knocking back the shots, which didn't bode well for later. I had offered for them to bring their partners and/or children but had been met with a unanimous response of "Fuck off, god no! Why would we do that?"

Propping up the other end of the bar were a couple of David's friends from Newquay, and I was made up that they had travelled all the way up here for his big night. They definitely wanted to raise a glass to David on his birthday I'm sure, but, and I might be a little bit cynical here, I'm bloody sure they were here on the sniff as well – Tariq was married, but may as well not have been for all the notice he took of his vows, and Adam was recently divorced and back in the game. They had better stay away from my married friends, Ali and Mikita – I would safely direct them towards some of the other female punters in the rear bar area later; I didn't want to be partially responsible for any extra-marital rumpy pumpy taking place and have to deal with the fallout.

As soon as David spotted his mates, he was over there like a shot and there was a lot of back slapping and mickey-taking, as was par for the course with them all. Red in the face and sweating a little, probably at the thought of spending his recent lottery winnings (£46.90), Billy joined them with another round of pints and no doubt a recently acquired dirty - bordering on filthy - poor-taste joke, as they were soon all laughing loudly, spilling their pints on their shoes without even noticing.

I sighed, contentedly, satisfied that everyone was having a wonderful time and, most importantly, David was happy. I glanced over at him again and he immediately turned and caught my eye and I was rewarded with his cheeky wink. Even at opposite ends of the room it's like we were completely in sync with each other, knowing when the other was about to make eye contact, feeling everything the other one was feeling. Dare I say it, soulmates.

The evening was a roaring success. Being a Saturday night, there was already a cheesy DJ and the obligatory karaoke booked to entertain the usual pub customers, and it wasn't long before Kirsty and the girls were up belting out such classics as 'I will survive' and '9 to 5'. There was also a shouty rendition of 'Mr Brightside' from all of the lads in the room, accompanied by the majority of the other pub-goers, which near-on deafened my poor old mother and almost rattled the steamed-up windows out of their weather-worn frames.

I didn't usually partake in much karaoke until I was about eight-drinks-in but Kirsty sneakily gave my name in to the DJ, who bore more than a passing resemblance to Alan Partridge, and before I knew it I heard, "And next up guys and gals, we've got a young lady called Louise? Where's Louise then? She's not in the toilets again, is she? Ah, there you are - come on down love! Louise will be singing 'I'm your man' for us tonight...bit of classic Wham! to entertain you all..."

David cringed and shook his head in mock despair...he knew I couldn't sing for toffee and had heard me warbling on in the bath many a time now to a George Michael tune. He was laughing though and eventually cupped his hands together around his mouth and yelled "Go on girl! Show them how it's done!"

It really was a brilliant evening, with everyone laughing, *drinking*, chatting, *drinking*, dancing, *drinking*...you get the picture. And David was beaming all night long, often drifting off from his friends and family to touch base with me - to take my hand or cuddle me; to kiss me gently or nuzzle my neck and tell me what he was planning to do to me later (unlikely after consuming approximately ten pints, but a girl could live in hope).

It was another amazing memory to add to the collection I was amassing – along with those precious ones from when we were sweet seventeen, when we met for the first time and fell hopelessly in love…strolling the tourist-choked streets of Newquay hand in hand, splashing around in the waves of the Atlantic ocean, rolling around in the golden sand exploring each other's young bodies and wishing the days and nights would last forever.

And there were the more recent memories to cherish, from when I had nervously looked him up and Kirsty had eventually found him some thirty years later - when we had clung on to one another never wanting to let go, when we had made beautiful love for the very first time and realised what divine pleasure we had been missing out on all of these years.

What a spectacular photo album we had created, all of those snapshots of our perfect days and nights together; an everlasting record of a love that lasted a lifetime – a love that nothing and no one could ever take away or destroy.

"I love you David White," I said as he stood in front of me now, his blue eyes sparkling and his silvery grey hair glittering in the darkly lit room. "Please don't ever stop loving me; please say that you will love me always and forever, here on earth, and wherever our spirits may ping off to in the next life."

Wow. I don't know where that came from, and if I'd heard it spill out of someone else's mouth I realised, to my shame, that I probably would have laughed and mocked them, but it was heartfelt and I needed him to know.

"And I love you, my beautiful Louise. It's always been you, only you, my heart was only ever destined to be yours. Always, forever, until the end of time. I don't deserve you but you don't know how happy it makes me - the knowledge that you love me right back, and nothing could ever change the way I feel about you. As I used to write in the sand on Towan Beach – "David luvs Lou 4 eva."

"Always My David."

"Always My Louise."

Chapter 2

SUZANNE

There was a definite date and, in fact, a precise moment when I realised I wasn't bearing up so well.

It was the 18th of October. It was Dave's birthday.

I hadn't had anyone over to the house in a long time – had declined all offers of company; had made excuses as to why I wasn't open for visitors.

I had visited my parents at their home on a reasonably regular basis and had lunched with friends in town - providing excuses so that no one was tempted just to call on me on spec.

Once you've put those well-meaning friends off several times; once you've withdrawn from them sufficiently, then the message seems to get through and they begin to leave you alone. You see, I don't have a really close mate to look out for me and share the best and worst of times with.

And I don't have the friendship and comradeship of "mums from school" as most women of my age do – when you don't have the children you don't do the school runs or the parents' evenings or the assemblies. I don't get to gossip at the school gates about milestones and achievements and, on the flip side, poor sleeping habits and naughty behaviour. I've never had that privilege.

I was quite nervous and withdrawn at school; a quiet little soul really throughout my formative years, music eventually bringing me out of my shell. Singing lessons followed piano lessons and I was often complimented on my voice for being pitch perfect and a joy to listen to. Rather than take on a 9-5 job locally or head off to college to gain further qualifications, I knew from a very young age that I wanted to sing my heart out for a living.

My confidence grew as I matured and I kicked off my singing career by offering my services for free at charity events, before dad took the plunge and invested in some higher end equipment for me. Once word got out, I was offered permanent paid contracts, singing at least five nights a week throughout the summer season at the more upmarket hotels dotted around the town, and occasionally even slipping in the odd matinee performance as well.

On the whole I thoroughly enjoyed it – entertaining became my life and I was perfectly happy belting out Jennifer Rush's 'Power of love' night after night to intoxicated holidaymakers. In fact that particular tune even became my wedding song...

With the exception of post-performance drinks with a few of the other staff and customers at some of the venues, I didn't have a great deal of time to socialise or get too close to anyone – but I think I honestly preferred it that way. I hadn't really missed that close bond with a female friend – I still had mum, and dad...and later Dave, and that was enough.

So, no one came to the house to check on me, to see if I was okay, and eventually Charlotte and Trudy and the other ladies I lunched with faded away and let me be. Peace and quiet at last.

I was relieved when mum and dad eventually departed on their annual month-long jaunt to Aunt Irene's villa in Portugal, because it meant I wouldn't have to keep plastering on make-up and a fake smile when I drove over to visit them every few days, in an attempt to prove that I was fine and moving on with my life. When everything fell apart and Dave left, mum had offered to postpone their holiday but I had insisted they go, re-assuring them time and time again that I really was coping and absolutely wasn't about to go under.

So, despite mum's fretting and dad's ever-increasing worry lines etched on his face, they departed for the sunshine and golden beaches of Portugal and we communicated by short text messages.

More comfortable by myself, not having to listen to other people's mind-numbing smalltalk while in my head thinking, "Shut up, shut up, shut up!", I stayed at home where I could remain in my pyjamas and listen to music and *sleep* – god knows, I was so exhausted these days – if I had slept for a month it wouldn't have been anywhere near enough to re-fuel me.

In my waking hours my brain seemed to be stuck on one continuous loop, torturing me over and over by replaying my memories of the last twenty-four years, starting with that fateful summer night in 1990, back where and when it all began for me and Dave.

"I seem to be getting a lot of feedback Stu – could you adjust your microphone a smidge for me please?"

"Well, m'lady, seeing as you asked nicely, I will do just that! Any better?"

"Much...I think someone must have been fiddling around with your equipment as I don't usually have these problems here."

"Mmmm...I am going to resist the temptation to pass some smutty comment about fiddling around with my equipment because I know that would make you blush like a baboon's bum and set your pulse racing! I'm guessing there's still no chance of me taking you out for a hot date to a luxurious Spud-u-like any time this century then?"

"Not in your wildest dreams darling...now, I need to go and beautify myself before the hordes of drunken tourists descend upon us...one of whom I am sure will take you up on your more than generous offer of an overdone, overpriced baked potato....you really do know how to push the boat out, don't you?"

"No expense spared with your little Stuey! What can I say? I'm a generous guy!"

Smiling to myself, I disappeared backstage into my tiny dressing room/glorified storage cupboard for a mug of strong tea - Stu was a character alright – a flirt and a practised charmer; the original lovable rogue. The first year I had appeared at the Towan Reach he had asked me out on a date, on average, once every week. Eventually, having been turned down, on average, once every week, he had succumbed to the attentions of the man-hungry, sun-kissed female holidaymakers and now had a steady stream of girlfriends throughout the summer season, who were usually to be found sobbing into their Bacardi and cokes on the last night of their holiday.

It wasn't that I didn't like Stu - I even found him quite attractive, with his floppy fringe and cute little dimples. But he was more like a brother than a potential love interest. I'd been on several dates with local men and even a few tourists; had a couple of relationships that had lasted seven weeks, and six months respectively, but I'd never been smitten with anyone - certainly never fallen in love. It would be amazing to meet that someone who had that certain 'quality', that special something that other men didn't have. I wasn't sure what that quality was yet, couldn't actually identify what exactly it was I was searching for, but I knew I was holding out for it and wasn't content satisfying for anything less.

When I met Antonio, he of the six month relationship, everyone else seemed to think he was "the one". With his exotic dark, swarthy Italian looks and his ridiculously well-paid job – general manager of the most modern, most luxurious hotel in Newquay – he had a certain presence – a confidence that you don't get from working on the buses or being merely blessed with average looks. But I knew, from the outset, that he wasn't going to be "the one". I couldn't put my finger on it – he was gorgeous, generous, attentive and loaded – on paper he was perfect, but I quickly realised that I couldn't see a long-term future with him. Maybe he was just a trifle too perfect – not rugged enough, too polished. I wanted someone who would instantly take my breath away; I longed for that moment when I would just know that I had found that mysterious something and someone I had been looking for all of my life.

Ah well, I was still relatively young and still had plenty of time to fall in love.

Draining the last of my tea, I double-checked that the door was firmly locked before changing into my dress for the early set. I always wore something long and slinky for my first appearance on stage, when people were still sluggishly returning from their evening meals, when the dining room was still emptying out. Not too many sequins but something a little classier than could be purchased at the likes of Top Shop or Dorothy Perkins. I tended to buy most of my stage clothes from an exclusive boutique in Truro; to invest in some quality pieces at the beginning of the season that would see me through until the end. This particular number was a Hattie Betona original in deep lilac that was one of my favourites. It clung to my figure and gave me confidence, and I set it off with a single large amethyst ring and matching necklace.

I diligently applied my make-up with a practised hand, knowing that I needed more on stage under the unforgiving harsh lights than I would ever chose to wear in daylight hours. Using the curling tongs to add a few subtle waves to my long, golden hair, I looked critically in the mirror. Ah, that was better. Not long till show-time now.

I completed all the necessaries in the bathroom, listening to Charlie, the compère, warm up the crowd for the evening. A few titters from the audience (they would be a lot more raucous by the end of the night), the clattering of empty plates being cleared and returned to the frantic kitchen, a telephone ringing in the distance. I knew when I heard Charlie begin his silly rendition of the Madonna classic 'Holiday' with its alternative lyrics which were borderline crude, that it was almost time for me to go on; his deafening but tuneless attempt at singing was my cue.

"So you lovely lot, let's give a big Towan Reach welcome for a stunning young lady who's going to entertain you tonight...I just know you are going to be knocked out by her astounding voice....put your hands together and welcome the one, the only...the gorgeous SUZANNE SIXSMITH!"

Any nerves I had, disappeared as always when I was only half way through my first song. Starting with an upbeat classic, encouraging the audience to clap their hands and join in, I was soon in my comfort-zone. The customers enjoyed the music of course, but also the banter between myself and Stu, half-hidden as he was behind his keyboard almost in the wings, and not forgetting Adrian on the guitar, who pulled ridiculous faces at the children, grinned like a Cheshire cat at the dads and cheekily winked at the mums, who adored him. He was a born entertainer and I wasn't surprised to hear he'd been a bloody good Pontins bluecoat in a previous life.

The set list had been carefully selected so there was a little something there to suit most tastes and it warmed me to see the room filling up nicely with cheery holidaymakers, full of good food and strong alcohol. The forty minute set seemed to fly by and before I knew it, I was exiting the stage to appreciative applause, choosing to walk the length of the room to enable me to stop by and say hello to our regular customers and return holidaymakers. As I was almost out of the lounge bar, I was brought to a halt by Bernie, the jovial but highly efficient hotel manager, who was seated with some people I hadn't met before....a cheery, smiling, middle-aged couple, a less-smiling teenage boy who had obviously been forced into his best bib and tucker for the occasion and who looked decidedly uncomfortable and...oh my word...who on earth was THAT?

He was blond. He was tanned. He was fit. He was muscly but not overly so. His smile was amazing, the most kissable lips opening wide to reveal perfect, gleaming white teeth. He was wearing smart black trousers and a buttoned-up black shirt. It suited him, but then I think he could have worn rags and he would still have looked as devastatingly handsome. He was laughing heartily now at something a man at the bar had leant over and whispered to him. And now he was staring right at me, smiling broadly, holding his hand out confidently to shake my own.

"Hey, I'm Dave, nice to meet you Suzanne. You have an incredible voice, you know; we really enjoyed your spot."

Even his voice made the hairs on my arms stand up to attention. It wasn't a local accent...there wasn't much of any accent there. He was different, he stood out. Well to me he did. This was ridiculous! How could this guy be having such an instant effect on me? Who the hell was he?

"Hi...I'm glad you liked it...if you're here for the rest of the evening I'll be back on again after Happy Hour and the warbling compère! Pleased to meet you Dave."

We shook hands, very formally, but his hand was warm and strong and held on to mine a little longer than was necessary.

"Yes, we're here for the duration now, so we'll definitely be around to see you perform again. We've just been to the new Italian place for my dad's birthday meal. This is my younger brother Mark – as you can see, he'd rather be out with his no-good mates but he's been dragged here instead, kicking and screaming...haven't you Marky boy? See, he loves it really!"

He affectionately ruffled Mark's hair and although the younger boy instantly coloured and it was blatantly obvious that he would rather be anywhere else than here, he didn't seem too put out by the teasing and hair ruffling. There appeared to be a genuine bond between the two brothers and I could imagine this Dave looking out for his younger sibling, protecting him and steering him in the right direction.

I had a sudden vision of Dave ruffling and stroking my own hair whilst leaning in to chance a kiss and I almost had to shake myself to drag my mind back to the present. What was happening to me? I needed to get a grip and show this man that I was actually an articulate, interesting person, worthy of his attention!

"Hi Mark, nice to meet you. So...Dave...are you holidaying here then? Or are you resident here in our lovely town - one of the locals?" I asked him quickly, as I knew I didn't have long before I had to perform a quick change and prepare myself for set number two.

He smiled in response - such a dazzling, warm smile that lit up the room and made everyone else's smile dim in comparison.

"Actually, for years we used to be holidaymakers – each and every summer, without fail, we came to Newquay, until we upped and moved here in 1985, so it's been a good half-a-decade since we were tourists! Mum and dad bought the old Hamiltons' cafe in '86 but they've put it up for sale now – it's time to admit defeat for the sake of their finances and their sanity! Bernie pops into the cafe almost every morning for a coffee and cake so that's how he struck up a friendship with mum and dad. In fact it's an acquaintance of his who's interested in buying the business, isn't that right Bernie?"

"Oh yes, this wonderful lady, Barb, makes the best flapjacks in Newquay, I'll have you know!" Bernie beamed his ear-to-ear, people-pleaser, on-duty smile and clapped Dave on the back, almost launching the poor man off his chair.

"And this young fella - best worker I've ever employed! Not one of those bloody cowboys. He works for old Arthur McKenzie at the DIY place on Clifton Street and came highly recommended when I was looking for an emergency plumber." I was impressed. Bernie had a deep-seated dislike for most tradesmen, having been let down and disappointed by them more times than he cared to remember. This gorgeous man must be REALLY good at his job.

"My parents are thinking of replacing their bathroom suite, so I'll tell them to call in shall I and ask for you?" I said, scratching around for any reason to have to contact him in the near future. Actually, they had only mentioned the possible revamp of the main bathroom in passing but no need to disclose that. I could easily persuade them that the current fittings were indeed looking tired and in desperate need of updating.

"Sure, but I can drop by and given them an estimate if you like..."

"...or I could get your number from Bernie and give you a call instead, now we've been introduced, Dave...?" I hoped I wasn't being too glaringly obvious. This was not my style - I did NOT do the running. But this man was in a different league entirely, and I didn't want to miss out on this opportunity, to have him slip away and some other lucky lady snap him up.

He tilted his head to one side, a knowing twinkle in his eye, a grin on his handsome, tanned face.

"Yeh, I think that would be a better idea...and I'll need your number of course in case I need to get back to you...strictly for work purposes you understand!"

Obligingly, I scribbled my number onto a slightly torn beer mat, before folding it over and tucking it into the pocket of his trousers, adding, "I'll call you then. I have to dash now...but will I see you later?" I sincerely hoped so.

"Well, only if you promise to dance with me before the night's out..."

"I promise," I assured him. "It's a deal." And with that, I gave him one last smile and walked away, swinging my hips from side to side as I went, praying he would be watching, and that he liked what he saw. I didn't cut out the carbs and slog my way through double shifts at the gym for nothing; I hoped he was appreciative of all that effort.

I probably looked as cool as a cucumber on the outside but inside my heart was racing and my pulse rate was no doubt dangerously high. This was the first time in my life that any man had ever made such an impression on me. I liked Dave very, very much – I knew I had to play this just right.

After a quick change into a tiny red dress and my sexiest high heels, minor adjustments to my make-up and numerous deep breaths, I took to the stage again. I couldn't remember experiencing nerves like that before, not even when I first started in the business as a naive young girl with stacks to learn. Belting out some more family favourites, I was acutely aware of Dave's eyes following me around. Even from that distance I could sense his gaze on me and I repeatedly smiled over in his direction as I shimmied across the stage, offering silent thanks to God that tonight I had slipped on some expensive glittery tights that showed my legs off to their full advantage.

Fortunately the holidaymakers were exuberantly throwing themselves into the dancing as well and there was a definite party atmosphere in the room. It was both flattering and exhilarating and I adored that feeling of being the host of the best party in town. Finally, after a medley of summer tunes, I left my audience wanting more with a wave of my hand and a loud "Thank you, and good night!"

Following a quick trip backstage to check my hair and make-up, making the decision to remain in the tight little red number rather than change back into my "civvies", I glided out into the bar area, noticing how Dave's eyes were out on stalks when I approached him and I was satisfied that I had his full attention. And what amazing eyes they were, glittering and sparkling, like precious diamonds in the semi-darkness of the room.

"Wow…I like the dress. I think I can confidently say that every man in this place is gut-wrenchingly jealous now that you're here with me and not with them. And you were amazing again up there you know; you had the audience eating out of your hand. That's a real talent."

He pulled out a chair for me to sit down and said "Here, let me buy you a drink – that must have been thirsty work!"

I noticed his family had discreetly relocated to sit at another table and were laughing and joking with a group of local pensioners. So it was just me and Dave then; I had his undivided attention. Perfect.

"I'll just have a small glass of wine please Dave as I'm driving - the house white would be lovely."

He was served quickly and returned with my drink and a pint of lager for himself, drawing his chair up closer to mine before he sat himself down, making my heart thunder in my chest. We comfortably exchanged stories of his early years before his family relocated to Newquay and of my fairly cosseted upbringing in this busy, bustling Cornish town; of life in the unpredictable world of plumbing and how it felt for a relatively shy girl like me to entertain holidaymakers throughout the summer season. We laughed over trivial, silly things, were surprised to find out we had a couple of mutual acquaintances...and all the while we never took our eyes off each other. I desperately wanted to touch him, to feel his skin on mine, to feel his hands on my body; I hoped it wouldn't be too long.

There was definite electricity crackling in the air - an atmosphere loaded with lust, with wanting, with anticipation. Finally, he took my hand and led me to the packed dancefloor, where we fooled around to some recent popular dance tune that had stormed the charts...and when the music dialled down to a more mid-tempo number he pulled me towards him and we swayed along to it together, singing, laughing and, in my case, wondering if he was just as turned on as I was.

When the first of the slow songs began to play, he didn't hesitate to further draw me into his personal space, and I rested my head against his chest whilst locking my arms around his shapely back. We were both hot, inside and out, and when he suggested we slip outside for some air, I struggled to respond succinctly and in the end merely nodded my head.

We were barely out of the fire exit door before he pushed me against the rough brick of the outer wall of the building and kissed me hard, probing inside my mouth with his soft, sensuous tongue. I was gasping for breath whilst aching for more - much more. Eventually he drew away slightly and that sexy smile was back in place.

"Well, Suzanne Sixsmith, I certainly wasn't expecting this tonight. I'm a lucky, lucky man, that's for sure."

"Actually I think I could be the lucky one, Dave White, if that kiss was anything to go by. I don't usually do THAT after work, I can tell you! But...right now I'm afraid I'm going to have to go back in and clear my equipment away from the main stage. Do you think you could possibly help me...?" I asked him, knowing full well what his answer would be.

"Of course, beautiful lady...I'm at your service for as long as you want me..."

I raised an eyebrow and replied, "I think I'm going to require your services for quite some time. Let's go." I grabbed his hand and we headed back inside to disassemble some of the equipment, pack the essentials away and load everything into my car boot along with my bags from the dressing room. Dave was a quick worker, in more ways than one, and I couldn't help but stare at him when he was bent over, at his delicious firm buttocks and his long, strong legs.

Once everything was in the car, Dave nipped back into the hotel to inform his parents he would be hitching a lift home with me and they assured him that they wouldn't be back for another hour, clearly anticipating that I would be invited in for coffee – an offer I gladly accepted when we reached his parents' place.

We never drank the coffee – the kettle boiled but the cups remained empty. Within moments of entering that kitchen I again found myself pushed up against a wall and we desperately forced our tongues into each other's mouths, almost devouring one another, and our hands were everywhere, exploring each other's bodies. I wanted him so badly, and the feeling was definitely mutual. Not yet though. There was time enough. I wanted to go to bed with him but not so soon; not tonight. It would be a wrench, to detach myself from him tonight, but I had to make him wait. I wasn't that kind of girl and I didn't want to get this wrong. We eventually tore ourselves away, panting and trying to catch our breath.

I stroked one slender finger down his neck and his chest whilst kissing him gently then on the lips. "I have to go Dave...as wonderful as it's been...it's time for me to say goodnight..."

He sighed and reluctantly released me from his grip. "I know, Suzanne. I don't want you to leave but I suppose this amazing night has to end sometime. I will call you though, soon

- very soon. And I'm not like most men around this town, because I do actually mean that!"

I didn't doubt it for one second; I'd met a lot of the fly, lads-about-town with a line for everything who had left a trail of broken hearts behind them. I could see Dave wasn't one of them – he would be a man of his word.

We kissed for one final time that evening but, as with the audience from the hotel, I left him wanting more. When I drove away that night it was with a massive smile on my face and a positivity I hadn't ever felt before. As I made my way home, my lips still stinging and swollen from his forceful yet tender kisses, I pictured his face in my mind and knew that was an image that would stay with me forever.

The incessant hammering on the door left me with no option other than to answer it. My parents. I must have looked terrible as mum clamped one hand over her mouth, clearly in shock, tears steadily falling from her anguished eyes. She never usually cried; she came from a generation where you kept it all in, you didn't show emotion – it was almost like a sign of weakness.

"Suzanne...oh darling...oh my lord...look at you! We've been so worried...your mum's here now, everything's going to be alright, you'll see."

I couldn't remember the last time I'd showered or when I'd dragged a brush through my hair or even cleaned my teeth. I glanced down at my once-fresh silky, magnolia pyjamas and saw that they were tired and grubby. When was the last time I had changed them or actually got dressed? Who knew. When you're sleeping so much and so often it's difficult to remember, when all the days and nights are blending into one.

Dad pulled me into his steady, comforting arms. He wasn't a man for physical contact but on this occasion he hugged me tightly and kissed the top of my fuzzy head, all the while barking instructions to mum – "Open those bloody windows woman! It's like a furnace in here and the air is stale. And check what's in that fridge – there's an appalling smell emanating from that kitchen!"

Eventually I found myself sandwiched between my parents on one of my designer settees, each of them holding one of my hands. Dad's ashen face and mum's tear-streaked cheeks made me feel a little ashamed. I hadn't meant to worry them – I just couldn't deal with the outside world at the moment. I had no strength, no purpose, no idea how I was going to continue to drag myself through each day.

"Suzy, we came back a little earlier darling because you frightened us half to death – we couldn't contact you and didn't know what to think. Call it mother's intuition, but I knew something just wasn't right, so we flew in this morning. You can't go on like this love...you need to take better care of yourself...and if you can't do that then your father and I will step in and take over. You've stopped taking your tablets haven't you? Well we need to get you back on that medication...perhaps the doctor will up your dosage...no, no protests sweetheart – you're clearly not coping with Dave's departure and you really do need some TLC, so you're coming home with us today. You can't stay here – and especially not today, of all days! We'll find you some clean clothes and get a decent meal inside you. You're a bag of bones for goodness sake! When did you last eat something?"

"I...er...I'm honestly not sure mum...I haven't had much of an appetite really...." I couldn't recall eating at all recently, but then I was struggling to remember anything from the last few weeks now. Everything was fuzzy, everything was blurred. How long had I been there? When was the last time I had left the house? I really didn't have the answers to either of those questions.

Ignoring my protests, they bundled me into the car, with my knee length military-style coat over my tired nightwear, in an attempt to avoid creating a show for some of the nosier neighbours.

As dad eased his gleaming white Mercedes off our spacious block-paved driveway, I glanced up at the house. My lovely, lovely house. Our lovely, lovely home. Where Dave and I had loved and laughed together. Where, despite my crippling depression in the later years and our ongoing difficulties, I had thought we would grow old together. Where dreams had been borne and dreams had been burnt. The recently erected 'For Sale' board was clanking about in the breeze, the one outward sign that everything was changing, that the Whites were moving on, and not together. I bowed my head as the car began to ease off. I couldn't stand to look at it, couldn't bear to think about the fact that I had lost Dave now and he would never come home to me again. My Dave. My wonderful, wonderful Dave. Gone forever. How could I live without him?

As we sped through the back streets of Newquay, I stared at my feet and tried to blank everything out of my mind. It's funny though, but when you are desperate to forget, all you can do is remember.

Dave was true to his word and rang me the very next day, when we arranged to meet that same evening as I had a rare night off from work. He took me to a fabulous restaurant where he thoroughly wined and dined me and then later kissed me until my lips were sore and my body ached inside for the promise of what was to come. As well as being a top grade kisser, he was also interesting and attentive and funny – he didn't just make me giggle, he made me belly laugh and wish the night would never end.

Date after date followed - we wanted to be together at every available opportunity; talking for hours on end about everything and nothing – family, friends, work, achievements, and dreams and aspirations. One evening, after a trip to the cinema to see some forgettable bad-boy action film, we sat huddled together in the quiet snug of an olde worlde pub while the rain bounced down outside and the conversation soon turned to ex-boyfriends and ex-girlfriends. I shyly confessed to my relative inexperience with men – my couple of previous boyfriends, a few disastrous dates I had had the misfortune to even turn up for and the three sexual partners I'd rather forget about.

"So..." I whispered in his ear, nuzzling into the soft skin of his neck. "What's the deal with your past history? Lots of love-smitten girlfriends and willing bed partners? Or have you been saving yourself for me?"

He hesitated just a second too long before he replied, "Oh, only a couple of girlfriends while I was still at school - one that even lasted as long as six months when I was sixteen. But then we moved down here and I was far too busy working and helping mum and dad with their business to think about the opposite sex! The years have passed by so quickly, and with the exception of a cute but strange girl from Mawgan Porth who I was seeing for all of about three months last year and a couple of ill-advised, unsatisfactory rolls in the sack with some very, very bad beer-induced choices last summer, that's it, nothing much to tell!"

"No way! I can't believe you've practically been living the life of a monk!" I leant forward and twisted my head around to look into his eyes as I gently teased and metaphorically probed him. "I mean, I can't believe you've been basically single from your school days right up until last year...are you sure you've not omitted anyone of any significance? No

dirty secrets that you're trying to hide? Nobody from your teenage years who you're still carrying a torch for who I should be worrying about, is there?"

I really was kidding, but I caught a glimpse of it then...that revealing look of intense sadness that briefly flitted across his face. I'm sure he thought he'd given nothing away, but he had. There wasn't time to dwell on it too much though as he moved forward to kiss me again, and for the time being all worries about previous lovers vanished swiftly from my mind and were replaced by feelings of sheer wanton lust.

We rapidly became a serious couple and I glided around with a permanent smile on my face and a big halo of happiness surrounding me. I cursed not having a place of my own, as did he, and eventually we gave in to our wanting, needy bodies and booked a double room in a random, anonymous hotel on a quiet back street where we initially gave in to all that pent-up lust without even stopping to remove our clothes. He unbelted his jeans and I urgently dragged them and his boxers below his waist whilst he roughly shoved up my leather-look skirt and ripped the sheer fabric of my underwear to one side. We had waited long enough and I needed him to be inside me; it felt like we were out of control.

When he started to moan my name as he was on the verge of coming, he looked deeply but quizzically into my eyes, as if he was searching for something there but then all at once he let go and lost himself completely inside of me. Once our first coupling had taken place we slowed down, but only a little. Dave was insatiable and I was desperate to have that connection; I never wanted him to stop – I felt empty when I was alone; when our bodies weren't clamped together.

Our hotel arrangement became a weekly occurrence and we lived for those precious hours. I purchased numerous sets of exotic lingerie, eager to please my man in fine stockings and lacy suspender belts and he bought champagne and condoms. Our parents asked no questions – they accepted the fact that we were old enough to make our own choices. If they had imagined our naked, sweaty bodies writhing about between the rumpled sheets all night long, they may have been rather less understanding.

I introduced him to my parents and they adored him from the outset – well, who wouldn't? They could see the sunshine he had brought into my life and I knew they were praying he would become a permanent fixture. Dave's parents were decent and pleasant and treated me well, but I think his choice of girlfriend took them by surprise, to be honest. I know I probably came across as quiet and somewhat reserved to them and his dad even nervously joked about my "posh accent". Already planning my future with Dave, I hoped that they would grow to like me more and that eventually I would feel more relaxed in their company.

Mixing with Dave's circle of friends was the biggest challenge for me. I constantly seemed to clam up and stumble over my words and struggled to let my personality shine through. When I tried to join in the conversation I always seemed to say the wrong thing and ended up kicking myself for my foolish behaviour – and so, unfortunately, I remained a bit of an outsider. Dave still persisted on dragging me along to every occasion though, proudly showing me off to all his friends and acquaintances, oblivious to how I was churning up inside and desperate for him to take me home. It was never better than when it was just the two of us and my heart sank when he made arrangements with others without consulting me first.

When I was initially introduced to Dave's best friend and partner in crime, Billy Lomax, I saw a look pass between them when I smiled and said hello. Almost a "Really? This woman?" I tried extremely hard to not dig too deep into what that could have meant; why I might have been seen as an unsuitable partner for Dave - surely he didn't think that I wasn't good enough for him? Maybe he thought I wasn't attractive enough? Or perhaps he thought I might be too quiet or too serious for him? Or it could be that I just wasn't his usual type, whatever that was. I just hoped with all of my heart that it didn't mean there was someone else on the scene; some other girl I was going to have to contend with.

Maybe I should have asked more questions then, dug much deeper, not been so keen to bury any seed of doubt.

To give him his due though, Billy was polite and funny and tried his hardest to involve me in everything, for Dave's sake I'm guessing. He was very kind and likeable and probably the one member of the group I could cope with being sat next to, besides Dave of course.

Billy's girlfriend Jenny was altogether another matter.

From the moment I met her I sensed that she disliked me intensely and the feeling was very much mutual. She was badly dressed in a cheap neon pink dress which did nothing to disguise her ample stomach and wobbling thunder thighs. She wore matching bright pink, scratched high-heeled shoes and if I wasn't mistaken that looked like an old plaster peeping out from the heel of her right foot. Eugh! Her make-up was badly applied – too *much, too bright, too tarty – and her short dark hair was frizzy on top but shaved at the sides. Before she opened her mouth I knew she was from the scruffy council flats – and I realised that was terrible of me to stereotype someone in that manner, because I've since met a variety of other people from that estate who have been lovely, and often inspiring and gone on to make something of their lives – but she really got my goat with her abrasive laugh, her smutty innuendos and the sarcastic way she spoke to me - that is, when she deigned to involve me in any conversation at all.*

I guessed she thought I was snobby and reluctant to mix with the likes of her – she didn't attempt to disguise her feelings and even once referred to me as "Lady Muck". However, Billy was besotted with her and they stuck to each other like superglue – and as Billy was Dave's best friend, avoiding the pair of them was simply out of the question. It was always a relief for me, to say goodnight to them, and all the others – I liked nothing better than being alone with Dave again; cocooned in our little world.

Just the two of us.

Arriving at mum and dad's house, I was quickly pushed upstairs and propelled towards the shower, where I reluctantly washed my hair and shower-gelled my body, before slipping into a freshly laundered pair of mum's rather old-fashioned pyjamas. I looked around the luxurious bathroom suite with its top-of-the-range Jacuzzi bath and expensive, stylish fitments. There were memories of Dave everywhere; I couldn't escape from them. He had indeed fitted a new suite here all those years ago but that had been replaced on two occasions now....each time the work being carefully carried out by Dave, with his full attention to all the tiny details. He was a fantastic workman – precise, meticulous and so very good with his hands. Oh yes, he had always been very good with his hands.

Slightly more fragrant now, I hesitantly joined mum in the dining room, where she had prepared us a light supper. I really wasn't hungry but I knew I had to try to force something down to stop her worrying.

"I've made you an appointment with Dr. Patel, Sue...he's already agreed to up the dosage of your tablets. You *have* to take them darling, or he'll suggest we look again at other options..."

"Don't worry mum, I'll take the pills, whatever strength I'm prescribed; however many milligrams do the job. Because there's no way I would consider admission to hospital, if that's what he's been inferring! It's not easy for me to say this mum but I....I...I think I hit rock bottom after Dave left; after he closed that door for the final time and I was left to wallow in my own misery. Even though things had been anything but perfect between us for a long time, he was still my whole world, and that just crumbled when he left. And I crumbled. I had no direction; didn't know if I had a future – and I couldn't see a way forward...it was all just more than I could handle at that point in my life." Never had I spoken truer words, but now was the time for honesty - to lay myself bare to the people who loved me most.

"I could wring his neck with my own bare hands Sue, I really could. How could he do that to you, after all you've been through? To leave you in the lurch like that, after all of these years, to go off with some...some...tart! I thought he was better than that." Mum's face reddened with anger whilst her knuckles turned white.

I knew she wanted to hit out at Dave but I had to put her straight; present her with all of the facts – I at least owed him that.

"Mum, it wasn't all his fault – we were both equally culpable as far as the breakdown of our relationship was concerned. We had been living together as brother and sister these last few years, man and wife in name only, sleeping in separate bedrooms. After the failed IVF treatments, disappointment after disappointment, I felt like such a failure. My body had let me down and I pushed him away from that body - I got it into my head that he wouldn't want me in *that* way anyway once he realised I couldn't give him the son or daughter he had waited so long for. I didn't need him *pretending* to want me – for our love-making to have become just *sex*." I cringed and squirmed, embarrassed to be sharing details of our private life with my mother. And it was painful to recall how we'd tried so hard to make a baby but how our dreams had been ultimately shattered.

Despite those images I'd had of Dave and I with a couple of adorable children in tow, for many years I had refused to even consider starting a family. Once our finances were on an even keel I wanted to live a little – to spend time as a couple before we added to our numbers. So that's what we did - we ate out at every opportunity and we partied hard and flew off to foreign shores and money was no object. Occasionally Dave would try and gently broach the subject of making babies but I would put him off again by telling him that I wanted us to make the most of our time together first - just the two of us.

Besides, I was reluctant to give up my singing at that stage; to let it take a back seat. And, if I'm totally honest, I was terrified at the prospect of actually giving birth. I liked the idea of being stylishly pregnant - as long as I didn't get too huge - and everyone making a fuss of me and my bump…and of course I did dream of producing tiny, scrumptious little babies who were half me, half Dave – who most definitely would be gorgeous and perfect and doted on from the day they were born.

No, it was the rest of it that brought me out in a cold sweat – the morning sickness, the labour, the actual process of a living, breathing little person forcing its way out of my body. I had always been so slim, and I fretted that I wouldn't be able to lose any baby weight I gained.

And what if Dave didn't like the new mummy-me – the one with stretch marks and sore breasts and cracked nipples and the excess baby weight. Supposing he looked at me one day and wondered what on earth had happened to the old body-conscious, elegantly turned out Suzanne….and began to look around for a younger, trimmer replacement…or alternatively, started to reminisce about someone special from his past…

It was ridiculous really as in my heart of hearts I knew that Dave would no more commit adultery than he would murder. But I couldn't rid my mind of those disturbing thoughts.

So I had put him off for as long as I could, but by the turn of the millennium Dave had become increasingly broody, speaking longingly of his friends' young families and the prospect of becoming a father himself.

Fortunately, he didn't have to wait much longer because, as if someone had flicked a switch overnight, my hormones suddenly seemed to kick in, and the realisation hit me that I was in my thirties and getting no younger to become a first-time mother. All those fears I'd harboured within me were suddenly swamped by the need to feel that tiny human kicking inside me; to deliver a baby, our baby, and see the love in Dave's eyes as he cradled his new-born son or daughter to his chest.

Dave of course was delighted when I threw my contraceptive pills into the kitchen bin in a grand gesture and had one last large flute of pink champagne in celebration. And at first of course we had great fun actually trying to get pregnant…jumping into bed at every available opportunity and experimenting with exotic sexual positions we had never attempted before. We kind of accepted then that it would take a few months for the contraceptive to completely work its way out of my system; for my body to return to its natural state.

By six months down the line, the sex had become somewhat more organised, ruled by dates and my body cycle.

"You need to be at home more next week darling...I'm ovulating from Tuesday onwards."

We were still convinced at that stage that it would happen for us...we were just frustrated at how long it was taking. I'd bought Dave lots of new, loose boxer shorts and binned his favourite tight-fitting jeans – he always used to joke that they "showed his arse off a treat", but they had to go.

The diet became more regimented as well. Dave dropped in several comments about eating what he called "rabbit food" morning, noon and night and jokingly claimed I was trying to starve him into submission.

By the twelve month mark, when I instigated a complete alcohol ban for both of us, despite Dave's protests that he needed a weekend pint after a long, hard week at work, we were both becoming a little concerned and wondered if anything was amiss. Parents, friends, colleagues and even our GP merely told us to relax and "let it happen", without putting too much pressure on ourselves.

Thirteen, fourteen, fifteen months....the sex had deteriorated from a loving and exciting coupling to an angry, desperate chore.

And yet the periods kept on coming....some months lighter, some months so heavy they drained the life out of me...and it wasn't just the pain in my stomach and back that was agony. It seemed like everyone I knew was expecting, was with child, was able to have what we so badly wanted. When the stomach-ripping cramps came every month and the world was a dark, hateful place, I curled up on the bathroom floor, crying and cursing and dreading having to deliver the news to Dave when he returned from work.

Two years went by, then three, then four, and yet I still shrank from seeking any further advice about our situation – I was terrified of what some medical professional might have to tell us. Eventually, Dave's patience wore out.

"We have to see a specialist Sue...this is killing us...and it might be something we can get help with, if there's a problem there at all. We have to do something love. Doing nothing isn't an option anymore."

"It's my fault Dave," I would sob, hugging my hot water bottle to my useless, aching body, trying to sooth the pain deep in my belly. "I put this off for years - always wanting more possessions, more holidays, more money, more time...and all because I was scared...terrified of bringing another life into this world. How could I have been so selfish and so stupid Dave? How could I have thought that all of that material stuff mattered more than having a baby – our baby?"

And Dave - my loving, caring, understanding husband - repeatedly insisted that it honestly wasn't my fault – that everyone is individual and must make the life-changing decision when the time is right for them, whether they are 22, 32 or 42.

An appointment with a specialist was eventually booked in. We attended at the private, unassuming offices and pristine medical rooms....we underwent test after test it seemed and finally returned for one fateful meeting with that quite matter-of-fact doctor, who had no doubt been the bearer of bad news on many occasions prior to dropping the bombshell on us.

The day of reckoning, 6th April 2004, was when one of the worst, most devastating moments of my life occurred while we were sitting there; legs crossed, palms sweating, hearts pounding, and hearing the words that translated into what I'd known all along – that it was my fault; my pathetic useless body, for all it looked good on the exterior, was a mess inside – not fit for purpose. My fault, my fault, my fault.

Dave had carefully taken my hand in his and whispered empty promises that it would all be okay, we would somehow work it out...there were other roads we could take. Despite the fact that there was nothing wrong with him, he was blameless, his body was in good working order – despite everything, he never once blamed me.

We'd tried IVF, of course we had. Two disastrous, failed attempts. No amount of advice and warnings in the world could have prepared us for this painful, devastating process. Each unsuccessful attempt was both mental and physical torture...and the pain was permanently etched on both of our faces. I walked around like a zombie and Dave went through the motions every day – working, eating, sleeping, attempting to comfort me. He *dragged me to counselling but I was beyond that...after two unsuccessful attempts I could take no more – I knew, without doubt, that I was never, ever going to become a mother and felt like it was my punishment for interfering with nature for so long. No one could reason with me – not Dave, not mum, not dad, nor the lovely counselling lady who had been through it all herself – no one.*

I poured scorn on Dave's suggestion that we look into fostering or adoption – I didn't want anyone else's abandoned child; I wanted my own! And besides, I was already on the happy pills now, having been steered into the doctor's surgery by mum one day when she called by to the house and discovered me sat on our back lawn in the pouring rain, oblivious to how wet and cold I was; not caring, not feeling anything at all by that stage.

I looked at Dave one day and saw what he had become - heartbroken, defeated and incredibly lonely – and yet I couldn't reach out to him, and he especially couldn't reach me. It was a time of such emptiness and sadness and the days became weeks which became months...and Dave and I were further apart than we had ever been. I watched him carefully, searching for signs that he had endured enough, that he was going to leave, that he didn't love me anymore. But there were none. He was still as achingly handsome as he had always been and still as loyal and faithful as the man I had first met. Somewhere along the lines his beautiful blond hair had turned silvery grey, his face more lined, his smile a little more forced most of the time. But he was still Dave, and, despite everything, I couldn't let him go.

The years rolled by and we continued to live together, but apart. Side by side but as if on different continents. Both just going through the motions and doing what we had to do to survive. I'm sure Dave must have despaired of the situation; I knew deep down that I had lost his love somewhere throughout this journey and I convinced myself that it was because he blamed me for my infertility. How could he find me attractive now? Maybe my knackered, useless body repulsed him now and all he saw when he looked at me was a miserable, barren, poor excuse for the woman I had once been.

"Oh Sue, I'm sure he didn't feel like that..." whispered mum, clearly at a loss for what to say in response.

"To be honest mum, in hindsight I honestly don't think he did, but the problems were in my mind as well as my body and my heart; I couldn't think straight. I was heading to a nasty, dark place and I needed to leave Dave behind rather take him there with me. Even when I was prescribed the medication and my mental health began to improve, I still struggled to believe that he could ever want me again, you know, in that way. When I admitted to myself that he was desperate to leave, when I realised that it was killing him to stay..." I struggled to continue.

"...I made it easy for him by assuring him that I wanted out as well - that I was in a much better place and more than capable of surviving without him. And I even told him there was another man on the scene...someone I'd met through a mutual friend...entirely fictitious of course, but like a fool Dave eagerly believed me because he so badly wanted it to be true!" My heart was heavy thinking about the undisguised delight on his face when he realised he had been let off the hook and had in effect been granted the freedom to go to *her*.

"Oh darling, *why* on earth did you do that?" asked mum shaking her head in disbelief, clearly a firm believer that you did whatever it took to hold on to your man, regardless of the circumstances and your personal pride.

"Because I didn't want him to stay with me out of pity and some awful misguided sense of loyalty! I didn't want him to stay with me purely because he was terrified of what would happen if he left! I wanted him there because he still loved me - because I was still the centre of his world, as he was, and is, mine. I only wanted him to stay if he loved me more than anyone else – but he didn't mum, he really didn't." The tears started to fall now...rapidly and relentlessly down my face, as if they were racing against one another to the finish line – which appeared to be somewhere further down my neck.

"I don't know what was going on in that man's head but I'm sure he did love you," mum replied angrily, stabbing her fork into the salmon on her plate, which so far had remained untouched.

"Mum, I *know* he did love me – but he loved her more. And I think deep down I've always known that," I answered sadly, only re-confirming the old saying that the truth really does hurt.

"Always?" Mum was incredulous. "Even from the beginning? I don't think so madam because I'll always remember how excited you were when you first met him; how you were on cloud nine when you were courting and how much he adored you. I recall the joy on your face when he proposed and you were throwing yourself into all of the wedding arrangements and planning your honeymoon, and the house was filled with sample invitations and bridal magazines and exotic holiday brochures. The way you two were together – laughing and holding hands – always so tactile. My goodness, you were inseparable for the first few years!"

I nodded my head in agreement whilst a wave of unbearably happy and sad blended memories washed over me and threatened to drown me in despair.

We were two years into our relationship before we started to discuss marriage. Neither of us were going anywhere, we were happy together, and it just seemed perfectly natural to be thinking of when we eventually would become "man and wife" and create a family together. Imaginative and spontaneous was what I would have wished for; my dream scenario would have been Dave whisking me off to sample the delights of Paris and proposing at the top of the Eiffel Tower, whilst crowds of tourists clapped and cheered us on.

If it had been down to Dave, we would have just quietly made the trip to the jewellers and chosen a modest ring together and not made an ounce of fuss.

In the end we met somewhere in the middle...he knew what it meant to me, so on my birthday he arranged a surprise meal out for both of our families and proposed officially somewhere between the main course and the dessert. It wasn't quite the getting-down-on-one-knee whilst declaring his undying love situation I'd always fantasised about but it was still wonderful – to see him suddenly, nervously stand up, clear his throat and quietly ask my dad for permission to marry his daughter. The ring he produced was beautiful, a single diamond surrounded by tiny amethyst stones – but the sizing was a little out for the appropriate finger so privately we agreed I would wear it on my other hand and we would return to the jewellers and buy the actual ring I'd quietly had my eye on all along.

It was such a special night and the months that followed were like living in a dream world, planning our lavish wedding and laying down the foundations for our future. I'd anticipated I would have become Mrs White within two years but it didn't quite work out that way. When Dave's employer, old Arthur with the croaky voice and the permanent odour of WD40, started making murmurs about imminent retirement, it was decided that Dave would purchase the business from him, but there were insufficient funds in our pot at that stage. When my brother Michael offered to raise finance to enter into a partnership with Dave it was the answer to all of our problems and eventually, by 1994,

'White's' was the name above the shop door, Dave having contributed the majority of the funds.

Everything continued to fall into place when we stumbled across the house of our dreams one day, strolling past hand in hand just as an old man was knocking the 'For Sale' board into the front lawn. It was considerably over our budget, especially having recently purchased the DIY and plumbing business, but mum and dad hastily produced a hefty cheque to make up the shortfall for the deposit and we agreed to pay the full asking price rather than haggling, to ensure we secured this stunning house with its sought-after sea view.

There were a few delays with the mortgage company due to our self-employed statuses, but eventually we managed to complete our purchase, and I almost had to pinch myself on moving-in day, when we collected the keys and entered our new home, Dave carrying me over the threshold despite my short, tight skirt and his dirty, oil stained overalls. It really was an incredible house and I had already pictured in my mind which bedrooms our children would occupy – the long, narrow one for our son at the back of the property which I imagined painted in shades of blue, with shelving fitted to accommodate his collection of football trophies, and the wide, airy room above the garage, where there was ample space for a dressing table underneath the front window - where I would teach our darling daughter how to apply her make-up when she reached her teenage years. Ha. Those dreams, how they would eventually return to haunt me.

Dave being Dave, of course, insisted we had to pay back every penny of the deposit; he was too proud to take so much money as a gift. So we worked our backsides off and saved like mad to pay off our debt, and the wedding was put on hold until the funds were there for us to make a decent contribution towards it - the father of the bride, my lovely dad, at least being allowed to pay for the rest of it. There was no expense spared as far as my wedding dress and the other traditional elements were concerned, but Dave drew the line at string quartets and the releasing of white doves after the ceremony. I needn't have worried though because the day couldn't have been any more perfect.

A strange feeling came over me once we were married – yes, there is always that anticlimax, but it was more than that; I think I felt rather smug. It seemed I had it all – I was blessed with this handsome, funny, clever, hardworking husband of mine and I was filled with joy every single day, living in this stunning home we had bought and decorated *and filled with beautiful possessions. Dave had his own successful business, I loved singing for my supper - which was all I had ever wanted to do - and we had decent cars and designer clothes...and exotic holidays planned for the next few years.*

We were truly living our best lives.

"We were happy mum, there's no denying that. We had some truly wonderful times together...such special memories...but there was always a tiny seed of doubt there for me; an inkling that I was second best. I ignored it as best I could and swept it under the carpet really but that didn't make it go away. I knew Dave loved me and I of course loved him – so I didn't dwell on it, otherwise it would have ruined everything. And I couldn't have asked for a more devoted, hardworking, infinitely good man than the one I had. When everything was going along swimmingly, it was just magical between us. In my wildest dreams I couldn't ever have imagined finding a better man than Dave." I meant it; I wasn't exaggerating. He was one of a kind – if we hadn't met when we did then maybe I would never have settled down and married; maybe I would have spent the rest of my life searching for that perfect match I was so sure was out there somewhere. I was looking for perfection and in Dave I thought I'd found it.

"But right from the beginning of our relationship I knew there was something there, buried inside of him, that he was hiding – way down deep below the surface - that he wasn't prepared to share with me or even admit to himself. I couldn't put my finger on it, and it's hard to raise something when you don't know what it is you're dealing with; what's making you so uneasy. He had closed down that part of him; had thought he had hidden it from view completely but *I* knew, I could sense something had touched him and hurt him badly, but it wasn't up for discussion."

I anxiously twisted the rings on my finger – the gigantic solitaire diamond 18 carat engagement ring that had cost an arm and a leg but I had so desperately wanted – we had foregone holidays for two years to pay for that. And the thick plain gold wedding band, that I'd taken, along with his matching ring, to have engraved with our names on the inside, to surprise him. I laughed, bitterly, to myself. I should've asked them to engrave the name 'David' on the rings...now that WOULD have been a surprise for him at the altar! Oh and if I'd known the score back then, maybe I could have asked the jewellers to add the name 'Louise' as well, rather than my own – no – don't go there – don't let yourself think about that woman; she doesn't deserve to occupy the headspace.

I thought I'd had the last laugh back then, on our beautiful wedding day – when the sun had shone brightly all day and every tiny detail went according to plan – when I'd got to say "I, Suzanne Maria ….take thee David…" On the one occasion when it mattered more than anything, it had been ME saying those words, not her. DAVID said his proper name loud and clear then and I genuinely thought there was no hesitation in his voice when he promised to love and take care of me for the rest of our lives. Now I wonder what went through his mind at that precise moment in time. He was all smiles on the outside, a picture of happiness and contentment. But who knows what was going on inside his head – maybe there was a minute when he thought of her; perhaps a second of regret.

We talked late into the night, as I dissected my relationship and voiced my own regrets. Mum asked if I would revert to using my maiden name and I responded angrily, with a resounding "NO!" – it was the one thing I wouldn't allow him, or *her* to take away from me.

'White' - how I'd loved becoming Mrs White, taking his name. How proud I was to produce my marriage certificate to alter my name on my bank books and other documents. I adored being his wife. I loved the fact that he had chosen me - not anyone else – but little old me to share his life.

Whatever happened, even divorce, I would remain Suzanne White forever.

Of course, he would no doubt be a "David" again now, seeing as *she* was the one person he allowed to use that godforsaken name.

Don't get me wrong, there's nothing wrong with the name 'Dave' at all, nothing whatsoever. But I thought 'David' suited him much more than 'Dave' – which always put me in mind of a cockney wide-boy selling a nice line in watches, rather than a professional, mature adult with his star on the rise.

Suzanne and David. Yes…it was much more in keeping with our status as a professional, comfortably well-off couple.

David and Suzanne. Mr and Mrs David White. That had quite a ring to it.

I wanted to nip this 'Dave' business in the bud early doors, so I casually mentioned it to him at the beginning of our relationship.

A big, fat, regrettable mistake. To me it was nothing really, just the small matter of him using the name he had been given by his parents for goodness sake. To him, it was obviously more than that - much more.

We were sat having a few drinks one evening, in a quiet bar away from all the crowds of holidaymakers. He had been teasing me, complimenting me on my "tight, peachy backside", and I had retaliated by swatting him with a ripped beer mat whilst saying in a mock cockney accent "Da-ave!" As he laughed and pretended to duck away from me, I merely added, "Do you know, from now on I think I'll call you 'David' if you don't mind – it's much more you, and a much sexier, more mature name!"

His face abruptly fell - that sadness in its purest form in his beautiful eyes again - and I wished I'd just kept my stupid mouth shut and not broached the subject at all.

"I do mind actually. No one calls me by that name now. I hate it." His face almost looked angry, one of the very rare times I was ever to see him like that. But his eyes remained sad – they gave so much away, despite his huge efforts to keep it all in.

"I'm sorry Dave, I didn't know it was such a big issue with you...I mean, it's just a name, isn't it - the name your parents chose for you..."

"It IS a MASSIVE issue for me and I'm not happy for anyone to use that name....not even you...so can you please just call me 'Dave' for future reference and let's move on..."

Despite my curiosity, at that point I was desperate to change the subject, to return to the easiness and joviality of just a matter of seconds earlier. "Of course, yes, let's leave it...I didn't mean to offend or upset you...now what were you saying before, about taking me sailing with your dad at the weekend...?"

And so I moved on at his insistence, and made a mental note to only ever call him 'Dave' in the future; I couldn't bear to see him annoyed like that. But again I knew there was something there, some event or some person in his past that had turned this small issue into a great big one, that had caused him pain and made him shut down, without reason or discussion. He was usually so open and transparent...but there was a small part of him that was out of bounds for me – I was aware of that already.

Of course, silly persistent me – I tried again once we were officially engaged and I was more surefooted as far as our relationship was concerned. I'd decided that I wouldn't ask the question this time but would merely drop the odd 'David' in when I was speaking to him or about him. It was fine when I was talking to mum and dad; if they thought it strange that I'd suddenly started to call him that, they never commented. When I referred to my fiancé as "David" to Billy, I received a raised eyebrow in response but he didn't make further reference to it.

Unfortunately, my usually placid and reasonable fiancé hit the roof after I called him David when we were out amongst friends one evening. He didn't actually say anything at all when we were in company, but that look was back on his face, and I didn't dare make eye contact with him. He quickly made our excuses to leave and we walked in silence back to my house, but once we were inside and the front door was safely closed behind us, I heard him shout for the very first time.

"Just what the hell do you think you're playing at? David? DAVID! You know I hate that name - I made it perfectly clear how I felt about you calling me that. I ask one small thing of you, to refrain from using it, and yet you're still determined to get your own way aren't you? You're just not happy until you have everything you want and everything is done to your liking! So spoilt and unaccumstomed to being told "No". My feelings on the matter just don't seem to count in your bloody eyes…"

I was shocked at his response, I truly was. Even now, with a ring firmly on my finger and a wedding in the early planning stages, it was a subject off limits – a ridiculous state of affairs.

"Dave, please don't swear at me!" I swiftly tried to catch hold of his hand but he crossed his arms in front of his chest, effectively removing me from his personal space.

"Look, I just don't see the problem…it's hardly the end of the world is it, me calling you David? I never thought it would elicit this response from you! I mean, it just seems like such a ridiculously small, insignificant matter for you to get so furiously worked up about…"

"…And that's just the problem isn't it? You can't open your blinkered mind to even consider how I might feel…you just can't see how anyone might have a different opinion to yourself! It's Sue's way or the wrong way!"

Becoming increasingly wound up myself now, I retorted angrily, "Look…there…in that last sentence, you addressed me as Sue! And I don't mind, I've always accepted that people will call me that and it doesn't bother me in any way, because it's NOTHING! But if you insisted on me being a 'Suzanne' all of the time, that wouldn't upset me either. I wouldn't be exploding like a bomb and accusing my fiancé of basically being selfish and uncaring, as you've just done. Your reaction is totally unreasonable and disproportionate and the way you're treating me now is so hurtful!"

Well, then I thought he WAS actually going to spontaneously combust before my very eyes, as his face reddened and his breathing deepened.

Instead, he picked up his bunch of keys from the coffee table and headed for the door, only pausing briefly to say, "It's all about you isn't it Suzanne? Don't talk to me about being hurt; you have no idea what that really feels like…"

He stormed out of the house, slamming the door behind him, and I was thankful my parents were away at the time and hadn't heard that little outburst. It really was a silly, stupid argument over nothing, but I was devastated that he had reacted in that way; in disbelief that something so trivial could have escalated so quickly.

Feeling desperately sorry for myself, I cried myself to sleep, but after a disturbed night tossing and turning between my sheets, I rang Dave first thing to apologise profusely and assure him it wouldn't happen again. Because it wouldn't, I would make sure of that. I couldn't lose this wonderful man, who possessed my mind, heart and body, over such a minor issue. To his credit, he apologised as well, for what he'd said and for raising his voice and swearing at me, adding that he shouldn't have treated me like that and that he knew I didn't have to put up with it. Frankly I would have put up with anything if it meant holding on to Dave. I was completely under his spell and couldn't contemplate a life without him now. Having to use a slightly shortened version of his Christian name seemed a small price to pay for a lifetime spent with him.

Chapter 3

LOUISE

"Good morning gorgeous! And how are we feeling on this fine autumn day?"

"Bugger off Mr, being so fresh and chirpy. You know full well that I'm rough as chuff and I can barely prise my eyes open."

"Well that's not a very nice way to greet your birthday boy is it?"

"Not your bloody birthday any longer matey boy so I can be as grumpy as I want! And just how are you managing to be so perky today when you sunk about ten pints last night?"

"Ah well, you see, I've had a lot of practice…and despite my best efforts, I couldn't seem to really feel the effects of all that alcohol last night…I think I was running on adrenaline…the shock of the surprise party and everyone turning up like that…turned out I didn't need the alcohol to give me that high after all!"

"As long as you enjoyed it…and your state of drunkenness - or lack of it - soon became apparent last night when I realised little David was still up and ready for action in the small hours."

"Er…'scuse me…we'll have less of the "Little David" if you don't mind…and yes, surprisingly enough, he was raring to go – must have been the sight of you in that little dress and those big boots that did it!"

"Mmmm…well I guess I could slip into them again tonight if you like…once I've come round a bit and had about eleven hours to recover."

"Well, I hate to be the one to remind you, but you kind of agreed to us going out tonight…"

I groaned…if truth be told, I wanted to lounge around in my pyjamas tonight with David, watching crappy television and dozing in and out of consciousness.

"Where, and what have I agreed to? God, I'm a dickhead."

"Yes, yes you are. Because last night you and Kirsty decided it would be a splendid idea to buy tickets to that '80s night at the labour club, which starts at seven-thirty prompt…you know, the party night that Mikita's been desperately trying to sell you tickets to for the last month...the one you had so far decided against because last time someone chucked a table through a window and two women had a fight in the queue to the toilets. Yes, that's the one...and by god, I'm beside myself with excitement now I've heard all about it!"

"Alright, there's no need for sarcasm! I can't believe she's suckered us in to buying tickets...what were we thinking? Why didn't you stop me?"

"To be fair, I don't think either of you were thinking at the time because you were playing drinking games in the vault and making more noise than all the rest of the pub-goers put together. I think Mikita tackled you when your defences were low and your alcohol levels were high. And I couldn't get a word in edgeways to try and dissuade the pair of you because you were all drunk and sweary and shouty..."

"Oh Christ, yeah, sorry about that...god, thank you for not breaking up with me last night then...I can be a bit of an arse when I'm leathered..."

"...no, you're just lovely....even when you're leathered...even when I have to pour you into a taxi, carry your shoes and handbag, and listen to your drunken ramblings while you sit peeing loudly on the loo with the bathroom door wide open..."

"Oh stop, stop, I can't bear it! Why can't I just be sensible and pace myself a bit more? Anyhow...if I'm to be in any fit state to make it out with Kirsty tonight then I need to *sleep* right now. Aw god, I'm so jealous of you being able to stay home and lounge around tonight..."

"Oh no...that won't be the case darling...because you know what you did in your infinite wisdom...you bought FOUR tickets for this thing tonight...one each for you and Kirsty...and ONE EACH FOR ME AND NATHAN! Now isn't that just fantastic?"

"Oh shit, once again, I'm sorry. But I'm kind of glad you're coming, for moral support...you know, in case some woman throws a punch at me or I need you to haul me out of the flightpath of airborne furniture. And I suppose it will be a laugh...and it's our era, right? All those '80s tunes...maybe even some that were around when we first met in '84...aw, it might be like a little trip down Memory Lane for us..."

"...or a little trip to A & E if it all kicks off. Right...now snuggle in here...and put your left hand down there...ah, that's better...time for a quick sleep before the phone rings or someone knocks at the door or Chloe comes in wanting money or food or both..."

I could feel my eyelids closing as he was still talking; my lovely, kind, understanding David...his voice gently soothing me into the land of nod...

"HOLY SHIT!" I almost gave David a heart attack as I shot up in bed, a sudden realisation hitting me like a ton of bricks.

"Jesus, you're trying to finish me off...I'm not insured you know. What now?"

"It's bloody fancy dress tonight..." I wailed, knowing that I possessed precisely nothing that would even be remotely suitable, whilst realising that all the fancy dress shops in town were definitely, firmly closed on a Sunday. For feck's sake.

"Only us...only me and Kirsty could agree to this without any forward planning, without any idea of what we could possibly wear. What are we going to do?"

"Well, I suppose you could always cancel...maybe Mikita would understand..."

"No, we can't, not an option...it's a charity do for the hospice that cared for her aunty...she'd never forgive us now we've promised to go...oh god, everyone's going to be looking ace in brilliantly thought out outfits or, at the very least they will have picked up bits and pieces previously to cobble together something decent enough to wear..."

Still wailing...still hungover...I leapt out of bed to grab my mobile and rang Kirsty, to give her a rude awakening...to inform her what stupid pissed-up plans we'd made last night. She was clearly still suffering and on another planet when she answered the call...and then we played the little blame game, deciding whose fault it was we had agreed to go in the first place (hers) and who had actually handed over good hard cash for the tickets (me, apparently).

Once we'd calmed down slightly, and she'd disappeared for five minutes to throw up and take some paracetamols, we had a bit of a brainstorming session, deciding who on earth we were going to dress up as and where the hell we were going to acquire everything from...before I crawled back into bed.

"We've no choice. The best we can come up with is Pepsi and Shirley. Kirsty isn't going to straighten her hair tonight so it will be naturally curly and bouncy and she was blessed with darker locks than me anyway…I'm struggling a tad with Shirley but apparently Kirsty's next door neighbour has a Rod Stewart wig she's going to try and trim down…and we're going to borrow the other girls' biker jackets and try and knock up a couple of flowery ra-ra skirts…or those puffballs things that, unfortunately, only look good on someone who's a size 10 or less…but needs must…"

David thought it was hilarious. I would soon put a stop to that.

"I don't know what you're laughing at. You and Nathan are going as George and Andrew."

"What? No! Bugger off! No way…we agreed to go with you but we're just going to prop up the bar in the games room or something…"

"Strictly no entry allowed unless you're in '80s fancy dress I'm afraid. Apparently Nathan's been told he's going as Andrew now…so you'll have to be George I'm afraid…and you'd better make a good job of it, him being the ultimate Greek god and all that…"

"Aw Lou…what the hell am *I* going to wear? I've left my jackets and everything at Billy's and I've only got a handful of outfits here anyway besides my work gear…"

"Don't worry, it's all sorted. Kirsty has a pair of aviator shades somewhere at home, we can buy you some white towelling socks and a cheap white t-shirt from Asda and I'm sure we'll be able to borrow some slip-on shoes from someone's granddad…and you already have jeans…and we'll ask 'Stink' to lend you his leather coat…"

"I'm not sure I want to be borrowing anything off someone called 'Stink'…"

"Don't worry, 'Stink' isn't his real name…"

"…well, I would hope not, but who the hell is he?"

"He's a lovely guy but he works on the bins…hence the name…he's clean, I promise you…him and 'One Skirt' have been going out for years…"

"… 'One Skirt'?"

"Someone once told her she looked slim in her little black skirt and now every time she turns out she's wearing it…lots of different tops but never seen her in another skirt, ever…"

"You're weird you lot, you know. What the hell is wrong with you?"

"What can I say…there were about forty kids a class in our primary school…we were kicked out every morning in the summer holidays to play and instructed to only come back for mealtimes…and our parents were too busy working all the hours god sends to spare any time to help us with our homework…we practically raised ourselves."

"Explains a lot. Can't believe you're making me dress up as George Michael tonight though…Christ, it's like your ultimate fantasy isn't it? You definitely owe me one for this."

"One what?"

One session in the bedroom in turned out to be…which left me feeling even more delicate than before so I snoozed off my excesses for a couple of hours more, before David cooked us all a fry-up…another good reason to love this wonderful man.

Kirsty and a slightly sulky looking Nathan arrived around six o'clock, as it had been agreed we would all help each other get ready at my house and leave together – in numbers perhaps the neighbours would realise we were actually going to an '80s night, rather than presume that was just how we liked to dress up these days.

If Nathan had been a little sulky-chops when we had been informed he would be dressing up as Andrew Ridgeley, then he was downright pissed off when he discovered that he had been allocated my old baggy 'Choose Life' t-shirt to wear and that Kirsty had produced from somewhere a pair of humungous white trousers that buried Nathan, even pulled up to his belly-button and with a belt on…and he ended up with the biggest turn-ups I've ever clapped eyes on.

David didn't look too bad actually once we'd applied the spray-in streaks to his hair, promising they would wash straight out (fingers crossed, ey) and sporting Stink's leather jacket and his own tightest blue jeans.

The boys had the last laugh anyway when Kirsty and I got our clobber on…her hair had a life of its own and, despite a further pruning, my wig was shocking and we ended up looking more like Wood and Walters than Pepsi and Shirley. Not helped by the flowery skirts…it turned out none of us were too clever with a pair of scissors and a needle and thread. David's 'skills', and I use the word 'skills' very loosely, were probably the best, but he would never gain employment as a dressmaker if it should all go tits up for him in the plumbing world. The hem on my skirt looked like a hungry dog had had a bloody good chew on it, but never mind, I'm sure no one would notice it in the dark.

We arrived at the club at seven-thirty on the dot, were unnecessarily frisked by Big Daddy on the door (god I hoped he had a big coat to chuck over his wrestling gear later or else he would freeze his nads off), and had our tickets checked by Charles and Di on the way in. And then it was like being in some weird timewarp for the next four and a half hours, where I counted five Boy Georges and six Madonnas (One Skirt amongst them of course – mainly, I suspect, so she got to wear her favourite little black number...which was looking slightly bobbly and more grey than black these days). Ashanti, Dawn and Mikita were, of course, Bananarama, looking magnificent in their denim dungarees and bovver boots and their hair backcombed and held in place with so much hairspray, it was to be hoped there wouldn't be a fire on the premises.

Michael Jackson, Kermit the Frog and Wonder Woman were behind the bar, while "Whitney Houston" was the star turn. And the room was filled with a selection of other 1980s stars...some recognisable, some not so much. I mistakenly thought Lionel Richie was Rustie Lee, and Cher was a dead ringer for Pete Burns. It was surreal. But hilarious. And much to my relief, there was no fighting...just a slight altercation at the food hatch when they ran out of pies (honestly, you would think Kirsty had never been fed).

All in all, once the boys had forgiven us and seen the funny side, it was the best of nights, with the best bunch of people...and I couldn't believe what an amazing weekend we'd had.

This is how I should have been spending the last thirty years...loving, laughing, living life to the full. Not just existing from day to day. No, this was the life. And with David right by my side, it could only get better.

Chapter 4

SUZANNE

Mum attempted to broach the more practical aspects of my situation the next morning, but I wasn't in that place yet – couldn't deal with the enormity of it all.

"Darling, I know it's probably the last thing you want to do, but you need to speak to Dave - otherwise, you'll never accept that you have to move on, if you don't step up and deal with everything. Dad and I will be here to help you at every stage, don't you worry," said mum, trying her best to reassure me. I noted each time she uttered Dave's name it was practically through gritted teeth. I'm not sure she could even be in the same room as him these days, whereas she'd previously treated him like another son and joyfully welcomed him into her home.

"I know mum. But the last time I spoke to Dave, just before he left, I'd told him I was fine, and he believed me. Please…I don't want him knowing I'm like this again. I can't let him see how he…how *they* have broken me. I can't." I almost begged mum. I needed more time…to get myself together. To not be the emotional mess he'd had to take care of for such a long period of his life.

Unexpectedly, his nan died, and I saw Dave cry real, mansize tears for the first time in years. When he took the telephone call from his brother who broke the news that Nellie, the delightful old lady who'd always had a kind word and a Glacier Mint for everyone, had passed away peacefully in her sleep, and I saw him crumple, I hesitated at first – it had been so very long since I'd last touched him – but then felt myself shifting towards him, sliding my arms around him and letting him cry onto my shoulder. Every cloud has a silver lining I guess…we were so very sad to lose his nan, but it broke the ice between me and Dave.

Years of estrangement meant we had a long road ahead of us, but we started to talk more, to share again; there were tentative smiles and even a little laughter. There was always the elephant in the room, mourning the child we had never conceived, but we at least were able to strike up a friendship again, even venturing out as a couple to family celebrations and accepting invitations to friends' dinner parties. There was a hint of the loving, contented couple we had once been, somewhere in there.

We hadn't shared a bed since the second time we had been informed that the IVF had failed...I had pushed him away and there had been undisguised relief in his eyes when I had transferred my belongings into one of the spare rooms. Of course he had tried to insist that I should be the one to remain in the master suite but I put my stiletto-clad foot down. At that stage I could no longer continue to share our marital bed with him...but I also couldn't sleep in it alone, without him there by my side...

He must have had yearnings over the years, that longing for sex that any fit, healthy male would have...but he never strayed, of that I'm sure. He was better than that; he didn't have it in him to let me down so badly. I'd no doubt that behind his firmly closed bedroom door he must have done the necessary to relieve the sexual tension built up inside of him but thankfully he never looked elsewhere, outside of the house. Many pretty girls had looked longingly at Dave, a few even dared to flutter their eyelashes at him and tempt him with their come-to-bed eyes, but he was disinterested, oblivious to their advances, unaware of the effect he had on most women, and even several men.

Over the next few days, once the heavy duty tablets kicked in, the fog seemed to lift ever so slightly. I knew it would never vanish completely; it was something I had become accustomed to heaving around with me – a heavy, cumbersome load that I was destined to be saddled with for the rest of my life. I had never had a big appetite but it had recently dwindled to almost nothing...but with mum's help and encouragement I was starting to eat tiny meals and gradually building up my strength.

I accepted I would have to sit down and talk matters through with Dave soon if we were ever to resolve our finances amicably, as we had agreed to do. Just a few more days and I would call him, arrange for him to come over after supper one evening when mum and dad were out at the golf club. It would take every bit of strength I had not to throw myself at his feet and beg him to come home.

Funnily enough, I had started to believe that possibly, just maybe, Dave and I could get back on track again and I found myself longing to be held in his arms once more...and for the first time in what seemed like forever, I desperately wanted him to take me into our kingsize marital bed and make love to me without there being a purpose to it...just because he wanted to, and I wanted to. And I would tell him I loved him - my god how I loved him. I hadn't said that in years. And he had eventually stopped saying those three precious little words to me – when he realised I didn't believe him; that I didn't understand how he could love me after the selfish way in which I'd behaved and, more than anything, how I'd refused to let go of the blame.

To be even considering any kind of reunion with Dave meant I was heading to a better place and I was finally casting aside some of my demons.

Secretly thrilled that I was taking the first steps towards normality and recovering a beautiful relationship that I thought I'd lost forever, I'd taken off on a shopping expedition to Truro, purchasing - amongst many expensive items of clothing and must-have pairs of shoes - sexy, seductive, flimsy underwear that I longed to wear for him, to remind him of what he'd been missing; to reignite the flame of passion between us. Mum and I had been thoroughly preened and pampered from top to toe in the luxurious hotel spa, and I'd returned feeling happier and lighter than I had in years; smiling, laughing and nervously excited in anticipation of the weekend to come.

But I'd taken one look at Dave's confused, bereft face and seen such pain in those blue eyes – and for the time ever I was terrified because I'd seen and felt deceipt...I could sense it, I could smell it, I could hear it in his stilted words. He tried to appear interested and attentive but it was those eyes, those endless pools of blue that were consumed with guilt, that gave the game away. Those eyes that said "It's her. She's back."

To anyone else, it would have seemed crazy to think that if he'd been unfaithful then it must have been with a girl he'd had a brief relationship with back in the '80s, when he was a teenager, rather than with someone he'd recently met through work or bumped into the pub.

But I knew.

It hit me like a sledgehammer; the realisation that the only other person who could ever have come between me and Dave was somehow back on the scene. How could it be, that after thirty years, god damn it, he was clearly still in love with this woman who he had last clapped eyes on when they were just seventeen, when she had brutally stamped all over his heart and ridden roughshod all over his feelings. I was convinced that there had never been any contact between them since they had parted acrimoniously...so what had changed?

Where had she come from? How had she found him? Why was she back after three long decades? I had so many questions that I didn't dare ask. He had never been tempted by *any other woman throughout the entirety of our rollercoaster of a relationship, no matter what life had thrown at us, no matter how much the bond between us had weakened - almost to the point of disintegration - yet the return of this woman heralded the beginning of the end for myself and Dave and told me everything I needed to know.*

I went into denial. Despite the indisputable, insurmountable truth, I carried on as I had before, trying to maintain that air of normality, pretending that everything was going to be fine and there wasn't about to be a Dave-shaped hole in my life. I studied his beautiful face when he was talking to me, watched his every move, listened to every emotion-filled sigh that escaped from his mouth and knew, as I lay awake night after night, that he was doing exactly the same in the room across the landing – unable to sleep, unable to see a way forward.

Every day it felt like the knife plunged and twisted a little bit deeper and I fought the urge to scream and shout at him and demand he give her up. Yet I acted as if everything was just fine and dandy, trying to keep my tone frothy and light-hearted, avoiding any serious subjects, making casual arrangements for us to go out with friends - to maintain some sort of normality. And Dave was present in body but not in mind. We shared conversations and meals and he forced laughter in all of the right places…but the laughter never quite reached his eyes and his mind was so obviously somewhere far away with someone else who I was unable to compete with, because the odds were firmly stacked against me.

Naively, I'd thought that I would try and weather the storm and bravely hold on to my husband, come what may. I'd clung to the hope that eventually, whatever secret liaisons had occurred, whatever they had shared, and may still be sharing, it would all peter out and he would accept that it was finally over for the two of them – and she would be out of his system once and for all. He would never leave me.

But I'd underestimated him and the depth of his feelings for her. He set off for work each morning with that pained expression on his face and he returned home later and later every evening, having taken on extra jobs that he hadn't really needed to, just to avoid coming home to me. His tortured expression mirrored my own, and I knew that even if he stayed it would only be out of his sense of duty and his promises made at the altar in 1997. This man would never again return to my bed, would never again tell me he loved me. It was ironic that after pushing him away so many times that I wanted him more than ever now, just when he was unattainable. I'd lost him. Game over.

"Hi Dave, it's me. Of course, you would know that. Sorry I've been a while getting back to you. I've just been busy, you know how it is. Anyway, can you come round to mum and dad's about eight o'clock on Thursday and then we can go through all the financial stuff and start the ball rolling. There's another couple of papers from the estate agents that you need to sign as well. Best to do it on slightly more neutral ground in the circumstances. Mum and dad will be out and she's leaving us some supper in the oven. No need to ring back to confirm, I'll just see you then. Bye."

I'd called his mobile when I knew he wouldn't be around to hear it ring, first thing on a Monday morning when they were sorting stock out, taking delivery of all the orders and prioritising any plumbing emergencies that had arisen over the weekend. His phone would be stuffed in the inside pocket of his waterproof grey jacket that would be hung up on the peg in the back room and he wouldn't be able to hear the ringtone over the sound of the ancient radio and the busy printer, rattling off stock details. I hadn't asked if the time and date would be suitable for him – years of living with this man meant I knew he would be sure to be available at eight o'clock on Thursday; he would wish to sort everything out as soon as was ever possible with minimum fuss and animosity.

Thursday came around all too soon and before I knew it, I was taking a deep breath and opening the front door to my nervous-looking, eternally handsome estranged husband.

"Hi, come in...you've just missed mum and dad." I spoke to him more formally, politely – that easiness between us had disappeared now, to be replaced by, if not quite *uneasiness*, then definitely a distance, a remoteness. Two old friends trying to re-connect; former lovers trying to find some neutral ground. A husband and wife trying to work out how best to divide up their lives and joint possessions and dissolve their marriage with the least hassle and expense.

"Thanks Sue. Sorry I'm a bit on the early side but I came straight from a job – as you can see from my dirty clothes and manky nails!" He was trying to lighten the atmosphere, to prove we could still be civil to each other – trying to make everything as painless as possible for me. Ha! If that wasn't so painful it would be funny. Every second of my life now was filled with soul destroying, mind withering pain; there was no escape from it, no matter how hard I tried to hide.

"It's fine, we can have a bite to eat and then start sifting through the paperwork, if you like," I responded, knowing full well that I would struggle to digest anything tonight while my insides were in turmoil, but wanting, *needing* him to sit with me so just for a moment I could imagine that we were still that couple, settling down after work to share a meal together and mull over the day's events.

"Erm..I'm okay thanks...I had a big meal at lunchtime...but you go ahead if you like and get something while I read through all this stuff that's come through from the accountants," he replied, not quite meeting my eye. Ah. The penny dropped. He never ate heavy meals at lunchtime, said it played havoc with his afternoon working hours and made him want to curl up and have a sneaky nap. *Louise.* LOUISE – god how I despised that name, I couldn't bring myself to even utter it most of the time. It was her – she would have reluctantly agreed to him popping over here to sort out finances and paperwork and all the necessary stuff but she wouldn't have settled for him sitting down to eat supper with me. That would have been a step too far in her eyes, much too coupley and civilised, with a faint possibility that supper and wine could lead to much more, if only for old times' sake. I pictured her smackable face and could almost hear her screeching "No way! You are NOT sitting down in your matrimonial home scoffing a cosy meal for two with your WIFE while I'm up here going out of my mind with worry!" She looked like the no-nonsense type, not afraid to speak her mind and take control of the situation – Dave would do as he was instructed.

She really had nothing to fret about though – Dave was clearly besotted with her and, having yearned for her all of these years, he obviously wouldn't risk losing her again by doing anything that might have been construed as inappropriate. She must have known inside what a good, honest, faithful man he was – mind you, she was probably frightened to death of him walking away from her again, of learning to live without him. I know I was.

The food remained untouched. The wine stayed in the bottle. Dave knocked back a couple of glasses of water while we jotted down lists, divided up possessions, worked out figures, signed papers – it was long and tedious and heartbreaking. When you set out on your journey together you don't ever envisage it ending it like this. It was so incredibly final and sad to be discussing the sale of the house, and when we moved on to arrange a date for him to collect the bulk of his personal belongings, despite my best efforts I couldn't prevent my eyes filling and brimming over with tears.

God, I couldn't bear to be the object of his pity and guilt.

"I'm sorry Sue...I really am. Are you sure you're going to be okay?" He tentatively reached out and touched my hand briefly and that was almost the undoing of me.

"No, it's fine Dave, honestly. Of course, it's unbelievably sad...but the end of any marriage is always going to be difficult. You...you've moved on now and I've accepted that. And I've moved on as well. It was over really a heck of a long time ago and we should have both laid our cards on the table then, rather than end up in the situation we did. Of course I would have preferred it if *you two* could have controlled yourselves until after *we'd* agreed to separate but there you go....it happened, such is life...and it was probably for the best as it forced our hands."

He had the grace to look embarrassed – I knew he wasn't proud of the fact that he had in effect been unfaithful to me and that his feelings for *her* were what had put the final nails in the coffin as far as our marriage was concerned.

"If it had been anyone else Sue, any other woman, I would never have gone there, you know that. But Louise...it was different, she's different. I can't explain...and you wouldn't want to hear it...but I couldn't let her go again. Life's too short."

Even those few words were like razor blades to my heart; they were sharp, stabbing, agonising and I struggled to form any kind of response.

"Anyway," he continued, clearly uncomfortable and desperate to get it all over and done with, "I'm glad you've met someone else too, that you won't be alone. Who is this mysterious man anyway - anyone I know?" He was attempting to lighten the atmosphere again, to ease the tension in the room.

Oh how I would have enjoyed telling him how incredible his replacement was, just to watch his face fall – but that was never going to happen, firstly because (a) there was no such man in my life; I had completely fabricated his existence and (b) it wouldn't have bothered Dave in the slightest *who* I was dating – all I would have seen in his eyes was a sense of relief that there would be someone else there for him to pass the baton to.

"No one you know; just a friend of Tara's we bumped into one night. It's not serious at the moment, but who knows where it might lead...although for the time being I'm just going to enjoy being footloose and fancy free!" I smiled an awkward smile; lying through my straightened, whitened teeth to Dave didn't come easily at all – it didn't sit comfortably with me. But I think he bought it as he didn't question me further, instead leaning down to gather up a pile of papers and slotting them into a file I had marked "SEPARATION".

We'd had a productive evening; waded through a lot and paved the way for all of the official stuff that would follow in the form of consent forms from banks and divorce documentation from solicitors and courts.

I'd heard his mobile bleep a few times, could hear the familiar text notifications coming through, although the phone remained inside his coat pocket and he made no attempt to retrieve it while he was with me. I'd no doubt Louise was texting him to enquire what progress had been made and wanting to know when he was likely to be out of here, to put her own over-active mind at rest.

"Did you ever really, truly love me Dave?" I cursed myself for blurting the words out but they were off my tongue before I could stop myself – I think they'd been festering within me since I'd first discovered his infidelity; when I'd realised he would soon be leaving me, for his one true love.

Relief flooded through me as I saw Dave's eyes fill with tears; to know he still had some feelings reserved for me, whatever they may be. He steadied himself on the scrubbed pine kitchen table and looked at me long and hard before saying, "Sue, I really, honestly did love you. If I'd never met Louise, if I'd never known her, there would only ever have been you. But I *did* meet Louise, long before me and you got together, and I can't deny how I've always felt about her, no matter how hard I've tried to suppress those feelings. I know I can't expect you to ever understand that, or forgive me."

"I understand Dave. Of course I understand...because the way you feel about Louise, that's how I feel...how I felt about you. You made me so incredibly happy, you were all I ever wanted – the man of my dreams. And I know everything got messed up...when we discovered we would never have children...but I never stopped loving you, with every fragment of my heart, with every ounce of my being – despite everything."

He looked uncomfortably down at the floor then, his eyes fixed on some invisible mark on the tiles apparently - not wanting to meet my eyes, not wishing to see the agony there, not wanting me to ask the next question, but knowing it was coming anyway.

"So...you always loved her more than you loved me then?"

Actually, in reality it was a statement more than a question.

There was silence for a few moments; you could have heard a pin drop in the room.

Eventually Dave nodded and spoke so low that it was almost a whisper.

"I suppose I did Sue, even if I didn't know it myself for a long time. I'm so, so sorry. I never, ever wanted to be the cause of any pain for you; god knows you've been through enough. But please, I beg of you, don't let all of this take anything away from what we had, because for a time it was fantastic. We fell in love and I entered into that marriage through my own free will, not thinking of anyone else. It wouldn't have been fair to anyone to go ahead with a marriage if I was still hankering after someone in the past. No, I'd put all of that to bed, found a fabulous woman and made her my wife because I loved her. Please don't ever think otherwise."

Chapter 5

LOUISE

"Jesus! What's up with your face, piglet? You found a fiver but lost a tenner?" Kirsty was her usual tactless self but I was pleased to see her; I could always rely on her to cheer me up.

"Three guesses! Dave's been summoned to the palace to discuss the separation and to sign all the paperwork. Despite my reservations, he was eager to go really, to get it all out of the way…but I would be happy if he never set foot in that godforsaken house again. I just don't trust that woman…"

"Couldn't she have just forwarded papers on to him for signature? Did he really have to drag his arse over there?"

"Unfortunately yes…with the business and the accounts and everything they jointly own…they need to get their heads together to divide it all up fairly, as well as put their signatures to the necessary documents. There was no way around it."

"Mmm…as long as they don't get their heads TOO close together eh…?"

"Don't. I can't bear the thought of her plying him with alcohol and trying to cosy up to him on the settee…all glossy hair and flawless complexion and Chanel perfume. I can just imagine her giving it "Oh Dave…you couldn't just look at the dripping shower while you're here…but you'll need to take your shirt off for the job though…"

"Bloody hell love, it's not a Carry On film you know…her bra's not suddenly going to pop open to the sound of a "Booiiinngg" and a "Ooh, er, Mrs!" Control your imagination poppet before it drives you crazy!"

"I bet she's got him pissed as a newt and is trying to mount him as we speak K! I've texted him three times and he's not even replied once! I'm going to go demented sat here waiting for him to get in touch. And my bloody head's killing me, especially after the day I've had at work. My boss was a bastard today…humungous files being chucked at me one after the other with a ton of awkward shit to do on each one and angry clients demanding to know why they won't be able to move at the end of the month after all…I've been running round like a tit in a trance all day…stressed out of my mind!"

"Aw, honey…you know what'll calm your nerves and make you feel more relaxed tonight?"

"Wine? You're going to say wine aren't you?"

"Er, no, actually smartarse…I was going to say BAILEYS!"

"Baileys? Are you having a laugh? On a school night? – It's not big and it's not clever!"

"Yeah…but there's half a bottle left festering in the kitchen cupboard from god knows when and it keeps winking at me every time I go in to get the coffee…and we don't want it going off now, do we?"

We certainly didn't. I had sickening memories of a large glass of Baileys that had curdled in the sweltering, non-airconditioned pit of a tiny room I had shared with a friend on holiday in Benidorm. We had heaved our guts up chucking it down the sink and had to dispose of the glass in the end, as we couldn't get the smell and the stain out of it. In fact, even recalling that distant memory now…I swear I could still smell it…

Oh well, best check we'd got some ice.

An hour and a half later, when the pair of us were half-cut and Kirsty was swearing like Gordon Ramsey on a bad day - and when we were howling with laughter at a tale from the funeral parlour, involving a deceased man found in a dubious position, a relative with a squint and a lisp, and a partner who wanted to dress said deceased male in revealing ladies' underwear - David finally rang to assure me that yes, it was all done and dusted and no, he had not so much as shared a morsel of food with her let alone bodily fluids.

I could finally breathe a huge sigh of relief and, what the hell, finish the bottle of Baileys…oh and the white wine as well that Kirsty had suddenly produced from the depths of her humungous handbag. Oh well, in for a penny and all that…

Down the hatch!

Chapter 6

SUZANNE

The new and improved happy pills made life slightly more bearable but I was rattling around in my parents' house every day and mum was driving me increasingly up the wall, watching me like a hawk and constantly suggesting a variety of activities I could participate in, to keep me and my messed-up mind more active and to give my days some sort of purpose.

When I returned to my own home on the pretence of collecting some essential clothes items, I refused to leave. I was an adult and I needed my own space. Mum became tearful of course, but I assured her I was more likely to remain sane there than within the walls of their house, feeling as suffocated as I did.

"Mum, I am FINE!" I repeatedly assured her but she took not a blind bit of notice, convinced I was incapable of looking after myself and assuring me she would be calling in every day to check up on me.

I wasn't fine; the paperwork was coming in thick and fast now with regard to our separation and every letter chipped away another bit of my already shattered heart.

I finally signed off the sales particulars for the house and within hours viewings were lined up. Other people wandering around our home, criticising our taste in decoration and furnishings, making plans for their future in our rooms and gardens would, I knew, send me spiralling over the edge. So I agreed with the estate agents that they could keep a full set of keys at their offices and conduct the viewings themselves. When the day of the dreaded first viewing arrived, I knew I had to escape to another location, if just for an hour, but the question was, where to? Even popping into town filled me with terror these days following a particularly traumatic event that had truly opened my eyes to the severity of our situation and forced me to accept it was the beginning of the end.

The day had started like any other day – after I had attempted to make small-talk with Dave and he had left for work, I had finished my coffee whilst gazing out of the huge bay window in our lounge, and then applied a full face of make-up before heading to the shops for a few bits and pieces. I bumped into a couple of people I knew and briefly passed the time of day with them before deciding to nip into the butcher's to purchase a prime piece of steak for dinner – Dave's absolute favourite, which I would serve with home cooked chips and grilled mushrooms and tomatoes. It would be a pleasure to watch him enjoy it and share a glass of wine over dinner.

"Hello dear, I haven't seen you around for a while...how are you doing lovey?" a croaky old voice piped up from behind me. I instantly recognised the dulcet tones of old Mrs Pearson, no doubt purchasing some offal for her long-suffering husband and I inwardly sighed. She was a pleasant old lady but, unfortunately, the worst gossip this side of St. Austell, and I was very wary what I said, as I knew it would be all round Newquay within the hour.

"Hi Mrs Pearson," I replied, attempting a smile. "I'm fine, thank you. You know how it is...not enough hours in a day! I don't have the time to get out and about shopping much these days. Anyway, how are you? And how's Mr Pearson's cough these days?"

When the old boy coughed I swear you could hear it three streets away. He didn't let it put him off his tobacco though, but I guess that was his one pleasure in life.

"Oh, he's still the same dearie, I left him coughing up an ace when I came out shopping today. You know what Frank's like though – he'll probably still make it to the bookies later. Anyway, I hear on the grapevine that you had a bit of a commotion in that shop of yours a few weeks back – was your Dave okay after all that trouble?"

She quite obviously realised that I hadn't the faintest clue what she was talking about and I swear to god it made her day, stirring the pot, waiting and watching for my reaction. I hated to have to ask her, but really had no alternative as I was completely in the dark.

"Sorry? I'm not sure what you mean, Mrs Pearson. What trouble are you referring to then?"

"Well, lovely, you know me, I don't like to gossip. But I heard from Albert Tattershall's brother-in-law that apparently, when Albert was in the shop looking for a new padlock for that old shed of his, well this crazed girl came flying in – I say girl, but I think she was about as old as you – and she came out with all kinds of foul language, hurling abuse at your Dave. Albert said he didn't know where to look; I'm surprised all that business didn't give him another heart attack – he's not been well, you know. Apparently, Dave almost dragged this...lady...well not so much of a lady if you ask me, using filthy language like that…into the back room and they didn't emerge for a good while afterwards, when she'd apparently simmered down and stopped shouting the odds at him.

The room started to spin and I could actually feel the colour draining from my face – of course Dave had never said anything. This was all clearly connected to the strange atmosphere at home, his unhappiness and his obvious desire to be elsewhere.

"I…I…I can't remember if Dave mentioned anything. I'm just wondering whether it might have been some disgruntled customer. I don't suppose Albert gave any description of this woman?"

"Ooh well now, I've heard that she was attractive, with dark hair - and she had a big chest to go with her big mouth - because she reminded Albert of some girl he'd oggled on page three back in its heyday – typical Albert! Oh and as well as a mouth like a sewer, he definitely said she had a Northern accent. Albert apparently wasn't sure if he'd heard Dave address her as "Kerry", or maybe "Kirsty", but perhaps he misheard as his hearing's none too clever these days. And that's all I know lovey; you know me, I don't like to pry."

She gave me a self-satisfied smile while I died a little more inside.

It seemed she'd managed to pry enough to get quite a comprehensive description of this angry woman who'd verbally attacked my husband.

"Well, that liver's seen better days if you ask me, so it'll be egg and chips for us tonight I reckon. I'd better dash Suzanne…say hello to Dave for me." And with that she was gone. Bustled out of the door, the little ray of sunshine that she was, no doubt to spread more of her sparkle and happiness elsewhere, while I struggled to remain standing and get my breath. I paid for the steak and left as quickly as I could, desperate to be back home, back to safety, where I could digest what I'd just been told.

It was all adding up now and I couldn't pretend that everything was going to be alright, because it clearly wasn't. My hand was shaking as I unlocked the front door, my head was pounding, and I threw down my bags and hastily poured myself a glass of ice-cold water, so much whizzing round and round in my overloaded mind, wondering where this was all going to end, but knowing what I had to do next.

I switched on the laptop, fired it up and opened up my Facebook account. Her name wasn't Kerry or Kirsty…I'd never forgotten it, but hadn't ever searched for it before. By the time I'd initially registered on the social media sites I'd naively presumed that this woman was just someone long forgotten in Dave's past and she was nothing to us. I'd never anticipated that I would have to seek her out; that she would ever be a threat to my marriage again.

Louise Robinson – good grief, there were an awful lot of women listed under that name – a common name that befitted a common woman it would seem. Two hours later I was still trawling through all the names, determined that I would find this elusive person who Dave had loved so much.

Hoping and praying that she had actually added herself on Facebook, I persevered until my eyes were blurry and the pounding in my head had reached epic proportions. I discounted many because of age, or geography (heaven help me if she had relocated elsewhere, as Dave had when his family had moved down to Newquay), eliminated others on sheer looks alone (cruel, but fair). Eventually, my perseverance paid off and I came across a few Louises listed but who all had different surnames to the one I'd searched for – obviously they had registered on Facebook using their married names but also added their maiden names – hence the reason they had appeared in the 'Louise Robinson' search results.

The first one – far too old; the second one – she lived in Chicago, and I'm sure Mr Tattershall wouldn't have mixed up an American accent with one from the North West of England.

The third name I came to...Louise Stewart....well she didn't have black hair and she wasn't particularly well endowed...but something made me stop and stare at her profile picture much more closely. Could this be her? She seemed to be roughly in the right age category, although the lighting in the picture made it difficult to tell. She wasn't stunning but she was quite pretty I suppose in a girl-next-door kind of way, with her dark wavy hair and big brown eyes - if the girl-next-door wore Primark clothes and cheap make-up. I delved in, searching her Facebook "wall" for more information and clues.

Ah ha! Another photograph; this time pulling an incredibly stupid face and clearly mucking about with another woman by her side, who more than matched Mrs Pearson's description of straight black hair, big mouth, big boobs. What in god's name where they wearing on their heads? Where did you even purchase hats like those? I'm assuming they acquired their matching headgear in the Poundland sale. And a comment to go with the *picture that read, "You see, this is what freakin' happens when Lou-Lou and Thirsty Kirsty drink too much on an afternoon sesh". Classy.*

This was her. Definitely. Without a doubt. I actually felt my face become momentarily paralysed as a chill descended upon my whole body. This was the girl who had stolen Dave's heart when they were barely out of school and who he had loved ever since. This was the woman who now shared his bed - who could proudly pronounce to the world that this was her man.

There were several mentions of Wigan on her profile page and a fair few pictures of drunken nights out. Thankfully there were none of Dave on there but there was one particular photo that took my breath away. A teenage girl, clearly a younger version of this Louise – obviously this woman's daughter. No pictures or evidence of any other children...but this was enough for me to deal with at present. Good old Louise and her fertile, albeit fairly chubby, body – able to produce a bonny, healthy daughter. Poor old Suzanne and her sensational but barren body – unable to produce a smile most days.

I heard a strangled sob emanate from my own throat and felt a hatred rise up inside me then that I had never thought possible.

What in god's name did Dave see in this hardly model-like woman? What made her so special to him? She didn't look anything out of the ordinary and by all accounts she had done the dirty on him when they were teenagers, so what made her the love of Dave's life? She must have a scintillating personality....or be outstandingly adventurous in the bedroom department – and that made me shudder to even think about it.

When I eventually closed down the laptop, the photographs of her disappeared from view...but they were captured forever in my mind now. I would never again close my eyes without seeing the face of the woman trying to take away my husband.

With precious little energy to do anything else, I set off on foot down to the supermarket to buy ingredients for meals I would probably never cook. Instead of concentrating on the task in hand, all I could think of was that there were strangers in our house – presumably admiring, financially planning and imagining their own futures there. Would the rooms we had designed and decorated for our children be used as bedrooms for other people's little ones? Or would the fittings be ripped out and replaced with office furniture or gym equipment?

Somehow I found myself at the till, and as I loaded my shopping on to the conveyer belt, I nodded at the disinterested young assistant, noticing she looked like she'd been tangoed and that one of her front teeth was chipped. Then she was staring at me quizzically and I heard the words, "I said that's £38.65 please. £38.65 PLEASE! Excuse me, are you okay? Do you have the money?"

I jolted back into the present tense, noticing that the couple at the checkout next to mine were gawping at me, staring at me as if I was slightly odd. God, what was wrong with me? I delved into my handbag to lift out my black leather purse...but discovered it wasn't there. I could feel the hysteria beginning to rise, the sweat beginning to trickle down my back, as I emptied the contents of my bag onto the conveyer belt and tears started to fall.

"Excuse me, excuse me...just a minute," barked a familiar female voice from behind me. "I'll get that shopping; here take my card and I'll come forward and pay for it. It's okay, I know her...she must have forgotten her purse; dizzy cow. Add a couple of those strong bags on to the bill will you and I'll pack this stuff up for her."

I half-turned to see Billy's vicious-tongued wife Jenny actually paying for my shopping with her credit card and haphazardly packing my bags for me. She was the very last person I wanted to see today and I tried to protest but couldn't seem to summon up the energy to do so. She propelled me towards a wooden seating area, with my packed bags stashed in my trolley, instructing me to "Wait there, for Christ's sake!" while she paid for her own groceries and then ordered me to follow her outside. She then insisted that she would drop me back home in her dirty, battered old Vauxhall – a vehicle I wouldn't normally have been seen dead in; Good grief, did the woman ever clean this old banger out?

When I arrived home I noticed Alethea from the estate agents just locking up and leaving with the interested viewers – a couple in their thirties I would say, with two young boys in matching sports gear. If they bought our house then the bedroom we had decorated so beautifully for the daughter we had never had – well it would be the first room to be re-decorated. Fighting back the urge to vent all of my anger at them, I watched the smiley family say goodbye and return to their car, and I turned to Jenny, who was watching me closely and had clearly had added "being bonkers" to her long list of my faults and inadequacies.

"Thanks for the assistance back there and the lift home but I'm okay now. And thanks again for paying the bill for me – I'll nip in and get the money now to reimburse you. I think I must have left my purse in my other black bag on the back of the bedroom door, silly me."

Ah there it was, the usual sneer on her hard, fat face.

"You're obviously not okay, you daft bint! You were on another planet back there in the supermarket...beam me up Snotty! Now we are going to take this shopping of yours in and put it away, and then I'll make you a strong brew and check you are back in the land of the living again before I have to leave. Stop protesting for god's sake! Don't be a stupid, stubborn cow all of your life; have a day off!"

I bit back my comment that she shouldn't join the Samaritans any time soon and thought of telling her to clear off now but could see she wasn't taking no for an answer. And I feared I would come off worse in any argument. I followed her down my path, noticing her massive backside wobbling perilously in front of me and cruelly thinking she should have reversing lights fitted on to it, it being such a large load and all. Her ancient tight black leggings did nothing to disguise her humungous thighs and chunky calves. God, had this woman never heard of aerobics? She was definitely no stranger to a fish supper.

I unlocked the door and Jenny made us a coffee so strong you could stand your spoon up in it, while I unpacked the shopping – my goodness, none of these random ingredients could actually be assembled to make a meal; I really hadn't been thinking straight in that supermarket.

When we retired to the lounge, Jenny bounced me up into the air as she clumsily sat on the other end of the settee I had recently sunk into.

I didn't know what to talk about to begin with; we didn't usually have anything to say to each other – we had nothing whatsoever in common other than our husbands being best friends. I guess we wouldn't even have that in common soon, when I wouldn't be able to claim Dave as my husband any more. At least I would never have to attempt to make polite conversation with this woman again.

"So, what the hell was that about back there then? Blimmin' eck...those bloody drugs you on sending you doo-lally are they?" enquired Jenny, in her usual forthwright manner, making disgusting slurping noises whilst sipping the boiling hot coffee.

"They are not drugs!" I replied hotly. "It is merely medication to make me feel calmer; to clear my head a little. I was just having a bad day, that's all, with viewers booked in to see the house. It's hard to think of strangers wandering around the home you love so much – the house that you are going to have to sell because of your husband's infidelity, I might add!"

"Oh piss off will you!" she quickly fired right back at me. "You and Dave have been living separate lives for years so don't try and pretend otherwise. You were trying to hold on to something that just wasn't there anymore. You know Dave is the most honest, decent man you could ever meet and he has put up with all your shit for years now, mollycuddling you and trying to pretend everything's okay. At least now, for once in your life, you have done the decent thing and let him go, given him a chance of happiness again."

How dare she! I couldn't believe the cheek of this woman, sitting there in *my* house, drinking *my* coffee, spouting off about my behaviour, as if she really knew anything about me.

"Happiness! Happiness? What even is that?" I almost shouted at her. "You sit there all smugly telling me I have been *mollycuddled*...do you have any idea what it is like to be childless; to be infertile? You, with your brood of feral little monsters! NO! You don't. So don't try and make me feel worse than I already do by insinuating that I was dragging Dave down with me and making his life a misery...because you will never know the emptiness that comes with finding out you will never be a mother! Never!"

She jumped up then, clearly angry, her face and chest red, which really did clash with her crimson t-shirt.

"Firstly, if you ever refer to my kids as "feral little monsters" again, I will knock your front teeth out. Secondly, no, you're right, I don't know what it feels like to be unable to have children. But I do know that I would never have made my husband suffer like you did, if I had been in your position! How do you think it was for him? He'd not only lost his chance of having children but in effect lost his wife as well, while you took a trip to La-la land! Christ, he was like your bloody carer for years – you, sitting there in your ivory tower with everyone doing your bidding and fawning over you! There are a shit load of other women out there who can't have children and they still have to get up every day and go to work and deal with it...but not you. Oh no, Miss Fucking Fancy Pants gets to take to her bed every day while mummy and daddy wait on her hand and foot and her husband slaves away, day in day out, to pay the bills! And don't give me that hoity toity look, just because I've used language you don't like...yes, people actually do swear you silly, sanctimonious bitch...welcome to the real world!"

I felt like I'd been punched over and over again; her words the punches, the pain they caused greater than any physical damage. How can anyone be so heartless?

"You're a cruel woman, Jenny – there's just no need to say those things. And don't think I haven't noticed that you always throw in a few extra swear words when you're talking to me – just to wind me up and make me feel uncomfortable!" I was almost whispering then, all the fight and stuffing knocked out of me.

"Yes I *fucking* do *Suzanne*! You're right. Because it seriously gets on my tits when you get all snooty when you hear what you class as 'bad language'. I mean, it's bloody ridiculous!" she replied, laughing her annoying laugh, and shaking her head simultaneously. "I'm not being censored by the likes of you! I mean, who do you think you are with all your airs and graces - the bleedin' queen? "

My anger was bubbling up to match hers now and I responded through gritted teeth.

"Of course not, you stupid, stupid woman! Just because I've been brought up to talk properly and I don't use profanities at every available opportunity...there's nothing wrong in that."

"Oh really, is there not. Well, while we're chucking the home truths out there, let's see how honest you can be. Admit it then, you purposely use big, long words when I'm around don't you? You try and discuss subjects and use language that you think I won't understand just to try and lord it over me and make me look a fool don't you?"

"I wouldn't have to try too hard, would I? It's not my fault you're uneducated and don't understand words consisting of more than one syllable!"

I did feel a little ashamed to be honest because that's exactly what I'd done - maybe it was tit for tat when she constantly tried to put me down and show me up in front of the others. And she was always so confident, so well-liked by everyone; constantly full of humour and good spirits – I faded into the background when she was around with her fowl mouth and cackling laugh. At least as far as looks and intelligence were concerned, I was leagues ahead of her.

"I knew it! I told Billy that, but he thought I was imagining it – you know what blokes are like. Anyway, just so you know, Mrs Mensa, I actually did really well at school and got nine GCSEs - I just didn't choose to use them. So not as thick as you make out, eh?"

A further unexpected wave of shame washed over me then - I had always assumed that Jenny had achieved precisely nothing at school and was definitely at the back of the queue when brains had been dished out. It would seem that I had made incorrect assumptions without any real evidence; that I had stereotyped this tough, outspoken girl from the housing estate and not given her a chance.

It nearly choked me to say the words but I had to get them out. "I'm sorry Jenny, I shouldn't have behaved in such a childish way. No wonder you hated me. In my defence, I'd never come across anyone like you before though; I always seemed to be tongue-tied whenever you were around and when I did speak I always said the wrong thing, and you were always so quick to make fun of me and put me down. You were so confident and I guess I was just socially awkward, even on Dave's arm. It was the only way I could show off a bit I suppose."

She looked at me in amazement as she said, "Hate you? I never hated you. Is that what you thought? It did my frigging head in, sorry, it did my *head* in - no swear word - that you spoke with that cut-glass accent and always had that superior look on your face that I just wanted to wipe off, but I certainly didn't hate you. We're just complete opposites, from totally different worlds. You buy your designer dresses at posh little boutiques where I can't even afford to buy my knickers from! I am Primark's best customer, but of course you wouldn't be seen dead in there! And you know what doesn't help your case - and this is entirely down to my own insecurities, I know - the fact you're so god damn beautiful of course! Elegant, immaculate, not a hair out of place, always looking a million dollars...and here's me with my rolls of fat and dinner lady arms!

She smiled then, the honesty bringing out a much nicer, more pleasant side to her. It threw me off balance a little – I wasn't accustomed to her being kind to me. I needn't have worried, it wasn't long before the old Jenny made a re-appearance.

"You and Dave though. I never got the two of you. Dave's amazing - a top bloke and a fantastic friend. Gorgeous, fit, caring, hard-working and funny as hell...a real catch. I suppose you made an attractive couple when you were together, but I never understood what made him choose you, out of all the women he could have had. Yes, you're beautiful and smart and I bet you've never had to use Clearasil in your whole zit-free life, but so were a billion other women and he could have hooked up with any one of them. I just didn't see that spark between the two of you, that connection - didn't sense that you were everything to him and that he was everything to you...like me and Billy..."

I couldn't prevent the "Christ!" that came out of my mouth. Her and Billy, would spoil another couple I always said, although Dave didn't like it when I did and told me that there was a "lid for every pot".

So I suppose I deserved what came next.

"Him and Louise though, I get them. It's there, that X factor, that missing ingredient you just can't put your finger on. It's like they were always *meant* to be together. They make each other howl with laughter, they're always touchy-feely and never let go of each other, and it's like they've finally found what they've been searching for all of their lives."

"Fabulous! Just fabulous. Thanks for sharing that. That's just bloody cruel, and *that's* bloody swearing!" I burst out, tears escaping one by one. "You didn't have to tell me that, I could have gone to my grave without knowing that thanks."

"I'm sorry but look, it's time you got some tough love," said Jenny. "Your mum and dad, your friends, and especially Dave, I know they've all had good intentions but they've all been guilty of smothering you with affection, of sheltering you too much, of never letting you really deal with the bad things in life. It's about time someone told you the stark truth without sugar coating it...otherwise you will never really accept what hand you've been dealt and never begin to truly move on with your life, without Dave in it."

It was strangely weird to hear Jenny speak like that...and what she said - albeit in her hard-hitting, unsympathetic, brutal way, did make sense – although it pained me to admit it.

I bit my lip and nodded my head, to let her know I accepted what she was saying, too choked up to reply. My humility seemed to bring out the kinder aspect of her personality again as she sat down once more, slid along the settee and put her hand over mine.

"I know you despise me Suzanne - no no, don't try and deny it! In a way, I can understand it, because I know I can be a real mouthy bitch! But I'm not totally without a heart – it does make me feel sad to see you like this, to see how much you're hurting. I know other women whose husbands have left them and I realise it's the pits, especially when *you* haven't fallen out of love but there's nothing you can do to save your marriage. I felt so bad for you today when I saw you in that supermarket, not your usual controlled self but a broken woman not knowing what the f...what the hell to do."

I appreciated her attempts to rein in the swear words.

She smiled at me, a smile that seemed to say, "We're all girls together; however we look, however, we speak, however we behave – we're all in it together and should support one another; have each other's backs."

I got it. I'd always judged too quickly – put appearances over everything and been quick to criticise. Maybe Jenny was happy with her looks, her weight, her situation – I needed to be kinder. At the end of the day, we were all equal...we all lived and died...who was I to judge?

"I never thought I'd say this to you, but if there is anything I can do to help then just give me a shout. I don't mean bleating on about your situation though – I'm all out of tea and sympathy for the time being – but if you need someone to take you out on the piss one night or you fancy joining our girls night in when we all veg out on the sofas watching trashy films and stuffing our fat faces with KFC whilst sinking a bottle each of gnats pee wine, then I'm your woman!"

Even in my rotten, distressed state, I could see that she was trying to show me some kindness, so I thanked her, saying I might take her up on it, whilst knowing that I never would. Hell would freeze over I think before me and Jenny ever became real friends. She knew it, I knew it – but it was a nice gesture, and I appreciated it.

"Anyway," she continued, "What's this I hear about some fella you're seeing eh? Back on the horse again are we? Tell me all about him then?"

"There is no fella Jenny. I made him up to make Dave feel better about leaving me," I admitted.

"No shit? Well, aren't you full of surprises? You have definitely gone up in my estimation. So instead of playing on your vulnerabilities like you usually do and pressurising him into staying, you told a little white lie to make it easier for him to leave, even though I know it probably killed you to do so. You loved him enough to let him go – good god, you're not such a bad person after all are you?" she nudged me, jokingly, making an attempt to raise a smile from me.

"No, there's the evidence that I really am a true saint…and look where it's got me. Louise – 1. Suzanne – 0. Final score." The smile was a weak one, having gritted my teeth again to say *her* name.

"But you have your dignity intact…well, almost, after your mad moment in the supermarket earlier when you'd left your marbles at home along with your purse. And you have the rest of your life in front of you. My friend, Abbie, she would love to be in your position; have the rest of her life ahead of her. But she has three months left at the most – terminal cancer – and she's only thirty-five. Not fair is it? And she would do anything to be in your shoes, to be given the gift of life, and to be able to grow old. So do me a favour, bloody enjoy your life now! Be happy. Travel, if you want to. Sing again, if that's what gives you pleasure. Let yourself go a little and maybe, just maybe you will find someone new - if you want to. Don't let the end of your marriage be the end of your life, okay?" She looked at me, head cocked to one side, awaiting some kind of response.

God, when did she get so wise – that was two decent speeches she had made in the last ten minutes, two occasions when she had actually made sense for a change and not just hurled insults and expletives at me.

"Okay Jenny, I will try, I promise…for Abbie. And…thanks…for bringing me home today…for the advice you've given….and for your kindness. Oh, and here's the money I owe you…thank you once again for helping me out today."

"Ha! Don't get too used to it love! But no worries, any time….and I promise to try and swear less in front of you if you promise to do away with the posh act and filter out the big words!"

I did actually manage a smile then. "Deal."

"Right well I had better be on my way or else the kids will have emptied the fridge again, little gits – I swear they are hollow inside. You don't need to see me out, you go and get a bath or something and relax for a while. Laters!"

She was almost out of the room when she turned back to deliver her parting shot.

"Oh…just one last thing though…if you try to get back at Dave, to make his life a misery – if you try to hurt him, to exact some sort of revenge – I will seriously bloody leather you Suzanne. He's been through enough."

I should have known she wouldn't have departed without dropping the niceties.

Seconds later the front door slammed shut signalling she was gone and I was left to mull over her words and contemplate the unappreciated life I still had ahead of me.

Chapter 7

LOUISE

What was taking so long? Why hadn't the bloody signed off those sales particulars yet? Why couldn't I just simmer down and stop being so flippin' impatient?

Everything had gone strangely quiet again as far as Suzanne was concerned, which was always a worrying sign – no good could ever come of a quiet ex-wife who held all the cards. Under daily pressure from myself, David had chased the estate agents on numerous occasions, to be told that they were just awaiting the return of the paperwork from *her* and then they were all good to go. Some young girl named Alethea had advised him there would be no problem whatsoever selling the house...properties in that particular area of Newquay were hard to come by and at least four lots of potential viewers were already lined up. Bloody hell, there must be more money around than I thought.

Christ, I just wish she would get her finger out. I mean, it's not like the woman had a job to go to; she didn't have to go out to work her ass off every day like the rest of us, for god's sake; it's not as if she was pushed for time. How hard could it be to sign some papers and take a short walk to the estate agents' office to drop them off and set the ball rolling?

When I'd expressed my concerns about the unjustifiable delays, David had just shrugged them all off – he was probably used to her making a meal out of everything - creating drama where there was none. No doubt she just wanted to stall as much as she could, to keep the tension up and make us wait; to dole out any small revenge whenever and wherever possible. Or was that just me being paranoid?

Kirsty had tried to pacify me by showing me a text message she'd received from Jenny, which stated that she'd bumped into Suzanne at the supermarket, and she'd apparently looked *awful*, and even though Suzanne did her head in, she'd given her a lift home and also delivered a few home truths - which meant she'd dissolved into tears again. On the one hand I was glad someone had given her a bit of grief; a taste of my medicine...but on the other hand I actually felt somewhat guilty that I was contributing to someone else's unhappiness – even if it was hers. I was probably being too soft for my own good, but it pricked my conscience – the fact that David had in effect dumped her for me and that no matter how I tried to dress it up and justify it, that was just the way it was.

So I'd tried my best to put the radio silence and suspected delaying tactics down to the fact that she might just have been struggling - without sharing those particular thoughts with David, who would have no doubt gone off on one and dashed off to check that the woman hadn't died of a broken heart in his absence.

Despite the bucket-load of nasty feelings I had towards her, I did also feel a fair amount of sympathy – I knew how tough it was to lose David and how hard it was to try and start over again; to attempt to establish a new life without him.

For the sake of everyone's hearts and stress levels, I just wish I could wave a magic wand and it would all be sorted and she would be completely out of the picture.

Because I was starting to get these niggling doubts.

Nothing to do with my relationship with David – no, my god I loved that man and he was so open and honest and transparent; I knew his love for me was real and pure, and he was straight down the line; no bullshit.

No…I just kept thinking that everything was going a little bit too well at the moment; that it couldn't continue to do so – that nothing ever went without a hitch. That somehow *she* was going to have the last laugh.

It was bugging me because I didn't like to be that glass-half-empty kind of person, but unfortunately at the moment I was. My stupid mind kept telling me that the bubble we had been living in this last couple of months which was filled with love and kindness and laughter and security was going to be unexpectedly popped without any warning…and I would be left picking up the scraggy bits of the balloon, knowing it could never be repaired…so that's why I was scared to death.

Eventually, Suzanne did get off her annoyingly pert little arse and returned the signed paperwork to the agents' offices and we were off! Of course, it was too much trouble for her to conduct the viewings herself – no doubt they would have interfered with her nail appointments or hairdresser visits – so the agents had been instructed to do it. Even though it would have made sense for her to be there, to answer any questions any interested parties raised, rather than them have to go through a third party. But why take the easy route when you can complicate things Suzanne?

Christ, but I was a silly cow, and then some. Stressing myself out about insignificant little matters that really didn't matter in the whole scheme of things.

Everything between David and myself was perfect. But I just wanted it to stay that way…I didn't want anything to ever change. Ever. I knew there would be obstacles and challenges ahead but I couldn't bear the thought of having to cope with them; outwardly I was a strong, confident, no-nonsense woman. Inside I was a weak, mushy mess.

Please god, leave us alone in our little, perfectly rounded bubble.

Somebody hide the sodding pin.

Chapter 8

SUZANNE

There had been four further viewings that week alone - two families, a single man and a young couple. It was the image of each family unit that almost brought me to my knees – a loving husband and wife and their picture perfect, high-achieving children settling into our house and making it their home; filling each room with their presence and belongings; making new memories and erasing the old ones that had been made within those walls. That crucified me.

I didn't try to kid myself that our house, sorry, *my* house would remain on the buoyant property market for very long. Such high demand in the area and the fact that it *was* a beautiful house and decorated throughout to such an excellent standard – it wouldn't be long before someone or some people fell in love with it. The views it commanded across Newquay and over the Atlantic had been one of my favourite reasons for putting down roots here. The master bedroom led out on to a small balcony were there was just sufficient room for two bistro chairs and a tiny matching table. I had once adored lazing out there in the morning with a freshly brewed coffee and a feeling of absolute contentment.

Dave had tended to wander out there in the evening after work, watching the sun set whilst sinking a pint of cold beer or cider. He hadn't done that for years though, to my knowledge, even when I had moved out of the bedroom we had shared. I couldn't remember ever hearing the familiar slide and clunk of the patio doors from within what had become just his room alone. Even one of the most desired vistas across Cornwall couldn't entice him out onto that balcony any more. Maybe to stand out there alone with his thoughts, wondering where it all went so badly wrong, would have been too painful in the end; too much to contemplate.

I slowly ventured out on to that balcony, not noticing the magnificent landscape in the distance, but instead glancing down again at the letter in my hand that had arrived that morning in the post from the agents we had instructed.

'Dear Mrs White,

Unfortunately, we have been unable to contact you by telephone on the numbers provided. We are pleased to inform you that we have in fact received two offers on your property, both for the full asking price....' And so it continued.

Not one, but two offers. No negotiation, no standard, anticipated attempts to persuade us to reduce the asking price. Straight in there, within a fortnight of appearing on the market, people desperately wanted my home as their own. God damn it, no, *our* home. It would still be our home until the date of completion when the property changed hands and we were no longer the legal joint owners.

I had missed the landline calls from the agents when I had been at the gym – I had resumed my membership there having let it slip for longer than I can remember, more to have an escape-hole to flee to when strangers were in my home. However, I had seen the agents' number flash up on my mobile several times but chose to ignore it, unashamedly burying my head in the sand for a little while, unwilling to hear the news that I knew was almost certainly coming my way, although even I hadn't anticipated it would have arrived quite so fast.

I couldn't dodge them now though - time to bite the bullet and ring them before they rang me.

Discussions with Alethea confirmed the contents of the letter and informed me that one offer was from the very first couple who had viewed with their children, on the day that I had gone into melt-down at the supermarket check-out. I knew, without a second's contemplation, that I was going to refuse that offer without even consulting Dave. I had *seen* these people, I could picture them settling into in our home while we were living elsewhere and I couldn't *bear* it. No, Mr and Mrs Tretheway and the junior Tretheways would NOT be moving into our dream home. The other offer was from an individual, a Mr Devine, who also had a cash buyer for his own property and was looking to simultaneously complete the two transactions around the end of June. Advising Alethea that I believed Mr

Devine would be the safest bet, I said I would discuss the matter with Dave and ask him to ring their office to confirm.

Hopefully they wouldn't even mention the Tretheways and he would happily go along with my wishes, as he had usually done in the past. The times they were a-changing though and I couldn't always rely on Dave letting me have my own way in the future. *Her* voice would be the one that mattered now, the one he listened to. He was no pushover, don't get me wrong, but without good reason he would previously always have trusted and accepted my decisions. Soon, our respective decisions would be of no business to the other – living lives apart with no reference to the person we had once intended to grow old with.

Reluctantly, I again left a message on Dave's mobile, explaining the situation with regard to Mr Devine, and asking that he place a quick call to the agents to confirm his acceptance of this offer, if he was in agreement, and requesting that he forward me a quick text to say he had done so, thanks.

The text arrived almost exactly an hour later, and I shakily poured myself a large glass of wine before telephoning the agents and confirming that yes, I was happy to accept Mr Devine's offer and that my solicitor's details, as previously supplied, remained the same.

So this was it…the start of the life-changing process…the beginning of the end of all my dreams.

Of course, Dave was ecstatic at the news…when I saw him next it was obvious he was trying to conceal his happiness to a degree, no doubt out of respect for my feelings, but it was apparent for, if not all, at least *me* to see. I bet *Louise* was skipping around her house in celebration – the time when I would be completely obliterated from Dave's life drawing ever nearer.

I'd left all the business dealings to Dave - I trusted him that he would see Michael right and the whole process would be handled quickly, fairly and with minimum fuss. I'd heard from Michael, via mum, that matters were progressing well and it wouldn't be long before Dave's name was taken off the paperwork and he would be free to trade on his own – where that would be I was unsure. I was positive that he wouldn't want to set himself up in competition with my brother but perhaps she would want him to move lock, stock and barrel up to Wigan anyway. I felt heartily sick at the thought that *she* may relocate to Newquay – good lord, in theory they could end up living down the road from me, along with her precious daughter and all her cheap and nasty belongings. That thought truly was inconceivable and unbearable.

My solicitor was astonished that I wasn't trying to take Dave to the cleaners, especially as he had already met someone else and I had effectively been dumped. In Mr Griffiths' experience, abandoned wives were usually bitter and twisted and wanted their pound of flesh and much more besides. But Dave had worked so hard for everything he had achieved and acquired – I knew that if I'd kicked up a stink he would probably have walked away with much less but I couldn't do that to him – I still loved him too much to hurt him unnecessarily or cause him any hardship. So a 50/50 split it was, incorporating the proceeds from the house sale, the business monies and savings in various accounts.

I had considered remaining in the house I loved so much, but not only would it have been difficult financially, but actually it would have verging on the ridiculous as the house was far too big for me to be rattling around in on my lonesome. It was a family home without a family at the moment and it felt so empty in there without Dave's presence. Everyone had agreed that it was the best decision for me to move elsewhere rather than cling on to the house and keep it as some kind of shrine in Dave's memory. A new start, fresh surroundings was what I needed, every man and his dog assured me. We would see.

Dave was lodging at Billy's for the foreseeable future, until everything was resolved. God help him there with the little terrors in residence, when they weren't roaming the streets looking for mischief or doing wheelies on their clapped out old bicycles in front of oncoming traffic. It seemed so cruel that I was unable to have children and yet for Jenny it was like shelling peas...and look what had popped out of the pod! I had to admit, they were actually quite sunny, funny kids when I did speak to them occasionally, but always filthy from rolling around in the dirt and cheeky as hell. I can't imagine what it must be like for Dave waking up to them bouncing on top of him, thrusting worms and other creatures in front of his face before he'd even had chance to prise open his eyes in the morning.

Actually, what I could imagine was Dave somehow fitting in amongst all the chaos, being the easy-come, easy-go sort of person he was. Chasing the little one around whilst pretending to be a pirate, or letting him mount him and ride him like a horse. And challenging the older ones to a battle on the Wi-U or the X-Box, when they should have been knuckling down to do their homework. Yes, he would probably love it, and they would love him being there. He was their godfather after all.

Thankfully, Jenny actually hadn't asked me to be godmother to their four children – maybe she had predicted that I wouldn't always be in their lives. Dave had repeatedly assured me though that it wasn't meant to be a slight against me - Siobhan had been asked to be godmother as she was Jenny's best friend. It was a blessed relief for me anyway – I had no great desire to be connected to this family of clampets and it would have felt like a cruel request in view of my own personal circumstances.

Chapter 9

LOUISE

"Da-da-da-da-da-da...hey! Da-da-da-da-da-da..hey! Na-naa-na-naa..hey! Na-na-na-naa...!"

As Kirsty, Ashanti, and I performed the conga around the cluttered coffee table, with Dawn bringing up the rear, Chloe stood in the doorway like a strict school ma'am, shaking her head in disgust.

"My god, you're all so childish! I mean, it's just not very dignified is it, mother dear? Singing and gyrating around the living room purely because David and that woman have accepted an offer on their house. AND you said you weren't drinking any more during the week. For the love of god, it's only Tuesday!"

"Aw, give your mummy a break Chloe love...don't be making her feel guilty when she's such a happy little bunny tonight!" I appreciated Ashanti trying to stand up for me, but when she was slightly inebriated and *she* could hardly *physically* stand up, well it didn't really help my case. "Oh and be a doll – set your alarm for the morning, as the chances of your mother waking you up for school are looking pretty slim..."

Breaking off from the conga, I danced my way over to by beloved daughter. "Sorry love...I just never thought I'd see the day when David was finally let off the hook! Bearing in mind how long I've waited for him...and bearing in mind how tricky *she* can be...let me just have a teensy weensy celebration tonight and then I swear from tomorrow all I will be drinking is a cup of cocoa every night and I'll be tucked up in bed by nine!"

It did make Chloe laugh that...I hadn't been in bed by nine since I was about eleven years old so the likelihood of that happening was pretty much zilch. She knew I didn't do this every night anyway...it may sound at the moment like I am some high-functioning alcoholic with serious mothering issues, but I was actually giving myself a break tonight. Being a bit of a light-weight, I couldn't usually drink any more than one glass of wine on week nights anyway, not if I wanted to get up for work the next morning – well, I didn't actually *want* to get up for work, but it was a case of having to, out of necessity to pay the bills and keep the wolves from the door – and when I wasn't actually at work, I spent most of my waking hours cleaning, cooking, washing and ironing. Oh, with a little bit of shopping chucked in as a special treat! Whoopee!

To be fair, my dull little life had definitely perked up considerably since the reappearance of David and I'd received a serious injection of love and was buzzing with happiness most of the time…but Suzanne was still the fly in the ointment, and to be shut of her once and for all would be a blessed relief.

Since the offer had been made and accepted by David on his old house, Suzanne had apparently spoken to the agents again and confirmed the price was agreeable to her. How could it not be really though? – I mean, they were getting top whack, no reduction in price…so far it was all good! I wanted to locate this Mr Devine, the guy who had made the offer, and give him a big smacker on the lips in gratitude! Unless he was old and smelly though…then I would have shook his hand and washed my own afterwards. But, oh god, I was so chuffed! Everything else seemed to have picked up a pace as well…the dealings with the solicitors, the disposal of the business, the financial affairs…I couldn't believe it. Soon David would be free! A day I never thought would come.

The ultimate goal was to have her deleted from our lives and to establish a place to call home all together…me, David, Chloe…and Fudge of course. I struggled without him in the week, counting down the hours until I saw him again…and hated to have to wave him off on a Sunday afternoon, as he hit the road back down to Newquay. And it was even worse when I travelled down to Cornwall to see him - our time together was amazing, but once I was on that train home, I was a snivelling mess. God help whoever was sat next to me.

The house felt so empty now when David wasn't there. And it was worse for him - the poor bugger must have had a permanent ringing in his ears from the noise at Billy and Jenny's. It was no five star hotel, let me tell you, and I'm just surprised that none of their neighbours had complained about the noise levels yet. Maybe they're stone deaf. I'm sure Dave must have longed for some peace and quiet and a comfortable mattress while he was there in the week…but he never moaned, not once.

And I knew when I rang him later, around 1 a.m., drunkenly serenading him with "Hopelessly devoted to you," or ruining some other absolute classic, he still wouldn't complain…and when I texted him from work tomorrow, moaning and groaning all day about my banging headache and chronic indigestion, he would just laugh and tease me a little, and think I was cute.

And do you know what I thought was cute? – The fact that when he looked at me - bypassing the rapidly ageing face and thickening body, underneath all the wrinkles and flabby bits and too many flaws to mention, he still saw that ditzy young girl who loved him with everything she had to give. Whatever he'd seen in me back in 1984, well he still saw it now and to him I was quite simply perfect.

Now, that's cute. And it's also true love.

Chapter 10

SUZANNE

It was always bound to happen. I knew in my heart of hearts that I would bump into the pair of them together one dark day, and probably soon in view of the fact she was apparently spending as much time as possible in Newquay, when Dave was unable to make the trek up to Wigan, but it still completely sent me off kilter – it still tore me apart.

Making a rare trip into town, I had only nipped into the gift shop on a whim, wanting to purchase a decent card for my friend Trudy, who was celebrating her fifth wedding anniversary that weekend. Approaching the till area, I heard Dave speak at the same time as I caught sight of them together, their backs to me, waiting in line to be served at the counter. He was wearing his black leather jacket and faded black jeans; his hair was trimmed slightly shorter than usual, but it suited him – always devastatingly handsome. Scruffily dressed in a baggy navy sweatshirt and faded jeans, she had her long, dark hair scraped up in a messy ponytail and she was throwing her head back, laughing at something that Dave had whispered into her ear.

I should have made a run for it, but I was frozen to the spot – the shock of unexpectedly stumbling upon them rooting my stiletto-clad feet to the floor. In a flash they were served and then they turned around and they noticed me. Presumably she had been sneaking around my Facebook profile as well, because there was an instant look of recognition; her face immediately coloured and her mouth opened and then quickly shut again. Dave's eyes widened in shock and then, remembering his manners, he managed to squeeze out a faint smile and said "Hello…hi…er…this is Louise…Louise – Suzanne."

No one knew where to look, what to say, how to behave. I was way too dignified to throw a punch at her or even throw a dirty look in her direction, but I was wary of how she might react – what garbage may spew out of her mouth or what stance she might take.

Instead I heard my trembling voice somehow reply, "Hello Louise. Hi Dave. The structural survey on the house has apparently been arranged for next Wednesday at eleven…I'll let you know when I've heard something further."

Dave seemed to have lost the power of speech as he said absolutely nothing in response but merely cleared his throat and nodded. I needn't have worried though because of course *she* took control of the awkward situation, smiled politely, albeit fakely, grabbed Dave's hand and said, "Come on David, Chloe's waiting for us in the car and she was hungry when we left her so she'll be *starving* now! Bye Suzanne. Nice to meet you."

I half-raised my hand in response and muttered a weak goodbye as they brushed past me; the chiming of the bell attached to the shop door announcing that they had vacated the premises.

I was having palpitations and could hear my own heavy breathing; could feel the palms of my hands become damp and clammy.

Eventually it was my turn at the till – I always double-checked that I had my purse with me when I left the house these days so I knew I had sufficient money to pay. Collecting my change, I grabbed my purchase and quickly left the gift shop, almost running back to the security of my car in my haste to leave the situation behind.

Once slumped in the driver's seat, I gripped the steering wheel, fighting back the tears, chanting to myself, "It's okay. It's okay. You're going to be okay."

For goodness sake, now I had seen her in the flesh I would never get her godforsaken face out of my mind. I had to concede, she was much more attractive in real life rather than when she was striking some silly pose for a photograph. She could do with losing a fair few pounds and investing in a decent hair stylist to trim those tatty locks but I couldn't deny she was naturally pretty, in a girl-next-door kind of way.

That one chance meeting with them had, it seemed, quadrupled the hurt and pain I felt because

1) I had seen her up close and personal and, god help me, could almost understand what attracted Dave to her and

2) I had observed them *together*. They were no longer just a regular feature in my worst nightmares. I had seen them in the flesh as a couple – and a touchy-feely, happy one at that and

3) She had mentioned her beloved daughter, Chloe. Sometime soon, when our house sale was through and all the ancillaries had been sorted, they would all be living together as a happy, complete family unit and, worst of all,

4) She called him David, and he didn't mind at all. He was used to it; he was familiar with it; it didn't offend or distress him in any way. Because he was deliriously happy and he loved the bones of her and clearly actually liked *her* using that name – the one I hadn't ever been allowed to utter without fear of upsetting the apple cart.

Oh god, please make this agony stop. Just when you think you are making slight progress and dealing with the huge un-wanted changes and the gut-wrenching hurt, you discover what REAL heartbreak actually is.

Eventually I gave into the tears. Unsure as to how long I'd sat there, at some point I realised that I needed to get myself home; my home for the time being, but not for much longer. I needed to get out of there before anyone I knew saw me practically collapsed over the wheel and either thought I had completely lost the plot or called an ambulance to take me away.

The journey home passed in a complete blur, on autopilot - but somehow I made it. Stumbling through the front door, I hurled my jacket and bag onto the stairs, splashed cold water on to my burning hot face in the downstairs cloakroom, and made the decision to retire to the security of my bed for an hour; to shut the rest of the world out.

I awoke to find darkness had fallen and, as I had no further plans for the day, I changed into my pyjamas and forced myself to eat something - strawberry yoghurt straight from the small plastic pot. Strangely I felt calmer; I think I was all cried out from earlier and too exhausted to even muster up the energy to weep now. My body felt like it had been kicked all over and the shock of the day hadn't deserted me, but I had still had my wits about me – there was still some fight left in me this time.

"Well girl, you sure as hell know what you're dealing with now," I muttered into the darkness to no one but myself.

Chapter 11

LOUISE

Mother of God…I couldn't believe I came face to face with the enemy! It was a knocking bet really that we would chance upon her some day while I was visiting David in Newquay. It wasn't *that* big of a town; well, not really. I mean, I once bumped into a long forgotten crush who I'd been to school with at a cash machine in Tenerife! So, I suppose I shouldn't have been surprised.

All the same, it *would* have to be when I was dressed in my ancient, baggy, totally unflattering sweatshirt, accompanied by my oldest, most machine-washed jeans – you know, faded, but not in a good way. I felt comfortable enough with David now to wear my scruffs when we were just knocking about at home or doing some shopping. At least she couldn't see under the sweatshirt that the button was a good inch off actually fastening and my ever-expanding belly was spilling over and out. I swear those bloody jeans had shrunk in the drier again.

Of course she was dolled up to the nines in designer gear and a suede jacket that probably cost more than my weekly wage. And who actually goes shopping in suede and fancy stilettos for fuck's sake? Bloody freak.

Her sodding mane was freshly washed and expertly cut and actually SWISHING for the love of god! – like the wig of an overpaid celebrity in a television advertisement for expensive hair products. I hadn't had time to even dry-shampoo my scruffy mop so had scraped it back into a bobble of Chloe's and hoped for the best (and David said I looked proper cute, like I was seventeen again with my little swinging ponytail, so I thought what the hell).

My god, I felt inferior stood next to this woman, even with the love of our lives firmly on my arm, not hers.

So, and I know it's not very dignified, but I took a cheap shot. I brought out the big gun, namely, my ownership of the name she was never allowed to use. I took a deep breath, pushed out my boobs and said, as confidently as I possibly could, "Come on *David*, Chloe's waiting for us in the car and she was hungry when we left her so she'll be *starving* now! Bye Suzanne. Nice to meet you."

Of course it wasn't *nice* to meet her, that was pure, top-of-the-range bullshit, but you just say it, don't you? I could hardly tell her that I'd rather come face to face with Adolf Hitler in the card shop on a pleasant Saturday afternoon than her and that I wanted to smash her immaculate doll face in and snip off all of her shiny, golden locks – no, scrub that; I wanted to shave her sodding head.

Anyway, listening to her posh, la-di-da voice really, really did my head in; Jenny had warned me that Suzanne spoke like the queen and turned her nose up as if there was a bad smell everywhere she went – she wasn't wrong.

I hadn't meant to drop Chloe's name into the brief conversation; it just sort of slipped out – I really wasn't trying to rub Suzanne's stuck-up hooter into it or anything, what with her being unable to have children and all that – I wasn't *that* bad of a person, honestly. Anyway, I didn't want to talk to *her* about *my* precious daughter…it felt like I was somehow tainting Chloe's name or doing her a dishonour even mentioning her to that woman and therefore in some way involving her in our lives.

No, I'd started jabbering on because of the shock of bumping into her and because of David's dumb and dumber act he was putting on by standing there like a plank - silent and useless. I could see he wanted the ground to open up and swallow us and could sense how uncomfortable he was with the situation…and he was probably worried in case we started name-calling and hair-pulling in the middle of 'Greta's – Gifts for all Occasions.'

We couldn't get out of there fast enough and practically broke into a jog as we escaped down the street, dodging groups of smoking teenagers and weary mothers with pushchairs and multiple bags of shopping. When we were safely out of her clutches I pulled David into a dark little alleyway, tried to ignore the distinct whiff of urine in the air, and held his hands while he shook his head and groaned and muttered something like "Shit, shit, and more shit!"

"David it's okay. The first time was always going to be awkward and, let's face it, it doesn't get more awkward than *that*. But we survived, she survived and everyone was civil and polite – no fisticuffs or spitting. Oh, I know, it was all fake and phoney and there's no love lost between me and her, and never will be, but it will get easier in time. She has her mysterious new fella now to take care of her…and you – you lucky, lucky devil – have me!"

Ah there it was – the smile was back. Phew. Explosive situation diffused.

"So David White, let's go and get those cheeky pints of lager we were considering nipping in for earlier and most definitely could do with now…and then we can chance a quiet snog and a bit of a feel-up in a quiet corner…unless you have any better ideas?"

Desperate to ring Kirsty, to squeal at the top of my voice down the phone to her, "I JUST MET THE BLOODY WIFE!" (itching to have an essential de-brief whilst calling Suzanne every derogatory and insulting name we could muster up between the two of us) I nevertheless managed to control myself when I realised my first priority was to bring David's pulse rate back down and reassure him...he had been clearly shaken by his past coming face to face with his present...and future.

Actually, to be fair, I had the triple whammy as I was also part of his past – the most significant slice of his history that had sealed his fate and given him a tempting glimpse of his future. So, she, with all her airs and graces and her perfect model looks and swishy frigging hair could, quite frankly, go and swivel.

Chapter 12

SUZANNE

It was a tough old week. A raft of long-winded forms to fill in, more telephone calls to make, and the dreaded visit from the surveyor, who was possibly the most boring, jobsworthy man on the planet. And everything I did was with the painful image of the two of them together lodged deep in my mind; even as I slept they appeared in my dreams; always together, always touching, always laughing.

I carried on popping my pills so I could function on a day-to-day basis, but I was deeply unhappy and I could see no end to this half-life, this state of loneliness and bewilderment. I tried so hard to pick myself up and start again, by firstly beginning the search for my new home – although my heart wasn't really in it - and secondly by attempting to re-boot my social life.

I attended a school reunion, practising my long-forgotten people skills whilst slowly dying inside when I had to tell former classmates that yes, Dave and I were amicably separated now and that no, I didn't have any children, so at least we didn't have them to consider when dealing with the separation.

Once upon a time, when I'd still had hope in my heart and dreams of a contented, rosy future, I would have shown off a little - drip-fed details of my wonderful, handsome husband and enviable life in our perfect house that most people could only ever dream of owning. I would have bragged of numerous exotic holidays abroad and expensive, top-of-the-range cars in the garage. But in the end, all that material stuff didn't matter, because Dave was gone.

For once, I took no pleasure in comparing myself and my life to that of one of my peers. So what if the school beauty, Josephine Rawlinson, had long since lost her looks? And who cared if Gail Chalmers' previously flawless complexion was long-gone and her face was now lined through years of smoking and other excesses? What did it all matter in the end? Gone were my days of taking pleasure from what I perceived to be someone else's failings – gone was the cattiness, to be replaced by eternal sadness, and even a little jealousy that many of these people were still happily married, some to their childhood sweethearts.

Why had I ever been so superficial? How had that kind of nonsense made me happy? Why had it taken me so long to realise that, in the end, all you needed was love.

I attended a number of charity lunches with mum raising funds for animal shelters and defibrillators in our community, and I even contacted an old friend, Timothy, who was now managing a sprawling hotel on the outskirts of Newquay, with a view to discussing a possible residency for me for the following season. I desperately needed to practise and hone my craft again; to try to unearth some of my old stage confidence – I didn't want to be a victim of stage fright on my very first night back at the microphone.

When I began to test out my voice at home I was relieved to find I could still hold all the right notes; it was still strong enough to fill a room, please the public and keep the management happy.

And yet I couldn't find pleasure in anything; couldn't feel any degree of optimism within me. Without Dave at my side my future felt pointless, I felt worthless and I didn't know how to make things better. I wished to god that I'd never blasted his little affair out into the open. I wished I'd just plodded on, burying my head and all that I knew.

I'd been a fool to think that honesty was the best policy and that he deserved to move on and that I was capable of making a fresh start.

Eventually I realised I couldn't continue to live a lie – I had to make him confess, bring it all out into the open and accept that this really was the end of the road for us. Taking Dave by surprise one evening when he was barely through the front door, I told him that we needed to sit down and talk, and he readily agreed; I could almost see the relief swimming around in his eyes; the knowledge that he wouldn't have to live this lesser life for much longer. That soon he would be free to spend the remainder of his days with the woman he worshipped above all others.

Anticipating a long evening ahead, I'd already opened an expensive bottle of Cabernet Sauvignon that we'd been keeping for an occasion – well, if this wasn't an occasion then I didn't know what was – although I had honestly hoped for a cheerier event. He didn't decline when I offered him a drink, and we retired to the living room with our glasses, which ironically were treasured wedding presents – part of a set received from some friends of my mother. He spread out on one sofa, and I was on the other - as had been the case for so many years now. Long gone were the days of snuggling up together, as close as we could physically get. The evenings passed with me lay across him with my head in his lap, while he tenderly stroked my hair – well they were long gone, almost as if they had never happened at all.

I decided to take the bull by the horns and come straight out with it.

"You're obviously not happy Dave, and neither am I, and we can't go on living like this. For so long now you've looked after me, when just getting through each day was an uphill struggle, and whilst I really appreciate all that you've done, it's no longer necessary. I know you've only stayed as long as you have because you're a loyal, decent, caring man but you deserve more. I'm a stronger person now…I can honestly cope in that big wide world on my own, without adult supervision. I promise you."

Dave looked thoroughly shocked to the core that I'd finally raised this trickiest of subjects, but before he could respond in any way and distract me from the little speech I had prepared, I continued.

"I'm not your responsibility any more Dave; no man should have to stay in an unhappy marriage out of a sense of duty and loyalty. You're not my carer for goodness sake! So, I'm setting you free – I'm handing you your life back; you should take it and run."

He started to try and speak but I cleared my throat and continued to maintain control of the conversation.

"Besides…you're in love with someone else aren't you?"

Boom! That completely took the wind out of his sails; he hadn't been expecting that bomb to be thrown into the conversation.

He paused. He swallowed. He ran his hands through his hair, making it stand on end in places, and I had to resist the temptation to lean over to smooth it back down.

"Yes," he quietly replied, looking contrite and ashamed, but quickly added, "I'm so sorry Sue, I truly am."

I knew, of course I knew, but nothing could have prepared me for his admission – I was winded, I was wounded and, if I didn't finish this off quickly, I would either be violently sick or collapse on the floor – possibly both.

There was no going back now – time to reveal that I knew who was – who had always been – my rival for his love and affection.

"It's her isn't it? That Louise girl – the Wigan Wonder. The girl you met on holiday when you were just kids? The one that got away?" It stuck in my throat, to even speak about her; to say her name out loud.

"She's the only reason you would ever completely give up on us; the only person who could ever make you want to move on."

I stared at the gold-framed clock on the wall. I didn't even have to look at Dave to know that he was nodding, replying "Yes, it's her." I'd recognised that sadness in his eyes - that look of hopelessness when he thought he would never set eyes on her again. I'd experienced it all before and it was an unwanted and uncomfortable feeling of déjà vu.

Revealing what I knew about this woman's trampy, foul-mouthed friend appearing in the shop giving him holy hell, I told him it was all around town and frankly how humiliated I'd been - and I noticed his face was drained of all colour as I then relayed the details of my secret Facebook search and the discovery of the pictures of this Louise and her precious daughter.

Dave provided me with the detail then - it all came spilling out – her numerous searches for him on social media (how I rued the day I ever persuaded him to sign up to Facebook for the sake of the business), her unannounced visit to the shop at the beginning of her holiday, his shock at coming face to face with her again but ultimately how they had been unable to let go this time around. I sensed that he omitted many details for my sake, in an attempt to save me from any additional distress, but I filled in a few of the blanks myself. I'm guessing he resisted at first, him being the faithful husband type, hence the hissy fit from her partner in crime in the shop – he claimed that this Kirsty was actually a lovely woman, just very protective of her friend. I silently begged to differ.

And all the while I just had to sit there calmly and listen – I couldn't scream and shout and violently attack him like I wanted to; I couldn't call her every abusive name under the sun and smash things around me to pieces as I longed to do.

Dave appeared as if the weight of the world had been lifted off his shoulders and I adopted a serene, understanding expression on my face, hiding the acute pain I felt inside.

Time to let him go. Too cruel to bind him to me by disclosing my hidden suffering, by admitting the truth - that I didn't know how I could go on living without him; that my life was nothing without him in it.

That evening I was no longer a singer but an actress and I gave the best, most heartfelt performance of my life. I could've won an Oscar for it, or at the very least a BAFTA.

I let him think that I was stronger, that I was ready to move on and that I truly believed it was best all round if he moved out immediately and we started to lead separate lives.

He was free to run to her. I loved him so much that I had to release him; to let him go.

Dave was to become David once more.

*

And then I began to formulate "the Plan".

I accepted what I had to do, knowing that it would hurt people in the short-term, but also that they would all get over it; they would eventually see it was for the best.

Dave of course would be upset; in fact he would be devastated. I know he still cared for me; unfortunately, once I had executed the Plan, he would remain guilt-ridden for the rest of his life, but so be it.

I still had a stock-pile of pills from last time. No one would ever have thought to look behind the panelling in the kitchen when they were searching the house for clues that I was intending to do the worst. The plinth slotted in but was easily removed if you knew how – a fact I had first discovered when I had dropped an expensive tiny diamond earring on the floor and somehow it had rolled underneath, necessitating a recovery operation that DIY SOS would have been proud of.

I needed more, to be on the safe side. I wanted Dave to see that this was not a cry for help – that I was beyond help now that he had abandoned me.

So I visited shops slightly further afield, where there was less chance of bumping into anyone I knew. I was sure to add some bottles of cola to my shopping basket and to vary the stores; I didn't want to arouse anyone's suspicion.

I felt calmer, now I had a plan. Everything had become so clear now – there was light at the end of this very long tunnel

Mum and dad, I think, presumed I was coping a little better; they would have been shocked to know what was inside my head. I hoped they would be spared some of the details and would see that this was the best outcome in the circumstances.

When Dave called round one evening to collect some of his old clothes, presumably to dispatch to a charity shop, unless *she* was planning on making him look as if he was actually still living *in* the 1980s, he seemed surprised but delighted to discover me happily singing along to the radio while I prepared my evening meal. As he left via the front door I tried not to think too much about the next time he would see me. I bid him a warm farewell and tried to concentrate on the task in hand, my shaking hands only hinting slightly at what I had in mind.

It seemed that Friday came around incredibly quickly; the days inbetween blending into each other, packing up boxes on the pretence that I was preparing for my house move and sorting out paperwork to get my affairs in order.

I had selected that evening because I knew mum and dad would be at the golf-club, Michael would be heading for a pint at his local with his friends, and Dave had arranged to call back to collect some of his CDs, before he disappeared - most likely to spend his evening with *her,* in various positions, in various states of undress.

I lined up everything I needed in the kitchen, and after a long soak in the bath, I slipped on my best and newest top and my most flattering trousers, applied my make-up, styled my hair and when I was satisfied I looked the best I possibly could, I returned to the kitchen.

Pausing for a moment to think about what I was about to do, it seemed like my life suddenly flashed before me…pictures fleeting through my mind of myself as a young girl sat on my daddy's lap, hugging my mum in thanks at my surprise 18th birthday party, belting out my favourite songs on the stage to tumultuous applause, meeting Dave for the very first time and savouring that first kiss from him, stood by his side at the altar feeling like the happiest woman in the world, lying on a beach in the Seychelles whilst he rubbed sun lotion into my back and whispered the words "I love you" into my ear….memories stacked up to form the basis of my life.

I had of course edited out all the painful memories...I wanted these few quiet moments of clarity to be positive ones, full of joy.

"HELLO! Sue...are you there? You'd left the front door unlocked; you want to be careful as there's a few unsavoury characters knocking about at the moment. Just as well though, I knocked about twenty times and you didn't hear me. I messaged you as well to let you know I was stood outside but your mobile must be upstairs – we did say eight o'clock, didn't we?"

Dave! He was slightly early – I should have expected that.

I didn't reply; I let him come and find me in the kitchen.

"Sorry Dave," I said, making sure I was treating him to my happiest, sunniest voice to cover up anything else he may have detected in there. "I had the radio on loud so I didn't hear you. At least the door was unlocked." Of course it was – that was intentional.

"Ah okay...you alright Sue?" he looked at me questioningly, concern in those sparkly, beautiful eyes of his. I missed those eyes, that smile, this man.

"Yes, I'm doing great thanks. I'm off out shortly, hence the get-up and the unlocked door!"

"You look....nice..." His voice wavered then, not sure if he should be telling me anymore that I looked nice - if that was allowed; if it was appropriate.

His eyes darted around the kitchen as we both struggled to fill the awkward silence.

"Anyway...I just need to grab that sports bag on the landing that's got my CDs and DVDs in, if that's okay, and then I'll leave you to it."

He left the room and I heard him take the stairs two at a time - obviously keen to be away as soon as he could – and once he'd got what he came for, he sprinted back down, smiling, almost shyly, as he said, "Thanks...for this and for...well, you know...not making things any more difficult than they have to be."

Sorry Dave, but your life was about to change again after tonight; for once I had the balance of power and was going to do what was best for me...and if it made life more difficult for you, then so be it.

I returned his smile. "It's okay. Bye Dave, goodnight."

And he was gone. He had looked at me in a peculiar way as he left, but I let out a sigh of relief when I heard the door slam and his car move off the drive.

"Goodbye Dave," I whispered, holding back the tears that were threatening to fall. "I'm sorry...but you've left me with no alternative."

Chapter 13

LOUISE

"Sorry love, I needed to pick up that bag of CDs before we left, otherwise I will have to endure listening to George Michael all weekend again!

"Oy, cheeky! You know you love him really…I've seen you wiggling your sexy little bum to 'Fast Love' when you think I'm not looking. I tell you what, I'm going to put an absolutely massive poster of him up on our bedroom ceiling if you're not careful!"

It gave me a cosy, warm feeling inside to refer to it as being "our" bedroom now, rather than just mine. It was my house, my home in Wigan that I had owned for a number of years, but it was also now David's as well. He belonged there more than Richard ever had.

Sometimes I almost had to pinch myself, to believe that I actually now was able to share the life, the house, the bedroom and of course the bed with this beautiful man who I had loved above all else, above all others for almost all of my life.

While David collected the CDs from Suzanne's, the house he had formerly called home, I waited anxiously in the car, fidgeting and biting my nails.

To be honest, he definitely seemed to be more relieved than sad when he talked of the property being sold. It *was* a beautiful house - at least it looked beautiful on the outside as I hadn't seen the interior and was never likely to - it seemed so wrong that it not be used for its purpose – to be filled with a happy family who would make memories within its walls. Anyway, it would be sold soon and then David and I would need to make a decision as to whether we stayed in my old house in Wigan or we bought something else, somewhere else.

I was beyond happy that it was Friday again and I was back in Cornwall, having begged the day off from work, with the promise that I would make the time up one Saturday (never going to happen). The weather forecast was promising…beautiful autumn days I was to spend with my devastatingly handsome man before I, unfortunately, had to wave him goodbye again on Sunday.

We had booked a last minute hotel deal to provide us with some privacy and, for once, a little luxury. Last time I had travelled the lengthy journey down to Cornwall I had squeezed in with David at Billy and Jenny's rented house and I was still recovering from the experience. A romantic, peaceful weekend it was not, with kids and dogs clambering all over me and following us both around but at least we were together, and nothing could spoil that. And it was generous of Billy and Jenny to welcome us into their home.

The ancient put-up bed was definitely only made for one – in the end we gave up and slept on the floor amongst the toys and other clutter. We were just happy to be together; when you've been apart for so many years and spent a lifetime longing for one another, it really does make you appreciate your time together. Even the random Lego bricks which painfully dug into your flesh if you had the misfortune to roll over on to them, didn't detract from the pleasure of David making love to me; I couldn't get enough of him and his body – if we spent the rest of our lives in bed together it would still, somehow, seem too little – but then we had lost thirty years when we could have married, had babies and grown up together – so maybe we were making up for lost time.

Yes, we were definitely looking forward to our hotel stay after last time – to sink into a double bed together and not wake up with back pain and stiff necks and small children peering into our faces.

I glanced over at David and noticed a frown descend upon his lovely face and realised he had something on his mind.

Squeezing his hand, I asked, "Are you okay love? Only you look worried, like something's bothering you..."

He was trying to concentrate on the road ahead, but I could see he was miles away, replaying the scene back at Suzanne's over and over in his head; mentally retracing his steps and scrutinising every word, every mannerism, every gesture.

"Sorry love, but yes, I am a bit concerned...I know she's the last person you probably want to talk about but...it's just...well, something didn't seem right back at Sue's there. Something felt really, really wrong...and I just can't put my finger on what it is..."

"How do you mean? You said she seemed happy today, right, and that she was dressed up and going out – surely that's a good, positive sign?"

"It is...usually...but...I don't know...it all felt like a bit of a front. Yes, she was done up to go out somewhere...she seemed cheery and more confident....the house was spic and span with everything organised and in its place like it used to be. The front door was unlocked though, which isn't like her at all, but maybe, like she said, it was because she was on her way out..."

"So everything's hunky dory then and you're worrying your pretty little head over nothing, David White!" I put on a mock stern voice and squeezed his firm, denim-clad thigh.

"Listen baby...she's finally got her big stretchy girl-pants on now and is forging a new life for herself so let's celebrate that! You're worrying about nothing and...."

"SHIT, SHIT, SHIT!!!" yelled David as he made a sudden u-turn, almost causing a pile-up, resulting in other drivers honking horns and yelling abuse, but that seemed to be the least of his problems.

"Get out of the fucking way you fucking shitty Mazda!" he screamed, while I almost jumped out of my seat, thinking that he had actually gone stark, raving, mad.

"What in god's name is wrong with you David? You're lucky one of those drivers back there wasn't one a loony-tune who wears a knuckle-duster and carries round a baseball bat! Calm down, will you! Jesus, you look like you've seen a ghost! And why the hell are we going back the way we've just come when we've got a booking at a luxurious hotel and a reservation for dinner?"

"Oh god Lou...Christ...Fuck...I know this sounds crazy, but I think Sue's planning to do something stupid!" I noticed the colour had drained from his beautiful face as he spoke, and his hands tightly gripped the steering wheel whilst he rammed his foot down on the accelerator and tried to ignore the blare of the horns of the other cars he cut in front of.

"What? WHAT? Jesus! Surely you're wrong...what suddenly makes you think that?"

"Oh Christ, it's going to sound stupendously stupid but, not only was the door unlocked, but she was just *too* cheerful and calm...and she had bottles of cola lined up on the kitchen unit..."

"Bottles of cola? As in fizzy pop? And that's what's causing you to drive like a maniac and nearly kill us both is it? Are you actually insane? What do you think she's going to do with this fizzy pop then – drown herself in it?"

"Oh god, I realise how crazy it must sound to you Lou…but a while ago we were watching a drama programme one night where this young girl took a stash of pills and drank a load of cola with them because she had heard that it would act as an accelerant…Sue was at her weakest around that time and I was really worried about her – so when I realised she was studying it all intently, I quickly changed over the TV channel. I was paranoid about anything giving her any daft ideas she could possibly act on…"

"Oh come on, surely she wouldn't have remembered that? I mean, it was just a stupid television programme – it's not real life! Chances are, anyway, that the cola theory is all a load of crap – I've never heard that one before – and of course it won't work and she won't have enough pills and she will just sleep really, really well tonight - like she's just had a couple of good gobfulls of Night Nurse."

"Lou, listen to me, I once found some stuff in her internet search history where she'd actually researched how many pills it would take to finish herself off! She tried to laugh it off and brush it under the carpet afterwards, saying of course she would never go through with it, but from then on we regularly and diligently searched the house, checking there was no hidden stockpile of pills anywhere. We did find a little stash at the back of a kitchen cupboard and we binned them straight away…and there was never a repeat of that incident…but now she lives alone, maybe she's been hoarding the pills somewhere and none of us knew…and she's bought the cola to complete the job…"

"Oh Jesus, she probably just fancied a soft drink or, god forbid, she's bought them as mixers to, sensibly, accompany the alcoholic drink of her choice…it doesn't mean she's going to top herself, you dickhead!" I was becoming increasingly annoyed - frustrated with his concern for his supposedly estranged wife, but it looked like he was taking no chances.

"I'm sorry Lou, but I know for a fact she never buys pop, not for herself, not for guests, not for anyone – she was passionate about not putting all that shit into her body – she was an advocate for 'clean living' and all that baloney – well obviously apart from the alcohol and pills. I know something's wrong. It was her demeanour as well – she was just too calm and collected. I can't just drive away and forget all about it. I've got to go back and see if she's okay…I have such a bad feeling about all of this and my instincts have always been on point in the past…I know this woman, inside out."

To be quite frank, more than anything I wanted to turn this woman's organs "inside out" but I didn't think anything could be gained from saying so.

David easily broke the speed limit more than once racing back to his former home, praying quietly to god that he'd got it all wrong, all the while guiltily glancing across at me, most likely taking in my furious face; my despair and disappointment at the prospect of our romantic weekend being spoiled or cancelled and him running off to his Mrs, to sort her life out again. If he was wrong, he would have to make it up to me over the weekend and I would line up the massage oils and the sexual favours…if he was right, well god knows what would happen if he was right…let's not go there for the time being.

We screeched to a halt at the end of their driveway and David flung open the car door. As he quickly jumped out and raced up the front path, I quietly mumbled, to no one but myself, "Well, I guess I'll just stay here again then."

The front door was still unlocked – I thought she was supposed to be going straight out – and my own heart sank as David ran like the clappers into the house, leaving the door wide open, and down the beautifully decorated hallway that was bigger than my living room, clearly dreading what he might find inside.

I also dreaded what he might find inside. And what it might mean for us.

Chapter 14

SUZANNE

My drink was poured and I was staring at the pills that were carefully lined up on the granite kitchen worktop, when I heard the sound of a car screeching to a halt outside, right at the front of my house.

Instinctively I knew it was Dave's car. I recognised the engine noise, heard the sound of his feet thumping on the ground as he raced up the path and flung open the front door. But even without all of the noise, I would have known it was him; I could sense when he was near to me; not miles away frolicking with another woman.

I had planned everything meticulously, but I hadn't been expecting Dave to return so soon.

Wrenching open the top drawer, I swiped the tablets off the worktop and into the plastic cutlery tray, making sure the drawer was firmly shut when a second or two later Dave burst through the kitchen door, banging it back almost against the wall, panting and panicking. My heart somersaulted like a young gymnast at the top of their game as I waited for him to react.

"SUZANNE!" he yelled as he barged in, knocking into one of the leather-topped breakfast stools and overbalancing it slightly. *"SUZANNE!* WHAT THE HELL ARE YOU DOING?"

I had to remain calm – to try and assure him that it had all been a figment of his overactive imagination.

"Dave! What on earth are you doing back here again? And why are you shouting and storming in like that? Is something wrong?"

He stopped short then, frowning and obviously doubting himself for a brief moment. I could see his bright blue eyes were scanning the whole room for traces of evidence, for some telltale pill packets or childproof jars to have been lying around.

"*You* tell me, Suzanne. Is something wrong? Because something *feels* very wrong. Something definitely isn't *right*."

"Just what on earth are you talking about Dave? I'm on the verge of heading out of the front door and you burst your way in here like a mad man, all crazed eyes and sweating forehead! Now if you don't mind, I need to get going, or else I'll be late. And I'm sure your *lover* out there in the car will be getting twitchy and nervous if you keep her waiting much longer..."

"Don't. Don't do that. Look at me Sue. LOOK AT ME!"

He slammed the kitchen door shut and leant against it, effectively barring me from exiting the room, and I was forced to stop in my tracks. I looked him directly in the eyes and he spoke again then; quietly, gently, deliberately.

"Why do you have a full glass of cola poured there Sue if you're about to go out? - notwithstanding the fact that you don't even drink the stuff! If you're just about to leave the house, as you stated you were quarter of an hour ago when I last saw you, then where are your heels and matching handbag? You never go out, to a bar, a restaurant, a club, to a house party or ANYWHERE without changing into your best shoes and picking up the matching designer bag. You always leave them in the hallway, by the side of the small table, so you can grab them literally just as you're about to depart. So where are they Sue, where are they?"

I hesitated then. Just a second too long. My god, he was good. This man knew me so well.

The brief hesitation was all he needed – before I could stop him he was wrenching open cupboard doors and emptying out bags and boxes, throwing them to one side as I began to protest.

"For God's sake, stop it Dave! Look at the mess you're making...I don't know what's wrong with you!"

He continued, undeterred...a man on a mission.

"Dave, please! I don't know what you're talking about...if you think there's something untoward going on here...if you mean..."

The drawer was wrenched open again and the assortment of pills were scattered about amongst the knives, forks and spoons - plain for all to see.

"FUCKING JESUS SUZANNE! *Not again!* Why, for fuck's sake? *Why?*"

As he was half-yelling, half-sobbing, he was throwing the tablets into a hastily grabbed carrier bag, all the time shaking his head, unable to take in that history was repeating itself all over again; that his estranged wife was so desperate as to plan on taking her own life.

I lost it then. It had been a long time coming, but coming it surely was.

"WHY? *WHY?* Let me bloody tell you why, Dave White…because I may as well be dead as carry on with the life I have now! Because the man I have loved with all of my heart from the minute I set eyes on him feels *that* way about someone else…and *always has*! Because although you're my absolute soulmate, I am not yours! You're someone else's soulmate. Because I can't contemplate existing like this for even one more god awful day…that's why!"

"Sue, I…."

"I HAVEN'T FUCKING FINISHED YET!"

He knew I meant business then – I never swore at him.

He tried to reach out to me to comfort me with his words and his touch but I was done with this crap and I needed to vent an awful lot more.

"Why? Because I can't have children, in case it's slipped your memory! Because I feel so useless and alone all of the time! Because you look at me with pity now rather than love! Because I have to put on this act in front of mum, dad, and every other bloody person I speak to. Because I have to pretend I'm absolutely fine and coping admirably to ease everyone else's guilt. Because when I told you I had met someone else to make it easier for you to leave me for *her*, you looked into my eyes and you actually BELIEVED me! How could you? How could you ever think I could ever love anyone other than you?"

I punched him then, I actually punched him. Hard as well, for a girly punch. Right in his gut. He looked like he was about to keel over; not just from the punch but from the shock of what he was hearing from me, and the swear words that were tripping off my tongue now; the venom firing out of my mouth.

I grabbed the lapels of his shirt – a grey patterned shirt that I had never seen before, possibly even bought by *her*. Underneath his jacket I could see he was obviously dressed up to go somewhere nice. Well, tough luck - shit happens.

"Do you know what it feels like to be me Dave? No? I didn't think so. My husband has abandoned me, my family are suffocating me, and my friends are mere acquaintances, at best. When I feel like all the world is against me, do you know what I want? I want great big squishy hugs from my children! Except that's never going to happen is it? – Because there is a space either side of me where my children should be. So DO NOT, you fool - you stupid, *stupid* man - ask me *WHY*? "Why not?" might be more appropriate."

He grabbed firmly hold of my arms, probably to avoid any more punches, or possibly a good old slap to the face which was certainly a possibility with the way I was feeling, but when he saw the torrent of tears pouring down my cheeks he pulled me tightly into his warm, comforting chest, where I soaked his new shirt whilst hurling abuse at him. It was extraordinarily satisfying and I don't know why I hadn't done it before. It was also tortuous, that familiar feeling of his arms around me; his aftershave, his skin, his breathing, his everything.

Eventually he released me from his grip and steered me towards the nearest chair. He pulled out another from under the kitchen table and sank into it, holding his head in his beautiful hands.

"I'm so sorry Sue. I know I keep saying it and you're probably sick of me repeating myself, but I really am. I never wanted to hurt you but I can't change how I feel about Louise…and I don't know how to make it better for you. I can't believe it's come to this; I really did think you were moving on. One thing I do know though, this isn't the way. You're not a selfish woman; you wouldn't want to inflict this pain on your parents, would you? Because to take this way out would completely destroy them."

It was to be hoped it was a rhetorical question, because I had no adequate response.

"Suzanne, you are entitled to be happy again; you *deserve* to be happy again. You WILL be happy again, even though you can't see that right now. You think you'll never meet anyone else but you will…there's a man out there for you who will love you wholly, completely and forever. And you will feel the same way about him. You've just got to give it a little time."

The anger was rearing its ugly head again; the mist had come down and I began to shout and rage again.

"How dare you! How fucking dare you! The last person I will take advice from about relationships is YOU! It's easy for you to sit there all smugly, lecturing me about what I should and shouldn't do when you're sorted for life now. And how much easier it would be for you two if I quietly moved on rather than signed off for good! If I chose to end it all now you would be eaten up inside and it would kill you and your precious relationship with that bitch! So excuse me if I don't take heed of your crap, kind Dave. Excuse me if I feel like taking the easy way out!"

There was a beautiful antique vase filled with perfect white orchids in the centre of the kitchen table and I desperately wanted to hurl the whole lot at him. I was so angry - so tired and angry. Sick of being nice and compliant and understanding. At that moment in time I didn't care if I was hurting him. *He* was going to sit and listen to what I had to say and *she* could wait and worry herself sick in the car outside, all by herself.

"So what do you suggest I do Dave? Come on then, let's hear Dave White's top tips for a suicidal wife! What's the matter Dave? Cat got your tongue?"

There it was - that was the catalyst; that tipped him. He stood up, flinging back the chair, matching my screaming and shouting with his own.

"I tell you what might help Suzanne. It might do you some good if you actually did something constructive to help yourself instead of burying your head in the sand. I get that there is no magic solution and it's a case of taking one day at a time. But there *is* help out there…how many times has the doctor suggested speaking to someone professional about your problems or passed you details of support groups you could attend? But you won't do it, will you? You'd rather break your mum and dad's hearts. You'd rather everyone worry themselves to death over you than shoulder a bit of responsibility and attempt to do something positive for once."

I lunged at him again but he was faster this time and grabbed hold of both of my tiny wrists, as I screamed right up close into his face.

"And if I go to these amazing, incredible groups Dave? Or if I speak to some random stranger on the telephone and pour out my heart to them? How will that change things? I have *had* to accept that I will always remain childless; that my body is useless. But what do I do about YOU? Because it's living without you that I can't stand; that's the issue here. I don't have clinical depression; it's the broken heart that's killing me! Being in this house on my own and you living somewhere else with someone else. How do I remedy that?"

He didn't say anything in reply; how could he respond to that? What could he say that would ease my pain?

We stood in silence then, probably just for a matter of seconds but it seemed like an age. He couldn't possibly have all of the answers, and I knew I wasn't being fair and that I was deliberately trying to hurt him. But, god forgive me, if I wasn't to be allowed to do something, *anything,* to blot out the pain, then it was all about self-preservation, and everyone else could go and whistle.

"The ironic thing, Dave, is that I can only do it *with* your help. If you were to support me, I know I could get through this."

"Sorry? What? Support *you* through *our* separation? How on earth could that work?" He shook his head and looked at me as if a madness had overcome me and I had taken leave of all of my senses.

"I'm going to ring your mother now and she will no doubt call the doctors and they will deal with you as a priority case and..."

"NO! NO WAY! I'm not having mum, wonderful as she is, sobbing hysterically over me and blaming herself for the state I'm in...and the doctor most likely showing me the way to the psychiatric ward..."

"Not necessarily Sue...but if, and that's just "if", they wanted to keep you in, they would only do it if they thought it absolutely necessary and you might just get the help you need and..."

"No way Dave! No fucking way! I'm not bloody crazy, I'm just heartbroken. I don't need treating for mental health issues when my only problem is that my husband has upped and left me for his teenage sweetheart!"

"Well there's obviously some serious problem there when you're genuinely attempting to take your own life! This is no trivial matter Sue...they will assess you and..."

"I said NO FUCKING WAY! I'm telling you Dave. If you blart all of this out to mum, or anyone else - doctors and mental health professionals included - I promise you with all of my heart that I will definitely finish the job off. I will still go ahead with it – some other place, some other time, some other way - I will just make sure I plan it better next time around! And then *you* will have blood on your hands because it will be all *your* fault!"

Trying not to think of it as blackmail – because that really is such an ugly word – I waited for his next response.

His head was back in his hands again and I could feel the despair radiating from him as the realisation dawned that he could not escape from this; that I was someone who he could not turn his back on; that everything in his world was about to be turned on its head again.

I hoped *she* was beside herself - anxiously waiting outside in the car, chewing her fingernails, impatient for news - wondering what all the shouting was about; worrying about her *David*.

Dave slowly dropped his hands to his sides and raised his head slightly and simply stared at me. He sighed, he swallowed, his mind worked overtime as he considered his options – how he could extract himself from this situation. He couldn't.

I was backing him into a metaphorical corner now, but it had to be done.

I lowered my voice and returned the steady eye contact.

"I also promise you faithfully Dave, that if you keep this to yourself and help me sort this mess out; if you come with me to the various support groups and you hold my hand, so to speak, all of the way, I won't go down this road again. If I can't have you as a husband then I need you as a friend right now. I miss your friendship Dave, your company and your positivity. I miss you. Please don't go. Please stay and help me through this."

"I...it's difficult for me to do what you're asking. You know it will cause serious issues if I'm spending time with you Suzanne..."

"But Louise will have you for the rest of your life! Good lord, she's waited thirty years for you! I don't think another few weeks will make much difference, if she truly loves you. I just need you as a friend for a short while, to steer me in the right direction and to be by my side when I attend these groups and try to open up to complete strangers. To listen to me in the early hours like you used to do when I'm rambling on and pulling my hair out with anxiety. You're the only one who truly knows what I've been through – who knows every single thing about me. I need you Dave."

"I want to help you Sue, I honestly do, but..."

He left the sentence unfinished. The fact that Louise would completely flip and possibly do him physical damage when she heard what I was proposing, well that hung, unsaid, in the air.

"Please stay with me here Dave, just until the house is sold. I don't mean *together*, you know as a couple...but just as we were before, while I seek the help I need. Separate bedrooms and all that. I can't bear it at mum and dad's – they try so hard to help but they lay it on so thick I feel I can't breathe - and I've nowhere else to go at the moment. I love this house but it's so quiet and empty without you here....I can't sleep, my mind's racing and I'm jumping at every little noise I hear. Please don't leave me here on my own. Consider it as a friend helping another friend. You at least owe me that. And I'll give you my word that I won't ever try to do anything stupid again."

Dave looked almost defeated - a decent, good, honourable man who would do the right thing no matter what it cost him. I knew I was taking advantage of that aspect of his personality, but what the hell; what did *I* have to lose?

I continued to beat him down, adding, "And it seems so stupid, you roughing it at Billy's and damaging your back on that ancient put-up bed with the springs popping through - when you can have your own room back here, hassle free, until the sale goes through. Maybe I will be able to sleep more soundly with you in residence, and then I will be able to think straight and make some real progress at last..."

It didn't take a mind reader to deduce that he was scared to death of walking out of that door just in case I followed through with my threats. Ditto if he informed my parents or the doctor. But on the other hand, he was obviously wondering how the hell he would explain his predicament to Louise - that he would have to look after me a little while longer; that I couldn't cope and he needed to support me while I sought help. He was trapped, and he knew it.

Chapter 15

LOUISE

Where in god's name was he? What the fuck was taking him so long? I'd heard banging and shouting and was hoping that silly cow hadn't murdered David as everything had gone ominously quiet. *She* clearly wasn't deceased or incapacitated because more than once I'd heard her screaming and screeching like a chimpanzee on drugs. And I was sure David had said she couldn't abide "bad language", yet I'd definitely heard her drop a few F-bombs in there today.

The trouble was, the more time that passed, the worse the scenario I pictured in my head. This was downright ridiculous – me, sat there like a total gobshite in my lover's car outside of his wife's house, anxiously waiting for him to escape…or, alternatively, waiting for a convoy of police vehicles and ambulances to arrive and to be informed that my man had in fact been bludgeoned to death.

After what seemed like an age, thankfully David appeared at the front door and slowly walked down the path towards me - I could see from his face that it wasn't good news. Jesus Christ, what now? And why wasn't he approaching the driver's side of his Audi? Why was he sticking his head through the open window on the passenger side to speak to me?

"I'm so sorry I've kept you waiting this long, Lou. It's not fair on you being stuck out here but I couldn't take you in there with me. Unfortunately, I was spot on - she had the pills and she was about to do the worst." His face was ashen, I noticed – he seemed to have aged several years in the space of half an hour. His magnificent broad shoulders were slumped and, I could see tears that had been shed as they glistened on his handsome face.

"But she's okay now, I take it? You got here in time…da da daaa!! – David to the rescue!" I couldn't keep the sarcasm out of my voice. Yet again he was the frigging knight in shining armour rescuing the delicate damsel in distress in her ivory tower. This woman seriously needed to get a grip and stop looking to others to dance on her attendance all of the freaking time. And when would David realise that he wasn't put on this earth to be the hero of the hour all of his godforsaken life?

David slowly shook his head and my heart sank to my black leather ankle boots.

"She's not okay, Lou, she's anything but okay. I can't leave her like this…I've snatched away the pills this time…but who's to say she doesn't have a load more secreted somewhere else? A Plan B in effect? She's in a terrible state, to be frank, and I can't just walk away and convince myself that she won't try something else. I'm scared to abandon her like this…and if I tell her parents what's just occurred or involve her GP at this stage, she's said she'll still do it anyway…and I seriously think it would send her over the edge…"

I knew it; I just fucking knew it.

"So she's blackmailing you, is she? If you tell anyone then she really will follow through with this threat…what a pathetic creature she is! And you, YOU, are falling for it all over again, you bloody muppet! Can't you see she's pulling the wool over your eyes? She clearly knows that this is the way to get you back and ruin everything we have! Why are you so blind that you can't see what is obvious to everyone else? For a highly intelligent man, you are an absolute moron as far as she is concerned!"

"I'm telling you Louise…this is no cry for help…she means it alright. And I can see why you would think she's bullshitting, but I know her, and I can assure you she's not. She's begged me to stay as a friend…she needs me babe…just to make sure she does actually seek professional help…to make sure she's okay and to get her on the right road…it will only be until the house sale goes through; she's struggling here on her own and…"

"So tell her to piss off to her mother's then! Or rent somewhere else! Like any normal person would do! Because when it's all over she will *have* to live by herself elsewhere…so why can't she do it now?"

"It's just overwhelming for her…seeking the help she needs without the support in place…her parents mean well but suffocate her and she can't think straight when they're around…"

"So let me get this straight…rather than seek proper medical advice today or let her parents and mental health professionals take over, she wants YOU to stay here with her to support her through *your* joint separation? Is this a bloody joke? Are you actually winding me up?"

"Unfortunately not. But I couldn't live with myself if anything happened to her Lou...and it's only for a short while and then we can finally move forward and spend the rest of our lives together like we've planned...me, you and Chloe...."

"NO."

"Please try and understand babe...she has no one else really she can turn to who understands her, who's known her for as long, who...."

"Oh spare me her tale of woe for Christ's sake! She's mugging you off David! She's latched on to that weakness that you have inside you...your desperate need to "do the right thing". She knows you're a sucker for her sob stories and she's outmanouevering you; she's doing all she can to reel you back in and stop us moving on together...can't you see that?"

He looked absolutely distraught, stood motionless, with his hands on his hips, his head clearly about to explode, and my heart turned over to see him so sad, when he had recently been so happy and almost carefree with me. What was she doing to him? What was she doing to us?

His voice broke as he asked "What am I supposed to do Louise? I can't take the risk – I can't have Suzanne's death on my conscience. She desperately needs help. I love you so much Lou and the last thing I want to do is hurt you, but I feel backed into a corner. She's begged me to stay, just as a kind of lodger until the sale goes through. If I say no, what will she do?"

"She's not your responsibility David, not any more. You have to stop running to her every time she snaps her fingers. And she knows this will cause a whole heap of trouble between you and me – she's a calculating bitch and not the sweet, innocent little lady you seem to have her down for. She knows you've moved on with me and yet she's still begging you to stay and help her...so what does that say about her?"

"That she's desperate and can't do this on her own?"

"No. That she wants you back. That she wants me out of the picture, for good."

I started to cry then; I couldn't help it. Big ugly gulps in between the tears as well and a full-on snotty nose.

"You said you would never hurt me again!" I wailed. "You fucking PROMISED that you would never leave me but you lied. I trusted you and opened up my heart, my home and my life to you and you're throwing it all back in my face! I waited thirty years for you David White and I thought this time we would make it..."

He wrenched my car door open then and pulled me out and into his arms. I should have kneed him where it hurt but instead I desperately clung on to him, wondering why everything always turned to rat-shit for me. Why I couldn't just love and be loved without seemingly being punished for it; without having it all snatched away at the drop of a hat. Like the star prize on Bullseye –"Now look at what you would have won".

"I'm so sorry Lou...I love you more than words can say...and you must believe me when I tell you that I honestly don't want to go back in there, but I have to. Because I'm not the kind of cruel, selfish poor excuse for a man who could just leave someone I once loved to attempt to end their life without trying to intervene. I don't think I could do it with anyone, let alone my ex-wife. And I hate to have to say this but I need to get back in there now, before she thinks I've disappeared...and does god knows what to herself. Please don't look at me like that Lou, I love YOU but I have no choice!"

I slowly released my grip on his shirt and took a small step backwards to lean against his car, furiously looking him up and down and wondering how we could be so close in some ways but yet so far apart in others.

"Oh no David, you *have* a choice – a clear, definite choice. You can ring her parents now so they can take over, and you can jump back in the car with me then and we will go to the hotel as planned – even though she has cast a dark shadow over these next few days for us and you will be stressed as fuck all weekend – or, the alternative is that you walk away from me, and despite your previous promises to the contrary, you go back in there and look after your delicate, vulnerable, little wifey - effectively giving *our* relationship the kiss of death."

He opened his mouth to protest but I hadn't finished yet.

"So, there are *two* choices in actual fact." I angrily brushed away the tears that were still insistent on leaking out and almost choked on my next words.

"But you - decent, loyal David, always doing the right thing – always putting your estranged wife's feelings before your own and mine - have already made your choice haven't you?

You're going back in there no matter what I say so I won't bother trying to persuade you otherwise."

Not sure how my legs actually carried me round to the driver's side of his car, I quickly moved and yanked open his door again, noting that his key was still in the ignition, having been abandoned when he leapt out of the driver's seat to rush to Suzanne's aide.

"I'm driving to the hotel now and I'm going to check in, alone. Humiliated and alone. I will wait in the room for you for precisely two hours, during which time you will speak to her parents and let them take over... and you will tell *her* that your days of being responsible for her are over – and then you will join me at the hotel. If, god help you, you don't arrive before the two hours are up, then you will find your car parked at the railway station, as I will be catching a train and making my way home, without you."

I was hurt and I wanted to lash out at him.

"You won't have a problem getting into the car, as I seem to recall you telling me your spare key is still here, in *this house*!" I almost spat the words out. "How very convenient for you."

"No! Lou, don't do this. Go to the hotel by all means...but I'll ring you later and we can talk everything through and..."

"Two hours David. Or I'm gone."

Chapter 16

SUZANNE

I heard the car door slam, the noise of the engine kicking in and then an almighty roar as Dave's cherished black Audi obviously sped off up the road driven by one hell of an irate driver.

For one moment I didn't dare breathe – was Dave driving that car? Had he left anyway, despite everything I'd said; despite practically falling down on my knees and begging him to stay? Did that bitch's happiness mean more to him than my life?

I almost collapsed with blessed relief when I heard the front door quietly opening again and realised that he was here – he *did* care, he *did* feel enough for me to come back. He thought he was merely doing "the right thing" but it was more than that – he just didn't know it yet. He obviously loved her, but it wasn't enough to race away with her today, no matter what she had said to him; however hard she had tried to persuade him to leave.

He didn't rush in to the kitchen this time; he shifted slowly down the hallway - his whole body language as he approached me alerting me to the fact that he truly didn't want to be here; that it wouldn't take much for him to walk out of that door again and fall back into her arms. His smile was weak, his eyes were wet with tears and his shoulders were slumped. He looked dejected, defeated and desperate. I would have to tread carefully tonight and make sure he knew exactly how much I needed him; that my very survival depended on his presence in this house, with me, for the immediate future.

Chapter 17

LOUISE

How the fuck had this happened? One minute David and I were the world's happiest, smuggest couple – sickeningly in love and wholeheartedly making up for all of those lost years. The next minute he had returned to *her* house; back to the matrimonial home – probably raking up thousands of memories from the past, reminding each other of happier times when they walked hand in hand, side by side, together as a couple.

And here I was, perched on the edge of a kingsize bed in a luxurious hotel room that I/we couldn't really afford – a fucking bed that would probably never see any action tonight – all alone, wondering what I must have done in a former life to have deserved all this crap that repeatedly seemed to get flung my way.

Two hours. I had given him two hours, one of which had already passed. Sixty long minutes. I had driven here like Lewis Hamilton on his last lap, tears streaming down my face, swear words tripping off my tongue, all the while picturing the two of them ramming *their* tongues down each other's throats, as they must have done once upon a time. I knew deep down that wouldn't really be occurring now as David wasn't that kind of man. Besides, he'd said that he loved me more than he had ever loved anyone and wanted us to be together forever – and I believed him. But was it enough? When this woman would always be around; popping up and creating drama every time we were well and truly settled and happy. Clicking her fingers and calling him to heel every time she thought he had made a successful bid for freedom.

I wanted to kill her. Jesus Christ, I had never been a nasty, vindictive, violent person – in fact I was a real wuss and probably too soft for my own good – but she brought out the very worst in me and I wanted to take a heavy shovel to that pretty little face of hers. God, I would end up doing time and I'd heard all about what happens in those women's prisons…they'd probably leave me alone though - with all my spare tyres, grey hairs and wrinkles…I was hardly catch of the year these days, even for a desperate hard nut on a long, lonely night.

Looking around the room, I squirmed as I recalled the embarrassment of having to check in without David, who I said may be arriving later. The look of heartfelt sympathy I received from the on-duty receptionist was almost more than I could bear. She had that look that said she'd seen and heard it all before and I think she was about to add a scathing comment about unreliable men but probably thought better of it when she saw the murderous expression on my face.

I wanted to pick up the phone and ring Kirsty and pour my heart out to her but she would have been like a raging bull - and would most likely have contacted David herself to scream blue murder at him and threaten what she could do with a pair of nutcrackers if he didn't get his arse out of that house *right now.*

The seconds were ticking by unbearably slowly and I felt sick to my stomach. This feeling…I remember this feeling from thirty years ago – when David thought I'd two-timed him and told me it was all over between us, when he'd walked away from me and left me with my poor little seventeen year old heart smashed to smithereens. When I'd thought that I could never live without him; when I'd learned the hard way that I would have to.

Chapter 18

SUZANNE

The tears were genuine; there were so many I didn't know where they were coming from and my face ached from sinus pain, and my whole body wilted with exhaustion.

We'd brewed up some coffee and moved to the lounge some time ago where we'd had a heart to heart and I'd admitted to David that there was no other man - that I'd merely been trying to clear the way for him and this *Louise* – that I'd seen how badly he had wanted to leave me but was too kind to say goodbye. That took him by surprise, and he had actually thanked me for *my* kindness. The irony wasn't lost on both of us that I was doing the exact opposite now; that I was dragging him back up that well-trodden pathway and blocking all exit routes.

He dug out some old pamphlets that I had received from the doctors' surgery and rang all of the relevant numbers, jotting down details of appointments made and support groups that I would be joining. Over and over again I told him I couldn't and wouldn't go without him and obtained his reassurances and promises to come with me. And he never broke promises so I knew he wouldn't let me down. He tentatively tried to suggest that he could stay elsewhere, that he already had accommodation sorted for the weekend and a temporary base at Billy's but I broke down again then and begged him – pleaded with him – to stay in the house with me, to give me that safety and security I so badly needed while I was entering the recovery process.

His bed was already made, both literally and metaphorically.

From time to time I saw him glance at the clock on the wall or sneak a quick look at his Gucci watch – a gift I had bought him to commemorate our fifth wedding anniversary. Eventually he delved into the pocket of the coat he had discarded earlier and took out his mobile phone. I hadn't heard it ring at all or noticed the familiar sound of a text message notification coming through. That was surprising – the lack of contact from *her,* giving him holy hell and demanding he leave this house immediately or face the inevitable consequences.

Muttering that he had to make an important call, he left the room – took himself off into the conservatory, no doubt to snatch a few moments of privacy. I desperately wanted to follow him; to catch a little of this clearly fraught conversation he was going to have, but my presence would have made him uncomfortable and he would have been guarded. I would just have to hope that the balance of power really had swung in my favour, because I genuinely couldn't bear it now if he was to walk out of that door and into her arms tonight.

Chapter 19

LOUISE

"Hello, it's me, Louise. Can you hear me? Are you ok Lou?"

Was he having a bloody laugh? Of course I wasn't okay – the events of the day had somewhat knocked the stuffing out of me.

I had wanted to snatch up the mobile and answer it the second I saw it light up, but instead I let it ring and made him wait. I stared at it, his name illuminated on the small screen, feeling nauseous and terrified. There was only ten minutes left before my deadline was up – part of me wanted to rescind it now – to go back in time and scrap the ultimatum. But it was too late. And there was no way I was backing down. If I gave into this, I would be making a rod for my own back - giving him the green light to run to her every time she cried wolf and begged for help – accepting that she always, *always* would come first.

I would just have to hope that he had done the right thing *by me* and had left Suzanne's house now and was on his way over. Please god, let that be the case.

"No, David. No. Funnily enough I'm not okay." I bit my tongue, not wanting to say more until I knew what the state of affairs was.

"I'm so sorry babe – I could never have imagined how today was going to pan out; never in my worst nightmares could I have foreseen that Sue could be so low as to think that this would be her only way out. I'm sorry Lou, we were both looking forward to this weekend so much and...."

"Where are you now then?" I interrupted him. I had to know.

"Well I've just ducked into the conservatory to call you, to let you know...."

"You're still there then. You have eight minutes left before you have to be here and yet you are still fucking there. Best flag a taxi down quickly David, or you are going to be late."

A moment's silence then and I knew. I absolutely knew.

I could hear he was trying to hold it together as he said, "I can't leave her Louise, I can't. She's in such a state and I promised her. It's only for a short while and I've already made a load of phonecalls and started the ball rolling...so it might not even be for as long as..."

"You fucking promised me, you bastard!" I was half-crying, half-screaming...he would have struggled to understand me if he didn't know me so well by now.

"You fucking promised you wouldn't leave me again...you wouldn't go running to her..."

"...I know Lou, I know and I'm sorry, but what can I do? I love you so much babe, you know I do - please don't think it's for any other reason than trying to get her well again...which will be better for us all in the long run and mean that we – me and you – can finally get on with our lives..."

Broken and incensed, I raged and wept, and he let me – I think he was crying too. Occasionally he tried to interrupt me and say my name and I heard the odd "Please don't, Lou."

When I finally got it together enough to speak, I glanced at my watch at the same time. Two minutes past the deadline. Time's up.

David tried to offer up some more reassurances but I cut him dead.

"You're out of time now, so I'm done. Goodbye David."

And I immediately cut him off then and switched off my mobile.

Chapter 20

SUZANNE

Dave seemed to have been gone an eternity; I didn't dare move a muscle, but just worried, and waited.

Finally, he returned to the room. He looked terrible – shocked, wounded, bewildered and above all, devastated. His sun-tanned face shone with tears that were still falling even now and he hastily tried to wipe them away with his sleeve. Whatever had been said, she had certainly done a good job on him.

Well, it was my job now to pretend that I hadn't noticed that he felt like his world had ended there and then during that one telephone call. It would be a painfully slow process but I needed his undivided attention and, eventually, maybe, he would remember how great we once were together. Maybe one day he would accept that it wasn't meant to be, between him and his little holiday romance who, it would seem, had been prepared to chase him to the ends of the earth in desperation. One day it might just all work out for us; for me and him; Dave and Suzanne – husband and wife.

"Oh Dave, thank goodness you're here; I was becoming so stressed again, even just on my own for those few moments. I'm so sorry I've messed up your weekend and everything…but you know I wouldn't have begged you to stay unless I was desperate. I think I've pretty much hit rock bottom now…I'm so ashamed of myself…but with your help and guidance I know I can get my head in the right place again…and then we can sell this place and go our separate ways. Thank you Dave, from the bottom of my heart - thank you for your kindness, your discretion and, above all, for being my best friend."

A rather weak smile was all I received in return before he started to busy himself and concentrate on practicalities. He hauled the suitcase containing the remainder of his stuff down from the loft to ensure he wouldn't be stuck for a change of clothes. He went to make us both a sandwich out of the sparse contents of the fridge and freezer and brewed up another coffee – he watched me force down most of my sandwich but, I noticed, he never touched his own and his coffee was left to go cold again.

He took the rubbish to the outside bins and then came in and switched the heating on. He drew curtains together and closed blinds; he tidied the living room that didn't need tidying and then switched on a comedy show on the television – a pointless exercise as he sat and stared into space for the whole of the programme. He then searched the internet for every bit of information and advice he could find about the medication I was on and the help that was out there for me.

Every so often he would ask me how I was, and offered his own assurances that everything was going to be fine now – that I wasn't to worry, and I was to let him know if I needed anything at all.

When he was satisfied that I was indeed alright, and out of any immediate danger, he reclined his armchair and leaned back into the head-rest, eventually falling into some kind of fitful sleep – his face troubled in slumber and his body twitching and jerking. I wanted to cover him with a blanket but couldn't risk waking him.

As much as I tried to shake it off, I felt guilty - incredibly guilty. Although I hated *her* with a passion, there was a physical ache in my heart when I looked at Dave. I didn't want to make him unhappy but I *did* need him here with me. I needed him much more than she could ever do.

With the passing of time, I'd realised that I couldn't continue to live without him. Foolishly so, I had tried to let him go - had even give him a gentle push in her direction - but then I had been left with a life that was simply unbearable. I needed Dave here by my side, even though, for the time being, I knew he loved her more. I could cope with that; well I would have to learn to cope with that. Because the alternative would kill me, of that I was sure.

Chapter 21

LOUISE

"He fucking did WHAT?"

I think the neighbours four doors down heard Kirsty's angry shouts, as I somehow calmly informed her by mobile that David had returned to Suzanne. Perhaps I was a little bit too calm as within ten minutes of saying goodbye I heard the screech of her car wheels and the sound of her heels clacking up the drive (and Kirsty hated any kind of exercise – she said running wasn't for folk like her who consumed three bottles of red wine over the weekend).

She was barely through the front door before I was gathered up in her arms, having the life squished out of me as I blinked away the tears and wished I could just go up to bed, crawl under my duvet and stay there for, oh, the next couple of months at least. Unfortunately, I had real life to deal with – a daughter, a dog and a house, and clothes to wash and iron before I was due back in work tomorrow. Sunday afternoons could, on balance, be pretty shite, but this one was the absolute pits.

"And the bastard let you catch the train back up here on your own without so much as a phonecall or text message to see how you were…"

"Well, after I cut him off, I blocked him straight away, threw my stuff back into my bag and drove his car to the station, where I found out there were no bloody trains until the following day so I had to check into *another* hotel and set off yesterday morning instead…changing trains FIVE…count them…FIVE bastard times…and just when the end was in sight they turfed us all off at Huyton and, guess what, I found myself on a replacement bus service back to Wigan, for my sins. I could've travelled to sodding Amercia in the time it took me to get home…"

"Wait! You blocked him? Why the hell did you do that? I thought it was strange he hadn't been in touch…hasn't he tried to reach you on your landline then?"

"No, because I unplugged it as soon as I walked through the door! I'm pretty sure he wouldn't have bothered to ring me anyway, as I seem to be at the very bottom of his list of priorities these days…"

"Now you know that's a crock of shit, honey, you know David's probably tried to call you about a hundred times since you upped and left. Even with the stupid bint there in the background listening to his every word. He loves you to death and, having lost you once, he's not going to relish the thought of it happening again is he? Now be a good girl and unblock him and plug that bloody landline back in. At least listen to what he's got to say; give the lad a chance, before I pay him a visit and kneecap him."

"And what if he's cosily settled back in now with that bloody limpet of a wife of his? What if he hasn't actually tried to contact me at all and doesn't intend to at any point in the future? I can't bear it Kirsty, I can't sit here waiting for the phone to ring; jumping every time my mobile bleeps – like a first class mug! I'd go insane! At least this way I get to take back a little control and salvage something from the situation."

"And live the rest of your life without him? Because that's what it could boil down to. If he can't see you or speak to you now, how on earth can the two of you ever sort things out? For Christ's sake Lou, you've spent the last thirty years bereft after losing him in 1984…do you want to spent the next thirty years feeling the same way?"

"I can't do it K! I can't be second best! I know he loves me more but she's got this peculiar hold over him. She starts to sink under the water and he's there, bravely diving in and rescuing her, probably ready to give her mouth to mouth resuscitation as well!"

"As if, you pillock! He'd never touch another woman Lou, not even her, not now he has you. I tell you what, I feel like holding this bloody woman down under the water myself, until the bubbles stop freaking rising to the surface…I don't care what she's been through - she's causing so many people so much pain."

"David always described her as gentle and kind and I believed him when he said she'd moved on and seemed happy to let him go. But, I tell you what, something has definitely shifted – it's like everything's been turned on its head. I think she wants him back K; she's well aware of his weakness - his need to do the right thing and live his life guilt-free - and she's homed in on it. She wants him back and he's falling for it. I mean, for god's sake, whoever heard of the estranged husband moving back in to help the estranged wife through their separation? They must think I'm a few nuggets short of a happy meal to fall for that one!"

"It's not quite as simple as that though is it? If she was genuinely intent on topping herself and he's worried she might actually try again if he doesn't keep schtum and support her, and she's giving him the full sob story and begging him to stay, then how can he ease himself out of that situation, as her husband? How can he walk away from that, without living the rest of his life in fear? I could throttle him for the pain he's caused you again, but try and see it a little from his perspective Lou. You've got to try and understand…"

"Bollocks! She shouldn't be his problem now! He should have contacted her parents and then that would have been his role in this unnecessary drama over and done with. It's down to them to ring the doctors and sift through all the paraphernalia and make all the enquiries to enrol her in the relevant help-groups. NOT HIM! He's already gone above and beyond the call of duty racing back there and preventing her from doing the worst…if that was ever her intention at all. If HE doesn't let go then SHE never will!"

Stamping my feet in temper, balling my fists by my side and almost blowing a gasket, I realised I was yelling at Kirsty when I shouldn't have been and taking my frustrations out on her, but I just couldn't stop myself.

"Hey, don't shout at me Louise Stewart! I'm just trying to give you my objective opinion on the matter. She might be a manipulative, scheming cow who has had this planned all along but there's no saying she wouldn't go through with it. She sounds desperate enough. I know you're devastated love and, in your shoes, I would probably be like the psycho-bitch from hell, but I've seen how David looks at you - how devoted he is to you, and how he would literally move heaven and earth for you and Chloe – even though she fleeced him for fifty quid last week for a new jacket that I *know* she got reduced for thirty-five – so him staying at that house, when he's finally escaped from her clutches, well, to him, it must seem like the only option."

"Oh my God, why are you defending him? I thought you of all people would be on my side, supporting me, as you've always done!"

"Oy, you cheeky little mare! You bloody know I'm on your side and I would kill for you, and on occasions very nearly have. Don't you dare and try make out otherwise or, heartbroken or not, I will tie you to that chair, force-feed you Marmite and make you watch repeats of Jeremy Kyle until you appreciate what a fine man you had, and could probably still have if we can get this mess sorted out."

Oh no, here come the god damn tears again. I thought I was all cried out by ten o'clock this morning when I, very early on it has to be said, entered into the angry, raging bull stage. But no, it would appear I'd just had a temporary reprieve, and my eyes were going to end up as red as those of a dirty old tramp, with donkey's years of White Lightening consumption under his belt. I'd used all the tissues and the kitchen roll was half gone. It was to be hoped there was a good supply of toilet paper in the bathroom.

"I'm sorry K," I hiccupped my way through my apology, crying and sniffing noisily. "I miss him so much already...his beautiful blue eyes, his silvery messed-up hair, his kind, gorgeous face, his broad shoulders and his sexy, firm chest..."

"...his highly squeezable, delectable bum...don't forget his arse love..."

"...yes, yes, his bum...his body...his smile...his *everything*. I never thought I'd be in this position again. All on my own. Without him. More than anything, I want him to walk back through that door now saying he's told her to piss off...and kiss me and make everything better. But that's not going to happen, and I can't let it happen. I'm *so* mad with him Kirsty and I feel like I've been taken for a fool. I've got to end it now because I can't spend the rest of my life waiting for the next crisis; the next time her feelings will take precedence over mine. I'm done. When I was seventeen and he dumped me on that beach I would have done *anything* to rectify that situation, *anything* to bring us back together. And when we finally became a couple, three decades later, I was the happiest woman on the planet. But this isn't what being a couple is about; this isn't *togetherness*. This is the next best thing and if I don't pull the plug now I can see I'm going to be yanking it out on a regular basis for the remainder of my years, never feeling secure in our relationship."

"Aw Mrs...I am so gutted for you. And, despite what I've just said, I really do understand where you are coming from. Don't take me on, I'm a cranky cow today as me and Nath had a bit of a ding-dong last night..."

"You and Nathan? But you *never* argue...he's the most easy-going man on the planet...what the hell are you two rowing about?"

"Must be something in the air eh? Oh...it was nothing really...just something stupid, nothing to worry about. Anyway, back to *you* and *your* problems...I'm going to say something to you, but only the once, and then I promise faithfully that I won't mention it again, okay?"

"Okaaayyy...why do I get the feeling I'm not going to take too kindly to what's coming?"

"The thing is Lou, it's like you've been expecting this, unconsciously or not. In your heart you've never believed you deserved the kind of happiness you've experienced over the last few months and you've just been waiting for it all to implode. Richard – god I hate that prick you were married to – inflicted some serious scars when he took off with tart-face from the office, when all you had ever done was wait on him hand and foot and - for some strange reason - love him. But just because he was a toe-rag, it doesn't mean David is. Richard was a smug, smarmy, less than average philandering twat whereas David is a handsome, gorgeous, faithful, well-above-average decent human being. I don't know what the fuck is going on with that wife of his, but he's just doing his best to hold it all together...and god only knows how much stress he is under at the moment. Whatever the circumstances, I know I couldn't have handled Nathan shacking up with his ex again and I would probably have smashed her face in and jumped up and down on his testicles several hundred times – but please, please, unblock David on your mobile. Plug your landline in again. Try and keep the lines of communication open. Put your relationship on hold if you absolutely have to but don't shut him out completely, because he probably needs you more than ever now. *Please*."

She gave me the puppy dog eyes but she hadn't dented my resolve or my natural instinct to protect myself and my daughter.

"He. Is. Living. With. His. Wife. End of. You can see why I might think it's time to call it quits, eh Kirsty? Only a total and utter gullible idiot would put up with that...and I've been an idiot in the past and I refuse to be that wimp again. So, whilst I appreciate your input, and I have to confess that a tiny, annoying part of me does feel sorry for David while she's pulling the wool over his eyes and taking advantage of him – oh my god, hopefully just literally and please god, not physically yet – for my own dignity and sanity, it has to be over."

Chapter 22

SUZANNE

We had an unexpected visitor the following day – Billy had heard from Jenny who had heard from Kirsty - who of course had been given the full run-down by *Louise*.

When Billy arrived on our doorstep, without even having the decency to text or call first to announce his visit, the first thing I noticed was that this usually placid, neutral-as-Switzerland, easy-going man was red in the face and clearly furious. Not wishing to speak directly to him, I let Dave answer the door, while I hovered in the background. After a hushed exchange of words in the hallway, Dave motioned to Billy to follow him through to the rear garden, telling me they wouldn't be long – in other words making it plain that this would be a private conversation between the two men, and he didn't want me present.

I silently crept upstairs, into the larger of the back bedrooms, where the window was already open to air it out, and initially I could hear every word that was said, as tempers flared and voices were raised.

"Aw man, Jenny is doing her bloody nut! And that Kirsty woman, who is possibly borderline psychotic, is apparently baying for your blood. I'm telling you, you don't mess with these women; they are terrifying when they are angry. I've had it in the ear from Jen since she found out – you'd think it was my bleedin' fault the way she's going on. I'm not lying mate, I'm on a complete bloody sex ban apparently until I've made you see sense. She said, and I quote, "Get your lazy arse round to 'White Towers' and drag him out by his fucking skinny ankles if you have to, or you can frigging whistle for any rumpy pumpy for the near future." You're lucky I've prevented her from barging in here herself and bitch-slapping Suzanne..."

"Shit, I'm sorry Bill...all I've been thinking about is Louise...and Sue...it never entered my head how much grief you would get...or that Jenny and Kirsty would want to tear strips off me. Sorry lad."

"Naw...it's alright I s'ppose...but Dave, you dickhead, what are you doing man? Louise is devastated and you look like shit. Suzanne has got you exactly where she wants you...under her thumb and back in this miserable house. It's like a five star prison. But even career criminals eventually get let out for good behaviour. You gotta hand this over to her parents, I'm telling you; this is not your shout. You can't be responsible for this woman for the rest of your life, just because of some vows you made at the altar in 1997."

"I wish it was that simple Bill but it's not; it's so god damn messed up and complicated. It's not just the vows I made – and I mean, I swore to be faithful but that's obviously gone out of the French windows – it's my friendship with Suzanne – because we have always remained friends, no matter what – I will always care for her and I can't just leave her in the lurch. She's so desperate, she needs me. And, I know you probably don't think so right now, but she's a really, really good person inside."

"She's not; she's a fucking conniving bitch who has you wrapped around her little finger. If she was half the person you make her out to be then she wouldn't be doing this. She'd accept responsibility for her own actions and she'd let you go. Especially knowing you love Louise, not her. Jenny says the woman has no pride; will stoop to any level to keep you in her clutches, and I'm beginning to think she's right. She wouldn't do this if *she* loved *you*."

"First of all, she is NOT a conniving bitch – don't ever say that again. You're out of order mate. And secondly, she was never exactly at the top of Jenny's Christmas card list, was she? I'm not being funny Bill, but you didn't witness it; you weren't here. She was about to take a shit-load of pills, and if I hadn't got here when I did, it could so easily have been too late. I'm racked with guilt because I should've *known* she wasn't right. I should've *seen* how miserable and lonely she was. I should have *realised* she needed help. And she does have pride, actually mate, no matter what you think. So I know if she's begging me to stay and help her, then it really is in desperation."

"And what about Louise? Or have you forgotten all about her? Because from what I've heard, on the grapevine, you've totally broken her. And at the moment she's saying she's done with you for good; that there's no going back. And I don't fucking blame her, because the way things are at the moment mate, she's too bleedin' good for you."

Silence then. I imagined Dave had sat himself down on one of the damp garden chairs, his body slumped and his beautiful face tortured as he thought about *her*.

"Louise. *Louise.* God I love that woman from the roots of her beautiful, shiny, brown hair to the tips of her cute little painted toes. I miss her so much I feel like I'm slowly bleeding to death inside, and I despise myself for hurting her. If there was any other way I would be out of here like a flash, begging and pleading with her to take me back..."

"I remember when you first met her you know, on Towan Beach, when we were just kids really - when I kicked that football and accidently bounced it off her head. You never really bothered with the girls much until she came along. One look at her and you were besotted. I got landed with her gobby mate, that Joanne – I took one for the team there, so the pair of you could get it together. And you were stuck like glue to each other all through that holiday, and I thought, "Fuck's sake, I've lost my wingman"...but I was chuffed to bits for you. And I really liked Louise. I mean, what's not to like? She was so genuine and funny and, sorry mate, but hot as hell. So I couldn't believe it when it all went tits up and you said you'd caught her dabbling with someone else at that party. I knew something wasn't right because there's no way she would be interested in anyone else – lease of all that knobhead, Stephen."

"And you were right, and I should have listened to you and trusted her..."

"Exactly. But at the time you were like a man possessed. I couldn't believe it though when you let her leave Newquay without even saying goodbye. And afterwards, I saw how you were. Mucking about with the rest of the lads, but somehow always on your own. And every summer, I saw you looking for her, searching for her...wondering if she'd ever come back for you...until you finally *pretended* to accept it was over – because, I fucking *know* you Dave, and I always sensed that deep down you still carried a torch for Louise, and part of you just never let go."

It was like an eyewitness account of Dave and Louise's love story from the very beginning, and yet I still couldn't drag myself away and spare myself the pain. Still rooted to the spot, on self-destruct mode again, I felt compelled to sit there and hear out the rest.

"When you met Suzanne, I was well fucking shocked I can tell you mate. Yeah, she's a bit of a looker and all that, but would hardly be a contender for personality of the year. And I couldn't believe you'd fallen for a posh bird and were settling down with her – it just wasn't you. She couldn't have been more different from Louise as well - looks and personality. I had my doubts but thought, well, if it's making the lad happy, let him be. But right from the off she had you where she wanted you. Yeah, occasionally you stood up to her over money and all that shit, but that big poncey wedding and this massive fancy house and all those bloody foreign holidays...that wasn't the Dave who I'd grown up with. All you really wanted was a cosy little house, a bit of cash on the hip, and Louise to share it with. Kids would have been a bonus. But instead you settled for Suzanne."

"I did NOT fucking settle for Suzanne. I wouldn't have married her if I hadn't loved her, you dick."

"But you DON'T fucking love her anymore, you wanker! After dreaming of Louise for thirty years you finally have her back in your life and now you're prepared to give her up to protect your devious *former* wife. You're mad Dave, bleedin' mad. But if you get your gear together now and get yourself out of here then perhaps, if you don't leave it too long, then there's the slightest chance Louise will take you back if you get down on your bended knees and plead for forgiveness. And then maybe, just maybe, there's the slightest chance I will get my end away before the week is out!"

It sounded like a poor attempt at a joke from Billy to try to defuse the situation, but I didn't hear Dave laughing. Instead, after a few minutes of definitely NOT companionable silence outside, I heard Billy scrape his chair back, clear his throat and say, "So you're not budging are you? You're still standing by Suzanne's side and waving goodbye to Louise in the process. You're a fucking martyr Dave. Well, I'm sorry mate, we've been friends a long time, but I won't be coming round here anymore. Jen would have my guts for garters if I even attempted it anyway. I might see you around, in the pub if she lets you out for a beer at any point, otherwise, look me up when you've seen sense. Stay there mate. I'll let myself out."

I couldn't believe it; I never thought I'd see the day when something - anything - would come between Dave and Billy. Surely they would sort things out. Although I'd be glad if I never had to clap eyes on his monster of a wife again – I think I'd be doing my shopping online in future to avoid bumping into her. She was scary at the best of times – I definitely wouldn't want to be beaten to a pulp in the middle of a supermarket aisle.

Quietly pulling myself up from the floor, I peeped out from behind the curtains, careful to keep myself hidden from view. I had heard the front door slam as Billy left, but Dave hadn't followed him. When I looked out into the garden, he was still sat there – not moving – just staring into space – his face emotionless; his mind unreadable.

I would pretend I hadn't heard a word of the heated conversation and knew nothing of his rift with Billy. Tip-toeing across the landing and into my bedroom, I lay on top of the duvet, as if I had been there all of the time. I tried to block out the way Dave had spoken about Louise with such tenderness in his voice, and concentrated on the positives instead. He had been adamant that he had loved me once – that he hadn't settled for less - and he said he still cared for me. That was something. We could work on that.

Chapter 23

LOUISE

My days were terrible and were consumed with disturbing thoughts, on one continuous loop – imagining what David would be doing; what *they* could be doing together – and the nights were even worse, when sleep evaded me and I imagined the absolute worst. I staggered through work as if in a trance and tried to put on some semblance of a cheerful face when I was at home and Chloe was around.

Kirsty had been good enough to brief my daughter and my mother, to bring them bang up-to-date on what had occurred, why David was notable by his absence and why I was in such a zombie-like state.

Chloe had been understandably upset – more so, it seemed to me, than when her brainless pillock of a father had run off with someone barely out of school and abandoned the pair of us. I had never been able to get my head round the fact that David thought, or hoped, he could maybe keep our relationship going whilst moving back into the matrimonial home, whatever the circumstances, and, likewise, Chloe was unable to comprehend how David could ever think that would be acceptable to me - to us – although she did infer that I was a daft old bat for refusing to speak to him.

Unfortunately for Josh, Chloe seemed to think it was acceptable for her to vent all of her anger and frustrations on him, and it would seem that they had hit a rocky patch. He only asked to meet her after school one day and I thought she was going to lynch him. A heated conversation followed about "control" and "boundaries" and then the poor lad was unceremoniously shown the front door. I'd offered him a sympathetic smile as he retreated with a puzzled look on his face, but I don't think it helped – and when I tried to tackle Chloe on the issue and suggest that maybe she had been a little harsh on him, I got the "all men are pigs" response. Fair play.

At least Chloe was no longer taught by Miss Waite, the geography teacher, who earlier in the year had shown an unhealthy interest in my rekindled relationship with David and who had often quizzed Chloe on the finer details of our romance during lesson time, when the kids should have been learning the important stuff that might just see them through their GCSEs. I'd been informed that Miss Waite no longer worked at the school – maybe she had been asked to leave as it seemed her mind wasn't really on the job and she was mostly away with the fairies. Anyway, thank the lord Chloe wouldn't have to divulge the news that I had been dumped by David, yet again...I don't think the woman's nerves would have stood it and I especially didn't fancy being the hot topic of gossip in the staffroom for another term.

Three hours after mum was informed, she arrived on my doorstep with a home-made steak pie and a family-sized tin of sweets – obviously if I was going to end my days as a sad, lonely, old singleton then I may as well get tooth decay and become obese as well. Kirsty was obviously of the same opinion as she had fetched pick 'n' mix and a whopping great big bar of chocolate, although she at least had the decency to sit down and scoff half of it with me, whereas all mum shared with me were her words of wisdom.

"I'm so sorry Louise. I just can't believe David would be doing anything untoward though; he's not that kind of man you know; not the philandering sort. Try and give him the benefit of the doubt in this instance, as difficult as it may seem. It would do the two of you the world of good if you could just sit yourselves down and have a little chat..."

"Huh! I don't bloody think so mum. What would that solve? He's not going to walk out on her now if he hasn't done already! So, he's gone; he's history. It's finished. Another one bites the dust as they say."

"Except you love him Louise. You've always loved him and you always will. No amount of time apart will ever change that. It doesn't just go away, you know – it doesn't just evaporate, all that love. And every relationship has its problems. You don't usually get to your forties without carrying some baggage with you..."

"SOME BAGGAGE! He's carting around enough baggage to fill a flippin' aeroplane hold! And it's killing him but he still won't let go; he's a sucker for a sob story, a bloody glutton for punishment I'll give him that. And since when have you become so understanding about an unfaithful boyfriend? Weren't you the one who told me I deserved better than to be someone's bit on the side?"

"Listen love, if I thought you were his bit on the side I'd give you BOTH a piece of my mind. But it's not that simple. If he'd walked away from the situation with his wife, do you really think that would have made everything alright again?"

"Well it couldn't have turned out any worse mum!"

"Look Louise, if she'd overdosed, the guilt would have ruined David, and your relationship would be over anyway. If he'd turned his back on her on this occasion, even if it had only been a cry for help this time around, then there would only have been *another* occasion - another crisis he'd have to deal with in the future…and then another…and another….and on and on it would go. Don't you see? This is his way of trying to sort it out once and for all. I'm not saying it's a foolproof plan; I don't know what the answer is and there are certainly no guarantees. But it seems to me that by sacrificing this time now, he's trying to protect your future."

"What future? Because from where I'm standing, we have no future. The only future he has now is with that woman who will never let him go! He has pissed on his chips now mum – excuse the language but he makes me so bloody angry! I HATE HIM!"

"You don't really though, do you Louise? You obviously still adore him and that's why it hurts so much and you're so angry. I know right now it seems like there's no solution to all of this, but things have a way of working themselves out in the end, you'll see."

It was okay for mum to say – I mean, she has my best intentions at heart but my dad passed away thirty years ago and she's never bothered with anyone else since, and she'd only ever had one boyfriend before dad anyway, so what experience has she of men and relationships, really? What does she know about crappy boyfriends and even crappier husbands and getting dumped and the likes? It was my forte!

Name: Louise Stewart.

Specialist Subject: Bastards, 1984 to present date.

Yes, I could comfortably sit in that big black chair on Mastermind and answer all of my questions correctly and be the unbeaten, unrivalled champion. Well, actually, not if Kirsty was a contender. Even my track record beats the shower of shit she'd taken up with in the past. Thank god for Nathan.

"Mum, I appreciate that you're only trying to help, but you have no idea what you're talking about. You've never been in this position so you don't realise how difficult it is…"

"Oh Louise! You really are your worst enemy sometimes you know!"

"Gee thanks! And just what do you mean by that?"

A huge sigh from mum. Here we go.

"I tell you what I mean. It's like this. You do it to yourself every time – you put yourself under so much pressure for everything to be absolutely 100% perfect and then when there's a tiny little hiccup, it's like the end of the world!"

"A tiny little hiccup? You're joking aren't you? I would hardly call him living with his wife again a tiny little hiccup! I'd call it a gigantic noisy burp! What was I supposed to do? Just go along with it like a fool and put the rest of my life on hold, waiting for him to come crawling back to me?"

"Of course not, you silly girl! But what on earth was this two hour deadline about? *If he doesn't come back in two hours it's over!* Well that's just stupid talk. It's like when you were a little kid – *If I don't manage to ride my bike by Friday then I'm giving up!* Or when you were a teenager it was - *If I don't get rid of these spots by Thursday then I'm not going to the school disco!* Or – and this is my absolute favourite – *If I don't lose two stone by the weekend then I'm staying overweight forever!* Why the deadlines? Why the pressure and the subsequent stress and tears if things don't turn out the way you planned - if you don't meet your target? I don't know where on earth you get it from. And don't look at me like that young lady – you're not too old for a clip around the ear you know!"

Always lovely to receive your mother's full support!

"Trust me love...you won't find anyone better than David."

"Oh thanks, that's cheered me up no end!"

"Love, I'm being serious. Have you *seen* the other available men around this town? Last week I bumped into that strange little weirdo who Kirsty used to date...there is something very wrong with that man!"

"I'm sorry, you're going to have to narrow it down mum...which strange little weirdo would that be?" I wasn't kidding – most of Kirsty's exes were freaks with borderline personality disorders.

"The one with the ruddy cheeks who still lives in his mother's back bedroom even though he's about forty...you know, the guy who buys kids' books from the second hand shop and who does that rather odd hand-wringing thing all of the time. I only stopped to ask after his mother and he must have done it about thirty times – I felt like I needed to go straight home and have a good wash after my encounter with him. Anyway, he's the type of man that's left on the market; do you really want to end up with someone like that, do you?"

"Well, clearly not. I don't want to end up in a shallow grave in his mother's back garden. Thanks for the pep talk though mum, it's been a great help."

Kirsty had of course been round on an almost daily basis, sometimes with the ever-lovely, ever-cheerful Nathan in tow. Despite wallowing in my own misery, I loved to see them, sharing private (dirty) jokes and fitting perfectly together like two pieces in a jigsaw. She positively radiated happiness when she was with him, and I sincerely hoped it would last. I prayed he would never hurt her. Mind you, I had never thought David capable of hurting me this time around but it just goes to show, you never can tell.

As an added bonus for Kirsty, she actually liked Nathan's ex-wife, Loretta. She'd met her a couple of times and, to my astonishment – knowing what a hot-headed psycho Kirsty can be at times – they'd hit it off and there was no jealousy or animosity; just pleasant conversation when they'd stopped by to pick up Jack. I did point out though that it was easy to be pleasant with a nice, normal woman, who Kirsty described as a "a bit of a plain Jane" and a "big unit". That sat a bit uncomfortably with me as I think I had ventured into the "big unit" territory of late.

Loretta also had a new partner, who was equally smiley and agreeable, and she was a great mum who was completely flexible as far as contact with Jack was concerned. And she kept her distance from Nathan - genuinely delighted that he had moved on and wishing him well. Perfect. What a breath of fresh air. Especially when you compared her to beautiful, slim Suzanne who caused endless problems and resolutely refused to let go. Christ. It was no wonder I had more grey hairs than you could shake a stick at.

A couple of texts had arrived from Billy's wife, Jenny, which read along the lines of "Me and B. are gutted. Have told him to sort Dickhead Dave out. B. knows he's dead meat if he sees D again while he's with that bitch." She meant well but, if anything, that made me even sadder, knowing how long Billy and David had been best friends and realising that the fallout from all of this was affecting more than just the two of us – three, if you included Chloe. And, if I'm honest, I didn't want Billy to stop knocking about with David, even if he was being a tool. He'd been a good friend to him and I wanted that to continue - even through my anger I couldn't bear the notion of David being isolated and having no one to confide in.

I had an overwhelming feeling that he was going to need his best friend more than ever in the days and weeks to come.

Chapter 24

SUZANNE

If I'd hoped to dodge the numerous appointments that had been lined up for me then I was truly deluded because Dave made damn sure I attended everything that was scheduled in the diary. Of course, it all seemed rather epidemic now – Dave was home and I was pretty sure that I no longer required the same level of support with regard to my mental health. But I trotted along to everything like a good little girl, and joined in when prompted and pushed - although I found it highly embarrassing and wanted to flee from the room when I had to describe the incidents with the pills and disclose some of my innermost feelings.

To my surprise, I actually found the local support group which met in the community centre rather beneficial. There was another woman there, Alice, who reminded me of myself - through no fault of her own, she found herself alone after her husband of sixteen years declared he was in love with someone else. She'd had three painful miscarriages prior to his departure and was struggling to come to terms with all that had happened to her; experiencing dark thoughts and days, when living for another thirty or forty years no longer seemed like a viable option.

I'd wanted to reach out and hug her and tell her nothing was so bad that it couldn't be overcome; that it was just a matter of small – no - tiny footsteps in the right direction, taking one day at a time. It shocked me into silence as I realised that was what other people probably saw and felt when they looked at me. It gave me a better understanding of my family's point of view and how frustrated and hurt they must have been when I had appeared unreachable to them.

Maybe Dave was hoping that it would be a miraculous recovery for me, if not overnight then within a reasonably short period of time. But I genuinely knew it wouldn't be – no one expected that of me – not doctors, not counsellors nor mental health specialists. They thought my problems went much, much deeper than that; that they'd barely scratched the surface, and who was I to argue? Instinctively, I knew as well that to save my marriage it was essential that the recovery progress be a reasonably slow one - to ensure Dave had reached the point of no return with Louise. I wasn't totally sure that particular line had been crossed yet – I wanted to be absolutely certain that she was permanently out of the picture.

I had an unexpected boost to my campaign when I checked his mobile and discovered that she had blocked his number. Well, well…she really was quite a feisty, determined lady – and I used the word "lady" very loosely – she wouldn't stand for any messing about.

I'd looked at the pictures on there as well but sincerely regretted it. The photographs told the story of a deliriously happy couple who were clearly crazy about each other. I felt physically sick when I saw the shots of them together at what looked like a birthday gathering for him in some scruffy, unfamiliar pub. Good Lord, there was Billy and that heifer of a wife of his, and even some other of the boys' friends from Newquay. I'd like to think that the evening hadn't been a roaring success – that he had preferred the romantic dinners for two we'd shared for many years on his birthday, rather than some knees-up surrounded by drunken louts and fruit machines, but unfortunately he was beaming with happiness on all of the images. Never mind - he would be happy again, eventually, once he had resigned himself to a life without Louise, and I had shown him exactly what he had been missing.

Chapter 25

LOUISE

"Kirsty, will you please have a word with mother and tell her to get a grip? We all miss David but moping around here all of the time in her ancient towelling dressing gown isn't going to help. We had cheese on toast *again* for tea last night; I can't remember the last time she cooked a proper meal. If it wasn't for the chippy and nan's care packages I would have starved to death by now! I never thought I'd say this but I actually *miss* vegetables, and there's not a hope in hell of us having a Sunday dinner today."

I could hear Chloe complaining to Kirsty in the other room and I felt ashamed, but it took all of my energy just to haul myself into work every day, and to keep us and the house clean and relatively tidy. Chloe had been looking after Fudge, our faithful old cocker spaniel – feeding him and walking him, although she drew the line at scooping any poop in the back garden – but I was pleased to see he was still drawn to me and still curled up on my lap while I stroked his fur. It was as if he knew I needed the warmth and the comfort; that he was reassuring me that *he* wasn't going anywhere.

"Right, get your coat on and go sit in the car. We'll nip for a carvery," I heard Kirsty say. She came through to the living room where I was stretched out on the settee and stood determinedly between me and the television screen, with her hands on her hips.

"And you, Mrs, you poor little soul who is driving her daughter to distraction, I don't suppose you want to join us? No? Shocker. Well, listen in, because I'm telling you now, this can't go on much longer. And I won't allow it. So, next Saturday, I am going to gather the girls together and we are all, you included, heading off into town to dance the night away whilst drinking copious amounts of wine-slash-beer. Have you got that? There will be no backing out - no protests about having nothing to wear. You've got all week to get yourself sorted and it will do you the world of good to get out of this house."

Of course, I did try and protest, an awful lot, but Kirsty wouldn't take no for an answer. So Saturday night I found myself squeezed into my old black dress, sporting new costume jewellery and overpriced handbag and shoes (despite the fact that I hadn't a pot to piss in these days) and dragged off into town to try and forget my troubles. To begin with it seemed like a terrible idea, but five wines in, I was feeling much more relaxed and the dancing had commenced.

Even looking well below par, I still managed to attract my fair share of nutters who just wouldn't clear off despite me being downright rude to them.

"Aw god, Kirsty, will you get this fucking limpet off me? He smells of hot pot and dances like my Uncle Fred. And he looks like a serial killer. If this is the best I can get then, fuck me, I'm never leaving home again."

"Ha! Wait till you hear this one. See that guy in the red t-shirt over there who's sweating like a pig – the one who's dribbling slightly – well he's just been trying his luck and do you know what he sang to me? To the tune of 'Ghostbusters' he fucking sang "Who you gonna call? Big Busters!", and then he tried to squeeze my tits, the lecherous old get. Anyway, I got my own back. He gave me a twenty to get us both a drink from the bar and he only received change from a tenner!"

"Kirsty, I think that's technically known as *stealing*. You can't do that, he might come after you when he realises he's a little short for his taxi fare!"

"Well I think what he did could be technically known as *sexual harassment*, so let's call it quits. Besides, I think ten pounds is a pretty reasonable figure for compensation - for embarrassment and distress caused back there. Come on honey, let's gather up the girls and move on before I clatter one of these knobheads."

So we staggered from bar to club, knocking back the free shots on top of all the other alcohol that was being thrown down our necks. If I'd been relaxed by the five pint stage, I was positively pissed out of my skull by the time I'd downed three shots and two ciders as well.

Unfortunately, I'd shifted on from the giggly and merry stage to the depressed and distressed one, as a curtain of sadness fell down on me and I remembered what I had lost. And I had that awful strange feeling - when you're in a group of friends, amongst a crowd of people, and yet somehow you're still completely on your own; by yourself.

Despite my protests, I ended up spinning round the room with two drunken women I'd never clapped eyes on before, who accompanied me to the toilets as I vomited in cubicle three, and then sat on the wet floor, in god only knows what, crying my heart out, telling them all about my David. Every so often I would hear a "Bastard!" or "Fucking scumbag!" as they sympathised with me and stroked my matted hair. No one is more supportive of a drunken woman in distress than fellow pissheads in the ladies loos at two o'clock in the morning. I recalled sobbing, "...but I love him and I can't live without him!" as they each took an arm and dragged me up off the floor and out of the, let's say water, that desperately needed mopping up.

The louder of the two women, whose names I will probably never know, checked all of our heels for stray toilet paper and then literally dragged me back up the stairs and into the bar area, depositing me with Kirsty and the girls before dancing off to order cocktails and fondle the bouncers. God love them.

As the others partied on, I propped myself up in a corner, noticing that I was seeing two of everybody and feeling the nausea rise up inside me again. I knew that me and my wet dress had to get out of there and back home into my lovely bed. This had been a stupid idea – what had I been thinking? - Leaving the safe confines of my lovely home to end up in this shithole with all of these drunken idiots. It only made me pine for David even more. Aw god, I seem to have gone back a stage – all the fury had dissipated for the time being and all I was left with was a broken heart and an empty space in my bed.

Stumbling out of the nightclub, I somehow tottered down to the taxi rank without going arse over tit in the silly, silly heels I had squashed my tired old feet into. Kirsty would probably kill me – I think she'd only gone to the bar (again) when I'd departed and everyone else was too pissed to notice I wasn't there anymore. But I would square it with her in the morning. Oh my god it *was* the morning. How in the hell had it got to quarter-to-four? I was too old for this shit now. This wasn't what I wanted – but then I couldn't have what I wanted. I could *never* have what I wanted but, despite all I had said, could I ever really accept that it was over for good between me and David? Every day I reiterated to anyone who asked that I was done with him – the day he had chosen to move back in with the wife-from-hell again was the day I had been forced to move on.

But oh Christ, I still wanted him, so very badly. I couldn't admit it to anyone, but I did. Only he could bring the sunshine back into my life again, only he could mend my knackered old heart – but he was the one that had shattered it in the first place.

And he'd gone. It was over. I just needed to accept that.

*

When I awoke, fully clothed and smelling like a sewer rat, at almost ten o'clock the next morning, Chloe was stood over me, frowning and revealing barely veiled disgust at the state I was in.

"Christ, what is that vile smell mother? Did you actually fall *into* the toilet last night or have you sprung a leak? You are MINGING! I've just got back from nan's and every light in the house is on and your shoes, bag and earrings are in various locations on the staircase. You do know you would absolutely lose your rag with me if *I* did that, don't you? I'm surprised you managed to even lock the front door behind you when you came in, but thank god you did or the place would have been cleared out overnight. Fudge slept on my bed you know? You didn't close the hall door so he sneaked up and he's spark out, upside down amongst my teddies!"

Oh god, Chloe's voice was loud, so very loud.

"Please stop talking now. Be a love and fetch mum the bucket before it's too late."

Looking me up and down as if I was a dirty old hooker, Chloe retrieved the plastic mop bucket from behind the bathroom door and placed it down beside my bed.

"Oh and Kirsty is absolutely furious with you! She messaged you about fifty times last night after you disappeared but of course you didn't reply - your phone was on silent and then you dropped it on the settee when you came in...so she thought you were dead in a ditch somewhere, and she is NOT impressed. She ended up ringing Marie - you know Marie with the feral kids, at number twenty-eight - at SIX O'CLOCK THIS MORNING, to beg her to run down to see if you'd got home okay. But Marie said, oh she didn't need to do that as you'd fallen out of a taxi around four-thirty and had dropped your bunch of keys about a trillion times before you'd managed to locate your own front door and got the key in the lock. Apparently the good old taxi driver waited to check you got in safely...so when you finally got the right key in and flung the door open you shouted "WHEY HEY! I'M IN!" to him...and woke half of the street in the process, including Marie's teething baby."

"Oh god, the shame! Marie will give me a right earful later – you know what a cow she can be. And Kirsty...oh Jesus. We never leave each other, it's the unbreakable rule. No one is left on their own, no one wanders off on their own and no one jumps in a taxi alone.

Kirsty's going to kill me with her bare hands when she gets hold of me – I'll never hear the end of it!"

I covered my squinting eyes with my hands, the shame making my cheeks burn, and then, as a hasty afterthought, added "And don't you ever, EVER, do what your stupid old mother did last night Chloe, do you hear me? Don't you EVER stray from your mates on a night out. Let this be a lesson to you."

My fifteen year old daughter actually sneered back at me. "I'm not that thick mum. I can't believe you did that. Anyway, you've got some apologising to do as far as Kirsty's concerned, and I've got a backlog of homework to at least pretend to make a start on before I disappear to Lilly's for a HOMEMADE Sunday lunch. Have a bloody hot shower mother and clean your teeth. Fresh as a daisy you are not."

I would let the "bloody" go on this occasion. I could hardly criticise *her* behaviour when I was a total and utter disgrace.

The slam of the bedroom door indicated she had left the room, but had at least deposited my mobile on the end of the bed. Charged up as well. Along with a small bottle of water and a packet of paracetamol. God love her.

The nausea came in waves but never actually resulted in anything more, even when I forced down the two pills. I eventually sat up on the bed, trying to find some clarity in my head; desperate for a wash but not knowing if I had it in me to drag my sorry arse into the bathroom.

Oh sweet baby Jesus, mum was coming over at eleven to return a couple of skirts of Chloe's that she'd taken the hems up on – apparently they weren't short enough these days unless your bum cheeks were hanging out for all to see. I had no choice but to haul myself into the shower then – it nearly killed me but at least I felt a bit fresher afterwards, especially after I had cleaned my teeth (oh-oh, minty...here comes that retching again). Clothes were a task too far so I just shoved on my faithful old dressing gown. It had a tendency to gape open when least expected, so it was to be hoped I wouldn't be welcoming any strangers into the house today.

Mum gave me short shrift when she arrived, telling me, yet again, that while my situation seemed dire at the moment and that a broken heart didn't heal overnight, I did in fact need to pull myself together.

"Don't you think you're setting a bad example to Chloe?"

"No, I think I'm setting a bloody good example to Chloe, actually. She took one look at me in shit-state this morning and I think it's put her off drinking alcohol for life. Job done."

"Don't swear. And ring Kirsty for the love of God. You were thoroughly out of order last night Louise."

Christ almighty, had Kirsty told everyone what an idiot I had been? Breaking my own rules, risking my own safety.

As mum departed, fairly quickly I noticed - probably in case I begged her to make me a brew and some bacon butties - I collapsed back onto the settee and took the plunge and rang Kirsty.

When she finally answered, I held the phone away from my ear as I took my punishment.

"YOU ABSOLUTE FUCKING DIPSTICK, LOUISE STEWART! What are you trying to do to me? Give me a bloody heart attack? We searched half of Wigan for you last night thinking you'd been dragged off into an alleyway somewhere! Ashanti interrogated all the taxi drivers – and she was pissed as a fart so god knows what they thought was wrong with her – and I rang you about fifty times!" (Slight exaggeration...I counted twenty-two missed calls). "Anything could have happened to you, staggering round the streets on your own, drunk as a skunk, and jumping into a taxi by yourself. Do you want to get abducted and chopped into little pieces and chucked into the River Douglas now, do you?"

"Oh god, *please* stop shouting before my head explodes and tiny bits of my *brain* end up in the River Bleeding Douglas. I'm so sorry Kirsty – you know I would never do anything like that normally. I was so drunk and so stupid and just on another planet. I never meant to cause you such grief and stress; I promise you I'll never do it again, honestly. I'm just all over the place at the moment..."

From god knows where, the tears started to flood out again, and I started to sob noisily into the phone. "I wish I'd never gone out K; I should never have left the house. Seeing all those other men – mostly knobheads – in all their glory in those clubs – oh Kirsty it only served to remind me what a brilliant, sexy, wonderful man I've lost. Not only was he heart-stoppingly gorgeous but he was the kindest, most thoughtful, hard-working, funny lovely, *lovely* man I've ever known in all of my life...oh K, how do I go on living without him? Look what he's reduced me to! I'm so sorry about last night Mrs, but my head is completely cabbaged and instead of all of this getting easier, it seems to just be getting harder every day…"

All Kirsty's anger was suddenly forgotten then and replaced by the words "I'm coming round."

In the short time it took her to whiz round to mine in her knackered old car, Chloe appeared again, but this time she knelt down by my side and pulled my head softly into her chest and stroked my damp, messy hair as I cried a thousand tears. It wasn't supposed to be like this. I should be comforting *her*, my precious child, not the other way round.

Kirsty looked remarkably alert for someone who had drunk like a fish the previous evening and slept for no more than three hours. She put her halo on and made me my coffee and bacon sandwiches, most of which Chloe ate, and curled up in her usual armchair, making herself comfortable. When Chloe was sure I wasn't about to dissolve into floods of tears again, she headed back up to "do homework" – I'm not sure how much was actually completed as she seemed to be on her phone more than buried in her textbooks, but there you go.

Kirsty and I covered the same ground – mostly repeating how wonderful David was but what a tosser he also was to agree to act as nursemaid and counsellor to that bloody wife of his. We did achieve the odd burst of laughter though when we recalled funny incidents from the previous evening – Ashanti's skin-tight leather-look trousers splitting as she was gyrating way down low to a Dirty Dancing classic; some intellectually-challenged guy actually telling Kirsty to get her crash helmet on as she would be going through the headboard later, and Mikita tripping and tumbling down the stairs in the first bar we went into ("Who in god's name decides that the best place to put the toilets is up THREE PIGGIN' FLIGHTS OF STAIRS?").

I noticed after a while that Kirsty had gone remarkably quiet, which was most unusual for her, so I gently asked, "You okay chicken? You have forgiven me, haven't you?"

"What? Oh yeah. Don't ever do it again or I will literally choke you, but yes, you're forgiven. This time."

She was fiddling with the zip on the cushion cover as she spoke; I knew she had something on her mind that she was about to disclose.

"Well…I've got some news actually – you will be the first to know."

"OH MY GOD, you're not…? Or do you mean you're going to get…?"

"No. And no. Sorry, no nappies or hat needed just yet."

"Oh right. And I should have known better than to think it was the first one as you're practically allergic to babies!" I wasn't kidding. She actually broke out into a cold sweat when she came into close contact with one and when we had worked together she had always made a run for it when anyone on maternity leave had brought their new little bundle of joy into the office for all to see and coo over.

"So what then? Do tell. Spill the beans. I'm in need of some cheering up."

"Well…this is going to come as a bit of a shock but…you see…the thing is…me and Nathan are splitting up a-week-on-Sunday."

"What? Say what? Did I hear you right then? You. And Nathan. Are splitting up?"

"Yes. A-week-on-Sunday."

"A-week-on-Sunday?"

"Yes. A-week-on-Sunday. Like I said. Sunday next week."

"So…you. And Nathan. Splitting up. A-week-on-Sunday?"

"Bloody hell, it's like dealing with a demented parrot. Yes, me and Nathan are going our separate ways, a-week-on-Sunday."

"Kirsty…Mrs…what the hell are you going about? You and Nathan are the epitome of love's young dream – well, young-*ish*. You've been happy as a pig in…well, you know…and you've been inseparable since you met and you're madly in love with each other. How on earth can you be splitting up? What the frig has happened?"

"We've had a difference of opinion with regard to a major subject, so the sensible thing was to call time on our relationship. A-week-on-Sunday."

"What? I mean…what? And only *you* could actually decide on an actual day to *split up*! Like, who does that? People argue, or are unfaithful and get found out, or someone drops dead and shuffles off this mortal coil...but no one arranges a bloody time and date to part ways for god's sake!"

"Well, we have. We are doing it sensibly, civilly and amicably."

"You? *YOU*? Sensibly, civilly and amicably?"

"Christ, you're doing your parrot act again. Yes, me – sensibly, civilly and amicably."

"Get the fuck out of here! Why Kirsty? Just...why?"

"I've got my cousin Trina's wedding on Saturday...we'd already accepted the invitation as a couple...I can't go and face all the family on my own when I've been bragging about this fantastic, handsome boyfriend I've got stashed away at home. They'd eat me alive. And Nathan would never leave me to face the music like that...so...we agreed we would go to the wedding and stay over in the hotel room we've booked, drive home on Sunday and say our goodbyes then..."

"I DON'T MEAN WHY ARE YOU BREAKING UP *ON SUNDAY*! Although, that had of course crossed my mind. I'm asking WHY are the two of you breaking up in the first place? What's this stupid difference of opinions you've had? Surely nothing can be so bad that you can't sort it all out and overcome your differences?"

"I want a baby and he doesn't Lou." Jesus. She said it without missing a beat. I was sure I hadn't quite heard her correctly.

"You? You want a baby? A baby? You?"

"Christ, you're doing it again...yes, ME! *I* want a baby. Little old me."

"But babies do your head in! You've always said you were never having children, that you'd just never had that urge to be a mother. That you couldn't bear the thought of all the dribbling and pooping and responsibility!"

"I know what I said. And I never, ever thought I would change my mind, not in a million years. But it's like this – when I met Nathan everything changed for me. I'd finally fallen in love with someone who loved me equally and it seemed *that* was what was needed for the maternal instinct to kick in. And now it's kicked in, it's all I can bloody think about. I've been deliriously happy with Nath over the last few months and I thought this was it, finally settled down at last. He was my future. But it doesn't feel like my, *our*, future would be complete without a baby we've made together."

"Good God. If I hadn't heard you utter those words with my own ears, I would never have believed it to be true…"

"I know – I can't believe it myself really. But you see, the thing is Lou, when we first met, Nathan said really early on that he didn't want any more children and I was happy with that, because I'd never wanted any little squawkers either!"

"Have you tried talking to him? Is that what you argued about the other week?"

"Yes, and yes. I tried to bring the subject up one night after we'd had some fucking awesome sex when he…"

"…yes thank you, I think you can skip those details…"

"…ooh okay Miss Prim and Proper, just 'cos you're not getting any these days…anyway, like I said, I tried to broach the subject and he pissed himself laughing – he thought I was messing about! So I tried again a few days later when we were having our tea and, I swear to god, his face fell like a ton of bricks when he realised that I was actually serious. We ended up having a proper ding-dong about it – he said I'd led him on - that I'd entered into a relationship with him under false pretences by initially assuring him that I definitely *wouldn't* be wanting any babies. We eventually made up after I tried to laugh it off and I insisted that it definitely wasn't a deal breaker - that if it couldn't happen, then so be it. But from then on I think we both knew our time together was coming to an end. He could see in my face that I was devastated at the thought that I'd have to rule out having kids…and when I looked at him I knew he could see right through me and the guilt was killing him."

"Aw Kirsty, I'm sorry hun – I had no idea. I've been so wrapped up in my own problems that I've not even considered that something might be amiss with you…"

"Don't worry, honestly babe, because I've been trying to cover it all up – to pretend none of it's happening…because I just don't want to deal with the reality of the situation – that I'm losing Nathan."

I don't think she even knew she was crying but I'd now gone out in sympathy with her. I dragged myself off my hangover-bed and moved over to sit on the arm of the chair, pulling her close to me, and we hugged for a very long time before breaking apart.

"So...presumably you and Nathan then had another little chat about the future..."

"I tried to avoid the inevitable but he got me in the car one night after we'd been to the chippy; he put the central locking on so I couldn't get out – to force me to have the dreaded conversation. He said it wasn't fair on either of us – if my biological clock was ticking and I really was so desperate to become a mother then I needed to be free to find someone new who wanted what I wanted. And when I tried to protest, to tell him that I didn't want a child with anyone else – that I could never be with anyone other than him – he wouldn't have it; said once that burning desire was there to be a mother, it couldn't just be crushed. And I hate to admit it, but I think he was right. It was awful Lou, so awful. And my bloody chips went cold as well."

"Is there no way he would ever change his mind? You know, he might realise that he just can't live without you and come to his senses and..."

"But he still wouldn't want another child, would he? So if we went down that route it would be under duress for him, and if I got pregnant then maybe he would end up hating me...and he might even end up blaming the child, which just wouldn't be fair. Besides...he's made it quite clear that there is no way in hell he will be changing his mind. He loves Jack to bits, but he says he's too old to start again, especially now he's finally got back on his feet financially. And even when Jack's staying with him, he's still able to have a life and go out when he wants to...and of course all that would stop if there was a little one to consider..."

"But he loves you K...and you love him...how can this be right?"

"You know what I keep thinking Lou? He loves me, but not enough. Not enough to never let me go. Not enough to want a little bit of him and a little bit of me to get it together and make a big, bouncing piece of *us*. Just not enough."

There wasn't a great deal I could say in response to that. Certainly nothing that would make Kirsty feel any better. Instead of the bubbly, positive ray of sunshine that usually curled up in my armchair, there was a sad, deflated woman there, and it pained me to see the change in her.

"How did we get to this eh Louise? How did we find ourselves here when not so long ago we were both living our best lives with the men of our dreams in our beds...and now look at us. Do you think we'll end up living together eventually, me and you? Like two batty old sisters who never go out except to venture into the garden to talk to the birds in the trees?"

"Quite possibly. At least you're giving me a counter-worry and taking my mind off my own problems for five minutes."

"Ah yes, speaking of your problems. Apparently, Jenny's mum saw David last week – just by himself in the chemist, picking up a prescription. And she said he looked *awful*. That he'd lost loads of weight and was very pale and that he didn't even notice her, even though she was right in front of him."

"Oh my god, you don't think he's ill do you? That the prescription was for him?" Try as I might, I couldn't stop myself from worrying about his state of health.

"No love...they shouted out that cow's name when the prescription was ready so it was definitely for her. But Jenny's mum said he looked a shadow of his former self."

Part of me was glad – that he didn't look happy and content as he had done with me; that he wasn't thriving while he was sharing a house and a life with *her* again. But another part of me – when I thought about him looking pale and vacant – ached so badly for him and just wished I could turn back the clock. Preferably to the summer of 1984.

Chapter 26

SUZANNE

Dave had collected all of his belongings from Billy's place while they were out – and had apparently posted his key back through their letterbox. One of the little darlings had probably discovered it and buried it in the back garden by now. I noticed that various items of his clothing, shoes, and personal effects appeared to be missing and could only presume that they were up in the north west of England at *her* house. Maybe she had destroyed them by now – it was almost the 5th of November after all, so perhaps she had burned them on a bonfire, as she had burned her bridges with Dave, it would seem.

Every day saw Dave treat our house more like his home again and we gradually fell back into the easy, familiar routine we'd had before *she* had made a re-appearance. He didn't laugh much but he smiled more and seemed to accept that he was here to stay now; that this was his lot. At least I thought he had.

Feeling much better than I'd done in years, I therefore had to concede that the help-groups and support network, the therapy and the adjusted medication were all working wonders and, yes, I know, I should have done it years ago. It felt like everything was finally coming together – it would be an indeterminable length of time before Dave would return to my bed, and I wasn't sure at what stage I would be able to officially confirm that we were a committed couple again – but it would happen, I felt certain, he just needed more time to realise that what he'd shared with me, what he'd always had waiting there for him, was indeed what was best for him.

With an air of confidence and a spring in my step, I called into the estate agents to tell them we were taking the property off the market. I didn't say there had been a total reconciliation but did mention in passing that Dave had moved back in again, so the girls in the office probably assumed that our marriage was back on track. I asked that they pass on my apologies to the purchasers and confirmed we would be responsible for their reasonable solicitors' costs and disbursements to date, as a gesture of goodwill in view of the inconvenience caused to them. It was a small price to pay.

After a lazy lunch that same day, my afternoon was spent giving the landing and the upstairs rooms a thorough clean while the house was empty. I was still up there, in my bedroom, wiping the slight smears from the full length mirror whilst humming one of my favourite tunes, when I heard Dave come home and, unusually for him, immediately make his way up the stairs. Without his usual cursory knock, he shoved open the bedroom door and, before I could even utter any kind of greeting, he asked, "Where has the sign gone Sue?"

"What? Oh…that…well I've instructed the estate agents for the time being that the sale is on hold until further notice. I mean, I can't even think about moving on from here and into new accommodation until my head's in the right place now can I? I said you'd moved back in, and they accepted they needed to put a stop on everything, for the time being. Now, let me just clear this mass of cleaning stuff away and I'll nip downstairs and lift your dinner out of the oven while you freshen up."

I'd tried to phrase it fairly innocently in an attempt to swerve an argument…but the most worrying aspect was that he didn't say anything at all in response. He looked haunted and defeated in equal measures and appeared to be studying me closely, no doubt wondering how I could possibly have cancelled the sale without consulting him first; clearly not sure he could trust my motives. In time, he left the room, closing the door firmly behind him, and disappeared into his own bedroom - his own private little world - and everything was quiet and still once more in the house.

When he emerged a full hour later to sit down for the rather congealed dinner I had plated up, he still looked shell-shocked and had very little to say. He wearily pushed a little of his food around the plate with his fork, but in the end left most of it untouched. I noticed he'd done that on quite a few occasions recently, his appetite clearly waning along with his lust for living. The extreme weight loss did not suit him and I wanted to rectify the situation – for him to rediscover not just his love of good food but his enthusiasm for life - but I didn't know how to. The removal of the signage had obviously been a step too far too soon – too hasty.

Time, Suzanne, give it time.

Chapter 27

LOUISE

Three events took place during the following week that sent me spiralling into a sorry state of self-pity again; too sad to even cry; too exhausted to fall into any kind of beneficial sleep.

Firstly, I received a brief telephone call from Jenny, who told me that (a) although she had only known me for a relatively brief period of time, she did in fact miss my company very much and thought I was a "top bird", and (b) she did now in fact thoroughly hate Suzanne and all she stood for, and would "knock her into next week" if she ever got her hands on her, and (c) the 'For Sale' board at the matrimonial home had quietly, unceremoniously, been removed.

So that was that then. It appeared a reconciliation was on the cards. Bastards...pair of bastards. Were David and Suzanne properly back together then? I couldn't allow myself to even entertain the idea that they may be in a physical relationship again; the very thought of it left me feeling sick to my stomach. As I said a hasty goodbye to Jenny, abruptly hanging up on the pretence that I needed to go and drop Chloe off somewhere, I felt myself retching again – no alcohol involved this time – and I snatched up the nearby fruit bowl from the table, letting the three semi-manky apples bounce off in different directions, and shoved my face into it.

He wouldn't, surely? He couldn't...could he? I'd never been in doubt about his love for me and I knew deep down that his feelings would still be intact. So what the actual fuck was going on? Had he decided that this would be best all round, for everyone, if he just stayed put and gave in to her advances? Or was this a temporary state of affairs? Billy couldn't even ask him because he was still out of bounds, in accordance with Jenny's instructions (sorry, threats).

I wanted to ring Kirsty, to fill her in and listen to her rant on about how she was going to string him up by his nuggets, but she had problems of her own to deal with. And besides, she worked in a funeral parlour, which was apparently seeing an upturn in business at the moment. I don't think the poor relatives of the deceased wanted to hear Kirsty screeching at the top of her voice, "The fucking twat, I'll lynch him!" while they were in mourning and trying to sort out burial arrangements for their loved ones.

Somehow, with the appearance of someone who had been dragged through a prickly hedge backwards on a blustery day, I forced myself to go into work the next day, which was when the second momentous event occurred.

The telephone rang incessantly that Tuesday morning - four whinging bastard clients, one after the other, with clearly nothing better to do than pester the already overworked and underpaid secretary, so when the phone lit up again and another call came through it was all I could do to wearily pick it up and force myself to say, "Good Morning...Cotton and Son...how may I help you?"

"Louise. It's me. I need to talk to you; I need to explain...no, DON'T PUT THE PHONE DOWN...*Louise*! DON'T CUT ME OFF, I just wanted to..."

Slam! I banged the receiver back down and stared at it in disbelief.

David.

Why on earth would he think I would ever want to speak to him again. Especially now. After all this time. And just when the house had been taken off the market and the only rational explanation seemed to be that he was back with that dollybird wife of his. He could seriously fuck off and stick his explanations up his deluded (but perfect) arse.

It rang again and this time I noticed the caller's number that came up in the tiny window on the telephone base station, indicating who was on the line. I pressed the disconnect button and cut him off before he could even get through. My heart was pounding, my forehead was sweating and my stomach was in knots.

Part of me wanted him to try and ring back from an unrecognisable or untraceable number, although I expect he dared not use the landline in that house for fear of retribution.

Hastily trying to think up some smart one-liner that I could deliver if he called again, I waited, and waited, and I could hear the tremble in my voice every time I had to answer the phone again. Each time the ringing started I muttered to myself "Fuck off, fuck off, fuck off," but I needn't have worried – when I answered it was never him.

He didn't ring again.

I made so many mistakes that day and probably looked so dreadful that in the end my boss must have recognised that I was a bit of a liability and insisted I go home and recuperate. Well that was a first.

Then, two days later, shit sandwich number three came my way, in the form of a text from Kirsty, on her way to work, who said "Soz but Davids mum told Billy that bitch's mother said they back together. Will hunt them down & beat them to a pulp if you like when get back from wedding. Luv u xx"

I packed Chloe off to school as usual, her skirt rolled up at the waist meaning her backside was almost on show and she would probably be the proud owner of a detention credit by the end of the day. Pushing her out of the front door with a kiss (blown, obviously – I wasn't allowed to touch the face when the make-up was in place) and a shaky wave, instead of then legging it upstairs to quickly dress for work, as was the norm, I picked up the phone to ring in sick. I wasn't often off sick due to illness – Mr Cotton would just have to suck it up. I was fit for nothing. And I gave no fucks. Precisely none.

Chloe was dining at my mother's that night, so she would be none the wiser when she got dropped off later. I often changed straight away into my pyjamas and slippers anyway when I came home from work, kicking my shoes off my aching feet as I burst through the door and catapulting my bra across the room as I heaved a big sigh of relief.

I'd had a productive day, crying into my knackered, old teddy-bear, punching the pillows, breathing in the last remaining scent of David from his shirts in the wardrobe, pouring his favourite shampoo down the sink and swiping through all the photos of him on my phone. I even tortured myself by taking out the treasured Kodak photograph of the two of us taken in Newquay in 1984, during that momentous summer, when we had only just discovered the delights of each other, when we were freshly in love and it seemed nothing could taint our happiness.

What sent me over the edge though was the picture of David in bed that I had cheekily snapped when we had eventually got down to the nitty gritty of mind-blowing sex, that wonderful, intense night just a few short months ago, when the thirty long years of wanting and waiting were finally over and it had seemed like the beginning of a new life for both of us.

I looked at that face and that body, and wept. I would never, ever be held in those arms again. He would never, ever be my David again.

If Chloe noticed my bloodshot eyes and swollen face on her return, she refrained from commenting. She was probably accustomed to seeing me looking a fright by now.

I just had to cling on to the hope that one day I would find happiness again; that some day in the future I would finally feel a sense of peace. There had to be something better out there than this. Although it was tough now, swamped as I was with misery, eventually I would truly hit rock bottom and then the only way would be up. I just had to persevere through the coming days and weeks without giving in. When I finally accepted that David's love had gone forever, I could move on. I just hadn't quite reached that stage yet.

Chapter 28

SUZANNE

The atmosphere at home was tense for a few days but then I noticed a definite change in David on Tuesday evening when he came home from work. Maybe he had experienced some sort of epiphany, accepted it was over with Louise and drawn a line under their relationship, but I sensed from then on that I could be a little more familiar with him and ease him back in gently to the former life he had shared with me. The occasional smile on his face never quite reached his eyes, and he seemed even more beaten down, if that was possible, but it was certainly a change for the better.

We settled into a routine; every evening I ran him a hot, scented bath when he returned from a hard day's work, and afterwards we would eat dinner and then he would join me in the comfort of the lounge, where we would share a decent bottle of wine whilst watching the latest film release on one of the cable channels and discussing anything of significance that had occurred during our respective days. Thankfully, the fractious issue of the house sale had been put to bed. Most of the boxes had been unpacked again and their contents stored away; if he noticed, he didn't ask why.

With the doctor's consent, I was easing off the medication, and had subtly cut back my attendances at the various groups and meetings, so in fact I only now showed my face once every fortnight at the informal self-help group in the local community centre. I knew in my heart of hearts that I no longer needed the assistance and medication offered to me, now it appeared that Dave was back for good. I knew it, and he knew it. His temporary stay at our beautiful home had now become a permanent one; I had him right where I wanted him.

To be fair, I was his wife and we *had* loved each other once and had been through so much together. We were friends again and hopefully, in time, that friendship would lead to more.

Mum was beside herself with pleasure when I confessed that Dave had moved back in, despite all the bad feelings she had harboured when he had left me for that *slut*. She agreed that Dave *had* been a great husband for most of our married life and that she would reluctantly forgive him for his minor indiscretion, especially in view of the pressure he had been under throughout the latter part of our marriage, and the fact that he had only succumbed to *her* when she had literally thrown herself at him.

I didn't exactly lie to mum by telling her that Dave and I were now reconciled as man and wife...but on the other hand I didn't put her completely straight when she cheerfully told dad that Dave and I were back together.

Dad obviously had his doubts; he was nobody's fool and had always been able to see through me, with an uncanny knack of knowing what was really going on. But all that he said was, "As long as you're happy Suzy love...if this is truly what you want..." I assured him that it honestly was, and that Dave was here to stay this time around.

Billy's birthday was looming and I anticipated that he may risk the wrath of his wife and invite Dave to join him and the other lads on the usual pub crawl around town but, as far as I was aware, he didn't get in touch. It would seem that Dave had been cast out into the wilderness.

And I managed to avoid bumping into Billy's *delightful* wife by shopping online and of course avoiding the various pound shops and chip shops dotted around town.

There was one little incident though that cast a shadow over our relationship.

We were due to visit my parents for Sunday lunch – the first time we had been back there together since we had split up – and we were all dressed and ready to go when there was a ridiculous amount of hammering on the front door. Wondering what on earth all the noise was about, I flung it open only to be almost accosted on my own front doorstep by some strange she-devil of a woman...oh my goodness it was Louise's friend – the vicious looking creature with the mass of hair and multiple chins.

"WHERE IS HE?" she hollered at me, attempting to roughly shove me to one side while she peered down the hallway. I stood my ground.

"Now just a minute! How *dare* you turn up here, banging on my door and attempting to barge your way in! Remove yourself from that step right NOW and don't..."

"Get. David. Here. Now." She had lowered her voice but her tone was almost menacing and I felt sure if she was to pick a fight with me that I would definitely come out of it more battered and bruised. "I'm Kirsty...LOUISE'S friend. In case you don't know. Now tell that fucking wimp to get his arse out here now before I REALLY get angry...."

"I'm here, Kirsty. And I'm not a fucking wimp." I hadn't heard Dave come up behind me; I sort of hoped he would rest his hands on my shoulders as a sign of defence and solidarity but instead he gently pushed past me, took this mad cow's arm and pulled her with him, down off the step.

Briefly turning back to address me, he said "It's okay Suzanne...you go in. I'll sort this out."

But there was no way I was retreating indoors, where I would have missed most of the conversation and action. I needed to know why she was here and make sure that it wasn't to persuade Dave to up and leave again. Whilst she didn't actually look like she was here to attempt a reconciliation on behalf of her friend, she did have an air about her of someone about to kill with their bare hands.

"You absolute fucking moron David."

All swear words aside, I bristled as I heard her use that name, trying to forget that he'd had another life as David, somewhere else with someone else, albeit briefly.

I expected Dave to give as good as he got – he was no troublemaker but he was a real man's man and could be strong and firm when he needed to be. But surprisingly enough, he just stood there, hands on hips, staring at this crazy woman gesticulating in front of him.

"What have you done, you total frigging dickhead? I tell you what you've done, you've broken the heart of my beautiful best friend who has loved you almost all of her life and you have devastated her little family unit! You've come back here playing the Good Fucking Samaritan, because this bitch has fluttered her eyelashes at you and played the victim. And she's played YOU, you absolute wanker!"

"Kirsty, look..."

"Don't you bloody "look" me, David White! Why do you think this FORMER wife of yours has taken this palace off the market, eh? Why do you think she's practically skipping around town with a huge smile plastered on her face, not bothering to correct all and sundry when they smile at her and say how fantastic it is that the two of you are reunited? Oh yes, I know all the details; Jenny tells me everything! Are you absolutely stupid? Can you not see what she's doing? You've even lost your best friend over her! She's isolating you, doing her best to make sure you're left with no possible way out!"

Oh god, deny it Dave, for god's sake deny it! Tell her we *are* back together! Tell her it's all been worth it, just to be reconciled with me. Tell her that you don't love Louise anymore, that it's over, and that she's just a distant memory now. Just tell her something!

"I'm sorry Kirsty, I truly am, for all the hurt I've caused. I miss Louise so much."

Oh god, DON'T tell her *that!*

"But I can't discuss this here and now. I had to do what was right at the time because I'm not a bad person, I'm really not. I thought I could intervene and sort everything out here – silly of me, I know – and Louise would understand – but it was too big of an ask that she accept the situation and wait in the wings for me – it was unfair of me to expect that of her. Anyway, she's made it clear it's over, no matter what I want now; no matter what I do. So I just have to accept it."

"Accept it? Louise would *understand!*? You stupid, deluded fool! You ballsed up the best thing you ever had in your life; you lost the one person who you loved more than life itself and you've given up on her already! You're pathetic, you really are. To think I had you down as an intelligent, smart guy, the perfect match for my amazing friend! Did you just think she would forgive you overnight for what you've done; for all the pain you've caused? That she would just wait for you with her arms and legs wide open and welcome you back into the fold as if nothing had happened? Did you?"

Dave covered his face with his hands and, with undisguised anguish, replied, "I don't know what I bloody thought Kirsty! Why are you even here anyway? Have you travelled all the way down from Wigan just to give me pain? Because that's going above and beyond the best friend duties I have to say."

"Don't try and be funny with me David or I'll lamp you one! I'm here, because I've come down to visit Jenny, and when I mentioned it in passing to Louise, she declined to join me but asked if I would drop off your belongings. Which I've done. Here they are."

I looked around, Dave looked around, but there were no belongings to be seen – not on the step, not at the front of the house, not on the lawn, not by the old oak tree – nowhere in sight. Was this woman actually insane?

Dave sighed, before asking, "Where are they Kirsty? What have you done with my stuff? I don't know what revenge you're planning here but I'm tired of playing games."

She smiled at him then, revealing clearly whitened but slightly crooked teeth with a hint of pink lipstick smudged on them, and gestured towards the road behind her.

"There they are. There's your stuff. I dropped them off, as I was asked to."

We simultaneously squinted to look further across into the distance, to the area she was now pointing to and, for god's sake, there *were* bin bags and items of clothing - strewn across the tarmac and up and down our otherwise immaculate tree-lined road. What was this stark raving bonkers creature thinking?

"I thought you were the perfect man for Louise, you bastard! I encouraged her to seek you out and take up where you left off and you let her down badly! You had us all fooled."

Ah, here it was, this is what she was thinking.

"I convinced her that you were worth all that effort and celebrated with her when she finally got her man. And look what you did to her! Do you have any idea how guilty I feel that I ever persuaded her to look you up? Do you? She'd already been through so much and she's so lovely and so genuine and no one deserves to be happy more than she does. I don't care what reasons you think justify putting Louise and Chloe through this...they deserve so much better. And you, you twat, will end up a miserable, lonely old man because *this woman* is not the woman for you...she might have dug her claws into you now, but one day you will wake up and realise what a HUMUNGOUS mistake you've made, when it's all too late. Because YOU don't love HER! YOU love LOUISE!"

Oh Lordy, I think she's going to punch him! Oh no...she's taken a step back...probably wondering where she's left her broomstick for the journey home. What a vicious tongue she had. What a nasty piece of work.

"I'm going now, thank god, because I have problems of my own to deal with and a heartbroken best friend to console when I get home. Goodbye *David* White. What a thorough disappointment you turned out to be!"

And then she was off, thundering down the path like a herd of elephants, muttering on to herself like she'd just escaped from the asylum...I'm sure I caught a few expletives aimed at me as well as she left.

I think we were both in shock, as we watched this she-beast clumsily climb into her battered old Fiesta, which was seriously in need of a good trip through the car wash. She roared off down the road, narrowly missing a tatty, torn bag that had fallen onto its side, and out of which various items of clothing were escaping onto the damp surface of the road.

Gingerly stepping out, I glanced at the house to the immediate left of ours…and sure enough, Hyacinth Bucket (not her real name) was curtain twitching as per usual. Wonderful, just wonderful. And here comes a taxi, pulling onto the drive of our neighbours three doors down…and out jumps the sweet old couple who've taken in parcels for me on more than one occasion. They glanced back at the road, taking in the messy scene of Dave's various possessions littering the tarmac, and then looked over to me and nodded, most likely wondering what on earth had occurred in our peaceful neighbourhood on this quiet weekend.

I was about to order Dave to go and collect all his belongings post haste but he was already on his way. As I watched him silently, slowly, move up and down the street, bending to pick up bags and stuffing wet clothing back inside them, I observed for myself the pain and humiliation in his eyes and, despite the circumstances, my heart ached for him.

Not a single word passed between us until we were back indoors, at which point I felt it necessary to voice my opinions on his *lover's* poor choice of friend.

"Dear god, is that what classes for a woman Up North is it? No class, no dignity, no decency…"

"….but stacks of loyalty, honesty, and compassion." He interrupted me to immediately defend her actions, which I have to say, took me aback slightly when she'd just made a holy show of him - of us - in public.

"Dave, who in their right mind does that for pleasure on a Sunday morning? It's like something out of one of those cheap and nasty magazines that are left lying around in the doctors' surgery! Trust the neighbours to put in an appearance while she was here as well – I'm so ashamed!"

"Suzanne, Kirsty is a thoroughly decent woman, so don't put her down like that. She didn't do it for pleasure – she did it for Louise. She loves her best friend to bits and she's obviously worried and looking out for her. I don't blame her really for what she's done. After all, I deserve it. She's just lashing out in anger after all that's happened…"

"Well she'd better not lash out again, or else she can explain herself down at the police station because I'm not putting up with that kind of behaviour at my house! It was embarrassing and unnecessary…"

Dave began to throw clothes from the bags into the washing machine, hesitating as he picked up one particular shirt, and I just *knew* that it was something *she* had bought him, that would always remind him of her. Well, that would have to go.

There was an awkward silence so I switched the radio on in an attempt to diffuse the situation and lighten the atmosphere. However, as the strains of George Michael's 'Freedom' filled the kitchen, it was as if I'd lit the blue touch paper.

"TURN THAT GOD DAMN RADIO OFF WILL YOU!" Dave roared.

I really didn't know what had brought that on but, realising we were expected at my parents' house in less than half an hour, I didn't want to dig any deeper. Maybe he was just annoyed after our unexpected visitor. So I let it go; I switched the music off, and tried to make small talk about everything from hearty Sunday lunches to pruning back the trees in the garden.

Dave was very unresponsive and clearly had an awful lot going on inside his head. I wanted to boldly take him in my arms and reassure him that everything was going to be fine, that we could find comfort in each other and forget all outside and irrelevant distractions…but it was too soon; it wouldn't have been deemed appropriate.

"Notwithstanding all these other people who seem to think we are back together again…do your parents think that is the case Sue, that there's been some big reconciliation gone on since I temporarily moved back in?"

Oh, now, this was unexpected and rather tricky – I didn't want to rock the boat but I suppose technically it was true that I had led everyone to believe that we were back on track again. I would have to choose my words carefully.

"Dave, they just jumped to conclusions, I swear. They worry about me. I didn't want to dash their hopes by putting them straight when they were obviously so pleased that you were back. I'll make sure I tell them what the score is when the time is right…"

"…and everyone else? I suppose every man and his dog has jumped to the same conclusion and it didn't occur to you that you should tell the honest truth instead of indulging them in pure fiction?"

"Stop it Dave! You know how I've been. I just didn't want to get into the nitty gritty with people because I didn't want them to know *why* you returned. That's no one else's business; it's private and I want it to remain that way. Please don't infer that I'm a liar!"

Slamming the washer door shut, Dave angrily turned to face me.

"The last thing I want to do now Sue is head over to your parents' place to play along with this little charade, but I suppose I'll have to – because if I don't turn up they'll just think I've bottled it – that I'm hiding away with my guilty conscience. Because obviously I'm the big bad wolf in all of this and you're the innocent party. I don't want to hurt your mum and dad so I won't cancel, but I'm telling you now, this isn't fair and I'm not happy."

Slam! That was the kitchen door in my face as I attempted to follow him out of the room. Christ, this friend of *Louise*, she had really set the cat amongst the pigeons. I would have to tread carefully; losing Dave again was not an option.

If mum and dad spotted anything was amiss, they didn't say so, but then dad had knocked back a couple of large whiskeys, as was his want on a Sunday afternoon when he snatched the opportunity to put his feet up in front of the television while mum slaved over a hot stove, preparing lunch for everyone. She greeted Dave like a long lost son and he was too polite to maintain an air of frostiness in her presence. So he took the proffered glass of beer and sat down to talk business with dad, and later attempted to enjoy the meal put in front of him.

We left as soon as it was decent to do so, Dave implying that he still had a raft of jobs at home to finish before he was due back in work tomorrow.

Only there was no work for him "tomorrow". Because that particular evening he opened a bottle of Scotch that we'd had in since last Christmas, and, with only a little ice thrown in to dilute it, he knocked back glass after glass until he'd drank three-quarters of it. I kept a close eye on him – I'd never seen him do that before. He was more of a lager man, who maybe would drink a little wine with his meal; whisky was not usually his thing.

And he had such a distant, distracted look in his eyes. He may have been physically present in the room, but he was miles away in his head.

He swayed and staggered when he eventually rose to his feet and tried to walk by himself. At least I got to feel his arm around my shoulders, as he clung on to me for dear life on our way up the stairs. My tiny frame struggled to support him but in the end, after what felt like climbing Mount Everest, we reached his bedroom door, which he booted open (as I winced at the thought of any marks or damage he may have inflicted on it) and collapsed fully dressed on top of the duvet.

Before rolling him on to his side, I unbuttoned his whisky-stained cream shirt and prised his arms out of it, dragging off his jeans and socks. Lying there, in his black boxers, even three sheets to the wind, and with his dribbling mouth wide open ready to catch any passing flies, he still looked unbelievably, unaccountably gorgeous. He always took my breath away. His body was tanned and lean – although I noticed for the first time that his usual colouring had faded a little and he had definitely lost a substantial amount of weight. I realised that it was a bit weird – me, standing there, gazing at him, but I loved him and I wanted to see him in all his glory, if only for a few moments. To remember how he looked, how he felt, how much pleasure we had once taken in each other's bodies.

Not expecting him to wake for hours, but at the same time not wanting him to open his eyes and find me standing over him, I reluctantly backed out of the room and softly closed the door behind me. My cheeks were flaming hot and my body was aching with desire, but I had to make do with the almost-naked image of him in my mind for now.

Unsurprisingly, he didn't make it into work the next morning, for the first time in history, and there was no Billy to stand in for him in his absence, whilst my brother, Dave's partner in the business, rushed out to emergency jobs that seemed to come in fast and furious at the beginning of a week. Michael had been on call over the weekend and was shattered, and more than a little piqued at Dave's no-show, but I invented a dire sickness bug for him, and agreed with him that it was to be hoped it would only be one of these twenty-four hour things, and then repeatedly checked on Dave throughout the day, supplying him with a bucket, headache pills and, eventually, tea and toast when he could stomach it.

He finally surfaced around four o'clock looking very green around the gills, and more than a little sheepish.

"Sorry, Sue. I shouldn't have done that. And I can assure you that it won't happen again, as I feel like hell today. To let Mike down like that…it's well out of order. I'll make it up to him, I promise. I can't believe he had to close the shop early today due to "staffing issues". I feel so bad."

We lazily occupied the settees for the remainder of the evening, whilst Dave gulped down pints of water and picked at the pasta dish I had prepared for him. I reckoned it would be a long time before he could face a glass of whisky again. His obvious discomfort didn't give me any pleasure but I had enjoyed taking care of him throughout that day, and neither of us had mentioned the events of the previous afternoon. Knowing Dave, he would feel terrible that I'd had to wait on him hand and foot, so would unconsciously be making more of an effort with me; to try and assuage his guilt. The icing on the cake for me though was that he didn't even enquire who had removed his clothes when he'd somehow made it to bed the night before – he must have realised it had been me, but it didn't seem to bother him.

Which meant I was definitely back in his good books and on the home strait.

Chapter 29

LOUISE

"You did WHAT?" I clamped my hand over my mouth as I cringed and listened to Kirsty's detailed description of how she had dumped all of David's clothes and personal items up and down the road in front of their house. "Oh my god, I bet she went APESHIT didn't she?"

"She didn't look best pleased but I could tell she was biting her tongue so she could try and maintain an air of superiority. When she spotted all his gear blowing about in the breeze, her face was a picture – like a bulldog licking piss off a thistle. I noticed Little Miss Perfect didn't attempt to pick anything up herself though – when I glanced in my rear view mirror I could only spot David wandering around in a daze, scooping up his smalls!"

Oh Jesus, Kirsty was an absolute liability. I'd only asked her to drop David's stuff off as I just couldn't bring myself to throw it away or donate it to a charity shop, and I'd accepted the fact that he was never coming back for it now. Not that I would have allowed him over the threshold if he'd turned up here. No way.

It was a killer though, packing away the remnants of our short time together and stuffing it all into bags; watching Kirsty ram almost every last trace of him into the boot of her car. I almost snatched everything back at the last minute, not bearing to part with the clothes that had touched his skin; the boxer shorts that often peeped out from under his jeans with a hint of promise as to what was tucked away in there; the aftershave that he had liberally dosed on his body, that smelled like pure, undiluted heaven on him. But I accepted it was a task that had to be done.

Rubbing her tired eyes, a humungous yawn escaping from her mouth, Kirsty collapsed onto the settee next to me, kicking off her shoes and whistling to Fudge to wander over for a cuddle (he obliged – he thought she had treats for him – he was wrong).

"Budge up sweetie, I'm dead on my feet. I tell you what though Mrs, he didn't look good, your David…"

I resisted the temptation to point out that he wasn't my David and probably never had been, but allowed her to continue instead.

"...I mean, he's a handsome guy...and *I* would...well you know what I mean...obviously I *wouldn't* but you get my drift...anyway, he looked like shit. All haggard and pale. Lost tons of weight too; his clothes were practically hanging off him. Don't know what the score is there in that house but honestly, it's not agreeing with him. He couldn't have looked more miserable if he'd tried."

"Really? Truthfully? You're not just saying that to make me feel better?"

"I swear on my mother's life...he looked so *sad*. His eyes were dead. He was so *lifeless*. So defeated and worn out. He's always looked so strong and tanned and fit before...but, after I'd stopped laughing, when I got back to Jenny's, it did prick my conscience a little when I remembered his unhappy little face; I did find myself worrying about him – even though I know I should totally hate him, and that he's Public Enemy Number One at the moment."

"Public Enemy Number Two. *She's* Number One. Bitch."

"Anyhow...you don't think she's had him trapped in there do you? You know, like that guy in that Kathy Bates film, 'Misery'? Maybe she's planning on smashing his kneecaps, to stop him doing a runner..."

"Good god Kirsty, the one and only time I saw her she didn't look like she was capable of smashing an egg, so I hardly think so."

I could see Kirsty was holding something else back, wondering whether to disclose it or not; I could almost visualise the cogs whirring round in her mind.

"Go on chuckles, spit it out. What it is?"

"Well...the thing is...he said he misses you Lou. So much. And looking back, I think those words were the only ones that came out of his mouth that had any feeling, any substance to them. He clearly does. To say it in front of *her* as well. He looks so lost without you. Pretty much how you are without him. Sorry - maybe I shouldn't have told you."

"No, don't be sorry. I'm glad you told me. It gives me a certain sense of relief - that he's not living the life of riley and wondering why he ever left his perfect little wife, and his perfect little house, and his perfect little life in the first place. I'm glad he's suffering as well...that his world isn't the same without me in it. Even if ultimately it doesn't change anything, I'm glad you told me."

"Well, thank god for that then! It could've gone either way." She squeezed my hand, assuring me of her unspoken solidarity, and then upended a carrier bag she'd had beside her, the contents spilling out onto the settee between us.

"Now get your laughing tackle around that lot while we settle down to watch your George DVD."

"Good god Kirsty, how much chocolate have you bought? And is that an actual *bucket* of popcorn, just for the two of us? You do know that Chloe has gone bowling with her friends and is staying overnight at Lilly's? We're going to end up a couple of real fat bastards if we sit here night after night scoffing until we burst! I keep promising myself I'll cut back but you're like one of those 'feeders' aren't you, who you see on those dodgy programmes on Channel 5?"

"Listen, if I'm going down, you're coming with me. And we've got to have a few pleasures in life now we are man-free and therefore sex-free, AND you've put us on this bloody alcohol ban!"

"Well, I'd been getting a little bit too chummy with Ron Bacardi over the last couple of weeks...and then, you may recall, I had that disastrous alcohol-fuelled night out which took me a full week to recover from...and you'd been hitting the sauce initially after Nathan and everything so..."

"...I know, I know...and it's not great when it's seeping out of your pores and you reek of booze when you work in a funeral parlour. So...anyway...bugger the calories and dive in!"

Reclining our individual seats, mouths full of Cadburys finest, we settled in for a night of undiluted George Michael; punching the air with our fists in time to the chorus of 'Freedom', sobbing through the emotion-filled verses of 'Careless Whisper'. Around midnight Kirsty wobbled out to her car – at least she didn't have to worry about being over the limit - there wasn't a junk food breathalyser and she wasn't going to get pulled up by the police and have to confess that she'd eaten about a hundred squares of Dairy Milk and enough popcorn to make her feel slightly nauseous.

I lay awake thinking about what Kirsty had told me - part of me *did* want him to suffer but, despite everything, I worried about David and what would become of him. I couldn't take him back, not that this was an option in any event, but I also couldn't stop loving him. Despite my best attempts to move on, again, it would seem I had no control over my heart –

the bloody thing was a law unto itself – and I was destined to miss him and yearn for him for the rest of my life.

*

We fell into a routine, Kirsty and I, spending our Saturday nights slouched in front of the telly, eating approximately triple times the amount of our recommended daily calorie allowance. Oh well. Chloe tentatively suggested that I might like to join a local gym "to tone up", but I immediately dismissed that idea, as the one and only time I'd been mad enough to sign up for gym membership, I'd almost hung myself from a piece of complicated equipment during the induction session and had to be rescued by a member of staff.

I knew something had to change though; I couldn't maintain this lifestyle forever - I felt unmotivated, lethargic – in fact, absolutely diabolical - and you could have fried eggs on my greasy, shiny skin.

Still pondering how on earth I could go about commencing a major overhaul of my sorry life without too much sustained effort, Kirsty announced, completely out of the blue, that she was off to a singles night! I was thoroughly taken aback – she had loved Nathan so much; she *still* loved Nathan so much and I couldn't imagine her wanting to start over with someone else. Especially with her track record of dodgy dates and freaky boyfriends. I admired her new-found, can-do attitude but prayed to god that anyone she might possibly pick up, be relatively stable and normal. It was unlikely, but I could live in hope.

"Are you sure, chuck? Are you positive this is the right route for you to take? Can you not stay on Single Street a tad longer before you venture down Arsehole Avenue? A singles night, really? With all the weirdos and cranks that are lurking out there, casting their net for their next unsuspecting victim?"

"Aw, your concern is touching, but don't worry honey, I've got my rape alarm in my handbag and I've been brushing up on my karate skills. Besides…I'm going with my cousin Stacey – you know the one with the fuzzy hair and the peculiar dress sense - so I won't be alone. This place is somewhere I've never been to before - a club just down the road from Stacey's house that's trying to raise some revenue before it finally admits defeat and goes under – so it's giving these singles events a go. On balance, it's got to be better than that awful dive near to the rugby club that I used to frequent back in the late 90s…"

"I thought you said it was packed out there though - wall-to-wall men…"

"Oh, it was. The odds were good...but the goods were definitely odd. They all seemed to be lacking something, if not physically then mentally..."

"Oh well, you might as well give this place a go then. Stacey though? - I thought you hated her – didn't you say she was a real wet lettuce and an extraordinary man-repellent?"

"She is, but needs must, seeing as I know there's not a cat in hell's chance you will come with me!"

"You're dead right there. Sorry K, I just can't, for a whole multitude of reasons. Tempting as it may be...or not."

"Ha ha. You're missing a treat. Anyway, best dash, these nails aren't going to paint themselves and I still have to iron my party clothes."

With a "So long, suckers!" Kirsty disconnected the call and I found myself just sitting quietly for a few moments, mulling over our conversation and contemplating my pathetic life.

At least Kirsty was making an effort. Look at me, for god's sake - slobbing out in front of the soap operas again with my wibbly-wobbly belly hanging over the waistband of my tatty jogging bottoms. What had I become? I think I was gaining all the weight that David had apparently been shedding! There he was – occupying my thoughts yet again. Most days I was able to hide my feelings behind an outwardly hard exterior, but inside I was shattered and it killed me that he was hurting so much, even if it was his own stupid fault. It didn't sound like he was in a good place and I hoped *he* wasn't ill or suffering from depression, as a result of all the stress.

I recalled his second weekend up here, when instead of the stupendous sex he was probably anticipating, he ended up nursing me for two days while I was incapacitated with horrific period pains and debilitating headaches – just when I'd thought I was finished with all that monthly mess as well! He had searched the house from top to bottom for a hot water bottle, and had sent Chloe off down to the corner shop for stacks of chocolate bars. Casting his own needs aside, he had run me a hot bath and later rubbed my back as I moaned and groaned on the bed beside him. When it had finally run its course he had pulled me to his chest and stroked my hair and neck, whispering I Love You's into my ear. And he had never once complained, despite the fact that it had ruined our weekend and he had then had to drive back down to Cornwall and drag himself into work, having had a couple of hours sleep on the put-up bed at Billy's home.

He was a diamond, I knew that. Magnificent and precious. The trouble was, he tried to be everybody's diamond. Everything to everybody – that was his downfall. Only David could have a fault that in effect was a quality.

And every day without him, I felt like I died a little more inside.

Chapter 30

SUZANNE

Life just felt…difficult…and complicated.

The occasional day was positive and it seemed there was light at the end of the tunnel. Take the evening when we all went out to celebrate Michael's birthday. I realised that Dave may only have been present because he liked Michael a lot and was still in partnership with him. But I reminded myself that Dave didn't actually *have* to be there – he could have ducked out and Michael wouldn't have made a big deal out of it. But he didn't…he was there…and it was almost like old times – leaving the house together, Dave driving us to the restaurant, and taking my coat. And when we were inside the restaurant - filling up my wine glass, passing me the vegetables and ultimately paying the bill. In my head we were a couple again but in my heart I knew we had some way to go yet.

I noticed he didn't drink anything alcoholic that night, and we were the first to leave the celebrations, but it had still been a thoroughly enjoyable evening and it had been a pleasure to put on a united front and return home together in Dave's car.

And then there were days when I barely saw him…when he left for work at the crack of dawn and returned home just in time to crawl into bed, alone, not even pausing to share a meal or pass the time of day with me. His mask slipped on those days to reveal a man in pain, showing a face full of confusion and regret.

Impatient to move things on, it took all of my willpower to resist pushing Dave forward; to keep myself from straying into dangerous territory, where I may not yet achieve the positive outcome I so desired.

Chapter 31

LOUISE

"So go on, spill the beans! Tell me, tell me!"

Kirsty had barely got her size eights through the door when I practically leapt on her wanting her to update me on how the singles night had panned out; desperate to hear all of the sordid details. She had rang earlier to inform me she was on her way down and had sounded decidedly shifty. Something had occurred, of that I was sure.

"Alright, alright, let me get a brew first!"

I trotted after her into the kitchen and stood sternly, with my arms tightly folded across my puffed-out chest, as she boiled the kettle and made us both a mug of coffee. She laughed as she reached for the biscuits and her face lit up – it was good to see a glimpse of the old Kirsty back – it seriously did my head in seeing her miserable and downcast. I didn't hold out much hope of getting the old Louise back though - I think she was gone forever.

"God, you're like a professional stalker, following me round the bloody house – ready to interrogate me. A big, angry-looking bloodhound, trying to sniff out clues!"

"Can you please not describe me as a big bloodhound. That really does make me paranoid about all of my chins."

"Sorry, touchy lady. Here, have a digestive. Are there no chocolate ones left? Bloody outrageous that and I think..."

"STOP IT! Tell me what happened last night before I forcibly extract the details from you! Now, did you pull or what? You did, didn't you? Oh my god, one of us is having sex again! So, go on, do tell. Who was he? What did he look like? Is he fit? Is he...?"

Oh for feck's sake. I knew then. I just knew.

She had turned a deep shade of crimson as I'd been talking, and I don't recall ever having seen a blush grace her beautiful face on any previous occasion – not even when a pair of tatty old Flintstones knickers had once dropped out of the leg of her jeans while she was shopping in the local Spar.

And only one man in particular had ever brought that twinkle to her eye.

"You didn't? Tell me, you didn't. It was Nathan wasn't it? You didn't bloody go to the singles night, did you? You went knocking on his door instead!"

"God, you're like a super-sleuth aren't you? How the hell did you work it out already? Yes, it was Nathan. But I'm not lying, I *did* go to the singles night. The singles night that took place just up the road from him. The singles night that his brother-in-law had persuaded him and their mate Lewis to go along to, in an attempt to try and cheer the pair of them up."

Lewis had been dumped from a great height at the beginning of the summer and therefore was also a complete, unravelling mess. We definitely needed to start a club round here for us under-achieving, over-indulging fat, feckers in our forties – all of us poor souls wandering around baffled and bewildered, wondering what the hell had happened to our younger selves.

"Whoa, whoa...rewind there my cheeky, sneaky friend. How did YOU know all of this? How did YOU find out that Nathan would be there last night, showing his face at some dodgy singles event when you *know* how he usually detests anything like that?"

Kirsty had now devoured all of the smart-price digestives and started on the family pack of custard creams. At this rate, my house would be a biscuit-free-zone before teatime, and I'd only done my Big Shop the day before!

"Well. As luck would have it, Lewis puts quite a lot of detail on his Facebook postings..."

"Are you friends with Lewis on there?" I demanded to know. "I wasn't aware you knew him that well..."

"Er, well, I don't really, if I'm being completely honest. And I'm not actually *friends* with him on Facebook, but he *does* tag Nath in quite a few posts and photographs so..."

"...so you're a bigger bleedin' stalker than me then! What are you like, lurking around, tracking Nathan's every move! I thought you were supposed to be finished with him, and with men in general, for good?"

"Oh Lou I know, but I can't help it – it's like a sickness with me! I'm obsessed, checking the accounts and comments of everybody Nathan may have come into contact with during the last twenty years or so. I can't bear it, not knowing where he is and what he's doing and what he's wearing and what he had for his tea! And when I saw that post about the singles night I nearly keeled over! I realised he would only be going there under duress – yes, he abhors anything like; it would be his worst nightmare. But I couldn't risk him hooking up with some other woman; it would've killed me – some old tart getting into his Calvin Kleins. And let's face it, a good-looking man like him, well the dollybirds there would have been on him like flies around sh…"

"Yes, yes, I get the picture. Was he not just a teensy bit surprised to see you there though? Did deafeningly loud alarm bells not ring out for him eh?"

"He was surprised, but unsuspecting – you know Nathan, he takes people at face value and just sees the best in everyone…a bit like your David…sorry…. Anyway, it turned out that we both felt the same way – he said he would beat the living shit out of anyone who tried to tap me up! Aw Louise…isn't that romantic? I don't know who made the initial move but before the first half hour was up we were chewing each other's faces off and it was like we had never been apart…god I've missed him…"

I could truly understand that sentiment. What I wouldn't give to chew the face of David again…

"So, are you two lovebirds back together then, for good? Or was it just the alcohol that made you throw off all your inhibitions and decide to take one last run around the track with him?"

"No, no alcohol involved whatsoever - I'm still abstaining actually, you'll be pleased to know! And no, unfortunately not – sadly, we are definitely not back together. I put on a brass front and in effect said, without words, let's have one last night together – friends with benefits but for one naughty night only. I just wanted to savour every single moment with him this time; to let him take to me bed one final time. So that's what we did, and it was wonderful – as it always has been. Sad, but wonderful." I could tell she was trying to stave off the tears; she had thought she'd found her perfect forever man but, as was the case for myself and David, the relationship had been existing on borrowed time.

"Hey, and guess what? He didn't even notice that I've put on about two stone since we parted company! He still loves me, wobbly belly and all!"

"Of course he does, you nitwit. As long as he didn't put a little sprog in that wobbly belly last night though, madam! I hope you were a clever, sensible girlie and put a jacket on "Little Nathan", in view of the circumstances, my spontaneous, dangerous friend!"

It was absolutely meant as an innocent, crappy joke, but one quick glance at Kirsty's face - strained, drained and all at once a picture of misery - and I gasped in shock, as everything suddenly, undeniably fell into place.

I glanced down at her slightly swollen belly – Jesus H. Christ!

She wasn't overweight – she was most definitely, 100% pregnant! Oh good god, oh my lord...how had I not seen this before? How had I missed the most obvious of signs?

No wonder she, Kirsty Noble, who was rarely seen without a half-empty wine glass in her left hand, and a lit cigarette in her right hand had so readily agreed to the complete alcohol ban and had been off the ciggies for weeks. No wonder she had recently been eating for definitely more than just herself. No wonder her emotions were all over the place, even taking into account her devastating split from Nathan. Holy Mother of God, I needed to sit myself down; I was absolutely shell-shocked!

Blinking hard a couple of times, I stared down at her swollen belly again in disbelief, before glancing back up at her sad, tired eyes - wanting her to pour her heart out to me before I had to ask the question, but kind of understanding why she didn't; why she'd kept it all in and not shared her most precious secret with me.

"You're not, are you? Maybe I'm way off course with this one. Oh K, you are, aren't you? You're in the pudding club! Aw babe...I don't know whether to congratulate you or cry with you. Nathan's? Of course. Sorry. But how, when, why? When he has adamantly refused to have more children! And does he know? For feck's sake, he doesn't, does he? Oh my god, I think *I'm* having a bloody panic attack, you're going to see me off one of these days with all your shenanigans!"

"Welcome to my messed-up world honey. Aw Lou...I can't believe the timing...I've dreamt of having a baby so often these last few months, so much so that it's completely taken over my mind and body...and then Nathan and I split up because he didn't want another child...and now it would appear that I'm having one anyway...everything's 'Arse about face' – completely and utterly fucked up and I don't know what the hell I'm going to do..."

Her voice went up a few octaves as she started to panic as she contemplated her future.

"Ssh..ssh...come on now K. Don't worry, we will sort everything out between us; we always figure everything out in the end, don't we? We're a team; a little unconventional family. I have to ask though...with the timing and everything...are you definitely planning on keeping this baby? Alright, alright, don't give me the Noble death stare again, I was only asking! Because you have choices and I couldn't just presume. Was it an accident then? Because I'm sure you said you were still on the pill..."

"Yes, of course it was an accident – probably that old chestnut of having a funny tummy and the contraceptive pill not working – remember when I ate that dodgy kebab meat even though I thought it was on the turn because I'd had eight WKDs, and I spent half the weekend in the bathroom paying for it – I reckon that's when I got caught out. No way would I ever have tried to trap him - I would never do that, I swear. But, accident or not, yes I AM keeping this baby, and it will be as loved as much as any other bambino - more so, because I will make damn sure of it. And I don't want anything from Nathan; not a penny. I'm going to do this on my own, so he doesn't need to know. I don't plan on ever telling him, as he would be bound to come to the conclusion that I'd done it on purpose - and I certainly don't want him to be a reluctant, mostly absent father. I had one of those, and it truly stinks - my child deserves better."

"Chloe had one of those too, but I honestly don't think Nathan would behave like that K – when he comes round, after the initial shock, he will be an amazing dad to your little one, as he has been to Jack. He might be a little bit furious at first, because it will hit him like a ton of bricks, but he does still love you, and I'm sure you can work it out between the two of you."

"No! I love him, and I always will, but he can fuck right off! He has no right to be part of this child's life! I adore him, and I'll miss him forever, but last night was our final farewell...he hasn't earned the right to have a say in this baby's upbringing; to be part of their life. He doesn't wish to be a father again, so I'm not going to *make* him be one. He can keep his precious freedom, and shove it up his tight little arse, to be quite frank."

Honestly, I despaired of her sometimes.

"But Kirsty, you *have* to tell him. You do realise that, don't you? It's not like you live on opposite sides of the world, like there's a billion-to-one chance of you ever bumping into him again – he's practically only down the road from you, and the jungle drums will be beating as soon as word gets out that you're expecting! And, despite everything he's said, he really *is* a good guy and you really *can't* keep this from him. God, how long have you *known*? I can't believe you didn't tell me Mrs!"

"I'm so sorry chicken, but when *I* knew for certain, that's when I realised it was imperative I spoke to Nathan one more time. Stupid, lovestruck, naive old me thought I would just test those stormy waters again, hoping he would have mellowed a bit, before dropping the bombshell. But it was practically a taboo subject – he was *so* adamant he didn't want any more children and that he didn't want his life filled with crappy nappies and teething rings again. So I kept quiet and tried to ignore what was happening to my body – until we had "the talk" – and we decided to split up anyway! And even though I was heartbroken because I love the very bones of that man, I thought, "Bollocks to it! I can do this on my own". And it would be better for everyone concerned if I didn't tell him; didn't saddle him with another kiddiewink and ruin all his plans."

"You know, you have some bloody funny ideas, woman. What I don't get though is how you didn't let it slip when you were with him last night - how you didn't break down and confess all. And how could he not have noticed something different? I thought he was an astute, intelligent man!"

"Well perhaps that's because I didn't have a sign nailed to my forehead saying "AVOID! Crazy lady with child!" – and I'm a bit of a chubber anyway, so unless he could *smell* I was pregnant, how would he have known? I mean, you know me so well and I spend half my time rooting round in your fridge and lolling in your armchair and yet YOU didn't cotton on!"

"True. Christ...what a mess. I don't mean Baby Noble – he or she is going to be a Noble then? Not a Talbot? Of course – if you're not going to involve him in any of this then you're certainly not going to give your child his surname!"

"Definitely not. One hundred percent, this baby's surname will be Noble on that Birth Certificate."

"Right. Can I just ask one last question though K? Why on earth did you opt for one more night of passion with him then, if there was even the tiniest, remotest possibility that he might rumble you? On some level, were you hoping he would notice the change in you and man-up?"

"Nope, at least I don't think so. I just knew, with my baby on board, it would be the absolute, final time I would ever get to be with him. We didn't break up because we didn't love each other anymore - we broke up because of the baby issue. This was my last opportunity to get intimate with the love of my life - to try to memorise every last thing about him, before I have to completely erase him from my life and start afresh, with my mini-me by my side. Because a little squawker does *not* feature in Nathan Talbot's big plans for his future."

Tears came streaming down her face then. She wasn't a massive crier, Kirsty, but I guess these were extenuating circumstances.

"Oh Jesus wept, you've got me crying again. At least it's a refreshing change to be blubbing over someone else's problems anyway, rather than my own."

"I can't *stop* frigging weeping mate. I cried like a baby again this morning, after I took one last look at Nathan in all his glory and crept away from his place for the final time. It's a good job he's such a heavy sleeper, otherwise he would have heard me sobbing before I'd even shut the front door. I was trying so hard to hold it all in – I wanted to remember our last meeting as a fantastic, happy one consisting of lots of mind-blowing sex – which it was, I must add. I didn't want it to be marred by me wailing the house down and begging him to change his mind."

I ached inside for her. It was just so unfair, so unbelievably sad.

Moving on to discuss the more practical issues – like where the hell she was planning on living with Baby Noble now she had been forced to return to her mum's house, what she planned on doing regarding work and childcare ("Not a clue mate - how does Chloe fancy a bit of babysitting?"), and how she was hoping to cope financially seeing as she wasn't great with money at the best of times, and there were no savings to cover all of the essential baby-related purchases she would have to make.

It was exhausting just thinking about everything...but I would help her as best as I could and I knew her mother, and my mum, would step up too.

It was a pretty desperate situation, so I had one last shot at talking some sense into her before she headed back to her mum's for a cat-nap.

"Kirsty, you *have* to tell Nathan. You are making this far, far harder than it needs to be. What's the worst that can happen? You're separated anyway! And even if you don't ask him for anything, I'm sure he will still want to contribute *something* – and you will need all the help you can get. I realise it will initially come as a huge shock to him, and he might even be a little bit mad at first if he jumps to the wrong conclusion, but I'm sure you'll soon put him straight! And, honestly, he will be an awful lot madder if he finds out *after* you've had the baby, which he *will*, I'm telling you - when he realises you've kept his child from him for so long, despite everything he has said in the past."

"No, no, NO! Are you listening to me? I'm not telling him, and that's that. And I don't care what he may or may not think in the future. My only concern is what's best for baby now – and my child will be better off having no father rather than one who resents them. So, one last time, just so you're clear on this point – the answer is NO!"

She was a stubborn so-and-so and I knew I had to leave it for now, or risk the two of us falling out. Maybe when she was waddling round like a weeble and panicking about the all the gory details of the childbirth process and the reality of managing a screaming newborn on her own, she might change her mind. I say "on her own" but I had a distinct feeling that this baby would be brought up and cared for by my family as well as Kirsty's.

Something else occurred to me then as well.

"Oh…you…you bitch! All those nights of you turning up with mounds of chocolate and family-sized bags of crisps for us to pig out on! You have your excuse for your big, wobbly belly - you're eating for two! Me – I'm just a fat bastard now!"

"Aw sorry chuck, but I didn't see it like that. I just thought, "What the hell!", as we both love our grub, and after all we'd been through, we definitely deserved to indulge in some comfort eating…"

"I guess so, but my bloody diet starts now, before people think I'M pregnant!"

After she left, taking her junk food with her, I sat alone in the chair for hours, many problems without solutions floating round in my mind.

David. Suzanne. Kirsty. Nathan. Baby. Chloe. David again.

God, we had all the makings of a good soap opera cast. I wondered how everything had gone so drastically wrong for me and Kirsty. We had thought we had it all, and now look at us. What a stinking mess this all was. How complicated our lives had become. How could Kirsty manage a baby when she could barely manage to look after herself? How could Nathan be kept in the dark about all of this? And would I get lumbered with babysitting duties every Saturday night while Kirsty went out on the razz?

Above all else though, I missed David, and I couldn't envisage a moment in my life when that would ever change. I wished to god that we could go back to the beginning again, when we were just carefree teenagers with our whole lives ahead of us, and I would have done things so differently. I would never have messed up, so we would never have split up, and hopefully he would never have met Suzanne, and we would have lived happily ever after. I knew that was all just fantasy, but the reality was too painful to deal with. I badly wanted to move on but I realised that I just couldn't let go of David, no matter how hard I tried.

But what if he had let go of me already? And what if I never saw him again?

Chapter 32

SUZANNE

My first booking in, quite simply, AGES! It was only to sing at some family friends' golden wedding celebrations, but it was a promising start. I'd been practising like mad and Dave, my parents and even my brother Michael, had assured me that I sounded wonderful; that my voice was back to its very best. I was climbing back on the horse, and it felt refreshingly familiar and yet exciting to be back in the saddle.

Dave was pleased that I had another interest in my life again; that I had real purpose to my days and I wasn't just drifting from one to another. But, as I explained to him, I couldn't have done it without him by my side, and it was only his continuing presence that gave me the confidence to tentatively return to work. The truth was, that I actually felt *ready* to throw myself back into work and it had only recently occurred to me just how much I had missed it – but no need to mention that to Dave. I couldn't take the risk that he might reach the conclusion that I could manage without him - because I really couldn't.

I felt so positive and calm now; everything was slotting into place. Since the unexpected return of Dave's clothes and our simultaneous doorstep humiliation, everything had quietened down and it seemed Dave was here to stay. Besides, he had nowhere else to go now. Returning to Billy's was out of the question and I understood Dave's mum and dad weren't happy at all with the situation...and he certainly wouldn't be welcomed back at Louise's little love nest after all of this time had passed.

Hopefully, he'd looked around him and finally begun to appreciate what a fine home he had here, what a lucky man he was, and what a charmed life he could lead with me. We were a strong team, always had been – it had just taken him a while to realise that.

The festive season was fast approaching and I was thrilled at the prospect of waking up on Christmas morning with Dave at home, where he belonged. There was just one remaining hurdle to jump – I needed him to willingly come back to my bed – where I would be sure to remind him just what he had been missing. Once we had made love it would be the beginning of a new era for us and there would be no going back to her - not ever.

It was imminent; I could sense it. He was all man, without doubt, and he had needs that I knew exactly how to satisfy. We now sat close together on just the one settee every evening, where I gradually snuggled up to him, and whilst he didn't exactly respond, he didn't object or attempt to move away either. When he left the house each morning for work, I gave him a quick peck on the cheek, numerous texts were exchanged between us throughout the day, and we always hugged when it came to saying goodnight. A little gentle persuasion, and he agreed we should venture out of the house occasionally – which meant we enjoyed a couple of meals at our favourite Italian restaurant in town and also took a trip to the cinema to see a film I'd been itching to see for a while.

The house sale hadn't been mentioned again and it was as if that 'For Sale' board had never been out there at the front of our home, threatening all I held dear.

Michael had of course originally intended to buy Dave out of the business, but he had hit unexpected financial difficulties himself when he had unearthed an extraordinarily high credit card bill that his wife had run up without his knowledge, and had also discovered a multitude of other outstanding debts. So after a major flare-up resulting in strained relations on the domestic front, and the necessity to re-assess their limited finances, Michael had confessed to Dave that unfortunately he wasn't yet in a position to buy him out. He could possibly have borrowed money from mum and dad, but I knew he was reluctant to admit to his wife's excessive spending and how he had been kept in the dark. I wasn't too concerned, secretly thinking that the transfer of the business wouldn't even be necessary now Dave and I were back together.

Tonight would be the night, I had decided. It seemed we were closer than we had been for an awful long time – I felt Dave's hand on the small of my back as he guided us through the door into the reception room. It dropped down to my waist as we stopped to congratulate Esther and Ernie on their fiftieth anniversary and made small talk with their group of friends. I could feel the warmth of his body penetrating through my delicate silk, jade green mini-dress and I hoped that he was now aware that I was wearing stockings and suspenders underneath, which were there purely for his pleasure later.

The room was packed and buzzing and when I took to the small 'stage' area at nine o'clock everyone was slightly sozzled and keen to hit the dancefloor. I thoroughly enjoyed belting out all of the old hits and was reluctant to finish at the end – how I had missed dressing up and entertaining; I hadn't appreciated what pure, unadulterated joy it gave me. The final song was always popular with the elderly contingent in the room – 'The Power of Love' by Jennifer Rush, which was also our wedding song. Dave didn't know it was on my set list; I had made the decision to add it at the very last minute.

Mum and dad's faces lit up like beacons when the opening notes began and they recognised the tune. But it was Dave's face in the crowd that I was seeking out; I needed to gauge his reaction to my performing our precious song tonight. Ah, there he was, chatting to some regular customers from the shop. He ceased talking and slowly turned to look at me, no doubt recalling how he had seen me perform this number in the very early days when we were together. And how could he forget how we had taken to the dancefloor on our wedding night as the band played this old favourite – silently mouthing the words to each other, our bodies moving as one in anticipation of what was to come in the bridal suite.

Looking directly at him, I sang "…I hold on to your body, and feel each move you make…" and he returned my gaze and his face broke into a tentative smile, and he raised his glass – toasting, I hoped, our marriage and imminent reconciliation. Forgetting everything and everyone else and please god, wanting what *I* wanted.

The song finished far too quickly and I delivered a brief speech thanking everyone and wishing Esther and Ernie a happy anniversary, and then I exited the stage area and made my way over to Dave. I took his hand and squeezed it, and then my dad nipped over to congratulate me on finding my voice again, and as he handed me a glass of champagne, I was almost overcome with emotion and so very, very happy that I had the love of my life by my side again.

This was a fresh start for me and Dave, and we would show everyone that we had overcome our issues and prove just what a strong couple we were now; a force to be reckoned with.

The evening was simply perfect and I remained by Dave's side throughout. We smiled and laughed and chatted and drank and I almost didn't want it to end but then I remembered that I was a woman on a mission tonight and that it certainly appeared Dave would be a man willing to join me on that mission, if his appreciative eyes were anything to go by.

We shared a taxi home with mum and dad and we were dropped off first. I unlocked the front door and switched the alarm off whilst Dave headed into the kitchen to uncork another bottle of champagne, which seemed appropriate after such a successful return to work.

He slipped his shoes off more-or-less straight away but I wanted to keep my heels on – they allowed me to feel so much more powerful and in charge – and I knew they were sexy as hell, even though they were agonising to wear.

We giggled and sipped our champagne and I sat as close to him on the settee as I possibly could, without actually sitting *on* him, which was what I truly wanted to do. I was waiting for my moment, and when I heard Dave's speech slurring a little more, I knew the moment was upon us...and he let me pull him unsteadily to his feet. I made sure I ascended the stairs a couple of steps in front of him, so he could almost see up the short dress I was wearing, and would therefore notice that my legs were encased in his favourite sheer black stockings.

When we both reached the landing we ended up face to face outside of my bedroom door, and as I looked at him then, all wonky smile and loosened tie, twinkling eyes and the body I knew so well, I had never felt so aroused and I desperately wanted to feel him inside me.

In the end it seemed that we were drawn together. Suddenly our arms were around each and I moved closer to kiss that delectable mouth, flicking my tongue around inside, as his lips and his body began to respond.

Oh the ecstasy! How had I survived for so long without this feeling? I pushed myself harder against him; his hands were on my bottom and I wanted him to slip one up under my skirt, to delve inside of me and relieve the aching that made me want to cry out and beg him to take me there and then.

I had dreamed of this for so long and now it was about to happen. Yes, for a while he had been intimate with another woman and wanted her more than he had wanted me. But tonight it was my turn. I was going to do everything he wanted me to and more besides. I was going to show him what he had been missing and he was going to be begging for more every day for the rest of his life...

"Suzanne....NO!" He roughly shoved me backwards, and I almost crashed into the table on the landing, shocked and bewildered at the sudden change in the demeanour of this man I thought I knew so well.

"I can't do this Suzanne...you know that! *I love someone else*; I love LOUISE, for god's sake!"

I tried to gather my wits about me as I straightened myself up and gave him my best seductive look.

"You know you want me Dave. You wanted me then just as much as I wanted you and you can't deny it. You weren't protesting when I had my tongue in your mouth and I could feel how much more you were craving…"

"STOP IT SUE!" He was raking his hands through his beautiful silvery hair and I could see a whole range of emotions pass over his face as he yelled at me.

"The only woman I want is Louise! I've had a lot to drink tonight, far too much, and, god forgive me if I gave you the wrong impression, but I just wanted to enjoy myself for a change and let myself go. But I don't want THIS!"

One last try. I reached down to seductively pull up my dress on one side to reveal a hint of stocking top and smooth, creamy skin that I had imagined, from past experience in the bedroom with Dave, would be faintly bruised when he had finally succumbed and given me what I wanted. And what deep down I knew *he* wanted, despite his protests.

"See these Dave - these are for you. I can go and kneel on the bed for you now darling and you can give it to me like you used to do."

Dirty talk didn't come easy to me and I'd never felt confident enough to ever behave this way with anyone else, but Dave brought something else out in me, when we were alone together – those animal instincts that had taken me by surprise when I had met him for the very first time.

"ARE YOU ABSOLUTELY OUT OF YOUR MIND? I. Don't. Want. This."

I didn't like it when he shouted like that – he rarely got so angry and I never knew how to respond.

"You *said* you just needed my help and then we could move on! You assured me that you didn't expect anything else and I *told* you there couldn't be anything more!" He shook his head from side to side in disbelief, looking at me as if for the first time - as if he'd never really seen me before.

"But Dave, so much has changed recently – I thought we were back on the same page again…" I tried to edge closer to him, to reach out to stroke his face, but he jumped back as if he'd been stung. This certainly wasn't going to plan.

"Please Dave, you *know* how good we are together. It's been such a long time…and Louise is completely out of the picture now…so you may as well take what's on offer…I know just what you like and how to please you…what man in their right mind would turn this down?"

He groaned and shook his head again, my Dave, and I had the feeling he was sobering up rather quickly.

"Oh god, what have I done? Everyone warned me that you would want this but I honestly believed I was doing the right thing, sacrificing my own happiness for the sake of your health. It was supposed to be temporary but somehow, somewhere along the line, it became permanent! I kept trying to reassure everyone that you understood that nothing could ever happen between us in the future…but you…YOU…had everything planned didn't you? I was so scared for you but all along you knew your actions would have me racing back here to pull you back from the brink…"

Oh god. Please make him stop speaking.

I couldn't even attempt to offer up a denial because he was, of course, right on the money.

I had always known that Dave would notice the cola bottles lined up on the worktop that night back in October; that he would almost immediately recognise the significance of them being there. I had known that he would spot that something was amiss and would rush back home to save me; I had been confident that he would fit all of the pieces of the puzzle back together and instigate a search until he found the pills scattered inside the kitchen drawer. He, Dave White, would be my knight in shining armour. He always had been.

"I've lost everything Sue…the respect of my parents, my friendship with Billy – and Jenny and all the other friends and family who have all given me a wide berth since I moved back in - my chance of freedom when the house was up for sale and the business was in the process of being transferred…but most of all I have lost the love of the woman who I was relishing the prospect of growing old with. And the fact that I have hurt her, and her daughter, so deeply and unnecessarily kills me inside…"

Silence. My mouth had ceased to actually work and I was struck dumb. I pulled my dress down at the hem and folded my arms across my breasts that were threatening to spill out, as I had discreetly loosened the shoestring straps a little in the taxi on the way home. And I so badly wanted to remove the god damn shoes, but I remained rooted to the spot, listening to the painful truth that was being hurled at me in such a cruel fashion.

"I've felt so trapped, Sue…so bloody trapped! I couldn't talk to anyone and it seemed like there was no way out. Night after night I've lay awake…the memories of those wonderful summer days… this beautiful young girl walking into my life and changing everything…I replayed them over and over again and grieved for the years we had lost and could never get back. I pictured us on Towan beach together, Louise and I, when we were so young and innocent and we joked about what the future might hold for us. Those long, long summer nights when I held her so tight and in my heart I knew that I would literally *die* for this girl, who was *everything*."

His voice came in sobs now, releasing all of the pent up heartache that had been inside of him – oblivious to the irreversible damage he was doing to me.

"I tried to gloss over what came after that – the split, and the years of waiting and wanting, and the realisation that she wasn't ever coming back to me. And also the years you and I were together – because although it was great at the time it pales into insignificance when compared with what I've had with Louise. But you and me - it is OVER and has been for as long as I can remember, you just need to accept that Suzanne! I don't know how to make myself heard – I can't be any clearer."

I stood there and took it – every hurtful word; every angry look. He couldn't humiliate me any more than I had just humiliated myself, let's face it, so I let him get it all off his chest.

"And then I remembered how I felt when Louise finally came to look for me, after three decades of being apart, and how it completely knocked me for six, but I knew I could never let her go again. How we finally made love and I found peace and contentment in her arms, where I should always have been. When we finally got back together…I'd never been so happy in all of my life Sue…and yet I let it all go. Trying to do the right thing. Kirsty was spot on - I've been such a wimp and turned into a shadow of my former self – wrestling with my guilt and letting you walk all over me in your two hundred pound, four inch stilettos. And now there's no way out for me; not even the slightest chance of any more happiness for me. I guess I got what I deserve huh?"

Oh god, that haunted look in his eyes again – I'd thought that had vanished forever but it had always been there – disguised but most definitely there. My overriding emotion was shame, that I had done this – reduced him to this. A gorgeous, self-assured, fine figure of a man had become a quiet, weary, weaker version of his former self, and I was responsible for his downfall. How on earth could we move on now? I needed to say something quickly, but what?

Too late, Dave was drawing a line under the conversation.

"I'm going to bed now Suzanne, alone. And I suggest you do the same. I'm sorry if my words have hurt you but, seeing as you're the only one I have to talk to these days, you've had to be on the receiving end of my outpouring of grief. I can't even contemplate what tomorrow might bring; how we can even rub along as housemates after this, but I suppose we will have to try. Goodnight Suzanne. Sleep well."

His bedroom door slammed behind him and I was left standing there alone, agog, adrift, on the landing. Seconds passed and yet I still couldn't move – I felt frozen to the spot; his icy words and actions leaving me out in the cold.

Eventually I retreated to bed, slipped underneath the duvet and willed sleep to come, but of course it didn't. I couldn't even cry, despite the irreversible heartbreak - despite the acute humiliation, despite the finality of everything.

I decided to creep back downstairs for a drink to soothe my nerves, but as I passed Dave's door, I heard the most awful sounds, ones that ripped right through me. Dave was crying, not quietly; no discreet, muffled sounds – no, he was howling with grief and his cries were so loud, like a horrifically injured animal caught and wounded in a trap, and it was a terrible, terrible thing to hear.

Shaking my head, I inwardly cursed myself for expecting too much too soon. He had seemed so happy though and I'd been sure the time was right to make my move. How could I have read the situation so wrong? How had I looked in his eyes and somehow seen desire within, when all that had been there was affection borne out of friendship. He'd merely wanted to celebrate my successful return to work and I'd behaved like a bitch on heat; like some deluded temptress, prepared to peel off her clothes and adopt the slut position just to procure her man. My cheeks burned with shame.

How low had I been prepared to go? Where was my dignity? Presumably the same place as my marbles if tonight was anything to go by. And I felt so *accountable* – as if I'd absorbed much of the guilt that Dave had been carrying round on his shoulders for the last two months.

I'd had no back-up plan, so where did I go from here? At least Dave had acknowledged that he had nowhere else to escape to, so I wouldn't have to plead with him to stay.

In the coming days my mother would be gushing about what a splendid night we'd had; what a stunning couple Dave and I made together, and how wonderful it was that we were reunited! How could I explain to her now that it was well and truly over between the two of us?

Whilst I accepted that this was a mess of my own making, how could I clear up the debris and go forward into the future?

How would I even get through the next twenty-four hours, let alone the rest of my life?

Chapter 33

LOUISE

The next few weeks passed in a flurry of activity. Kirsty gently confessed all to her surprised old mum, making her reluctantly promise to keep her secret, should she ever bump into Nathan – which was rather unlikely, bearing in mind Annie Noble barely went further than the end of her own street, and labelled Manchester as "exotic". She was quite an old-fashioned lady with very old-fashioned views - the complete opposite of her wayward daughter - but I was relieved to hear that she'd been incredibly sweet to Kirsty and even handed over a bundle of cash for a beautiful cot that Kirsty had immediately ordered along with a top-of-the-range travel system.

When we confided in my mum, practical as ever, against my will she forced me up into her loft where, amongst the thousands of cobwebs and gigantic spiders, I was amazed to discover a Moses Basket, baby bath and cot mobile, all of which had been shoved up there by my sister a good few years ago, "just in case" she changed her mind on the subject of having more children (never gonna happen).

Kirsty was throwing up morning, noon and night, and consequently her boss and colleagues at work had soon realised what was going on before she had plucked up the courage to tell them. Previously she hadn't given a toss about skiving off on the sick from work, and if she hadn't genuinely been ill for a while then she actually scheduled in the odd Monday or Friday to stay home for a "duvet day". However, the weight of responsibility was now bearing down on her and she was terrified of losing her only source of income and being unable to provide for her child.

I had assured her that in today's day and age employers couldn't just fire you because you were pregnant, and unless they were asking her to actually heave the bodies about in the funeral parlour, then she should be okay to fulfil her usual office and reception duties, albeit a bit green around the gills. As it happened, her bosses were genuinely thrilled for her (possibly secretly relishing the prospect of an extended break from their bolshyest member of staff, while she was off on maternity leave), and had already gifted her some Mothercare vouchers – which Kirsty had spent wisely within about three minutes of receipt.

As she had already declared that she didn't want one of those baby-shower-things that had recently become so popular, in an effort to keep the pregnancy and birth very low-key, I had just gathered our strange little group of friends together at my house and we had presented her with a variety of essential items including a monitor and steriliser, and of course vodka to help her recover from the shock of giving birth.

She had been unsure as to exactly when Baby Noble had been conceived as it would seem they had been at it like horny rabbits for the duration of their relationship, and Kirsty's periods had always been infrequent and irregular, and, Kirsty being Kirsty, she couldn't remember the date of her last one. But her due date had been estimated as 30th of May 2015 and, it was a date now highlighted on all of our calendars.

Excited and happy and emotional for her, I was busy as a bee zooming round doing all her errands, while she upchucked into the nearest container and swore to god that "Men had a lot to fucking answer for".

But every so often a wave of sadness washed over me when I allowed myself to imagine how it could have been for David and I, if we'd had a child together. Don't get me wrong, I adored Chloe (attitude and all) and knew I was incredibly lucky to have her, but I couldn't prevent my imagination from running wild and picturing David and I holding a bouncing newborn baby, a definite part of both of us encapsulated in one tiny little human-being. A blend of the best bits of the two of us that would possibly go on to have their own children…extending our love out into the future long after we had become just dust and bones and memories in our loved-ones hearts…

Christ almighty, I think I was picking up on some of Kirsty's emotions – despite the on-set of the peri-menopause and the realisation kicking in that it was unlikely I would ever be able to carry a child again (I was too bloody old anyway), my hormones were everywhere and I was returning to the unfortunate stage of weeping, angry, bitter, almost middle-aged woman again.

David, David, David. What was he doing now? Would he be staying with Princess Posh (our new name for her) for the rest of his life? Would they settle down and be happy again? Would he forget I'd ever existed? Had I been resigned to the past already? If he were ever to be single again, would I succumb to his charms once more or kick him in the nads and tell him to bugger off?

His charms. God, he had plenty and I missed them with all of my heart. That smile of his that could melt you like chocolate in the sun and make your insides spin round like an overworked tumble drier. Those eyes, those sparkling, flirty, mesmerising blue eyes that you lost yourself in and that seemed to penetrate right through into your mind and soul, instantly knowing what you were thinking and feeling, but not in an uncomfortable way. More in a way that said "Come here darling, let's show them all just how good we are together."

I longed to hold his hand in mine, just one more time. I yearned to feel his lips on mine, just one more time. I dreamed of having him in my bed and my arms just one more time. Despite all he'd done and all I'd said, the longing never subsided; it never went away.

He had bloody spoiled me for anyone else, that was for sure.

Funnily enough, when I discovered Kirsty's baby news, he was the first person I wanted to tell. All I wanted to do was ring him and blab "Guess what! Kirsty's up the duff!", but I couldn't. He was still blocked on my mobile and I'd arranged to get rid of our landline, and I wasn't giving in. He hadn't tried to ring me at work again. I don't think he even had a non-work email address and I'm sure he wouldn't have the time or the words to post me an old-fashioned letter via snail mail even if he'd wanted to. But I still checked my inbox and searched through the post every day, just in case.

So much to say, but I guess nothing more to say. So painful, so unbelievably sad.

Anyway, I had to leave my own self-pity party to deal with all Kirsty's requests and to try and look after my daughter, my dog, my home and my mother – she still came round most Friday evenings, when we put the world to rights over a bottle of ice-cold chardonnay and she would deliver endless lectures about the benefits of thrashing it out with the person who had broken my heart but who had attempted to reach out to me, if only over the telephone.

Mum was also in the habit of pestering and badgering me about Kirsty, harping on about the necessity for her to reveal her pregnancy to Nathan. I assured her that, on more than one occasion, I had slugged this out with Kirsty and I personally didn't think it was a good idea to keep all of this from Nathan – but it *was* her decision, not mine. It wasn't my secret to tell. And she *was* my best friend, so whatever her decision, I had to stand by her and be there to pick up the pieces if and when the shit hit the fan.

And so the days and nights rolled on. The highlight of one week was when Chloe and I bumped into her former teacher, Miss Waite, in the frozen food section at Asda, and she gave me a proper grilling about David. Not one mention of Geography though or how Chloe's studies were getting on…bloody hell, the education system was LUCKY to have her, that's all I can say. I'm not sure what I expected her to look like but she was far prettier than I'd imagined and had youth on her side, not to mention a man – a rugby-playing type – all hulk and bulk, but not bad…not bad at all. Dear god, if the slightly unstable and disturbingly obsessive Miss Waite was in a relationship and I wasn't, then something was seriously wrong with my life.

The next week was a real crappy one – and on one particularly diabolical day - a wet Wednesday when the hours at work had seemed interminable - I had arrived home exhausted and soaked to the skin to a freezing cold house (we still hadn't figured out how to alter the timer – you needed a degree or some other comparable qualification to understand it). The curtains and blinds were open but almost every light in the house was on and music was blasting out from upstairs. Toast crumbs scattered everywhere in the kitchen and the packet of butter left open on the worktop suggested Chloe had stuffed her little face when she came in from school but hadn't bothered to clean up the mess. Fantastic – welcome home!

Naively, I'd asked her to switch the washing machine on and feed Fudge but the clothes remained unwashed and the poor old bugger was still lying in his basket in the dark. When

I turned the light on I got that hang-dog, hard-done-by expression – it probably mirrored my own.

Half an hour had passed before I even had time to remove my coat, what with seeing to Fudge, clearing up the kitchen, closing all curtains and blinds, unpacking my shopping and shoving the shop-bought lasagne into the oven.

Chloe hadn't even stirred upstairs; hadn't even checked to see if it was a burglar clattering about downstairs, removing all of the family silver. I sighed, dramatically, feeling particularly sorry for myself. Sometimes, she could be so good - helping out and showing me consideration and respect – and other times she could be so thoughtless and selfish. I could hear her giggling now and knew she would be curled up on her bed, taking a call from one of her friends, discussing her on-off relationship with Josh and any other lads who had recently taken their fancy.

I was on a short fuse and I knew it. Stand well back because something was about to blow. Gritting my teeth, I made my way up to Chloe's boudoir, steadfastly refusing to knock and throwing open the door instead.

"Christ mother, you made me jump!"

"Jump? Chloe, I have been in this house now for thirty-five minutes and been banging about downstairs, clearing up all of your mess and doing all the jobs you've conveniently forgotten about again! How did that not make you jump? – Or is it that selective hearing you've got again?"

"Aw god, chillax mum...I've not been in *that* long and I'm well-knackered..."

"*You're* knackered? How do you think I bloody feel? I've been working all day and I come home to this? For god's sake Chloe, you need to start thinking of me for a change rather than just yourself...and your friends...and your boyfriends..."

"Boy*friend* actually. There's only the one. It's still just Josh. When he behaves himself that is. Oh, and speaking of Josh, he'll be round soon so he'll be joining us for tea."

"Oh, marvellous! Another mouth to feed! Another excuse for you to avoid helping me around the house, when he's here. Well, I tell you what, you two will be doing the dishes after tea, and you can take Fudge out for a walk later..."

"Oh Gawd…stop nagging will you! We'll do the flipping dishes and I *always* take Fudge for a little stroll in the evening. God, I wish David was back here again…you were never like this with him around…"

"Thanks. Thanks very much for that."

I bit my bottom lip to hold myself back from yelling at her and giving her a piece of my mind, and stormed out of her bedroom.

Pyjamas and wine - that was what was required. I was trying to lay off the chocolate but it was nearly killing me. I had bought a massive bar of Dairy Milk on Saturday with the intention of taking and eating two squares each night…but who even does that? The whole fecking lot had gone by Sunday. So I was having to abstain completely now and I don't think that was helping my mood – and I seemed to have acquired the caffeine withdrawal shakes. Still, there was a third of a bottle of a nice Malbec left in the kitchen that had my name on it.

I threw my pyjamas on, ignoring the pasta sauce stain down the front of the top half that had resolutely refused to be removed, even with half a bottle of some expensive liquid that had promised on the label "to remove all stains with one squirt". What a crock.

By the time the lasagne was heated up and a poor effort at a side salad had been hastily arranged on the plates, I'd managed to get a few of the necessary household chores under my belt, replied to a couple of texts and heated the house to a comfortable standard, so I felt I deserved my (large) glass of red. I'd just yelled up to Chloe that her tea was now going cold in the kitchen and was about to park my big bottom on the settee with my lasagne and vino when there was a hammering at the front door.

Just bloody perfect timing as always. And of course there was no way that Chloe could hear the noise over the racket coming from her bedroom. I slammed my glass and plate down onto the coffee table, warning Fudge not to dare going near my grub. Sighing to myself and chunnering all the way, I bounced down the hallway to the front door, and flung it open expecting to see Josh there, usually smiling, always nervous (I don't know who scared him most these days – Chloe or me).

Fuck. My. Life.

David.

At least I think it's David. Because he's lost a shed-load of weight and his face looks ashen and he's biting *his* bottom lip, something I've never seen him do.

"Louise."

One word, my name. Oh yes, it was definitely David, no one said my name quite like he did.

I wanted to slam the door in his face, but I just couldn't bring myself to do it.

In any event, I heard the sound of another body making their way up the driveway and before I could yell "PISS OFF YOU HEARTBREAKING TOERAG!" to David, Josh popped up behind him.

"Hi Mrs Stewart, is Chloe in?" He knew she was in. Of course she was bloody in when she'd just told him she would be in, for Christ's sake.

I just about squeezed out a smile and indicated he should come in, which he did, immediately followed by David. As Josh climbed the stairs, David closed the front door behind him.

"I never said *you* could come in!" I snarled at him, the anger that had been bubbling all evening, and in fact since the day I had lost him, simmering just about underneath the surface and threatening to explode in his face.

"I know. I made a bid for it while I could, as there was obviously a good chance you would slap my face and shove me out into the cold. But I figured it was worth the risk."

"So can I slap your face now?"

"I'd prefer it if you didn't."

I became conscious of hushed whisperings on the landing, which appeared to come from Chloe and Josh hovering somewhere up there, no doubt trying to eavesdrop on our conversation, so I retraced my steps back into the living room, indicating that David should follow me.

When we were away from prying eyes and twitching ears, I let rip.

"WHY ARE YOU HERE, YOU PRICK? WHAT THE FUCK DO YOU *WANT?*"

"Louise…I get why you're so angry, and you have every right to be. But I just needed to talk to you. I understand why you blocked me - why you effectively removed me from your life. But that was the last thing I ever wanted."

"So you think you can turn up here and charm me with all your bullshit after all of this time? And little Louise will say, "Oh, I understand David…I'm so sorry for wanting to ERASE EVERY LAST TRACE OF YOU FROM MY LIFE!" Do you? *Do you?*"

"To be fair, I have tried to contact you right from the beginning…but you made sure you were *un*contactable. No matter how I tried to get in touch, I was met with a brick wall."

"So you just gave up then - how noble of you!"

"NO! I never gave up Lou. I never stopped dreaming of the day we'd be back together…"

"What fucking planet are you on David? If you'd really wanted to make contact with me you'd have been on my doorstep a long time ago, begging for forgiveness, instead of turning up out of the blue now…wanting….well I don't know what it is you're wanting, do I?"

"Louise, I was terrified when I first went back to Suzanne's house – because it *is* her house now, it's not my home anymore – I was scared to leave her for five minutes in case she did something stupid. If I'd hot-footed it back up here to Wigan it may have sent her over the edge…and you wouldn't speak to me anyway and had told me it was all over…"

"What did you *expect*? You'd moved back in with your supposedly EX-wife and put our relationship on hold while you attempted to sort her shit out! What sort of mug do you think I am? Did you really expect me to be sat here, waiting for you, counting the days off until you returned? Piss off!"

"Like I said, Lou, I understand why you reacted the way you did…"

"Oh that's very good of you…you…pillock! How wonderful of you to be so *understanding!* That bitch says "Jump" and you ask "How high?" It's the way it's always been with you two and it's the way it always will be. And me? Little old me gets pushed to the sidelines, heartbroken and alone again…with just a load of broken promises and tainted memories to keep me company."

"I'm so sorry Louise, I truly am." He looked so crestfallen and distressed that I almost believed him, but I wasn't falling for it. I had to dig deep into my reserves of strength.

"Well, it's too late to apologise David. What's done is done and you can take those apologies and stick them right where the sun doesn't shine. Now I suggest you leave right now by the way you came in before I *do* slap that face of yours."

"I'm not leaving Louise. Not until we've talked, properly."

"Well you're not fucking staying. And I don't want to hear whatever crap you have to say."

"I repeat, I'm not leaving."

"I'll call the police."

"No you won't. And you know they won't turn up for about a week anyway, what with all the cutbacks and the crime wave round here."

There was a bit of a stand-off then, while I wondered if I could physically remove him myself – he'd lost weight but I was a bit of a weakling so I'm guessing he could still take me on.

In the end, I sat myself down and turned up the volume of the television on the remote, but he responded by leaning over and actually switching it off via the button on the side of the set. I glared at him as he began to speak.

"You were right Louise. All of you – Billy, mum and dad, Jenny, Kirsty, the lads. Everyone. I played right into Suzanne's hands. She *was* vulnerable and struggling to cope but she thought I was the answer to all of her problems, so she wanted me back. I'm still getting my head around the fact that she seems to have planned all of it – she's never been a devious person and I can't believe that she made a conscious decision at the start to deceive me...but there's no denying the fact that at some point she realised if she played on her vulnerabilities, I would feel guilty and responsible enough to return home and take care of her..."

"And you've only just cottoned on to this now have you? Not very smart are you? It's only just become apparent to you that she was on a mission to take back her husband, even though it was perfectly obvious to everyone surrounding you what she was up to?"

"To begin with, I took her and all her problems at face value Lou. Because I've been there before with her. She seemed in a terrible state when I moved back in but this time she finally agreed to attend some support groups and, because she insisted she couldn't do it without me and refused to let me involve her parents or anyone else, I felt I had no choice but to try and get her back on track. But what I began to realise somewhere down the line was that, although the advice and medication were doing *some* good, it was actually having me around that was making the difference."

"So why didn't you walk away then, when you knew?"

"Because I wanted to be sure that my suspicions were right – I didn't want to leave her again until I was positive that she really was going to be okay long-term…otherwise it would have all been for nothing and it could have happened again at any point…and, looking back, there was the veiled threat that she would do her worst if I abandoned her again…"

"Christ, do you know how pathetic you sound right now?"

"Yes. I do. And I'm ashamed. I ended up too scared to leave her, and with nowhere to go. I knew I couldn't live with myself if she followed through with her threats…but I knew I needed to get out of there, and fast. And yet I stayed, and we lived side by side…as friends I might add, absolutely NOTHING more…"

"Do you think that makes any fucking difference now?"

"Well it should do. Because in all the time I was with her, I never, ever wanted her. I never felt the slightest urge to return to where we once were. All that living with her did for me, was to confirm to me that I should have got out years ago. That perhaps I should never even have married her. I used to think, no, we had some great years together, even if she wasn't you - and I didn't want her to think that I hadn't loved her in my own way during those years. But now, now that I've had plenty of time to think, I've come to the conclusion that I should never have got involved with her. Because my heart always belonged to you, always."

"Oh sod off with your bullshit, because it really won't work this time. I've been a mug for too long and I'm not standing for it anymore. Just out of interest, what was the catalyst then, that's propelled you up here all of a sudden, completely out of the blue? Thrown you out has she?"

"Thrown me out? You've got to be joking. I've felt like that guy out of that film 'Misery' – you know the one who's trapped in that house with that crazy woman. Suzanne might not have bashed my legs in but the invisible restraints have been there. No, she's definitely not chucked me out. Something did occur a couple of weeks ago though and it's finally brought me to my senses and I've realised I can't go on like this. So miserable, so trapped, so caught up in Suzanne's little fantasy world where she believes we can become the perfect couple again, living that enviable lifestyle and shutting out the rest of the world."

I felt an ugly sneer descend upon my face as I sarcastically said to him, "Oh, now, this should be good. Let's hear it then, what's been occurring?"

A sigh escaped from him then that I swear had risen up from his trainers, as he came to sit by my side. I should've told him to park his backside elsewhere but, god damn it, my body betrayed me by wanting to feel him close.

"We went to a Golden Wedding anniversary party at this club – it was some friends of her parents' celebrating and they had asked Suzanne to provide the entertainment. I couldn't believe it when she agreed to do it and got stuck into the rehearsing – it was like she finally had her mojo back and she wanted something more than to stay at home with me night after night, watching the TV and making small talk. So I was made up for her, and myself, and encouraged her all the way. And on the night she went down a storm, and she was over the moon. As was I, because I thought to myself, this is it, an opening for me...an escape route...so I was celebrating the prospect of freedom as well as Suzanne's return to work. I knew if she was confident enough to get up and sing in front of all those people then she was confident enough to make a life for herself again, without me in it. So...we had a great night...and she got a bit merry, and I got absolutely legless to be frank..."

Oh no, I think I knew what was coming next and I couldn't bear the thought of them falling into bed together and resuming carnal relations. I knew I should have stopped him talking then but I was a glutton for punishment and let him continue...

"I ended up absolutely bladdered and I kept thinking to myself, "Louise, Louise, *Louise*! If it takes the rest of my life to make this up to her I will. If she hates me and tells me to do one, I will still pester her for the remainder of our days until I wear her down and she accepts that I was just an idiot trying to do the right thing and that I never stopped loving her..."

"Just feck off with your "doing the right thing" crap will you. You're like a broken record and I don't want to hear it anymore."

"Sorry, I'm sure you *must* be sick of hearing it, but it's absolutely the truth..."

"So, go on, finish your story...complete the torture..."

"No, no, honestly, it's not like that! As I said, I was totally tanked up and can barely remember getting back home...to the house I mean...but when I got in I thought, bollocks to it, let's open another bottle and we can celebrate new beginnings. I don't remember even drinking any of that champagne...next thing I knew Suzanne was helping me up the stairs after I'd started to pass out on the sofa...and then we were up on the landing and...god, it took me by surprise, especially when all I could think of was you...but she suddenly launched herself at me and tried to stick her tongue down my throat. In my pissed-up state it took me a second or two to realise what was actually happening and that it definitely wasn't *you* trying to delve inside my pants, at which point I shoved her away so hard, I almost hurled her down the stairs. Christ, I could've killed her."

I wanted to kill her.

"Well, what a surprise, she saw her opportunity and went for it...it was almost like that's what she had planned all along..."

"It was a bloody surprise for me, I can tell you. I've never sobered up so quickly in all my life, and although I was disgusted with her and disgusted with myself that I'd been so naive and hadn't seen it coming, I did feel sorry for her, throwing herself at me like that. I don't think I handled it too well and wondered if it was my fault and by agreeing to move back in for a while, it had led her to believe she would get the full package in time..."

"Of course you led her on, you dimwit!" I scoffed. "The minute you agreed to shacking up with her again in that fucking house she thought she had you back! And, because she has no pride and no bastard dignity, she throws herself at you, practically gagging for it, even though you've tried to tell her that's not how it's going to be. But does she apologise for getting hold of the wrong end of the stick and putting you both in an awkward position...no...YOU end up feeling guilty again because *she* feels so humiliated! Guilt, guilt, guilt! When will you ever let it go?"

"Sorry. I know you're used to men who don't give a shit and have no conscience whatsoever - who treat you like crap and walk away without a care in the world...but I'm not like that."

"Oh, nice one! Good put-down. Smashing way of turning it all around to try and make *me* feel bad for being angry with you..."

"NO! That's not how it is at all! YOU have done nothing wrong Lou. Let's get that straight from the off. *You* deserve so much better than any man has ever given you, including me. I'm just trying to explain how I can't change what sort of man I am..."

"...I know what sort of man you are now David. And do you know the irony of it all? In 1984 when I first met you and I believed that nothing could ever come between us...when that dickhead Stephen threw himself at me on the beach, you went ballistic and immediately dumped me! You didn't listen to what *I* had to say - even though I was practically down on my knees begging for forgiveness, for something I hadn't even done – you jumped to conclusions and cut me out of your life. And yet, you're sitting there now, telling me about Princess Posh throwing herself at you, and I, presumably, am supposed to just accept that and move on."

I balled my fists and gritted my teeth, possessed with fury and baying for blood.

"When I close my eyes now I picture the two of you cosying up at this party, while *I* was miserable as fuck, probably sprawled on my settee munching my way through a family-sized pack of crisps. I picture you on that landing, together. Lips together, bodies together. Even for just one moment, it still took place. And how do *I* get past that? Well, I'll answer that little question for you myself. I *don't*. I don't get past it. So there's no point in you being here any longer; you may as well just sling your hook right now. As they say - you made your bed, so go and lie in it. Because you're not lying in mine again."

He rubbed his eyes and I noticed how tired he looked then. The redness in them that hadn't been there before; the bags underneath that suggested he hadn't been sleeping well for a very long time. Part of me wanted to reach out and tenderly stroke his face, but then again, part of me wanted to punch his lights out as well.

"I don't expect you to forgive me overnight Lou, if ever. But when I realised what a gullible idiot I'd been, I knew I had to come and talk to you. Even if it was the last conversation we ever had, I needed to explain myself."

His blue eyes, which seemed to have lost their spark and sparkle and had become so sad and empty, filled with tears, and I didn't want to look at them. I wanted to remain angry and not let my guard down, ever again.

"I've spent most of my life trying to be a decent guy, trying to do the right thing. But on this occasion, I got it badly wrong. I couldn't see that the *right thing* was to leave Suzanne in the capable hands of the medical professionals and her parents, whatever she may have intended to do in the future. I couldn't see that the *right thing* was to walk away and back into the arms of the woman I love. That's you, by the way. To spend the rest of my life loving you, and leaving you in no doubt that you're the only one for me. But I got it all wrong. And found myself in a situation that I couldn't seem to extract myself from."

"Oh, poor you, living in your big fancy house by the sea, with your pretty, posh wife and..."

"No, I'm not saying poor me. I know it was worse for you. And the stupid thing was that you were the last person on earth that I would ever have wanted to hurt. I would have killed anyone else who caused you any pain!"

"But you did it, didn't you? You basically left me for her, whatever the reasons behind it. You made your choice and there was no going back."

"Louise, I did *try* and turn back. I tried over and over again to contact you. Even when you blocked me, I kept on trying, because I thought at some point you might just unblock me. And your landline – I kept trying to ring that but you'd unplugged the bloody thing! So I called you at work, because I was left with no other option, but you slammed the phone down on me and then didn't answer when I rang back. You made it abundantly clear that we were over, as far as you were concerned, that our relationship was dead in the water."

"Yes, that's because it was, and it still is," I bit back at him, but it was almost as if I hadn't spoken at all, as he continued to talk without barely pausing for breath.

"I even thought about sending you something in the snail mail. I started about ten letters but never finished them – Christ, how could I put it all down on paper – so much heavy stuff that I needed to say? And you were *so* mad, I thought she's just going to burn them and never read them! And I haven't a clue as far as e-mail and all that shit's concerned – Suzanne always used to do them and she has complete access to my email account. No - I needed to speak to you, but you wouldn't speak to me! I couldn't abandon Suzanne in that state, to come all the way up here, to probably get the door slammed in my face! But Lou, I felt so trapped down there...every day was the same...work...back to the house - which felt like my prison...tea in front of the television...sometimes excruciating silences. The days only broken up by the odd appointment for Suzanne or emergency plumbing jobs I had to rush out to. And then it felt like the net was tightening around me..."

"The net? What the hell are you talking about now?"

"Without even discussing it first, she took the house off the market, and when I tackled her on the subject she said she'd arrange to have it put back up for sale again when she felt better. But she never did. And then Michael had heaps of trouble on the domestic front and his finances went tits-up so the transfer of the business got put on the back burner. All our plans, our dreams for the future, me and you, were slowly fading into the background...it was like everything was being cruelly snatched away from me, and I was being left in a loveless marriage, in a house that I was gradually beginning to hate. I couldn't see a way out. I couldn't even speak to Billy about it. He and Jenny had washed their hands of me, and I was fucking devastated. I know they hate Suzanne, but, fuck me, I needed my best mate more than ever and he's always been there for me before whenever I needed him, even if it was only to take the piss – so I was lost without him."

"You let Princess Posh control you...pushing away all of your mates, especially Billy, who you've been friends with like, forever...and distancing you from your family and everything and everybody you had known before. Christ, you were putty in her hands!"

"I was a prick, you were right. I kept thinking that I only had to endure it until she was better...but once I realised she *was* better, I didn't know how to break away...I just felt shattered and alone and, more than anything, trapped, in a heap of shit of my own making, I know."

"Yes, it was definitely of your own making David. I took you into my life, and my daughter's life, and actually believed you when you promised you would never hurt me...that you would never go back...that you would never leave me again. But you did. When it came down to it, when you had to make a choice, the bottom line is that you chose her."

"I'm so sorry Louise for making such an appalling decision. I really thought she'd do something stupid if I just walked away, and I couldn't have that on my conscience for the rest of my life. I thought my best bet was to deal with the situation once and for all, and then you and I could get on with our lives without always looking over our shoulders. I did a really bad thing though, I know now, in causing you so much pain. But, and I can't stress this enough, I never stopped loving you. I've missed you so much – I can't explain how much – and it's been killing me. I can't sleep, I can't concentrate on anything, I'm making mistakes at work, I can barely eat..."

"...And how the hell do you think it's been for *me?* You abandoning me for your *wife*, humiliating me, devastating me and trampling all over my heart *again*! How do you think I felt when I checked in to that hotel on my own? Or when you didn't come back within the two hours? Or what about the journey home - crying like a baby all the way back to Wigan? Or, and this is a corker, how about when I had to explain to Chloe, and mum, and Kirsty and my other friends and every fucker else who asked me where you were and what had happened? HOW DO YOU THINK IT WAS FOR ME?"

I was shouting now, gesticulating wildly and almost giving myself a heart attack in the process. He had literally ripped my heart out and he had the cheek to sit there and tell me how awful it had been for him. Fucking men.

"I know...I get that it must have been horrendous for you and I hate myself for putting you through it. I can't believe I let you go...I can't believe I didn't go chasing after you...but...and I know this is a lot to ask, I'm asking you to please give me another chance, please Lou. Because now I've lived with you, I can't go on living without you..."

He'd grabbed both of my hands now and gripped them tightly with his own as I tried and failed to stop my tears falling, yet again.

"But you're going to have to David - you're going to have to live without me. You'll get used to it in the end. I've had to. Because, make no mistake, there are no more chances for you. You've used up all your chances, you've ruined everything...all we had is in the past now. And all that's left is to say goodbye now...and wish each other well..."

"*NO! NO LOUISE!*"

Aw god, please stop him crying before I relented a little...I couldn't give in now though. I'd come too far and I had to let him go, for my own sanity if nothing else, no matter how much I loved him.

"My life's nothing Louise without you in it...nothing. I can't lose you for good, I can't! I can't live the rest of my life without you! How will I survive without your love? Even if you don't want to go back to where we were...can't we at least just see each other as friends for now? And then maybe one day you will see you can trust me again and love me the way you used to..."

I had to stand firm; I would never let him hurt me again.

"No, that's never going to happen David. You've damaged me too much, and all that trust and faith in you that I had is gone forever. It's too late to rebuild anything at all from the ashes of our relationship. And Suzanne would always be lurking in the background, waiting to make her next move, ready to pounce and destroy anything we had - even friendship."

I roughly pulled my hands away from his, ignoring the searing pain in my heart and the nagging part of me that was telling me to bury my head in his chest and hold on to him for the rest of my days.

"I'm so sorry Lou," he openly wept, his head in his hands. "If I could go back in time and change everything I would, but I can't. All I can do is assure you that Suzanne will never, *ever* be an issue again, not after this…and tell you that no matter what happens, even if you don't want me back and I never see you again, I'm never going back to her; I'm never spending another night in that house. I'll have to nip back to get some stuff, but that's it. Even if I have to pitch up a tent in mum and dad's back garden and live there until I can find somewhere else to go, I'll do that, I promise you."

"But you see the trouble with your promises David White, is that you can't keep them. You looked into my eyes and promised me that you would never let me down again, but you did. So forgive me when I say this, but you can keep your promises for what they are worth. You take your promises with you when you leave now, and save them for the next girl you fall for, because I don't want to hear them anymore."

It had been the word "promise" that had been the undoing of me. No matter how much I loved this man and always would, I knew at that point I had to show him the door. I expected him to refuse to leave again, or to get angry with me then and shout "God damn it Lou, I am NOT letting it end like this!" But it was as if all of the fight had evaporated out of him. He had looked so done in and exhausted when he'd arrived - it appeared that this battle that he had lost had taken everything he'd got.

I refused to turn around as he uttered a muffled "Right" and I heard him shift across the room towards the door. He stopped though, just before he left, and said "Look at me Lou, one more time – just once."

I would have been within my rights to tell him where to go but instead, wanting desperately to see him one more time, I looked up at his tear-stained face - firstly seeing the boy of seventeen – all blond, messy hair, suntan and cheeky, dazzling eyes; carefree and with a quick quip for everything. And then I saw the man he had become in his forties – the silvery, shorter crop, the sun-aged but still-young skin and the much lusted after body.

And, now just a few months later but two years away from his fifties – the slightly tighter smile hiding so much pain inside; the eternally good man who just, occasionally, made bad, bad choices.

I almost said something, but no words seemed enough.

"Remember our song Lou - 'The Closest Thing to Heaven I Have Ever Known'. Well that's you - you're the closest thing to heaven *I've* ever known."

Silence again then. Just our hearts beating and the clock ticking.

And then he was gone.

The door slammed, the car engine started, the world ended.

I wandered into to the hallway and hesitated there, gazing at the door, as if doing that would make it open again and I would see David burst back, declaring his undying love and refusing to let me go. Shell-shocked at what had just taken place, I shakily sat down at the bottom of the stairs, scratching my fingernails through the wellworn pile of the carpet on the bottom step, the silent tears rolling down my cheeks onto my neck; my shoulders heaving, my body aching like when you have the worst kind of flu. So this is what it felt like when it was *really* over; when there truly was no going back. I'd felt anguish, and devastation and heartbreak before when I'd lost David, but not this. This was something else.

"And that's it, is it mum? You're going to let your pride rule your heart and let David drive on out of your life?"

"Jesus, Chloe! Where did you spring from? You almost made my heart stop, popping up out of the darkness like that!"

"We were listening on the landing, I won't lie. I heard you shouting and wondered what on earth was appertaining down there. Although I wish I hadn't bothered eavesdropping now, with the disappointing outcome. You really did put on a pathetic show tonight mum."

"WE? You mean Josh just heard every word as well?"

"Don't change the subject. It doesn't matter if a whole tribe of people were up here listening in, when you're going to come out with that kind of tripe and cut your nose off to spite your face. And it wasn't every word...you lowered your voices a few times so we had to fill in the blanks..."

"Don't be so bloody rude Chloe...cutting my nose off to spite my face...you have no idea what you're talking about."

"Don't be so flippin' patronising mum. I'm fifteen, not five. No idea what I'm talking about? I've heard all about your relationship with David remember, the beginning, the middle and, it would seem, the end. I've been there when you've described each other as "the love of your life" and watched you drool over one another. I've heard you laugh your socks off with him and also cry into your pillow over him in the dead of night when you think no one can hear you. When you were together as a couple, I loved the new, improved you – the one who finally realised life was for living and that she deserved to be loved. And you didn't nag *half* as much. And, before I learned to trust him and, I suppose, love him myself, I hung back and watched and listened and realised that someone like David only comes along once in a lifetime...and I thought to myself that if I ever found someone like him – no offence intended Josh – I would seriously never ever let them go."

Christ, it comes to something when your fifteen year old daughter delivers a speech so passionate and, unfortunately, mainly accurate, that you end up feeling ashamed to the core. I just wasn't sure if the shame was as a result of telling her she had "no idea" or whether it was because deep, deep down, I had niggling doubts that I might just have made a humungous mistake that I would regret for the rest of my small, insignificant life.

"And, the teensy matter of him running back to his wife every time she made a song and dance about something? You would just brush that aside would you and skip happily off together into the sunset?"

"You're doing that annoying patronising thing again mum. And I would hardly call a possible suicide attempt making a song and dance about something, would you? And yes, it looks like she wasn't as bad as all that, as it turns out; that she had a hidden agenda. But David didn't know that. He may have handled it badly...well, to be frank...he made a total and utter cock-up of it all – but it certainly wasn't because he had any romantic notions towards this silly woman – and it sure as hell wasn't because he didn't love you! If I was in your shoes? Well, yeah, I would probably make him suffer every day for the rest of his life. But if I still loved him so much and a future without him seemed unthinkable, then I wouldn't let it stop me being with him. Some things are more important that pride."

"Bloody hell, Marjorie Proops, how did I spawn such a sensible, knowledgeable child?"

"Trust me, I'm not that sensible – I get up to lots of daft stuff that you never hear about. Who the hell is Marjorie Proops anyway?"

Oh my, I forget how ancient I really am sometimes.

"Aw, it's irrelevant. But you'd better tell me now what daft stuff you've been up to behind my back before I have to starve it out of you!"

"Stop changing the subject mother!"

Of course Chloe was almost always top of my agenda and I would no doubt lie awake at night wondering what the "daft stuff" could have been, but tonight my head was filled only with thoughts of David and what I'd lost. It was like I'd slashed through an invisible cord that had joined the two of us together, and even though he was totally responsible for the mess we'd found ourselves in, I also blamed myself for not being able to absolve him of his sins, to enable us to move on and grow old together.

"'Scuse me Mrs Stewart. Thank you Mrs Stewart." I blinked hard and stood up quickly as I realised Josh was trying to slither past me on the stairs, no doubt hoping to escape from this madhouse and the curse of the relationships that were formed and smashed apart within it.

"Sorry Josh, love...and apologies if I've ruined your night..."

"It's alright, it's time I was leaving anyway as I've got a load of homework to finish. And it was more entertaining than Hollyoaks anyway. I'm sorry about David, Mrs Stewart. I always liked him; he was funny, for an old guy."

Oh goody, David had the seal of approval from some teenage squirt. Well that made all the difference.

On autopilot, I locked the door after Josh had made his hasty exit, and dragged my aching feet into the kitchen to make myself a mug of hot chocolate, although I was kidding myself if I thought that it may help me achieve a decent night's sleep.

I felt so empty inside. I couldn't even bring myself to ring Kirsty; I just wanted to curl up and die on my own. But oh no, Chloe wasn't finished yet, and had crept up behind me.

"Ring him, for god's sake, ring him. It's not too late. Tell him that this time YOU made the stupid mistake – that he's been a pillock but that you can't live without him and his cheesy jokes and knackered old Adidas trainers. Just do it…RING HIM!"

She thrust my mobile into my face and glared at me, whilst I stared at it as if I'd never seen it before and didn't know what the hell to do with it.

"I can't, Chloe, I just can't," I whispered. "It's been too long. He's had too much time with her – I've had too long without him. Sometimes you just have to accept that it wasn't meant to be and try to get on with your life. I've loved him more than I've ever loved anyone. But we should have seen it for what it was – a teenage holiday romance - and left it behind in the '80s with ra-ra skirts and leg warmers - not dragged it kicking and screaming into the twenty-first century. We should have cherished the old memories and not tried to make new ones."

"What a load of old crap. You're a coward mum. Scared of getting hurt again; too frightened to try, too proud to admit that YOU should have fought harder, as well as David. I get that dad did a good job on you – he's my father but no real dad to me, and not a very nice man either. But David isn't him. He would never, ever hurt you on purpose or cheat on you. He's a great guy and he's left a painful void not just in your life, but in mine as well now. I've never really had that father figure before, but if I'd had to hand-pick a man for the job, I would definitely have selected David. And if you don't contact him again, if you let this lovely, sweet man return to his dull 'Dave' life, then you will lose some of my respect and probably change my own view on relationships and scar me for life. Sorry. Just putting that out there."

The phone went clattering across the worktop as she almost threw it towards me and I couldn't even muster up the energy to chuck out the standard "If you've broken that young lady, then you're paying for it!" As she stormed upstairs again, muttering on about wasted opportunities, I heard a little whimper come from Fudge's direction and I felt my shoulders sag as I realised that Chloe had not, in fact, taken the little stinker out for a walk.

"Sorry, Fudge…back garden for a widdle it is then."

I thought of all the evenings David had taken Fudge out for a late-night stroll without even being asked to do so; of the mornings he had thrown some crumpled clothes on to nip to the local shop to pick up some emergency bacon; of the times he had insisted on driving Chloe to wherever she needed to be rather than me having to lug myself out of my comfy chair when I was half-asleep and worn out from work.

Many, many people had told me he was one in a million. I knew it myself really.

But in a way he had become a victim of his own success. One of his most endearing qualities had resulted in his downfall – the loss of everything that made him happy. Being the good guy had led to him being taken advantage of and brought him nothing but pain. He had been so trusting and so quick to jump in and help someone he had still cared for that he had been deceived and been unable to see the very worst aspects of that person's personality, that had been festering under their skin all of the time. That woman he had thought he knew had been a wolf in sheep's clothing all along. David had finally been enlightened when it was far, far too late and he had let the best thing he had ever had slip through his fingers, yet again.

Chapter 34

SUZANNE

Dave's sudden disappearance in the middle of the week was unexpected and unprecedented. He clearly hadn't been to work either as a quick call to the shop revealed that Michael was covering Dave's shifts once again, and was none too happy about it.

"Supposed to be taking Debs to that big, fancy shopping outlet, I was. She's not best pleased you know, and *you* don't have to live with her. She'll have my guts for garters if Dave doesn't make a re-appearance by tomorrow. And that scary woman who lives over by the church, who keeps sabotaging her central heating system to get one of us to come by her house out of hours, has only flamin' done it again! I feel like a piece of meat, bent over trying to check out her pipework while she stares at me, and makes horrible smacking noises with her lips, and asks me for the fiftieth time if I wouldn't like something stronger than a cup of tea. Dave owes me one for this. Big time. I mean, he told me nothing – only that the shop would have to close if I couldn't stand in for him - where even is he?"

Struggling to rustle up an answer without having to go into too much detail, much of which I didn't have anyway, I could only reply "He just needed a few days break, sorry Michael."

"Would that be a few days break up north by any chance? Perhaps in...say...the district of Wigan, sis?"

"Don't be ridiculous Michael. I know you're annoyed but I won't let you wind me up."

"Aah...come on Sue...just who do you think you are kidding with all this pretence? Mum and dad may have been conned into thinking that the pair of you are a couple again but I'm not falling for it. I'm not sure what went down, and it's really none of my business, but all I know is that Dave was finally back on form again and looking forward to a rosy future, with a massive grin permanently plastered across his face...and then suddenly...all change! He's back in the big house with you again, and he's looking and acting like a zombie. Surviving but not living. Something occurred - but you're just not prepared to admit to it, are you?"

"As you say Mike, it's none of your business. Everything's fine and I don't need you, or anyone else for that matter, interfering in my affairs."

He had a justifiable right to dig deeper really, seeing as he was the one picking up the slack as far as the business was concerned. But I couldn't confess that I had, in effect, blackmailed Dave into leaving behind his new life and moving back in with me - that he never would have stayed if he hadn't believed it to be a matter of life and death.

I had begun to feel a real sense of shame, and it wasn't just down to trying to wantonly seduce him when he was three sheets to the wind – practically throwing my scantily dressed self at him and being spurned like that, left in no doubt that Dave was no longer attracted to me in any way, shape or form. When had I become so desperate? How had I stooped so low?

Saying a curt goodbye to Michael, I slipped into Dave's room, to search through his belongings, to see if I could unearth any clues as to his whereabouts or what his plans may have been. I knew in my heart where he was though, even without evidence. If my instincts were right, he was probably in Wigan right now begging in the last chance saloon. I knew he still loved her – it was so very obvious and anyway, I could feel it deep in my gut. He had never stopped loving her, despite my best efforts to put a spanner in the works and bring him home forever.

So now all I could do was wait. And see if it was a yea or a nay from the mistress department.

Attempting to distract myself from the reality of my situation, I tried out some new songs and my practice session actually went quite well - probably because the tunes were a selection of modern love songs and were being sang from the heart. The neighbours were most likely wishing I would put a sock in it after a while, but it was good for me to belt out some of that emotion; best not to store it all up inside, I had realised, all too late.

By eleven o'clock that night, I had accepted that Dave was unlikely to come back this time, but to my surprise, I heard his key turning in the lock and he appeared before me, in the lounge, where I was drifting in and out of sleep.

He looked dreadful, worse than I had ever seen him, and merely said "I'll be back in the shop tomorrow, so you can tell Mike to keep his hair on. I'm going upstairs to grab some stuff and then I'll be checking into a hotel."

I opened my mouth to enquire if he was okay and assure him he really didn't need to do that, but he was already gone. Less than ten minutes later he was back down the stairs and out of that front door, leaving me shattered and once more alone with my thoughts.

*

Downright miserable. That's how I would describe the hours and days that followed. It was the week prior to Christmas already, yet there was little festive cheer in the air. I had ordered, taken delivery of and decorated an enormous tree which could be seen in all its glory in the huge bay window in the lounge, and I'd strung a few sets of lights up in the downstairs rooms and added some tasteful decorations that I had paid a small fortune for over the years. And yet Dave only mentioned the impending celebrations once, when he messaged me to confirm that he wouldn't be joining us for Christmas dinner at my parents' house or attending any further events with me, and I could tell people what I liked as he no longer cared.

I couldn't bring myself to confide in mum and dad yet; I didn't know what excuse I was going to make on the big day, but I just couldn't let on how awful my life was right now, and that while Dave had technically been living with me again, he had not actually been *living with me*. Not in the way that they had presumed and I had previously inferred. I couldn't even have described our situation as housemates in the end, because that description would imply that we had been *mates*, when the reality was that we barely spoken at all. And now he was gone and it would seem our friendship had not just been fractured but was almost completely broken.

Somehow I had picked up a few nights' work, here and there, following the memorable (for all the wrong reasons) evening of great celebration and ultimate humiliation, as I now referred to it. On a freezing cold Thursday evening I hauled all my equipment down to a less than savoury pub usually frequented by underage drinkers flashing fake ID, but on that particular evening it was full of drunken partygoers who had flooded in from the Chinese restaurant next door after feeding their faces with the all-you-can-eat Festive buffet. It wasn't one of my favourite jobs, I can tell you. The presence of bouncers on the door had given me an indication that it was likely to be a particularly raucous night and it certainly was. It paid reasonably well though, and the evening was rounded off with a drunken sing-a-long for all and I left the venue with lots of praise ringing in my ears, mostly in the form of

"You're a knock-out Suzanne – cracking voice – any chance of a snog?" At least it had felt more like Christmas in there.

The next evening was much more up my street, in an old-fashioned but immaculately clean sprawling hotel that was hosting turkey and tinsel weekends right up until Christmas itself. Setting up my equipment on and around the stage, I felt at home amongst the friendly staff and cheery hotel residents. More at home than I did in my own house at the moment, if the truth be told. It made a pleasant change to be away from the confines of those walls and the screaming emptiness that lay within.

I had an hour beforehand to run through some of the numbers with the band, and when they arrived, I was both surprised and pleased to see that I recognised one of them – it was my old keyboard player from back in the day, when I used to entertain the masses at the Towan Reach Hotel. It was Stu – the lovable rogue with the cute dimples and repertoire of dubious chat-up lines.

He looked just as shocked but equally happy to see me as he came over and immediately pulled me into a giant bear hug, squishing my chest to his own.

"Well if it isn't the number one vocalist in Cornwall - Posh Spice, with the sexiest of bodies and those come-to-bed eyes! They said they had a great singer lined up for us tonight and they weren't wrong."

"Stuey! Oh my goodness, it's been so long, I can't believe I'm working with you tonight...I haven't seen you in so many years! Where have you been?"

He threw back his head in laughter, as he had always done in the past, and said, "Well, lovely lady, I gave up my dazzling musical career for a very long time and actually knuckled down and got myself a proper job! I work at Tesco in the warehouse at the moment!"

"You? In a warehouse, where there's statistically more men than women? I never thought I'd see the day!"

"Ooh, still as cheeky I see. Well, let me tell you, there *are* actually more women than men there – we've moved on from the 1980s you know!"

"Ha ha, I do know! I suppose you've been chasing them all around the warehouse though, like in one of those not very politically correct Benny Hill sketches!"

"Oy! I'm a married man now, you know! The beast was tamed and I finally settled down to wedded bliss."

"Oh my god, I can't believe it, Stuey off the market. Last I'd heard, you were still bedding the poor unsuspecting holidaymakers and half of the female residents of Newquay as well!"

"I'll give you that one - I was fighting off the ladies every night and I did put it around a little – I always presumed I would be the eternal bachelor! But the "last you heard" was probably in the 1990s, as I relocated to the Welsh coast about fifteen years with my good lady, Davinia. Only came back a few months ago and picked up the old keyboard to continue as a bit of a hobby really, and then I got offered a few gigs with the band."

"Wales? Really? Wow, and you a pastie-eating, cider-swilling Newquay boy through and through. She must be quite something this wonderful woman, to tame you and your wild ways."

"She is. She's a wonderful woman. One in a million. I never thought I'd fall in love again; I'd given up on love after getting my heart smashed to pieces!"

"In love again? Heart smashed to pieces? What did I miss? When were *you* ever in love before, apart from with yourself, you naughty boy!"

Something weird happened then. His smile faded, and he lowered his head and I noticed he clenched his fists at the same time. Everything seemed to fall silent in the room, before Stu finally spoke again. Thank goodness, I'd suffered enough awkward silences to last me a lifetime.

He tried to shake off the strange moment by reverting to his usual jokey nature. "Never mind me! What about you and loverboy? I saw his work van tootling down the hill from where the rich and posh people live…I take it the two of you are still in residence up there at the manor!"

I could have just laughed it off. I should have just laughed it off. But instead I tearfully replied, "We split up Stuey. Long time ago really, but he only properly left me earlier this year. And then he came back, under duress, but he's gone for good now. We're not a couple any more. It's complicated, but we are definitely not a couple. He loves someone else, and I think he always has done."

I don't know why I chose that moment to let my heavily armoured guard down, with Stu of all people, who I'd not seen for years and who was daft as a brush. But I found myself literally crying onto his shoulder, as he shushed me and tenderly rubbed my back. It actually felt good to let it all out and confess to the big fat lie I had been living; to share some of the secrets I had been hiding way down deep inside of me.

Once I'd composed myself, he ordered two coffees from the bar, remembering after all of these years that I didn't take sugar and only liked a drop of milk in mine, and we quietly sat in an unoccupied corner of the room for a short while.

"I'm sorry Stu; I bet you didn't need that. I'm embarrassed really. I've not told anyone else the ins and outs of it all…but I guess it's because you've always been so easy to talk to - even though it's been so long in between our conversations. Sorry. Again."

"Hey! Don't apologise. It's me! We all need someone to confide in. Even you. I'm so sorry it didn't work out for you guys but, you know Sue, it happens. Even the happiest of couples don't make it, for a variety of reasons, and often it's nobody's fault; just one of those things."

He scraped his chair up so that it was considerably closer to mine and leant forward so I could hear him even when he whispered, "My turn now. Do you want to hear my dirty little secret? I'll share it with you, if you promise to keep it."

I rubbed my face where the tears had fallen, hoping to god that my make-up wasn't smudged beyond repair and I didn't have noticeable Panda eyes.

"Oh yes, please, do tell. I need to hear all about someone else's life to take my mind off my own. I'm all ears, as Mr Rabbit said to Mrs Rabbit – see, I'm even remembering your unfunny old jokes now."

"Well they were pretty unforgettable! Well, Suzanne…Sue… with the body of a goddess and a hard-earned degree in sarcasm. My revelation is…that…well you know how I said I hadn't thought I'd ever fall in love again? Well, that first woman who I loved really and truly *did* smash my heart to pieces, and the bedding of hundreds of lucky, lucky ladies - well that was just a cover-up really, to mask the pain, to try and forget the one that got away."

"Aw…Stuey…I can't believe someone was resistant to your persistent charms…who would do that to you?"

A brief pause.

"You. Suzanne. You did it to me."

"Ha ha! What? What are you talking about, you silly sausage? You didn't love *me*, you just loved winding me up – and you had a particular talent for that! I certainly didn't break your heart!"

"Sorry Sue, but I did, and you did. I just never told you before. I kept it all to tell myself."

I was struck dumb, still slightly suspecting that he was having me on, but one look into his honest, sincere darkest brown eyes told me otherwise.

"I was crazy about you from the moment I first met you. But you weren't interested in me. I was besotted with you from the off, but you wouldn't even enter into a conversation with most of the guys you worked with. You spoke to the other lads in the band, because you had to, when it was work-related, but you could still be incredibly frosty with them and they were all pretty wary of you. I asked you out a billion times of course but the reply was always a resounding "NO!", and I found that if I did my cheeky chappy routine and flirted with you and flattered you while pretending it was all one big joke, you were happy to go along with that and join in the banter, so we became friends. But I desperately wanted so much more."

"Oh God, Stu, I didn't realise...I honestly had no idea..."

"No, you didn't. You couldn't see how I always engineered every situation to ensure that I would be working closely with you. You couldn't see that it was more than a coincidence that I always arrived early when I was working with you, and never left until you had. You couldn't see that I was, in my own stupid way, initially trying to make you jealous when I was chatting up all of those women about two feet away from you. You couldn't see it at all. Any of it."

I felt awful then; more awful than I had felt earlier when I was telling him about my disastrous marriage, and that was quite an achievement. All that time, Stu hadn't been joking when he had kept asking me out, and I had been so ignorant of his feelings; so wrapped up in my own precious little world.

"I really am sorry. I was a silly, silly woman then who spent more time preening herself and putting on an appearance for others that I couldn't see what was right under my nose."

"To be frank, Sue, even if you had known you would have dismissed me outright and the banter would have stopped then. I kept on hoping and kept on trying, just in case you woke up one day and looked at me in a different light and thought, "What a handsome guy this Stuart is, I think I'll take him back to mine and ravish him all night long", but you never did."

"Ha ha. I always thought you were handsome Stu, a bit of a looker…and you *knew* you were! You were a really good-looking, funny, talented guy but…"

"…but I was never good enough for you, I know. You were always on the lookout for something better, waiting for your Prince Charming to come along and sweep you off your dainty little feet. Hotel managers, wealthy businessmen, guys with money and status – that's what you were interested in. Not little old me."

Feeling somewhat uncomfortable now, maybe because it was all a little too close for comfort, I shifted about in my seat and weakly tried to insist, "No, Stu, I just wanted to find my perfect match; someone who I could see myself growing old with…", but he was having none; he wasn't allowing me to get off that lightly.

"No, Suzanne. You wanted someone you could show off, like a prize trophy that you had won. You wanted to become one half of a respected power couple, and anyone who didn't meet the required standards, like me, handsome as I was, got kicked to the side. Not good enough. You wanted the looks, the body, the personality, the money and the *status*. You wanted it all."

"Hang on Stu, if I was that much of a social climber and as power-mad as you say, how come I ended up with a lowly old plumber then?"

"He took you by surprise, that's how. He took us *all* by surprise. You couldn't help those feelings that you harboured for him, right from the beginning. He was never who I expected you to end up with, I'll admit. When you met him that night at the Towan Reach, I watched you fall for him right before my tired, lovestruck eyes. Whatever he had, he had in spades, because once you'd seen him, there was no hope for me or anyone else."

"I *did* fall head over heels for him right from the outset Stu…he made my head spin and I wanted him so badly. I'd been looking for that Mr Right and I thought I'd found him."

"Well I wanted to hate him – after all, he had *you*, everything I'd ever wanted. But I couldn't even dislike him a tiny little bit – he was too bleeding nice. I could see what attracted him to you – he was a good-looking guy who had a great personality – one of the lads you could stand and have a pint with as well as being a smooth talker with the ladies. I still couldn't get my head around the fact you'd settled for a plumber though!"

"Aw Stu, I loved him, and everything about him. And he was just perfect as he was; faults and all – not that he had any. But do you know what I did? I took him and tried to mould him into what I wanted him to be – I boasted of how he had his own business that was raking in the cash, and later his own shop premises, and I made sure we were seen together in all the right places, in all the right clothes – showing everyone that we were the perfect, successful, attractive, financially secure couple. Cornwall's very own Posh and Becks! Dave was so wonderful and down to earth and happy in his own skin – and yet I somehow felt the need to try and turn him into something he wasn't. All for appearances' sake. So strangers would look at us and think, "Wow! Look at them! I wish I had what they had!" He was gorgeous and fit and funny and kind and considerate but it still wasn't enough for me! I still wanted more."

"Alright, alright…I can do without you listing all of Dave's wonderful, superior qualities when he's the actual bloke who stole my dream woman right from under my nose!"

"Sorry; add tactless to *my* list of *inferior* qualities. But, sorry again, he *was…IS* wonderful. And I was a stupid, stupid shallow woman who never really appreciated what she had. Or thought she had. Because, you see Stu, before I even met him, he'd fallen in love with a young girl who had broken his heart and he had never really got over her. Oh, sure, he loved me in his own way for a while and did a good job of pushing her to the back of his mind, but there was always that deep-seated connection to her fizzing away inside of him – a part of him that was unreachable and the subject was *not* up for discussion. He tried to bat me off when I attempted to bring up the topic of his exes, and he inferred there had been no one of any significance prior to me in his life. But I did my research and heard mutterings that there'd been this girl, a tourist from up north, when he was seventeen, who he'd been besotted with and who had left him in bits. I tried to brush it under the carpet myself, but I found that I couldn't ignore it in the end when it came to a head. That slimy toad Stephen McAvoy – I don't know if you know him, he may have gone to your school – had been mouthing off in the pub about this girl, and Dave, who usually wouldn't hurt a fly, laid into him and apparently had to be pulled away before he really did him some serious damage."

"God, yeah, I remember that Ste McAvoy – he was two years above me at school but he already had the makings of a complete tosser then; constantly in trouble with the coppers, repeatedly bunking off. And there were rumours that he practically tried to force himself onto a younger girl at the old youth club once and the girl's parents had gone ballistic and got the police involved."

"Really? I had no idea. Maybe what I heard later was right then – that this *Louise* – the love of Dave's life – who he'd thought was messing him about, was actually the innocent party then. At the time she was apparently painted as this two-timing, flaky young girl when actually she'd just suffered at the hands of this dangerous predator."

"That's what I heard."

"What you heard? Why, what else do you know?"

"Suzanne, you *know* what Newquay's like for gossip – once the holidaymaker contingent and all of the seasonal workers and those just passing through are taken out of the equation you're left with a town where everyone seems to know everyone else's business; you couldn't keep a secret here if you tried."

"Tell me what you know Stu before I have to sabotage that precious keyboard of yours and beat you about the head with my microphone..."

"Okay, okay. Don't get your knickers in a twist! I don't know much really; I just made it my business to find out what this Dave was all about when you took up with him – I suppose I wanted to uncover some unscrupulous business dealings or unsavoury lovelife details so that I could dish the dirt on him to you – but he was as clean as a whistle. The only information I gleaned was about his family and friends, where he lived and worked and all that jazz – except a lad I knew was an acquaintance of Billy Lomax – Dave's best mate. And he mentioned that Dave had been all loved up with this really pretty girl on holiday one year and that they'd been forever down the beach, necking and other stuff, as you do when you're a teenager...not that you would want to hear about that...but that they'd split up suddenly and Dave had been really cut up about it. He'd dropped her like a hot potato, but had regretted it for a long time afterwards..."

"Oh. There seems to be a recurring theme here. Everyone seems to recall that Dave and Louise were crazy about each other - and that she was apparently blameless and he shouldn't have given her the elbow...and that they were both devastated afterwards. It would appear that maybe she was 'the one' after all. Kind of a bitter pill for me to swallow though...because he was 'the one' for me."

"And you were 'the one' for me Sue – life's a bitch, but we all have to move on. It's agonisingly painful, but nobody's life ever ended just because their partner didn't love them anymore. There *is* a promising future out there for you, you incredible, lovely woman...you've just got to go and grab it for yourself. Stop living in the past and do something with your life that is just for *you*."

"Aw Stu...you've got a good head on your shoulders when it comes to doleing out advice. It already feels like a weight off *my* shoulders to be opening up to you like this – and I'm glad you've felt you could do the same with me. And, again, I'm sorry if I've been insensitive to your feelings in the past and failed to notice what a fabulous, fine man you are. Because you really are a fantastic guy, Stu. Your Davinia is an incredibly lucky lady to have you, and I shall tell her so, if I ever meet her one day."

"Well...the thing is....she's not my Davinia, as it happens..."

"How so? You just said you married her and that she was a wonderful woman – one in a million and all that...?"

"Yes, I *did* marry her, and she *is* wonderful. I'm just not married to her anymore..."

"Aw Stu, you little fibber...."

"No, no, take that back. I never said I was *still* married to her. I'll never stop loving her, but we've both moved on. She has mostly moved on with another man, who she has much more in common with, and they live in a massive renovated barn with acres of farmland surrounding them...whereas I, unfortunately, have moved on to a pokey little flat above a launderette and a freezer compartment bursting with dinners-for-one again."

"Well, I'm sorry to hear that, I really am."

"Nah...it's fine. We fancied each other like mad and we had a real good laugh together. And when we tied the knot she really looked after me with her home-cooking and almost manical cleaning up and organising. And she's really thoughtful and kind, and good company to boot."

"So what the hell went wrong? God, you're as bad as me!"

"Nope, no one's as bad you, you naughty little girl! Oy! That hurt!"

"It was meant to! Now, carry on...tell me all the juicy details..."

"What went wrong...well, she's Welsh – not that there's anything wrong with that – we met when she came down to Newquay on her friend's hen night – and she really didn't want to leave Wales; or 'The Holy Land', as she used to describe it as. So, all loved up, I relocated up there and tried to settle in the valleys, but it was difficult. I didn't know anyone and a lot of the guys my age round there were part and parcel of the farming community, which clearly, I was not. They probably weren't, but it felt sometimes that they were deliberately excluding me from their conversations. I'm sure they spoke more Welsh when I was around – and I know that's their native tongue, but I'm crap with languages, and just couldn't get it to stick in my mind. Davinia said I barely made an effort with either the language or trying to interact with anyone – and it caused a considerable amount of conflict between us. So...we ended up staying in more than we went out...and, whilst I like a good telly sesh with a cup of tea and a packet of hobnobs as much as anyone else, I wasn't quite ready for my pipe and slippers..."

"I can't imagine anyone less likely to vegetate in front of the TV...you were always a bit of a party animal!"

"Oh those days are long gone...but I still need the occasional night out...I still wanted a bit more excitement in my life. But, we were still in love then, and so we persevered, despite the arguments. And it wasn't just that – we didn't seem to share any of the same interests! She had a penchant for country music for god's sake and it did my head in. She tried to persuade me to go line-dancing – me! With two left feet! And all those reality shows she used to watch. And I only have the odd cheeky ciggie, you remember, when I'm leathered, but she used to go mad about it and made me stand outside with the dog. I suppose there were lots of little arguments..."

"...which add up to something much bigger in the end I suppose. It was a different situation for me. Ex-girlfriend and love-of-his-life aside...it was the *big* things that caused the massive problems between me and Dave for a good proportion of our married life. I couldn't have children – my defective, stupid body wasn't up to carrying a baby...and it tore me apart..."

"It was the same for Davinia...she'd had all kinds of gyneological problems and my sperm were apparently only part-time workers...so we were unable to conceive as well..."

"God it's more common than you think, isn't it? It's so painful discovering you can never have a baby and then trying to continue as a couple with that hanging in the air and a quiet, empty house which should be filled with children's toys and laughter..."

"Oh, ours ended up filled with toys and laughter...and lots and lots of noise...we adopted three year old twin girls – Macey and Rochelle – don't get me started on the adoption process; it still haunts me when I lay awake at night – and our peace and quiet was shattered forever! But I wouldn't have missed out on them for anything – despite the split, they've been smothered with affection and have given us so much joy...and in turn we have given them a roof over their heads, security and more love than they can handle. Seriously, I would die for my girls. "

The shame was back with a vengeance. This was something I had fiercely fought against. Adopting someone else's unwanted babies. But Stu's face had lit up like a beacon when he was talking about his precious daughters. He and his wife had opened up their hearts and homes to two little girls desperately in need and he clearly loved them as much as anyone could possibly love any children. I had been too selfish, again, too stubborn to open up my mind to the possibility of fostering or adoption and, serves me right, I had missed out on so much love. How different my life might have been if I had taken that route.

His daughters were apparently eight now and it had been the hardest thing he had ever had to do, to move back to Newquay, but he had instinctively known that it had been the right decision for him. He was back amongst his friends and family and the girls came to stay with him every other weekend and in the holidays; they thought Newquay was "ace" and loved to play on Towan and Great Western beaches, building sandcastles and begging for ice lollies, even in the freezing cold winter months.

His wife was apparently an outstanding mother and he knew they were in good hands when they were with her, even with mother's new partner on the scene – it pained Stu to say it but "Ian" was a nice guy, who was able to provide them all with a higher than average standard of living, and he took good care of the kids and had an easy relationship with them. He even let Stu bunk down in their annexe when he travelled up to see the girls, as often as his work schedule would allow.

A few discreet coughs emanating from the stage area indicated that it was time to stop chatting and start working, and I reluctantly returned my cup and saucer to the bar and made my way over to greet the drummer and guitarist, who were keen to slip a quick rehearsal in before the punters arrived.

Despite my head being filled with all kinds of pictures of what might have been and what never should have been, it turned out to be an amazing night and we performed encore after encore and almost raised the roof of the place. Complimentary drinks were sent over again after we had finally finished and we all stayed on a while, unable to get sozzled as most of us were driving home later, but enjoying our pint of beer or glass of wine and reminiscing about how it used to be round the pubs, clubs and hotels of Newquay…in politically incorrect times when all kinds of scandalous stuff went on! What happens backstage, stays backstage!

I came down to earth with a huge bump when I returned to my morgue of a house. The high I had been on since completing the set at the hotel and sharing banter with the band had vanished into thin air and all I was left with was a feeling of loss. The loss of my marriage, the loss of the baby I could never have, the loss of the last fifteen pointless years of my life – when all I had done was mourn and grieve and feel sorry for myself – whilst trying to cling on to the remnants of the life I had once lived with Dave.

His old trainers by the front door and one of his coats hanging from the peg in the hallway meant I still felt his presence in the house whilst simultaneously feeling his absence. All was silent in the house, but the lights from the Christmas tree were twinkling in the darkness and it was a strangely comforting sight. I poured myself a large glass of wine, slipped my shoes off and reclined in the chair by the tree. The night's events and conversations had given me food for thought and, as I sipped my glass of Chile's finest, I came to a decision. A decision I should have made years ago.

I couldn't go on like this. I couldn't stand to live this half-life any longer. Not so long ago I thought I couldn't survive without Dave in my life, even if he didn't love me - that any life with him was preferable to life without him. Wrong, wrong, wrong! That was no way to live – circling around each other, trying to think of civil words we could say to each other. So perhaps it was for the best that he had moved out.

I thought of Jenny's friend who had so badly wanted to live but how cancer had cruelly robbed her of that wish. I had been given the gift of life but here I was, wasting it.

I knew what I had to do. This time I would get it right.

It was for the best for everyone. Mum and dad would be upset initially but they would eventually realise I had done it for all of the right reasons.

Time to put my new plan into action. A Christmas gift for everyone.

Chapter 35

LOUISE

"Merry Christmas Motherfu....Oh hello Mrs S...didn't realise you had arrived already! Not come in the car? Tell me you didn't pay for a taxi on Christmas Day? Ooh good...robbing dogs they are on Bank Holidays, that firm round the corner from you. Anyway, I am the designated driver this year so you can all drink to your hearts' content and I will give everyone a lift home later."

My crowded living room livened up immediately with the arrival of Kirsty, piled high with presents, food and Christmas cheer, her belly entering the room before the rest of her. She had stopped throwing up everything she ate and said she was looking forward to a double portion of Christmas dinner, seeing as she was packing it away for two now.

We had experienced a bit of a depressing run-up to the big day, not helped by Kirsty's unplanned pregnancy which meant she was unable to consume any alcohol, so we couldn't get pissed and hungover together. We'd had a girls' night out early December with the other ladies, although we treated ourselves to a meal first at the new Bengali restaurant in the high street, so I wasn't quite as off my face and morose as the previous time. But Kirsty, intensely disliking being the only sober one amongst the pack of girls, declared "This is shit" at precisely 9.40 pm so we saw her off safely into a taxi and then just lingered around for a couple more drinks.

Anyway, we eventually pulled ourselves together and decided that, despite all our woes and worries, we were going to have the best Christmas we possibly could, in the circumstances; we refused to lay down and die - spending the festive season by ourselves, sobbing into our Harveys Bristol Cream whilst eating chocolate brazil nuts by the boxload – well, that was simply not an option.

We had both expected to be celebrating Christmas with the love of our life...but sometimes things just don't work out the way you expect them to...and we came to the conclusion that we had to make the best of a bad situation. So we bought sacks of gifts, spending a ton of money that we didn't have (that good old Argos card came in handy), filled my house with gaudy decorations and a freezer full of party food and of course a table full of drink (a few non-alcoholic beers lined up for Kirsty) and blasted out Christmas tunes all day and night and even in the car. Wham!'s 'Last Christmas' gave me a bit of a wobble, and I couldn't even skip that song because I bloody love it, but otherwise, we were surviving – just about.

Christmas Eve saw Kirsty, Chloe and I touring round the town visiting various friends and relatives in Kirsty's little rust bucket of a car, which was soldiering on, no doubt inspired by our collective words of comfort every time Kirsty tried to fire up the engine ("Come on Freddy, you can do it. Come on lad, we'll buy you a nice Christmassy smelling air freshener, if you behave yourself!").

We were like three little Santas – well two of us certainly had the bellies for the job - delivering gifts and cards, having belted out "We wish you a merry Christmas" on everyone's doorstep, like three very poor, out of tune carol singers. It was unexpected fun actually, although if I ate another mince pie I would explode. The aching hole was still in my heart but what I could do? I couldn't allow myself to contemplate what David might be doing – whether he would be spending Christmas with that bitch in that soulless mausoleum of a house with its imposing pillars and endless rooms. Not so long ago, we'd had a discussion about Christmas one evening, and I'd discovered that he adored it just as much as I did. So I presumed he wouldn't be hiding away somewhere, pretending it wasn't happening.

Bastard.

God, I missed him.

In a fit of generosity and madness, I had invited not only my mother, and Chloe's boyfriend Josh, and Kirsty's mum and her new man-friend Rodney to our Christmas Day gathering, but also my brother and girlfriend, my sister and her clan, and a couple of our friends – Ashanti and her latest beau, and Dawn and her girlfriend Leanne. Thankfully my brother Neil said thanks, but no thanks, as he and Clare were off to the Carribean until well into the New Year (Phew!), and Dawn and Leanne were off to Leanne's parents for three days, which was a damn shame as Leanne was a bloody scream after she'd had a few glasses of cheap plonk.

Even counting the emergency chairs, we didn't have enough furniture to go round so we had turned Christmas Dinner into an unconventional buffet – but at least people could just take as little or as much as they wanted, and everything was devoured as people just kept nipping back for "another roast potato" or "one more slice of turkey", as they downed lethal quantities of alcohol. Chloe had been pre-warned that neither she nor Josh would be drinking in excess of one small glass of wine with their stand-up meal – I didn't relish the prospect of receiving a dressing down by his parents; god knows what they already thought of us, what with Chloe dumping him every five minutes and Josh sharing tales of the unhinged mother and her soap opera love-life.

My stomach groaning with the weight of the food I was forcing into it, I was just clearing away a stack of plates when Kirsty squealed and announced that she'd forgotten that she'd left my main present in the car, but would just nip out and get HIM. Fully expecting a squashed up, greased up stripper to be dragged in by his ear, I slunk back into the corner, but the present was truly an unexpected, delicious surprise.

"Is…is that what I think it is?" I gazed in wonder, mentally picturing Kirsty's car with its lack of space and piles of rubbish and was clueless as to how she had squeezed my gift in, along with everything else that was permanently stashed in there.

"Yes. Yes it is. It's a six foot cardboard cut-out of George Michael clad in a purple suit and looking incredibly handsome. Isn't it fab? Got it off t'internet. Now you'll never be lonely."

She clasped her hands to her belly, adding, "I'll have my baby, and you'll have George."

Chloe put her head in her hands but everyone else erupted into laughter and cheered, before breaking into song, 'Last Christmas' being the appropriate ditty for this special moment.

I threw my arms around Kirsty - well, as best as I could owing to her current shape - and planted kisses all over her pretty face as I drunkenly slurred "Aw my beautiful Kirsty…she buys the best presents…ever! I bloody love you, I do. And I bloody love George…look at him…sex on legs…what a man!"

As if on cue, everyone in the room began to warble "I'm your man" and leapt up to dance around my wonderful cardboard cut-out. By the end of the drunken, laughter-filled evening, everyone had boogied with George - even mum who had agreed to stay the night and knocked back a few extra Babychams - and unspeakable things had been done to him (I was holding Kirsty and Ashanti wholly responsible) and a good time had been had by all, a few of who would be suffering through the entirety of Boxing Day for this evening of merriment.

There was a moment, just after mum and Chloe had disappeared to their respective beds, and everyone else had departed and the place was littered with bits of food and half empty glasses, when I was seriously drunk and so unwisely decided to have a quick look at my favourite picture of David on my mobile – the one of him that I had secretly taken when he had been fast asleep – when we had finally ended up in bed together after a thirty year separation.

I hated him, sometimes, but I clearly didn't hate him enough to delete his pictures. Jesus wept, look at him! So very gorgeous and sexy and so wonderful and talented in the bedroom department.

"Happy Christmas David," I whispered, to no one but my inebriated self and my phone, as my eyes shone brightly with tears I was trying to hold back, for I was determined not to cry on what had been such a successful, joyous day.

"Happy Christmas, my love."

Chapter 36

SUZANNE

Christmas Day was absolute torture. I had purchased token gifts for my closest family and sent vouchers to Trudy and the other ladies I kept in touch with from time to time. And I'd picked out and posted a jokey, slightly smutty card for Stu, along with a bar of his favourite cheap-and-cheerful chocolate – I could have sent him a much more luxurious, high-end gift but it would have been pointless when he was just as content with his sugar-laden treat.

But for the very first time, I didn't purchase anything for Dave - everything I'd considered when I'd been shopping for gifts seemed entirely inappropriate. Just what do you get for the man who's lost everything? It did cross my mind that, whilst unlikely, he may turn up with a small gift for me and I would have nothing to hand him in return. But I needn't have worried, because he didn't even text let alone visit on Christmas Day and I therefore received precisely nothing from him. If I'd harboured any hopes that he would have secretly picked up a bottle of my favourite designer perfume or perhaps had quickly nipped down to the jewellers in his lunch hour to select a pair of diamond earrings, then I would have been sadly disappointed. There was no peace offering, and therefore no peace.

I decided to bestow upon my parents the best gift of all – the whole truth, and nothing but the truth. My conscience was killing me, and so, over copious amounts of dried out turkey and mountains of sprouts that seemed to lodge in the back of my throat despite them swimming round in a lake of gravy, I confessed that I had, in effect, blackmailed Dave into returning home; that he'd never wanted to come back but he'd been left with no choice. I tried to cover most ground, only omitting the details of my attempted disastrous seduction of him and subsequent humiliation, which no parent needed to hear. Fighting back the tears, I explained that we had never been reunited as a couple – he still loved the other woman, unfortunately, and his feelings for me were merely platonic ones. Hence his absence from the Christmas "celebrations".

The reaction received was mainly one of obvious disappointment, but after a few sighs and head shakes and weak words of consolation, we tried to carry on with the day as if I hadn't just dropped a mammoth bombshell on their toes. Mum had had high hopes for a reunion; I'm pretty sure she'd already mentally chosen an outfit and handbag for a renewal of vows ceremony. My continuing sense of shame was actually overshadowed by a surprising sense of relief that the truth was finally out there.

And I still had my plan, which I intended to go through with before the year was out.

Having stayed the night in my old bedroom at mum and dad's, I arrived home the next morning to a cold, silent house. Properties up and down the street were quiet but lit up inside with fairy lights and television screens, as neighbours lounged on their sofas trying to recover from the excesses of the previous day. A few youngsters were pedalling furiously up and down the road on their brand new bicycles, and I heard the smash of bottles as they were dropped into wheelie bins, no doubt as people cleared away the remains of the Christmas Day celebrations.

The loneliness hit me like a big, hard slap in the face, as I switched on the heating and peeled off my clothes to take a quick, scalding hot shower. As the water gushed out and poured over me I wondered where Dave was. There'd been no note to say he'd popped in to collect more of his belongings, no message to wish me a "Happy Christmas", no phonecall to enquire of my wellbeing. Just his absence. A space in each room where he had once been.

A single tear slid down my face and slipped away into the water raining down on me from the shower. I would always love him but it was time to finally, and forever, let go.

I wondered if he knew the end was coming. He'd always looked forward to the festive celebrations and despite everything, I hoped he'd enjoyed the 25th of December.

"Merry Christmas, my love," I whispered.

Chapter 37

LOUISE

The father of all hangovers, because I am quite, quite sure that those bastards are male, hit me like a ton of bricks as I prised open one sticky eye at some point on Boxing Day morning.

Holy mother of God, there was a man in my room! Oh, no…my mistake…it was just George, draped in tinsel, and sporting several smudged lipstick marks on his handsome face, which had *better* wipe off, or else there would be hell to pay.

"Morning George", I croaked as I tentatively, slowly, began to ease myself out of bed. Oh this was going to be a Nurofen-every-four –hours kind of day; I could feel it in my water – speaking of which, I was desperate for a wee.

Oh my lord, I'd promised to go back to mum's with her to help her prepare a buffet for when all the tribe descended on her for her annual Boxing Day party tea. I wondered if I could quietly disappear into her conservatory for a quick snooze at some point in one of the wicker chairs while she was busy in the kitchen.

From downstairs I could hear mum and Chloe singing tunelessly along to the Christmas album as kitchen cupboard doors slammed and cups and plates were clattered about. I waited until I heard the toaster pop up before I gingerly descended down the stairs, very aware that I still had bits of party poppers stuck in my wig and that I probably smelled like a brewery.

I was greeted by all smiles from the pair of them (how did mum manage to look so bright and well after a night on the pop – maybe she was just more practised at it than me?) and a litany of sarcasm and rude comments in the vein of "Oh god, here she is, the living dead…looking like an extra from The Addams Family…the Ghost of Christmas Present".

Allowing the comments, which were probably fair and just, to wash over me, I gratefully accepted the proffered mug of coffee and rounds of buttered toast, as Chloe took the piss a little bit more.

"You and that cardboard cut-out last night mother! Honestly, you're an embarrassment when you've been on the ale! Thank god it was just family and friends here – I hope no one recorded you and stuck it on You Tube or else I'll actually die of shame!"

"Alright, alright Miss Goody Two Shoes! –I was just enjoying myself, and if you can't do that on Christmas Day then when can you do it?"

"She's right love. Leave your poor mother alone – it's about time she popped her gladrags on, let her hair down and put everything else behind her."

Good old mum, jumping to my defence.

"You'll like this one though love…"

Oh, what now mum? I was barely awake and struggling to even formulate sentences at that point in the proceedings.

"Guess who rang this morning on your mobile? Go on, guess."

Let it be David, despite everything, please let it be David.

"Only that good-for-nothing ex-husband of yours, finally wishing Chloe a belated "Merry Christmas" and promising faithfully that her present is on its way - when we all know he'll just put £20 in a card sometime in mid-January!"

"Tosser."

"Chloe!"

"Well, he is! I know he's my dad but god above mum, where on earth did you find him?"

"In the pile of men that no other sane women would want. What can I say, my defences were low."

"Anyway love," mum attempted to continue. "He wants to speak to *you* this time. He's ringing you back in quarter of an hour, at ten o'clock, or so he says."

"Oh God, what on earth for? This, I can do without. And why am I out of bed before ten o'clock on Boxing Day? I must have received a blow to the head last night or maybe I've just taken leave of my senses."

I dragged myself into the shower for a quick freshen up, in an attempt to recover my wits, which I would need about me with Richard on the phone, no doubt requesting money, or a favour, or a limb – none of which he could have. He was always late so I didn't rush to get myself dressed and ready, and my mobile eventually buzzed almost knocking on ten-thirty.

"Ola! Merry Christmas Louise!"

"Yes. What do you want Richard?"

"Well that's a fine way to greet me when I'm ringing all the way from Spain and I just wanted to see how the festivities were going at your end, you know, now that you're *single* again."

He made "single" sound like a dirty word and I could already feel my hackles rising.

"Oh…god…look, we've had a wonderful Christmas Rick (he hated it when I called him that because he knew we always followed it with "…the Dick") thus far, as no doubt you have, in the sunshine, with your latest slip of a girl – a Spanish one now isn't it? I've had a great time, Chloe's had a great time – because she's stopped expecting anything in the form of a gift from you and accepted that everything comes out of my purse…and right now, if we've finished exchanging pleasantries, I really do have to go as my head is banging like a drum and I've got a billion things I need to do before…"

"…well, there was one small favour I needed to ask love…"

Oh, here we go again. I knew it. Always on the scrounge for something.

"…you see, Luciana and I have parted ways…she was just too…*Spanish*…but because we were living in her father's basement, I am in effect now homeless…but the good news is I've had an offer of a job in the UK, in your neck of the woods as it happens, for the rest of the winter months, and I need to take advantage of the health service over there anyway for some bits and pieces so…I was wondering if I could just bunk up with you for a few months while you've got plenty of space now…well it's sort of my house anyway isn't it?"

I blinked, rapidly, about twenty times in succession, in disbelief. Was this man for real?

After everything he had done – screwing around, abandoning me and Chloe, stealing most of my furniture and belongings, emptying our joint bank account, mostly ignoring our beautiful daughter - which had led initially to her indifference to him followed by barely disguised disgust...and he still thought I was such a desperate, soft touch that I would open up my house to him again, and let him live here rent-free for the foreseeable future. Because there would be no money forthcoming, of that I was sure. And it was now MY house, not his. The paltry sum he had invested in it had long since been paid over to him and I'd almost thrown a party when his name came off the deeds. Just how much of a mug did he think I was?

I cleared my throat, took a deep breath and braced myself to deliver the only acceptable reply in the circumstances.

"PISSSS OFFFF!!!" I screamed down the phone, before pressing the red button to disconnect him and then switching the mobile off completely.

My mother and daughter stared at me, wide-eyed and shocked, before erupting into peals of laughter, and I soon joined them as I realised the ridiculousness of the situation. I filled them in on the whole conversation and we laughed some more at Richard's extraordinary thick skin and his inability to comprehend that he had actually done anything wrong , as I declared "that bloody phone" was staying off now for the duration of Christmas, as I did NOT want to be speaking to that pillock again, under any circumstances.

Mum packed up her car with all of the gifts she had received, remnants of a cheesecake and a gateaux, and unopened boxes of Christmas crackers and I promised to follow her over in the next hour once I'd cleared up my own house, which closely resembled a bomb site, despite mum's efforts with the dishes and the duster earlier while I was still in bed. One mention of cleaning had Chloe running for the door, shouting that she was just off to Josh's for an hour or two before the celebrations re-commenced at her nan's.

I was just sweating out a litre or two of cheap vodka by vacuuming the downstairs carpets with my temperamental Henry Hoover when there was a loud knock at the door. Reluctant to answer it in my slightly delicate state, a worrying thought occurred to me – this had better not be Rick the Dick, already here and waiting with his knock-off Gucci suitcases, possibly having phoned me earlier from a motorway service station en route, rather than an apartment in Spain. I wouldn't put it past him...and I would wring his bloody neck if it was.

Or carol singers. Carol singers should only be released into the community at night time, when everyone was wined-up and therefore feeling more generous and Christmassy.

With trepidation I unlocked and opened the front door, and there, like a vision from my ghastliest nightmare, in the pouring rain stood the ex-wife from hell, Suzanne.

"Good Morning, Louise."

I was speechless; I was actually speechless. Where the hell was Kirsty when you needed her and her self-taught self-defence skills. She'd left the party relatively early last night, assuring me she would be round first thing in the morning but still hadn't appeared. God damn her and her inability to arrive anywhere on time.

"I expect you're wondering what I'm doing here?" Suzanne's cut-glass voice sliced right through me and I wanted to grab her by the throat and squish her windpipe.

"Funnily enough, it had crossed my mind. What the hell do *you* want? Not content with stealing my man, have you come to steal Christmas as well now, like the frigging Grinch?"

"Good one; very amusing. I suppose I had it coming. Look...I realise that I'm probably the last person on God's earth that you wish to see right now, but I do need to talk to you...so can I come in for a moment?"

"Nope. You can stand out there in the pisspours of rain and get soaked. You. Are. Not. Coming. In. This. House."

"Fabulous. And very mature, might I add. So we have to air all of our dirty laundry on your doorstep, with the neighbours practically hanging out of the windows, desperately trying to catch the gist of the conversation?"

"Well they won't get to hear much, will they? Because I have ball-all to say to you, so you can jump back in your brand new four-by-four and PISS OFF back to your massive posh house and eat your caviar and drink your champagne or whatever it is you do in there!" I gave her a quick shove which took her by surprise, and she staggered backwards, having lost her footing on the step.

She didn't attempt to hop back up again, which left a larger gap between us, but was still too close for comfort in my opinion.

Unfortunately, losing her balance didn't make her shut her mouth.

"Just for the record – as you seem to believe I am some kind of spoiled millionairess who's never had to work for anything and never wanted for anything – I'm sorry to disappoint you but I only drink champagne on special occasions and I have never, ever in my life, consumed caviar. And I'm sorry if my lovely house and car offend you but..."

"I'LL TELL YOU WHAT BLOODY OFFENDS ME! The woman who ruined everything, who took back the love of my life, having the cheek to stand outside *my* house and expect me to listen to what crap *she* has to say! That's what bleedin' offends me! Now LEAVE before my next push knocks you off your feet! Did you hear me? Do one NOW before I..."

"HE LOVES *YOU* LOUISE. NOT ME. IT WAS NEVER ME. HE LOVED YOU *BEFORE*, HE LOVED YOU *DURING* OUR MARRIAGE AND HE LOVES YOU *NOW*! LISTEN TO ME!"

Wow, that woman had a set of lungs on her when she wanted to get her point across. It was impossible not to listen to her when she was shouting her mouth off at full volume. All the young kids in the street hopped off their scooters and turned around to see what the commotion was about.

She was crying now, this stupid, silly excuse for a woman. Her eyes were red but her tears just looked like raindrops, plopping down her perfect face and making a mess of her perfect make-up.

She lowered her voice now, still sobbing, but clearly determined to spit out what she had come all this way to deliver.

"I always knew there was someone in his past, somebody he had loved with all of his heart before me. When I found out about you, I decided I would do everything in my power to make him forget you...and for a while, he was mine...and then the heartbreak – the fertility problems and the breakdown in relations. And in the end we could never really paper over the cracks. Dave supported me for so long when I was in the worst kind of place because he *is* a good man, through and through."

"I knew that. I know that. But he was too good to be true in the end – galloping back to you when he should have seen through your bullshit and stayed well away. Can I ask you something Suzanne? - Why let him go only to haul him back in at the first opportunity that presented itself? To offer him a glimpse of what true happiness really was and then snatch it all away from him in the cruellest of ways. Why do that?"

"Because, like you, I loved him, and life was nothing without him. That's why I genuinely considered swallowing a load of pills at one point – I wanted to fall sleep and never wake up

– but Dave saved me, he was there for me when I needed him most. This time around, I saw an opportunity to make him stay and I went for it. I am *not* a bad person, despite what you think. But I did do a bad thing – preying on his fears and blackmailing him into staying with me, even though I knew it was destroying him. Knowing it would wreck your relationship but reserving that glimmer of hope that he might just eventually get over you and decide there were worse things than being married to me. But, stupid me, I misjudged him and his all-consuming, everlasting love for you. Because you remained everything to him. His love for you could not be diminished; not in the slightest, no matter how hard I tried to blow out that flame."

My blood was boiling, just listening to her high-pitched voice and smelling her sickly, cloying perfume – I wanted to hurt her in the worst possible way.

"He came here, you know…not so long ago…asking to try again; wanting to pick up where he had left off. But I sent him away with his tail between his legs…and it was the hardest thing I've ever had to do. You would think I would be used to it by now - getting over him; moving on. But no, it's as painful now as when we first split up in 1984 - when we were just kids with dreams of a future together that was ultimately blown apart."

"So why not give him another chance now then? It wasn't his fault; the wrongdoing was all on my part. He is still the beautiful, decent, faithful man that he always was. And, most importantly, you clearly still love one another."

"Because it's not that fucking simple is it? And why the fuck do you care? You've used every trick in the book to keep us apart and now I'm supposed to believe that you want us to get back together; that you're trying to reunite us out of the goodness of your heart! What the hell is going on in that mashed-up mind of yours?"

"Look, I'll level with you. I really couldn't care less about you and your feelings. If you hadn't come back into Dave's life when you did, we may well have stayed together. But I *do* care about Dave. I care that he's a mess now, trying and failing to get over you. I worry that I've brought about this situation that has caused him so much pain, and I do want to make amends and make it better for him. I can't change what I've done in the past, but I can change the future for him…"

"So, you're being a real good sort and giving him back to me now are you, since you've finished with him? Well, thank you very much for that *delightful* gesture, but you can stick it! What it boils down to is that he had to choose between the two of us that night...and he chose you. So that's it. It's over. No going back."

"Oh for goodness sake, stop being so pig-headed will you! I'm not *giving him back* to you...for a start, he's not mine to give! I wish he was! He's yours and he always has been, for some strange, inexplicable reason. Because lord only knows what he sees in you. I'm just here to try and repair the damage...to beg you to forgive him, for something that really wasn't his fault, and ask you to contact him and get your relationship back on track. Please don't let him go. If I was in your shoes, I would never let him go."

"Yes, well you're not, are you, and I'm not a crazy psychopath like you."

"Call me all the names you like; I really don't care. I did something terribly wrong purely because I loved the man so much and didn't think I could survive without him. But I can, I know that now. Because I will have to; there's no alternative. I have no right to hold on to him; to prevent him from being happy. So...here I am...not celebrating Boxing Day like a normal person - eating and drinking excessively in the company of my nearest and dearest like everyone else. No, I'm here instead - the last place I would ever want to be; opening up my heart and apologising to my husband's mistress. Let me tell you, travelling up here today, coming face to face with the woman who has all of the heart of my husband - the woman who didn't even leave a little bit of that heart for me - well, it's nearly killed me. Just looking at you, breathing the same air as you...it's ripping me apart inside."

"Ditto. Now let me tell YOU something. *I hate you* - with a passion. Knowing that David married you, loved you, shared a bed and a life with you...I just can't bear to imagine the two of you together...and that's all I've done over the last couple of months thanks to you, your lies and your deception. So, if you know what's good for you, you will leave here now and never, ever contact me again - ever."

"Trust me, I'm going in a minute because I've done my bit and my conscience is clear now. You can lead a horse to water but..."

"...and just supposing I contacted David...and we gave it another go...how do I know that you wouldn't pull another stunt in couple of months time, or maybe even in a couple of years time? How do I know that he won't try to be the hero of the hour again and abandon little old me to sort out your bloody shitty life again?"

"Because I give you my word that's never going to happen again. I know, I know, my word probably means "ball-all" to you - but prior to all of this, I have always been straight down the line with David. I may have been a mess and not even known what day it was sometimes but I've never purposely done anything to hurt him; never lied to him or tried to manipulate a situation before. This...these last few months...have been totally out of character for me, and it was only when I completely misread a situation and made an absolute fool of myself that I realised what a selfish cow I'd been, and I'm so ashamed."

"And so you should be. Yes, I heard you threw yourself at him and he had to practically climb out of the bedroom window to escape your clutches!"

"Well, I wouldn't go that far but I did completely get hold of the wrong end of the stick. You see, I wanted him back so badly - but when I saw the look of horror on his face when I tried to kiss him, that's when I knew it was well and truly over – that anything we'd ever shared had been dead and buried a long time. And shortly afterwards I had an indepth heart-to-heart with a wonderful old friend and he really made me see clearly again, for the first time in years. I realised then that I had to make massive changes and actually *want* to move on – the first step being to speak to you, to try to make you see how much Dave still loves you - how he is slowly dying without you."

Respect to her - as much as I despised her. At the end of the day, she was stood there, in the pouring rain, soaked through to her underwear, on Boxing Day, trying to persuade "the other woman" to take back the husband she herself loved more than anything in the world.

I still couldn't force myself to be nice to her though.

"Yes, I've seen the state of him. What the hell did you to do him anyway? He looks like he's wasting away, he's lost so much weight, and he's aged about ten years since he left me. Christ, he looks so pale now - it's like you're sucking the life out of him."

"He barely eats Louise, and he has no social life whatsoever – although that is my fault I'm afraid as I wanted him to stay home with me all of the time and I think he felt guilty for even setting foot out of the door. The only place he really goes to is the shop, and he works all the hours god sends, and I don't think he sleeps well at all – we did, of course, have separate bedrooms before and after he came back, but I could hear him moving about sometimes in the night so I knew he was awake more than was good for him. He's staying in a hotel now as far as I'm aware...but he is deeply unhappy and I worry for his future. He's pining for you – and if anything he seems to be struggling more as each day passes by. He needs you."

Don't cry. Don't let the bitch see you cry.

"And if it's any consolation, I won't even be around anymore."

Oh Jesus, not another stash of pills somewhere. I wanted Baileys and Quality Street on Boxing Day...not a trip to A & E while my arch-nemesis gets her washboard stomach pumped out.

"No...I don't mean *that*...of course not. I have plans for the future now, real plans. I'm emigrating to Portugal and I can't wait to bask in the sunshine and build a new life for myself there."

"What? Is this a new line in bullshit you've thought up?"

"No, no bull. It's true. I have an aunt who has lived there for almost seven years. She is well-established there now, and her villa has a spare bedroom, which can be mine for as long as I need it. And most importantly, I also have a job lined up, singing in a luxury hotel in Albufeira, so I can pay my way doing something that I love."

Well it would have to be a *luxury* hotel she'd be working in – no kids club, all-you-can-eat-buffet, bog standard place for her.

"I've contacted my solicitor and basically left instructions for Dave to deal with the sale of the house. The secretary will just forward the necessary documentation to me for signature when it's time. I've also popped a letter through the estate agents' door – they're closed for the Christmas break – confirming the sale is back on. I really don't think Dave will have any problem disposing of the house – prospective purchasers were quite literally queuing up at the front door the last time it was on the market."

"And what about the business and everything else? You don't expect me to believe all of this, do you?"

"Believe what you like...but you'll soon find out it's the truth. My brother Michael recently mentioned that his father-in-law had expressed interest in becoming a silent partner in the business, to help out, seeing as it's his daughter who's got her family into such a financial mess. That might be one avenue to explore. There's no rush for the money in any event.

Once Dave is back on his feet he can sort the ancillary stuff out. I've enough to be going on with."

"Do you know what, I don't care if you do bugger off to Portugal – it doesn't change anything. And quite frankly I'm sick of having to listen to you whine on. I have to go now - it's Christmas, and *I* have a life to get on with. One last thing though. He's not Dave. His name is *DAVID*."

I could see that wounded her, which childishly gave me great satisfaction.

"Yes, I get it, he was always your David. Never my Dave. I'm glad you felt the need to point that out. But, speaking of one last thing...I have something in the car for you."

Oh god, please don't let it be loaded.

Partly because I couldn't think straight, and partly out of curiosity, I waited at the door while she disappeared to her car; it was difficult to see just what she was retrieving, with the driving rain relentlessly coming down, not letting up for even a second.

Next thing I knew, three overflowing binbags were hurled onto the front lawn and, as I looked up at her in shock, I saw a wry smile creep over her face – beautiful when even tear-streaked and missing half of her make-up.

"There you go...I'm returning Dave's belongings – the ones your foulmouthed friend dropped all up and down my road in some ridiculous attempt to humiliate us. He does of course have more clothes and bits and pieces at the house but I'm guessing this is the gear he's been wearing lately and therefore is probably most in need of, and it should always have stayed here, at yours. I would pick it all up sooner rather than later, if I was you, before everything gets soaked and ruined in the rain. And ring him - ring him soon - because you'll always regret it if you don't."

Gobsmacked, I stared down at the assortment of clothes spilling out of the bags and didn't look up even as I heard her car door slam and the engine start-up. It would be a long drive back to Cornwall for her, especially in cold, wet clothes, but it was no more than she deserved.

Resisting the temptation to kick the bags out into the street or load them straight into the bins, I reluctantly dragged them into the hallway and slammed the front door shut. I saw my favourite black shirt of David's on the top of one of the bags and couldn't stop myself from bending down to stroke the fabric of it, choked up with emotion inside. I could picture him wearing it and me slowly undoing each button as...

"She's right you know."

"Bloody hell Chloe, where did you pop up from this time? You have to stop doing that, especially if you want me to live to see fifty. I thought you'd gone over to Josh's house, to eat all his After Eight Mints?"

"I did. I'm back. I shouted to you when I came in but you had the hoover on."

"God above, my heart's pounding love. I think you're trying to finish me off."

"Your heart's *broken* mum, and you know how to fix it. You know what you have to do. That woman is out of the picture now. You heard what she said. Not that she's ever really been *in* the picture, it would seem."

"I can't Chloe, you don't understand. I've come too far without him now. I can't do it again. I can't invest all my emotions in this man who's hurt me so much, time and time again."

"He was a prick mum – and don't you dare try and reprimand me for using bad language after the stuff I've just heard spill out of your mouth! But he knows that, and, bless him, he's tried to contact you, tried to apologise, tried to show you how much he loves you. But you...you ran away at the first sign of a problem. You didn't fight to keep him. You just crawled back into your shell, feeling sorry for yourself...and you'd rather wallow in your own misery than admit you feel exactly the same way and take him back. You're your own worst enemy!"

Crushing the urge to yell at Chloe for downright cheek, I bit my tongue because deep down I knew she was right. But I was just so terrified of him hurting me again; I didn't know how to trust him again and if I could ever get over that.

"I'm sorry mum, but you need to have a word with yourself and at least talk to David, properly, and try to make things right. Because you'll never be happy without him – your first love. You know it, I know it and everyone else knows it, apart from maybe David who probably thinks you hate him now."

She gave me a big hug then and it was exactly what I needed at that moment in time.

"Please just think about it mum. Don't be so stubborn."

Ha! There was no one more stubborn than Chloe – but I guess she was a chip off the old block.

"Okay, I'll think about it."

"Good. And well done on giving that woman holy hell – you were terrifying! Oh and before I forget, me and Josh have split up, for good this time."

"On Boxing Day? Have you no heart Chloe? Especially when he bought you that lovely bracelet out of his pocket money!"

"Er, I'll have you know, it wasn't just down to me this time – and I bought him that overpriced aftershave, if you recall. So we're fair and square on the present front. No…it was a mutual decision. We're too young to settle down and…to be honest…I've had my wandering eye on someone else. But I don't feel so guilty now, because Josh has just admitted that he's been on a couple of dates behind my back, with a girl from Year 10 who's fancied him for ages. It was nice while it lasted but, there you go, such is life. So he won't be joining us at nan's later."

And back out she trotted then, off to her friend Lilly's, to no doubt fill her in all the juicy gossip. Her break-up didn't seem to have affected her very much anyway as she seemed perfectly happy and was almost skipping out of the front door.

Oh to be young again, when you could just move on from a broken relationship so swiftly, without any lasting effects.

My life had never been like that though. I didn't have much of a relationship history from my youth…the only male of any significance had been David, and look how that had turned out.

Thirty years later and I still couldn't move on!

Acutely aware that slumping on the stairs was not getting the hovering finished, but still shocked to the core by the unexpected visit from Princess Posh, I heard another vehicle pull up on to my drive and through the frosted glass in the front door I could just about make out the outline of another caller.

Christ, why wouldn't people leave me alone on Boxing Day of all days?

Oh, panic over. It was okay – I recognised the knock. It was Kirsty – better late than never.

Wearily opening the door, I stepped back to let her in as she burst into a tuneless chorus of a Shakin' Stevens Christmas classic and I wondered whether I should point out that she had chocolate smudged all around her mouth and down her new top – she had clearly guzzled half a tin of Celebrations for breakfast.

"Bloody hell, who's been haunting you? You look like something out of a horror movie! That'll teach you to knock back the spirits from mid-morning on Christmas Day."

"Who's been haunting me? I'll tell you who's been haunting me K…only the bloody wife…that's who's been haunting me!"

"What? Are you still pissed? What are you going on about?"

"Suzanne. *Sue*. Princess Posh. She only bloody turned up here!"

"Shut the front door! Are you kidding? You're not are you – you're deadly serious! *She* turned up *here*. And she didn't firebomb the house or produce a rusty machete from somewhere or…wait a cotton-picking minute…are *they* what I think they are?" Eyes wide, mouth open wider, she pointed to the telltale bags of David's clothes squished into my tiny hallway.

"Er…yes."

"Are they on a frigging elastic or something? Because last time I clapped eyes on them they were littering a posh road in deepest, darkest Cornwall."

"She brought them back!   Got her sodding revenge by dumping them all on my front lawn and then roaring off in her top-of-the-range 4 by 4. Bitch!"

"Ewww…they're wet…she's not, you know, extracted a bit more revenge has she…? I mean, you hear of these women urinating on…"

"For God's sake Kirsty, dial it down a bit! They're wet because they've been out in the rain, albeit briefly…when it was absolutely piddling down. And, to be fair, they actually smell of Persil now as they've clearly been washed since you unceremoniously dumped them in the road."

"Bloody hell. They're more well-travelled than I am those flamin' kecks and shirts!"

"And the undies…don't forget the boxers…"

"Aw…do you miss the body and bits that pack out those boxers Mrs?"

"Of course I do. And you can drag your mind back out of the gutter, because I don't just miss his nether regions…I miss all of the man - every last hair, bone, muscle and millimetre of skin. The same way you probably miss Nathan, I'm guessing?"

"Oh don't get me started. I'm trying to lie low, for obvious reasons, but I'm frightened to death that I'm going to hear on the grapevine soon that he's picked up with someone else…someone younger and prettier and not so desperate to drop a sprog."

"At least you'll have your little sprog to occupy you and keep you company as he or she grows into a lovely little cherub. My lovely little cherub, my Chloe, well she grew into this big independent cherub who needs me less and less each day. I'm more alone now than I've ever been in all my life…"

"Well this is a bloody cheery way to spend Boxing Day! Now turn that frown upside down and go and get yourself tarted up and we'll head straight off to your mother's, where you can eat yourself into a food coma. You can tell me all about your little visitor on the way…Christ, I wish I'd been here to give her another mouthful."

"Perhaps as well you weren't…I think I was scary enough on my own…"

And I *had* been scary, but I was kind of proud of myself for standing up to her. For so long now she'd been this monster in my head – beautiful on the outside but ugly on the inside. In reality she was just another woman with faults and flaws and she'd looked fragile and pretty lost stood out in the rain while I ranted at her and wished her dead.

She'd kept on at me to contact David; she'd told me how much he loved me and whilst I took everything *she* said with a pinch of salt, I *knew* he still loved me.

I knew.

The love was still there. It would always be there. But was it enough?

Chapter 38

SUZANNE

Well, I had done it...and I would earn my rewards in heaven.

The look on the woman's face when I had returned Dave's belongings...it was priceless.

She was pretty hardcore though – within five minutes of driving away from her nondescript little house I had found it necessary to pull up again in some dead-end street, as I was shaking like a leaf, and it wasn't just because of the wet clothes I was wearing, which were stuck to me like a second skin. Despite my relatively tough exterior I was still mainly broken inside and I'm sure that any counsellor would have told me that I wasn't yet strong enough to do what I'd just done.

But I'd been a good Samaritan – despite her appalling behaviour, I'd apologised, returned Dave's stuff and left the door open now for her to take the appropriate steps through it, to take back her man.

What she chose to do next, well that was anybody's guess, but if she had any sense at all she would make it right with Dave and hold on to his love. He was a once-in-a-lifetime catch and she was the luckiest woman alive because she had hooked him, not me.

I wasn't totally convinced that she deserved that man but he was hers for the taking, and I was no longer going to dwell on the fact that I should never have settled for less.

Right now, I was heading straight for Asda – not my usual store of choice for fashion but I desperately needed to buy a warmer set of clothes than the one I was currently wearing.

Next stop would be McDonalds, for a coffee to see me on my way. Hardly likely to be the freshly ground beans I was used to in my favourite coffee lounge back home, but needs must, and I was dipping my toe into the waters of the real world.

Dave was gone, but my life had to go on.

Chapter 39

LOUISE

After a rowdy Christmas, and an even rowdier New Year, which took me to the second week in January to recover, we all staggered into 2015, wondering what the hell this year would have in store for us; where we would all be in 365 days' time.

I was on a diet, Chloe was on a mission to snare some other lad she fancied who knocked about round the park and sounded decidedly dodgy (come back Josh, all is forgiven!), and Kirsty was either eating, crying, or raging at someone. To say pregnancy didn't agree with her some days was a bit of an understatement – but she had permanent indigestion and was obviously still off the booze, at a time when she was more desperate than ever to go out and get lathered, so we were all attempting to show her some compassion and understanding...whilst trying to stay under her radar.

January was a long, long month and I was bloody glad to see the back of it. Against the advice of almost everyone I knew, I had held back from contacting David...but I was still a lost soul without him...and the dreaded Valentine's Day was approaching fast.

I felt marginally more positive about life in general though – which may have been down to a telephone conversation that had taken place between Kirsty and Jenny – the latter having confirmed that David had definitely moved out of the mausoleum, had briefly stayed at a cheap and nasty budget hotel, but was now back under their crowded roof again (she was fattening him up and cheering him up apparently), and Suzanne had indeed flew out to live with relatives in Portugal, and by all accounts was thriving over there in the sunshine and was definitely not planning to return.

David and Billy were back to being partners in crime, and therefore David was apparently a hell of a lot happier and had even gone for a few beers with "the lads", and they had all raised a glass to his new found freedom, whilst telling him - nudge nudge, wink wink - that they didn't think it would be long before he would be scratching at my door again, begging for me to forgive him and take him back.

Hmmm.

The original buyers of David and Suzanne's house were back on board, despite Suzanne previously mucking them about so much, and apparently desperate to exchange contracts and complete their purchase, probably before she changed her mind again. All the property information forms had been completed previously and all searches were still in date, and therefore exchange of contracts was expected within the next month or so.

Michael's father-in-law had stumped up the cash for David's half share of the business, but David had agreed to stay on as a paid employee for the time being. Taking a step back from the business had meant that he had much more free time and, so Jenny said, he had been visiting the gym regularly and also walking the beautiful beaches of Newquay, filling his lungs with fresh air and blowing away all the cobwebs that had been so intricately spun across his previous life.

That nugget of information made my heart ache and left my body longing for him…a fitter, healthier David with colour in his face and fire in his heart…it was wrong of me but I hoped he wasn't beating off a host of attractive admirers. I didn't really think it would happen, but I couldn't bear the thought of him being with anyone else. Picturing him kicking up the sand on Towan Beach with his scruffy old trainers, gazing out over the Atlantic and pondering his future…my favourite man in the world in my favourite place in the world…that was crushing…knowing I wasn't there with him, by his side.

I couldn't even begin to get over him, but I couldn't bring myself to ring him either. What I did do, a day or two before Valentine's Day, was unblock his number on my phone.

Just in case, you know.

In the event, the evening of the 14th of February was spent devouring a family size pack of Maltesers and an indecent amount of crisps with Kirsty while we both lamented our lost loves and kicked off over the fact that, yet again, neither of us had received one single Valentine card. I didn't even get one from Chloe these days - gone were the days of the handmade paper efforts with the stuck-on foil hearts and penned squiggle that represented her name; those precious cards I had received when she was still a little pipsqueak who would sit on my knee and tell me how much she loved her mummy. No delivery of flowers to work for either of us. No serenading in the street. No visit from the Milk Tray Man.

Fucking men.

I was royally pissed off.

I had been clutching my mobile all evening, itching to fire off a text message to David, if only to ask "Where's my bloody card then, if you still love me so much? Gobshite."

But my pride prevented me from contacting him. Ah, what would be the point?

Eventually, when all hope was gone, I headed off to the reassuring comfort of my bed, where I still curled up on the right hand side, leaving David's side empty, and could feel myself twitching and nodding off as soon as my aching head hit the pillow.

Bleep-Bleep! Bleep-Bleep!

For God's sake, what the devil was that? I sat up quickly in bed, not really knowing what planet I was on, and wishing I hadn't eaten the rest of those crisps before bedtime, and sleepily reached out for my phone.

"*I miss you X*"

Jesus Mary and Joseph, it was a message from David! Woo hoo! I know I'd said there was no going back, I know I'd said I couldn't forgive him, but no words could describe the relief I felt when I saw those three simple words and that big kiss at the end.

I sat up sharp, dithering then over what would be an adequate response - there was so much I wanted to say but couldn't. I began to type a reply, deleted it, composed another one, deleted that...and in the end plumped for a similar text to the one I'd received from him.

"*I miss you too David x*"

He didn't reply to that, but somehow I knew he wouldn't. And you know what, it was okay. He had held out until five-to-midnight and then had given in to the urge to send *something*, even though he knew it would probably bounce back because he was still likely to be blocked on my phone.

Presumably, he'd been hanging on to see if I would contact him first, but then the last of his willpower had evaporated and he'd just wanted to let me know I was still the one he loved; still the one he wanted above all others. And by replying in the same vein, almost immediately, he'd know now that I had actually unblocked him from my phone and that my feelings had never really changed either. His love was circulating in my blood, and mine in his. This was never going to be over.

*

Since Valentine's Day I'd had no further contact from David and it was pissing me right off. I felt like my life was on hold – that I was in limbo, yet again. I know I'd insisted there was no going back the last time we had met, but after our "miss you" messages on 14th February I'd thought there was a glimmer of hope - but now there was radio silence and I hadn't heard a single word from him.

Kirsty hadn't spoken to Jenny at all in recent weeks, and I couldn't just ring her up myself or else she would know for certain that I was fishing for information about David, or - worse still - David might be there in the background, eavesdropping on every word that was said.

Maybe he just wanted to give me some time and space to think about everything again, but the trouble was, I'd done nothing BUT think, and now I was in the *overthinking* zone, imagining him giving in to some trollop's persistent advances and indulging in a spot of rumpy pumpy on his put-up bed at Billy's house amongst the deadly Lego and broken Peppa Pig toys.

I hoped to god that he hadn't got sick of waiting for me and thrown in the towel, despite everything I had previously said.

There was no use pretending - I'd finally had to admit to myself that I really, REALLY wanted him back, but I'd been careful not to admit it to anyone else. Because I actually wasn't sure if I could trust him again, and if this all went tits up then I didn't want to be the one looking like a goon again at the end of it.

When I wasn't at work or running around after Kirsty (I swear to god you would think she was having three babies, the size of her, and she was forever struggling to negotiate crowds with her humungous bump in front of her, swearing at innocent passers-by), I spent most of my time idly staring at my phone, willing it to ring. My pride just wouldn't let me be the one to call first.

It was only one week until Easter; the end of March was just around the corner, and I felt like I was going slowly round the twist. What I didn't need was a hot date with Kirsty to Mothercare yet again, but that was I was getting on this super-exciting Saturday, like it or not, as she'd finally cobbled together enough funds to purchase the last bits and pieces she needed.

As I waited impatiently by the desperately-in-need-of-a-clean front window, wondering if eleven a.m. was too early for wine time (it was bloody Saturday for god's sake!), having given up on trying to persuade Chloe to crawl out of her pit and into the shower, I sighed again, for the about the billionth time. Life was bloody hard. To think, all those decades ago I used to fret about whether my perm was too tight or whether you could see the fat on my bum through my pedal pushers! Oh to be a teenager again.

Still no signs of Kirsty, and I couldn't even complain about her tardiness at the moment as baby Noble pressing on her bladder meant that every time she was about to leave the house she had to turn back to use the loo, or risk springing a leak in public.

Poor Kirsty. She was trying so hard to put on a brave face but I knew underneath that bravado, that confident personality and booming voice, there was a frightened, lonely woman, silently screaming out for Nathan to be back in her life. The thought of bringing her baby home to her mum's was stressing her out to the max as well. We'd looked around at flats in the locality, but I swear to god, you wouldn't put your worst enemy in one of those flea-filled, overpriced hellholes. Well, maybe Suzanne. Maybe I'd stick her in there for a while with only Marmite to eat and non-alcoholic wine to drink. That would serve her bloody right, the hussy.

I still hadn't got over the flaming cheek of the woman turning up on my doorstep, telling me what to do, but I knew deep inside it was a good thing, as it had finally allowed me to see clearer and admit my true feelings, if only to myself. David. That's all I wanted. Even though I didn't know how I could begin to forgive him and move on, he would always be all I ever wanted.

His bin bags of stuff had now been shifted to a corner of my bedroom, but I had resisted the urge to pluck out an item of his clothing and take it to bed with me; to hold it close against my body and try to imagine he was in it. So far. I didn't want Chloe to think I was even odder than she already suspected.

Aah, at last, here comes a car tootling down the road, dodging the kids on their scooters. It had better be her or else I'm uncorking that last bottle of vino in the fridge and having a slurp.

Oh well, not her – it wasn't a car, it was a van. Probably next door having some major works done again – it was like bloody Changing Rooms in there every fortnight.

Except the van said "White's" on the side. And it was pulling up outside of my little house. It couldn't be…no…I'm pretty sure it wasn't…oh my freaking god it was. David! And me in my oldest jeans and faded t-shirt with my unwashed hair – well that would certainly show him what he'd been missing!

I didn't wait for him to knock but instead silently opened the front door, wide enough for him to come in, wordlessly accepting that after all this time he had made the epic journey to see me, for us to have a heart-to-heart and perhaps figure out if we could make things work for us again.

We came to a halt in the middle of the unhoovered lounge (pining for David had turned me into a domestic slut this last couple of months), staring at each other intensely, each waiting for the other to take the initiative; to make the first move. To be fair, after his mammoth journey up here, when he was probably still shattered from work yesterday, I thought it only right that I should say something.

"Hi David." Well, it was a start.

He leant forward to kiss me on the cheek and as I breathed in his aftershave and felt the light touch of his lips on my skin, it was all I could do not to move that kiss up a notch and stick my tongue down his throat. Maybe, if we really couldn't get past my insecurities and his guilt, perhaps we could be friends with benefits after all. Christ almighty, I wanted him right now.

He straightened up, rewarding me with a slightly shy smile and the words "I still miss you Lou."

Ah bugger it, in for a penny.

"And you know I miss you too, even though I could kill you for what you did."

A full-on sunbeam of a smile then. Aw god, I'd missed that smile

"Ah, there's the Louise I know and love."

"You still love me then?"

"Always have, always will. I don't know what the hell you did to me when we first met, but I've never been able to get over you - no matter how hard I've tried."

"It must have been my Exclamation! perfume that did it. Or the plastic bangles and the cut-off t-shirts I used to wear that I thought made me look really sexy!"

"*Everything* made you look really sexy. You have always oozed sexiness!"

"Eugh, I don't know whether I like that sentence or not, it makes me sound like I secrete some weird bodily fluid!"

He threw his head back in laughter, in that cute way he had always done. It was good to see him smile and laugh again. We had a lot to deal with; some deadly serious conversations to plough through, but for now, I was happy to see *him* happy.

"Hey, speaking of when I first met you…guess who I bumped into last week in the drycleaners? Only Trisha!"

"Who the hell is Trisha? Please tell me she's not some ex-girlfriend you're going to chuck into the mix now!"

"Don't be daft, you plonker! No – I'll give you a clue… "Davey-boy…you couldn't lend me a few quid to get some ciggies could you? Pleeease…Aw, thanks babe…you're a star!"

He'd adopted a West Country accent and shrugged his shoulders a couple of times as he was speaking and I knew instantly who he meant.

"No way! Trisha from 1984…who never had two pennies to rub together but somehow managed to blag her way into some fancy London job in finance…my god that's a blast from the past!"

"Isn't it? She literally walked in the cleaners, threw a load of gear onto the counter and barked that she would be back on Wednesday to collect everything…but I immediately recognised those dulcet tones and tapped her on the shoulder as she was about to dart out of the door. She didn't know who I was at first – it's probably the grey hair – but when I introduced myself she was all hugs and smiles and it was like she'd reverted to being that sixteen year old kid again!"

"Aw I'd love to see her again…I bet she looks completely different from the double denim girl with the backcombed hair!"

"Totally – she's so glamorous now and she's married to some guy who's loaded because he's got some fantastic job in London dealing with hedge funds or something similar that I have absolutely no knowledge about. And they have some mega-bucks apartment in the city!

She's only back in Newquay for the week, visiting her old folks while she's got a few days off."

"God, I can't imagine her with a husband and billions in the bank! I don't suppose you mentioned me at all..?"

"Er...actually I did, as it happens! She asked if I was still married and I explained briefly that I'd split with Suzanne...but that me and you had finally got back together. She was so shocked! She said it felt like time had stood still in Newquay and almost made her want to dust off those old denims and party on the beach again to all those classic 80s dance tunes. I didn't want to go into the finer details about our relationship though Lou – the fewer people know what a dickhead I've been, the better. I just said that you're still as wonderful now as you were back then and we both agreed that you and I were destined to end up together."

Oh. Right. Straight in there with the serious stuff then. Better steel myself for an emotional conversation.

"Listen David, I..."

Bang bang bang! Oh god, that must be Kirsty – except it didn't sound like her knock, and the door wasn't locked so she would normally just walk right in without hesitation.

Oh crap! David, who I gather still speaks to Nathan on a regular basis, doesn't know that Kirsty is with child! Oh my giddy aunt! What to do? It wasn't *my* secret to tell. But as soon as he clapped eyes on her it definitely wouldn't be a secret anymore - there was no disguising *that* baby belly!

Hopefully it wouldn't be Kirsty and I would be able to shoo away any unwanted caller whilst grabbing my mobile off the hall table and texting Kirsty to warn her to stay away for the time being. I don't know how she thought this was going to remain a secret – if my unscheduled meeting with David today went well then he would have to be told very soon.

"Sorry David. That will probably be Kirsty, arriving for our shopping trip, not realising it's already unlocked..." I was just about to say "because she has a severe case of baby brain" before I managed to stop myself just in the nick of time.

"Oh no, I think it's Nathan...he was in the van on his work's mobile taking a call when I pulled up so I told him just to knock on when he was done."

JESUS H CHRIST! Please god, no! Please don't let Nathan be here, at my house, when heavily pregnant Kirsty is due to roll up any minute. Oh my good god!

Before I could invent an excuse as to why Nathan could not come into the house on this occasion, David had already let him in.

"Alright Louise. I hope you don't mind me gatecrashing like this. Only I've kept trying to contact Kirsty and she seems to have gone to ground. When I spoke to David last night he told me he was coming to see you today so I asked him to pick me up as a favour en route. I know if I'm struggling to find Kirsty she will either be here already or will turn up later! We've just called at her mum's but I don't think there's anyone home; I knocked and knocked on the door but there was no answer.

NO, because her mother's gone on a day-trip to Bury markets with a load of other pensioners and Kirsty is probably on her way over here RIGHT NOW. Dear god, I was sweating. How did Kirsty always manage to get me into such a colossal mess? What the hell was I supposed to do now?

Nathan must have clocked the look of abject horror on my face but interpreted it as probable disappointment that my longed for liaison with David was being hijacked like this.

"Oh, jeez...sorry, I know you two need some alone time and I'm hanging around like a spare one at a wedding. I tell you what, I'll just nip up and use your bathroom if that's okay and then I'll go and wait in your kitchen for her - make myself a brew and read my newspaper. I know she'll turn up here at some point!"

My mobile. I needed to grab my mobile and discreetly text Kirsty. I would kill her later.

Nathan opened the hall door, which meant I could now hear the said mobile vibrating noisily on the small table in the hallway; I must have switched off the ringer last night and forgot to turn it back on.

It all happened so fast then. As it vibrated, it lit up and Nathan picked it up to hand it to me, only to see the name 'THIRSTY KIRSTY' large and clear on the screen in front of him, identifying the caller.

"See, there you go, I must be psychic. I won't answer it, don't worry – she still might not want to talk to me after all of this time anyway! Here you go, make sure you tell her I need to see her though."

My heart was pounding through the walls of my chest as I swiped my finger over the screen to answer the call. Before I even had chance to form any words whatsoever I was almost deafened.

"AAAAGGGHHHH! Lou, is that you? Where the fuck have you been? I've been trying to ring you for Christ's sake and you're not picking up…and your bastard house phone is still disconnected. I'm dying Lou, I'm bloody *dying*. Get your arse over here quick before I give birth on the sodding kitchen floor!"

"Kirsty! Ssshhh. Listen…I'm really not in a position to speak right now because…"

"AAAAAGGGHHHHH! I'm warning you Louise Alicia Stewart, you had better get down here quick…this baby is coming RIGHT NOW….I'm telling you…I'm about to give birth and I don't want to be by myself Lou!"

"No, get away with you…don't be daft…you can't be….you're only thirty-five and a half weeks and…."

"GET OVER HERE *NOW* LOUISE!! You're supposed to be my birthing partner…and these pains are coming thick and fast….I need you, you muppet…AAAGGGHHHHH…."

"Oh, sweet Jesus…you're not kidding are you…shit a brick! Okay, okay, I'm coming babe…I'm on my way…just hold on for god's sake until I get there and we'll get you straight to the hospital…"

"HURRY THE FUCK UP THEN….I need gas and air, I need gas and air!"

Assuring her I would be right over, but begging her to ring 999 anyway (she wouldn't), I ended the call, and realised that both Nathan and David were now stood side by side, absolutely still, gawping at me, open-mouthed, and that Nathan was as white as a sheet that had been bleached to within an inch of its life.

I don't suppose there was the slightest, remote chance that he had missed any, or at least some, of that conversation…and perhaps was ignorant to the facts of the matter…

"Kirsty? Pregnant? Thirty-five and a half weeks?"

Shit. Maybe not then. And I could see he was now quickly doing the arithmetics in his head.

"She's having my baby. Kirsty's having my child. I'm having a baby; another son or daughter. And no one told me; I've been completely in the dark. I never knew."

"Nathan…I…"

"She hid it from me all of this time. This mammoth secret. A baby. My baby. She most likely planned it, even though she knew how I felt about becoming a father again. She did it anyway; she got pregnant on purpose. I suppose that's why she came on to me at the singles night…"

I saw blood red then…no way was the cheeky-mouthed fucker getting away with that.

"Listen here, you emotionally retarded, self-absorbed, selfish swine! She did NOT plan it. She was already in the early stages of pregnancy, by accident as it happens, when she broached the subject of babies again to you and YOU, you TWAT, couldn't even consider her maternal feelings for one minute…YOU, arsehole, responded by deciding that you would break up with her! Even though you were supposed to be head over heels in love with her. Even thought it broke her heart, you walked away from Kirsty, pretending you were doing it for her sake…when all the while you were just being a selfish pig!"

I was on a roll then.

"And another thing! *She* did not come on to *you* at the singles night…and *she* was already up the duff by then, like I said…but she loved you so much she just wanted one last night with you before you had to say your goodbyes. And *you* do the maths, dickhead! If she's thirty-five weeks now then she was clearly expecting when you had your little reunion. And don't you bloody dare try and blame Kirsty for getting pregnant…it takes more than one person to make a baby you know…and you were more than willing to take another roll in the hay with Kirsty!"

"…but…but she surely would have told me if she was pregnant then…"

"She was too bloody scared of what *your* reaction would be! She couldn't even tell the man she loved that she was having his baby because she knew he would run a record-breaking mile…you were so frigging adamant you weren't having any more children that she decided she could never, ever in a million years tell you that she was pregnant!"

"But I was completely honest with her Lou! She *knew* where I stood on the matter and yet, strangely enough, she managed to get herself pregnant *by accident*…"

"You total and utter fucking bastard! Don't you dare imply that she did this on purpose…that she would have chosen to go through all of this alone…I swear to god you will eat your words when…."

"LOUISE! NATHAN! I think there's a screaming pregnant lady, who isn't getting any happier, waiting for her best friend to arrive to rush her to the maternity wing, so, as lovely as this is, can we please continue this shouting match another time?"

It was a good job that David intervened before it got any more heated and I clobbered Nathan with the nearest available object, which happened to be a particularly heavy (and ugly) wooden ornament mum had bought me as a souvenir from a trip a few years back, and before I forgot that I was actually supposed to be on my way to collect Kirsty.

"Shit! It's all happened so early that I'm not prepared! I have no bloody petrol in the car," I wailed. "That's why Kirsty was taking us on this shopping expedition today - I was going to fill up later in the week, just in case she popped the little one out earlier than planned!"

"Jesus Lou, do you ever have petrol in that car? Right. Only one thing for it; we'll all climb in my van…"

"I am NOT getting in the van with that knobhead!" No way, I'd walk first.

"GET IN THE FUCKING VAN LOUISE!" They both shouted in unison, as I realised it would probably take me about two days to walk to the infirmary, even if I broke into a jog.

Muttering abuse at Nathan, I jumped in the van, up front, next to David. In other circumstances, I might have been tempted to squeeze his thigh, but instead I forced myself to concentrate on supplying him with directions as to the shortest route to Kirsty's mum's little semi-detached house. It probably only took us five minutes to get there but it seemed like an age to me, and when we arrived Kirsty was already waiting impatiently in the open doorway, her hastily packed bag-of-sorts at her swollen feet. She doubled over in agony as I jumped down, almost breaking my ankle (it's a long way when you're as short as I am), and raced up the garden path, and her screams were lengthy and ear-piercing. I'm sure the neighbours must have thought she was being battered to death with a blunt instrument.

"Where the hell have you been?" She was sobbing now. I could see the veil of fear covering her face as I grabbed the leather hospital bag and she pulled the front door closed behind her. It was at that precise moment that she noticed our mode of transport, and the two men running towards her to help.

"Louise, that's David's van. He's here...oh you've made it up...that's brilliant...and...and...what the feck is *he* doing here? Did you tell him? Did you? How *could* you have, after everything I've said?"

David swiftly took the bag from me and slung it into the back of his relatively clean van as he returned to give me a hand with Kirsty.

Nathan just stood there, shell-shocked – as you would be, I suppose, in those circumstances – when one minute you were a father-of-one, and the next you were about to become a father-of-two.

"I did NOT tell him K! He turned up earlier with David out of the blue, searching for you actually, and your bloody screaming down the phone at me alerted him to the fact that you might happen to be just a tidily bit pregnant, you idiot!"

Kirsty glared at me then before breaking into heart-rendering, heaving, sobs and, thank the lord, Nathan came out of his trance-like state, and rushed towards her to enfold her in his capable arms, and she actually let him. Another wicked contraction chose that exact moment to rip through Kirsty's lower body, but Nathan held on to her, whispering words of comfort and rubbing her back, as she screamed the whole street down.

It was decided that Nathan and Kirsty would travel in the back of the van, after we'd bunched up our coats to improvise as a form of pillow, and Nathan lay quietly by her side, in what looked like a horrendously uncomfortable position - although it was nothing he didn't deserve - holding her hand and talking to her softly. I was hoping he'd come up trumps after all; at least he was with her when it really mattered.

We drove to the hospital at break-neck speed (I was ready to yell "SHE'S HAVING A BABY!" to any passing officers who dared to challenge us), having called ahead to warn them there was a crazy lady about to explode on her way in.

The sense of relief was immense when we finally arrived and I was able to hand over a wailing Kirsty to a nurse with a wheelchair who rushed her off to the maternity suite, Nathan running alongside. My birthing partner duties had been forgotten in the chaos but I was happy to be tossed aside and for Nathan to man-up and take over the role. God help the midwife. No amount of me saying "Remember your breathing K," had made any difference…she had just carried on screaming and yelling abuse at everyone in the vicinity.

Having finally slotted the van into a dubious parking spot and paid a small fortune for the privilege, David went to purchase two coffees and then joined me in the waiting area, depositing the scalding hot drinks of dubious colour onto the floor and pulling me into his familiar arms as I promptly burst into tears and soaked his navy blue polo-shirt. It had been quite a morning, and to be frank I wish that I'd brought the wine supply with me, although I suppose it might be frowned upon - actually necking it inside of the hospital building. The shock of coming face to face with David again, the even bigger shock of Nathan joining us, the resulting tension when Nathan discovered the scarily big secret and now the imminent birth of Baby Noble…I was overcome with emotion.

When I had ceased crying into his chest (I almost wanted to squeeze a few more tears out to remain in his arms), David gently released me but stayed close - very close.

"How on earth did Kirsty think she would get away with it? I mean, keeping a secret is one thing, keeping a child from their father is another!"

"Hey! She wanted Nathan to be a father but he had made it very plain that wasn't on his agenda…that he wasn't prepared to alter his lifestyle in any way, shape or form to accommodate a squawking baby…so don't you dare blame Kirsty! She wanted a baby, sure, but only as the result of a happy, healthy, loving relationship, not like this…but it happened…and she felt that doing it alone was the best for everyone involved."

"Sorry…I shouldn't be so judgemental. I love Kirsty, and I suppose she was just doing the best she could in the circumstances. God it's complicated isn't it?"

I let him off the hook.

"Yes, it is. And I *did* try to persuade Kirsty that she had to tell Nathan – we all did - but she was adamant. She swore us all to secrecy, but we hoped at some point she would change her stubborn mind and inform Nathan that he was going to be a daddy again. Christ, I thought she had another five weeks to go yet – I don't even know if she has everything she needs in that bag or even at her mum's."

"Don't worry; it will be fine. Some girls apparently come into hospital and have babies, yet they have nothing. But those babies are still fed, clothed and looked after. If she's missing anything here I'm sure the nurses will sort it out - and there's time yet to pick up any stuff she might need for when they get discharged."

He was so practical, so comforting, so reassuring…I was so thankful he was there with me and I wasn't hanging out, waiting anxiously for news, all on my own.

After several cups of coffee, numerous mini-packs of chocolate chip biscuits, and a frantic search for the toilets, I slouched down into my chair to close my eyes for a while, luxuriating in the feeling of David's fingers stroking through my hair and occasionally drifting down to massage my aching neck. I must have nodded off eventually because I felt a sudden nudge in my ribs and awoke with a start to see a female nursing staff member stood in front of us, the bearer of good news.

"Your friend had a beautiful little girl at four-fifty-seven – eight pound one ounce. Mother and baby doing exceedingly well. Father an emotional wreck. I can let you glance in on them for a few minutes if you like…"

Yes, I would like!

When I entered that room I was met with a sight that I had never in my wildest dreams imagined possible – Kirsty holding a tiny newborn baby, her baby, to her ample chest, weeping inconsolably, but with sheer joy rather than the misery of the last few months when, despite being surrounded by friends and family, she had encountered loneliness the likes of which she had never known.

She was beautiful, her daughter; the impatient little girl who had refused to endure forty weeks' incubation and had wanted to be on the outside and in her mother's arms rather than remain in her tummy until her due date.

Nathan was by Kirsty's side, gazing down in wonder on his newborn child; still shocked to the core but already in love with this perfect little girl.

As we whispered our hellos and offered congratulations, Nathan struggled to contain his emotions.

"I wasn't around for Jack's birth; I was too immature to be there for my wife and await my son's arrival at the business end. If you'd suggested that I might be present for this, I'm ashamed to say I would have taken off faster than the speed of light. But I *was* here and it was happening before I even had time to make sense of it, let alone make a bolt for the door.

And it was such a wondrous, wonderful thing…I mean, so much noise and goo…but to see her head appear, to hold Kirsty's hand as our daughter entered the world and to hear that first cry…it's the most special time…something you can never get back…I can't believe I nearly missed it…I've been so stupid and selfish…"

I understood what the nurse meant about daddy being an emotional mess. He had a lot of making up to do, a tremendous amount of ground to cover. But, as he clearly bore the scars of Kirsty's agony (deep nail wounds in his forearm and hand where she had dug her talons in when in the final throes of labour), I would let him off for now. All my raging anger of earlier had subsided and I felt choked up with love myself…for this new life that had surprisingly joined us on what had promised to be a dull, dreary Saturday…for my best friend who had suffered throughout this pregnancy and had produced her first child…a little bit for the gibbering wreck that was Nathan…and, of course, for David, my David who – as luck would have it – had been with us to share this beautiful day.

Our eyes met, over the top of Kirsty's sweaty head which was lowered to gently kiss her daughter, and I saw reflected in David's eyes what was in my own. So much love; too much love. And also some loss – the loss of the opportunity to have our own child together; a part of me and a part of him that would go on to do amazing things in this world; a part of us that would be around when our time on earth was over. I had Chloe, a beautiful, intelligent girl I was unbelievably proud of and who David had already grown to love. But the chance to have a baby together, well that ship had already sailed. It was too late. We were too old, and my body was already changing and putting an end to my baby-making days; I would never be able to bear another child. The euphoria of the day was tinged with melancholy on our parts – but we would never let Kirsty see that – this was her day. And Nathan's, in the end.

Chapter 40

SUZANNE

I had done the right thing. Painful, but necessary.

And I felt at peace with myself and proud that I was winning, against all the odds.

I had a future now – it just wasn't the one I'd envisaged.

I had let him go. Not my Dave now. Somebody else's Dave, or David, or whatever she wanted to call him. In the end, it was just a name. It was what was inside that heart that mattered. And in Dave's heart it was a mass of love for a woman who was my polar opposite; a young girl he'd never even started to get over.

I wished him well. I hoped he was happy now. I hoped he had found everything he had dreamed of for all of his life.

She was the one for him, for sure. Not me. Never me.

But maybe the one for me was out there, somewhere. Maybe here in Portugal, maybe not. I wouldn't be going searching for love – if it happened then that would be wonderful. But if it didn't, I wasn't going to sit around mourning my loss and feeling sorry for myself.

For the first time in my adult life, I was happy to be single. And for the first time since I'd met Dave, I finally felt free.

Chapter 41

LOUISE

After eventually managing to contact Kirsty's shocked mum, and Chloe of course, to deliver the good news, we left mother and baby quietly resting, then drove Nathan to his brother's house to collect his car (they had been out for a few sherberts the previous evening, a night out which I think he was sincerely regretting now). He had been immediately dispatched off to Asda to buy flowers, chocolates and a few toiletries and smaller sized babygrows, and would be returning to the hospital later to spend time with Kirsty and their little bundle of joy. I pitied him when Kirsty came down from her new-mother high and remembered that he had refused outright to consider having another child and had broken up with her as a result. By the Christ, she would make him suffer.

It had only been a few hours since David and Nathan had arrived and yet so much had happened in that short space of time. Waves of exhaustion were lapping over me, and when we arrived home I noticed for the first time how tired David looked. He had, after all, been working all week and then driven all the way from Cornwall, *on a Saturday*, which was to be commended. The house felt chilly and, after letting Fudge outside for a few minutes, I switched on the fire and lay down on the rug in front of it, beckoning to David to join me. His arms circled me, and I hugged them to my waist, his chest pressed up against my back, our tired bodies spooning, breathing as one.

As we drifted off into sleep he gently whispered into my ear, "A lonely boy and a lonely girl…" and I quietly sang back, "…they can't say where they're going…"

Lyrics from "Our Song". So meaningful. So apt. They whirled round and round in my head as I drifted into unconsciousness.

For once I was glad that Chloe was absent from the house, buying a stack of bath bombs and other pricey stuff she didn't need from the Trafford Centre. Whatever happened in the future, I needed David now, and he in turn needed me.

*

"Well, just look at you two lovebirds all warm and cosy in front of the fire!"

I wasn't sure how long we'd been lying there; how long we'd slept for, but the house was in darkness, the front room illuminated only by the glow of the fire. I hadn't heard Chloe's key in the lock so her arrival took us by surprise.

David pulled himself up, and took my hand to haul me up off the floor, both of us feeling the after-effects of lying there for an hour or three. It was strange to think that I could have slept in a builder's skip when I was a teenager and still been raring to go the minute I woke up (except when it was a school day of course).

I kind of liked the two of us being described as "lovebirds". It seemed quite apt. We *were* like two little birds, nuzzling up tightly together in our comfortable nest, me occasionally ruffling my feathers, David having taken flight a couple of times but now back with me and my little chick. And Suzanne – well, she was like a frail little sparrow with a broken wing, who had finally been nursed back to health and was now spreading both of her wings and flying away. Let's hope after her initial migration that she didn't decide to return home in the spring. Who knows, maybe she might even meet a little lovebird of her own on foreign soil.

"Fab news about Kirsty mum...can't believe that crazy lady is actually a fully-fledged mother now! I jumped off the bus near the big Tesco on my way home and bought baby a gorgeous little teddy and a pink hat...proper cute they are! Anyway, don't do me any tea because nan's picking me up in ten minutes and I'm staying with her tonight. She said, *apparently*, that you two need space to talk in private, without me butting in every five minutes...as if I would do that!"

Her cheeky grin confirmed that, given the opportunity, she would DEFINITELY do that!

Bag of treats packed, pjs and change of clothes slung into a shoulder bag, I hugged her tightly and told her I would see her in the morning. David stood almost shyly to one side, probably trying to second-guess Chloe's reaction to his re-appearance – after all he had hurt her as well as me with his disastrous decision to move back into the former matrimonial home to nurse his flailing wifey back to health.

When she stepped up to hug him too he was clearly relieved and glad to move on, although he did add a most sincere "Sorry Chloe, for messing up, and for everything. It's no excuse, but we all make mistakes sometimes, even daft old sods like me."

"I know that. I live in the real world. But, I'm telling you now, if you make another mistake, there will be no further chances – but I think you already realise that. I won't hold a grudge if you look after mum like you did before and make her happy again. But if you hurt her again, there will be a queue of people wanting to knock you out, and I will be at the front of it. Okay?"

"Okay. Message understood. But I'll never cock up again, I promise. Whatever happens, whatever your mum decides – whether she still wants me or not - I won't ever hurt her again; you have my word on that."

"Good. Now lend us a tenner. Ha ha, only joking mum…I have at least…ooh let me count…50p left in my purse to last me all week."

"Be gone with you, scavenging child!" I laughed, proud and touched that she had stood up for me and had got her point across to David.

The departure of Chloe, in a flash of bodyspray and air kisses, into mum's awaiting car, left the two of us alone once again – and it wasn't awkward, but I did wonder what was next for us. As I walked into his arms again, I knew one thing, I was going to take a leaf out of Kirsty's book. Maybe we could sort things out and this would be a fresh start for us or, perhaps, a continuation of what had gone before, but without the shitty, painful stuff in the middle. However, if I couldn't leave the past in the past and this was going to be the end of the road for us, there was something I really, really wanted to do. And it had to be before we attempted the peace talks – because if all that went downhill fast then it might be too late afterwards.

"Excuse me for ten minutes," I told David, switching on the television for him. "I won't be long."

Ten minutes, thirty minutes – all the same really. It took me half an hour to shower and change into my sexiest underwear and my favourite red Quiz skater-dress that I knew David loved. I dried my hair of-a-fashion, hoping he could excuse the shaggy dog look, but applied my make-up carefully, scrubbed my teeth and, even though we weren't going to be leaving the house again tonight, my highest strappy, sparkly shoes went on. After quickly checking that the bedding was reasonably clean and that Chloe hadn't spilt tea all over my duvet cover or left it full of toast crumbs again, I stood at the top of the stairs, hoping that David hadn't nodded off in the half hour I'd been missing.

Thankfully, he hadn't, so when I shouted his name, he came straight up, and his eyes were almost out on stalks when he saw me. Good. Whatever the future held for us, I wanted him to remember me like this – not in my dirty old scruffs or Disney pyjamas.

"Louise," he breathed. "I was just wondering what you were doing up here...but now I know. Christ you look beautiful. Is this...is this for me?"

"Yes, David, of course it is. Because you've only ever been the one for me. And I need you so badly it actually physically hurts. I think the phrase is "gagging for it". Not with anyone else though. Just you. That's if you want to, of course."

"Bloody hell, of course I want to, you gorgeous woman. But I don't want you to think I'm taking advantage of you, when we haven't even talked or made any decisions yet..."

"Oh, please, take advantage all you want, and then we'll talk later. I'm all yours, any which way you want. Now do you want to take this dress off me, or shall I?"

"Me. Please. God, let me unzip it and then you can unzip me and...Christ...is that a life-size cardboard George Michael propped in the corner?"

"Yes, David, it is."

"And presumably he's staying there?"

"Yes, David, he is."

"So, we're going to do this with him watching?"

"Sounds like a plan to me."

"Good god, I must love you Lou."

"You do. And I love you. Now are you going to keep me waiting any longer?"

I didn't get a reply. In one swift movement he was in my personal space, unzipping the dress with one hand whilst his other hand crept up the skirt. What followed was, I'm sure, the best sex I've ever had in my life. There's usually what I call "love sex" – when each party takes their time, caressing and stroking and prolonging the act – and then there's also hard, fast fucking that blows your mind. This was a combination of the two, and when it was over, when he was spent and I was panting like I'd just jogged a mile up a hill, I clung on to him, not caring how hot and sweaty we both were. Not caring that my stockings were ripped to shreds and that the rest of my underwear had took a hit as well. Not caring that there was a heap of dirty washing on the floor by the bed that I'd forgotten to shift earlier. I felt like I'd waited all of my life to experience this and, if I'm honest, I wanted to cling on until he was good to go again. Which I'm sure wouldn't be long now.

I knew he felt the same way. Now definitely wasn't the time for talking. Apart from a little swearing and a lot of panting, we chose to go with actions rather than words.

"Kneel up Lou," he eventually growled, which would have been pretty scary if it had come from anyone but him. Well it would have been rude to refuse, so I assumed the position.

Although I would never have thought it possible, that night just resulted in me loving him even more. It's like we had formed a connection on another level, that had always been there somewhere, but had just needed cementing in place. I was scared to let go of him – to break the spell and lose some of the magic – and even when we weren't making love, I was curled into his chest or holding his hand under the duvet.

Some time in the early hours, we nipped downstairs to grab a drink of orange juice from the fridge to top up some fluids and stave off possible dehydration. He sat on one of the rickety old kitchen chairs, a bloody vision in just his black boxer shorts, and I brazenly straddled his legs, hoping the chair would take my additional weight. My only item of clothing was a pair of never-before-worn French knickers (I'd bought them because I'd thought they looked sexy and chic but they'd been shoved in the back of my underwear drawer since about 1992), and as my boobs wobbled up and down, I said my prayers that my nosy neighbour wouldn't be out of bed at such an early hour, as I'd omitted to close the blinds the previous evening, when passion had dominated over practicality.

"We have to talk Lou."

Aw jeez. The spell was broken. I knew I couldn't put it off any longer but I'd wanted the high of the night to last forever. I buried my head in his chest, reluctantly muttering, "I know David. You go first."

"I think you know what I'm going to say. I am so, so sorry for the pain I have caused you Lou. I had my priorities all wrong, trying so hard to be Suzanne's saviour, when the most beneficial way to help her would have been to walk away from her for good and let her stand on her own two feet for once in her life. I was unbelievably stupid and it kills me inside that we have lost all of this time together, having only just found each other again. But I can't change what I did. The same as you can't change what happened on the beach in Newquay in 1984. The same as I can't change what a stubborn fool I was afterwards…I'm stuck with what I've done in the past unfortunately. But the present and the future, well that's a whole different ball game."

"Yes, but the road ahead is clear now so that's easy for you to say. But what if *she* comes back with a whole new bag of dirty tricks and obstacles she can throw in front of us? What if that road gets blocked again? How will I know that you won't be sucked back into that toxic relationship? How will I know that you won't break my already-knackered heart again?"

"It's a big ask, but I'm begging you to trust me again. You know that I love you with all of my heart and I always have. I'm nothing without you. But we can't really try to make this work again if the trust has gone. You have to believe me and try to forget what's in the past if we can enjoy our future together. Because it will be an amazing future, I can promise you. And I don't just mean the sex. Because, Christ, that is amazing. Spectacular. We were on fire last night, on it like two twenty-somethings who had just found out the end of the world was nigh. But can you trust me Louise? It all rests on that. Can you push all the other crap to one side and live your best life with me, without punishing me for all the mistakes I've made in the past? Can you?"

I don't know where the tears came from but suddenly they were streaming down my cheeks and on to David's bare chest. I so badly wanted to assure him that all was forgiven and we could continue as if nothing had ever happened, and drag him back upstairs to my bed, but now was not the time to bury my real feelings. I had to be straight with him.

"I just don't know babe. To be honest with you, I'm terrified of losing you again, especially to *her*. I'm scared to death that you will leave me in the lurch again; I just don't think my fragile little heart could take it. I *want* to put all of my trust in you again but I don't know how to bring that back – the trust that I once invested in you. How do I get over that? How do I stop myself from imagining all kinds every time you go back down to Newquay? How can I stop myself from being on edge every time you receive a text; every time I walk in on a call? How do I forget these last few god-awful months? I want to wipe the slate clean, because god knows I love you enough and I can't bear the thought of spending the rest of my life without you…but I'm just not sure if I can."

I slid down from his lap and reached over to yank an almost-dry, seen-better-days sweatshirt off the radiator and pulled it on – somehow it just didn't feel right, having such a serious conversation with my boobs swinging freely about and all my spare tyres visible and stacked up.

Pulling out another chair, I plonked myself down on it, wondering what the hell was wrong with me. Why couldn't I be like other people who would take the attitude that what's done is done, and get on with their life and endeavour to be happy? The last few hours had brought me such joy and a sense of fulfilment and yet here I was, waving that white flag again and practically waving David goodbye. I could see from his face that I hadn't said what he'd wanted to hear, but I'd had to be truthful. What was the point in lying at this stage?

He stood up abruptly, his face tense and frustrated. "I'm angry Lou. Not with you – but with myself for allowing this to happen to us. For taking away that positive, joyful woman and making you so sad and distrustful. I've tried to give you space and time and hope that it would be enough. I actually came here yesterday to tell you that the house sale's gone through. It's not my property anymore. And it's not Suzanne's either – and her half share is already in her bank account. And I also now have the funds from the disposal of the business in my account to add to the proceeds of the sale. I'm working for White's as an employee now – on a rolling contract basically which I can walk away from whenever I like. And all the other assets have either been sold on or divided up. Wait – there's one more thing. I wanted to commence divorce proceedings but Suzanne pipped me to the post! So instead of irreconcilable differences I'm now going to be outed as an adulterer. But you know what? I don't give a shit. In fact, in these circumstances, it's great to be the bad boy. Because I got to commit adultery with you! And it's not as if it was just some fly-by-night affair. Me and you, this is for life. At least it's what I want."

"You know I want it too!" I did, I really did. But if the trust was gone…

"So there you have it. We are trying to fast-track the divorce as far as we are able to. And, because everything else was so amicable, we have sold everything up and divvied everything out in record time. The solicitors were almost redundant. So, now I truly am a free man. Now it has to be down to you. Please think about it carefully Lou. Please try and forgive me and learn to trust me again. I don't know how I'll live without you if you can't. See…you're making ME cry now!"

His tears were less obvious but present all the same and I could see he was desperately hoping for an immediate answer – but I just couldn't say yes. I needed some quiet time to digest everything and David, of course, sensed that was the case. I was still devastated to see him run upstairs though to pull his clothes back on. I looked at the clock – only seven-fifteen now – where was he going to disappear to at this early hour? I hoped not back down to Cornwall, not yet – and I didn't want him falling asleep at the wheel; he'd had so little sleep over the weekend.

He kissed me gently on the cheek before saying, "Think about everything Lou. And remember, I love you."

And then he was gone, and I was sat alone in the kitchen, half-dressed and fully gob-smacked. I stared into space for quite some time whilst trying to make sense of everything in my head. David's arrival, Kirsty's baby, the night of intense passion, the revelations regarding his divorce and division of their assets….and the ultimatum I was now faced with.

To say, "Sorry David, can't trust you anymore", and watch him walk back out of my life – well, that was unthinkable. To say I trusted him whilst not really *knowing* if I did, purely to keep him – well that was unacceptable. Which only left trusting him implicitly as I had before, so we could spend the rest of our lives together – but was that unachievable? My head was spinning, and I could hardly ring Kirsty for advice while she was installed on the maternity ward, demanding she put down that baby and give me her thoughts on the situation.

And the other girls were good friends and great sports but bloody useless when it came to doling out advice - sensible or otherwise.

I toyed with the idea of calling Jenny, who was very similar in so many ways to my little new-mum partner in crime, but I didn't think it would have been fair. David was living with her and Billy now, and their assortment of cute but cheeky monkeys, and it would have been difficult for her to remain impartial.

Chloe mainly saw everything in black and white and was most definitely in Camp David, so to speak – not that I could ring her before eleven o'clock on a Sunday ("It's a day of rest!").

Mum was out of the question because she had reached that stage in life when her philosophy had become "Life's too short"…and I fear her judgement would be a little clouded by the fact that she adored David and got on like a house on fire with his parents.

My sister Sarah would definitely instruct me to tell him to fuck right off! Even though she has a soft spot for him, and even though he hadn't actually been unfaithful to me while he had been living under Suzanne's roof again, her mantra was still "all men are bastards", stating that they were all only one step away from adultery, despite having bagged herself a decent husband who hadn't dared even glance at another woman in all the time they had been married.

And I'd only ask my brother Neil for his views on my quandary if I wanted a bloody good laugh.

Tossing a coin didn't seem like much of an option.

So I did what any reasonable woman would do in my position. I ate a shed-load of chocolate ice cream straight from the freezer at the crack of dawn, I ran a stupidly hot bath, and I lay there in it, bubbles spilling over the side, as I sobbed along to my favourite Wham! cd and wondered just how other people got their shit together, when I couldn't for the life of me seem to get the hang of it.

The trouble was, David had crossed a line when he'd put Suzanne's needs and feelings before mine. I wonder how he would feel if he came back and I'd installed Richard in the third bedroom, complete with his bullshit and saggy underpants. No, I couldn't do that, even in the name of revenge. I'd probably last about an hour in my ex-husband's company before fastening some cheese wire across the stairs and digging him a shallow grave in the back garden.

Besides, I wasn't in the business of evening up scores. I just wanted us to be deliriously happy like I knew we could be, if only I could forgive David and crack on.

I was pretty peeved off that he'd disappeared; by ten o'clock I seriously felt sick and was half out of my mind – if this was a taster of my future life without David then I didn't much fancy it. Christ, I missed him like crazy already and he'd only been gone three hours!

By ten-thirty I just felt angry. Where the hell had he gone? Why had he not texted to say where he was? Maybe he was intending to give me some space and I wouldn't see him again until next week or next month or next bloody year, and we weren't going to resolve this after all any time soon. Men!

No freaking way was I texting him though; he could piss off if he thought I was ringing him either.

Lunchtime saw me ringing him, of course – willpower out of the window again. But no answer! Was I actually going mad? Maybe I was invisible.

When my mobile eventually rang I practically jumped on it, but it wasn't him. However, it was lovely to hear from Kirsty direct from her hospital bed. She was doing okay – but being kept in for another day or so as her temperature was slightly high and baby girl (as yet unnamed) had a touch of jaundice. To be honest I think she was pretty relieved they weren't discharging her yet – she was enjoying being treated to the care of the fabulous nurses of the NHS and seemed terrified of being let loose out into the big wide world with her little one, despite, it would seem, Nathan being around now to ease the burden

She had a selection of visitors lined up for the day so I said I'd see her, hopefully, the next evening after work – whether she was still in hospital at that stage or back at her mum's house.

She didn't really mention David, and I didn't want to take the limelight off her new arrival by rabbiting on about my never-ending troubles, so I kept it all in, and consequently felt like screaming and shouting when I finished the call and was left alone with my thoughts again.

Resigned to a day of housework and a life of loneliness, I sulked and stomped around, but was ecstatic to finally receive a text message from David.

"Sorry had to leave but necessary. We need to speak & think we need to get out of house to do it (Otherwise end up in bed!). Meet me at Bull @ 7. Love you babe xx"

Christ, what was going on? Why 'The Bull'? We'd not been there since his birthday party; maybe he wanted me to remember what a fantastic night it had been and how wonderful we were – *are* – together? He did really like The Bull and had joined in some banter with the landlord, Dirty Brian (he wasn't a pervert, he'd just told one really rude, funny joke that had spread like wildfire on the night he took over the tenancy of the pub, and the nickname had stuck).

Running the iron over my work clothes, I pondered over whether this could possibly be our last supper together, or whether we could come to a truce and all would be well from hereon in.

I knew one thing; if there was a chance it might be the last time he saw me, then it wouldn't be in tatty old clothes again, with my hair stuck out at all angles. No, I was going to dig out something decent from that old wardrobe of mine – chuck on some gladrags, slap on some make-up, tame my badly-behaved hair into the style it was supposed to be in, and show up with a smile on my face, however I felt inside.

*

For crying out loud, still no petrol in the sodding car. I didn't want to chance it, trying to limp along to the nearest garage. The way my luck was going, it would conk out on that one stretch of road where there were hardly any street lamps or houses and I would have to hobble along in my high heels, turn up late and probably find that he had given up and left.

Taxi it was then. I rang rent-a-wreck, who weren't the cleanest but at least you knew they would turn up. I was tempted to sit on my coat on the back seat to protect my suede skirt but I didn't want to offend the tattooed, toothless driver who was more than a little odd, but seemed quite harmless anyway.

The journey was spent listening to him waffle on about Rugby League and taxi-vomiters, and I couldn't wait to jump out at the other end. Tipping him heftily, just so I could get rid of him quickly by not waiting for my change, I straightened my skirt, pulled my little top down and hoped my favourite perfume would mask the smoky smell that had filled my lungs in the taxi.

Noticing that I was already five minutes late, I pushed open the double doors to the bar area, hoping that it wouldn't be packed full of students and under-age drinkers, making me feel older than old.

"SURPRISE!"

I almost jumped out of my skin as David, dressed in a carbon copy of my favourite black jeans and black shirt combination (the originals were still languishing in a bin bag in my bedroom), leapt out in front of me and for the first time I glanced around the room and found myself actually speechless.

There, on every available wall, mirror and notice board, were pictures of George Michael. Photocopied, enlarged and erected for my pleasure.

Bloody hell. And there was a Wham! track blasting from the wall-mounted speakers.

David nervously steered me in the direction of the wall nearest to the bar area.

Oh. There, next to the super-sized television screen, was pinned an absolutely enormous poster, with the 1980s photograph of the two of us indecently enlarged at the top and a more recent photo of us huddled together with Chloe at the bottom. But it was the huge words printed in between these pictures that caught my attention.

Wondering what the hell was going on, I slowly began to read out loud.

"Louise.

You got to have *Faith*. When we first met we were *Young Guns* but I thought you were *Amazing*. I never gave up hope of seeing you again – I was *Waiting For That Day*. I'm not one of the *Bad Boys* and I don't want my *Freedom*. I still think you're *Flawless* so let's give us just *One More Try*. You know it babe, I love you and quite simply, *I'm Your Man*.

David."

OH MY GOOD GOD.

Only David could love me enough to do something like this. Only he would ever go to this much effort to get all of this done in such a short space of time – I'm guessing Nathan's brother Keith who works in printing had a hand in it. Not one other man, not even my ex-husband – *especially* not my ex-husband – had cared enough, had been thoughtful enough to incorporate George's back catalogue into a declaration of love for me, so publicly as well.

Thank Christ he'd left out *I Want Your Sex* though or I would have been the butt of filthy jokes in the pub for years to come.

For about the trillionth time in the last year, my eyes filled up with tears, but this time for all the right reasons.

Turning to look at David, I noticed for the first time that look of steely determination across his face.

He took one step towards me.

"I hope you like it Lou. Bri's kept this bar area private for the time being so I could turn it into your own personal George lounge. Please tell me you love it. It's a good job the printing was done by someone you know, or otherwise they would have thought I had serious issues. I mean it though babe, everything it says on that poster and so much more besides. There's only ever been you for me. I love you more than you can ever comprehend and I just don't work without you. I've asked you to give me another chance; I've begged you to let me in again; I've *shown* you what effect you have on me…"

"I know David…I know you have…and…"

"Nope. Stop. Right there. Because I can see you're about to start dithering again and I am NOT taking no for an answer this time. I'm done with being such a wimp and letting you slip away quietly. Even if you fire me off today, I will be back tomorrow. And if you still say no then, well I'll be back the day after that. And the day after. And the day after. And…well you get the point. I'm not giving up on you…on us. Even if you punish me and make me pay for what I did for the rest of my life, I'll have to just suck it up – because I deserve it anyway. And it's a small price to pay for spending the rest of my life with you."

It would have been rude to turn him down then. And pretty stupid. And I've done a lot of stupid things in my time but this wasn't going to be another one. Just what was I achieving by sending him away again anyway? I couldn't stop loving him, he couldn't stop loving me, and what we had was too special to let go.

Plus I was dying to bump into Miss Waite in the supermarket again just to say "Ha! You may have a man now but I have THIS man…beat that, you nutjob!"

A tiny smile escaped from my lips as I said, "Listen, Captain Caveman. You might rue the day you ever said you'd put up with me making you pay for the rest of your life! I won't, of course, but I can't promise there won't be times when I ridiculously question your whereabouts or sling something at you in an argument. Not that we'll ever argue, of course."

His eyes were shining bright now, daring to hope that I was taking him back.

He took a second step towards me.

"Does that mean what I think it means?"

"You know it does. Don't ever hurt me again though David White. Because this is your very last, final, ultimate chance…got it?"

His third step brought him directly in front of me again; my chest against his, his fingers reaching out to take my hand, his lips moving closer to gently kiss mine.

"Got it. I'll take care of you, and Chloe, and Fudge and Cardboard-cut-out-George…and you'll never regret being my girlfriend again, and I'll be so proud to be your boyfriend."

"Girlfriend? Boyfriend? Really? It's like we're teenagers all over again. Back to that sacred summer."

"A lonely boy and a lonely girl."

"Dancing to our song underneath the stars."

 "Seventeen and falling in love for the very first time."

"And the very last time."

"On the beautiful beaches of Newquay."

"Back where it all began."

"But never really ended."

"My Louise."

"My David. Always my David."

EPILOGUE

JULY 2017

LOUISE

Suzanne never did return to Newquay, having opted to settle permanently in Portugal. I thought she would eventually shack up with a Mediterranean god who was rich in compliments and spirit as well as in monetary terms, but to my surprise, she quietly said "I do" again – apparently the groom was an old musician friend from the UK who had also been married before and who had always been waiting in the wings, or so her mother said.

We actually bumped into her mother and father one day while out shopping in Newquay. I can't say her mum was overly friendly, although she was polite, but her dad was a real sweetheart, thanked David for having been a wonderful son-in-law over the years, apologised for what their daughter had put him through and smilingly told me he was glad that "Dave" had found himself a lovely lady like myself. I wanted to kiss him for his kind gesture and words but just in time remembered exactly whose father he was, so instead gave him a genuine smile in return, quietly thanked him and we said our goodbyes.

Billy remains completely henpecked by Jenny but loves it and wouldn't have it any other way. The eldest of their offspring, a big lad named Karl with a mass of hair and a jelly belly, who is actually a kind-hearted soul with a goofy grin like his dad, had a brush with the law and I believe his mum almost knocked ten bells out of him and grounded him for, oh, at least six months. Needless to say, he hasn't strayed since. It's unfortunate for them all that they do all look like little thugs, when in fact they're just high-spirited cheeky monkeys who have no fear and no filter. I can't think where they get it from.

We sadly lost Fudge early last year and we were all heartbroken. At least the old fella passed away peacefully in his sleep, in his comfy old basket, bowing out of the most charmed of lives, having loved and been loved for almost fourteen years. David tentatively and gently enquired if we'd like to consider buying another dog, not to replace Fudge but to fill that empty part of our lives and that empty corner in the kitchen, but we've declined for now. I'm thinking next time around it will be a rescue dog we shower our affection on and take into our hearts...but it will be a little while before we take the plunge yet.

Nathan is still atoning for his sins. To the surprise of her life, when Kirsty left hospital with their baby, Nathan had fitted the car seat into his Mercedes and drove her straight to his house where he had installed the bassinet into the main bedroom and erected a brand new top-of-range cot in the small third bedroom. He had also, god love him, worked long into the night every night that Kirsty remained in hospital stripping and decorating that particular bedroom and transforming it into a little pink nursery for the new arrival – David and I having selected and purchased the wallpaper and other fittings on a mad dash to B & Q, flashing David's credit card willy nilly whilst making puppy dog eyes at each other.

Having had a dickie fit when she was firmly told she wasn't returning to her mum's following her release from hospital (kept in there for four days in total – driving all the poor nurses and medical staff insane), Kirsty's face was a picture when she entered Nathan's house and initially saw all of the baby bunting and banners pinned across the lounge, followed by all of Nathan's handiwork and hard work in the upstairs rooms. She handled her tiny little bundle to me while she (finally) headed into Nathan's arms, sobbing – and still calling him a dickhead but at least thanking him and telling him she loved him. He'd declared his love for her several times, both publicly and privately, since she'd had the baby and was clearly relieved that he hadn't completely blown it after all. I have to say though, it's a brave man who takes an angry Kirsty on, and I think he ate humble pie at least once a day for that first year.

And their beautiful little girl, well they finally bestowed the most gorgeous of names on her – Beatrice Rose. I had tried to persuade her to go for "Georgia Michelle" as a tribute to my wonderful George, but she was having none. The 'Rose' bit I understood as it was Kirsty's much-missed grandmother's name. 'Beatrice', rather than having any royal connections, was actually the name of a lady who had practically brought up Nathan and his sibling when his mother had run off with the Betterware man; a lady who had been kindness personified when she'd taken care of the two boys while their dad was at work, and she even helped them financially through college and, in the absence of any children of her own, left them a considerable amount of money in her Will. Nathan had relayed this touching story to Kirsty one night over dinner and she had never forgotten it. When she had informed Nathan that she wanted to name their little girl 'Beatrice' he had choked up and it had dawned on him there and then just what a woman he had, unwillingly it has to be said, chosen to be the mother of his daughter.

Beatrice, whilst stunningly beautiful with her big brown eyes and her head full of curls, had now hit the terrible twos and Kirsty was on the receiving end of the screaming Abdabs almost on a daily basis. To Nathan's relief, I think it had put Kirsty off wanting any more kiddies, and besides – she'd only just fitted back into her leather kecks after the first one.

Chloe sailed through her exams making me proud as punch, but I was gutted when she announced that she no longer wanted to be a vet and was taking a year out after school to decide what she wanted to do with her life. I think her work experience at the local veterinary practice, coupled with the loss of Fudge, had opened her eyes to the reality of working with animals and dealing with birth and death every day, and she no longer wanted to be part of it.

She began waiting tables in a restaurant close to home, just to put her on until something better came along and she knew where she was heading, but she turned out to be a fantastic waitress and loved the job. She won employee of the month more often than she didn't, and each time a promotion came up she was successful. Hard to believe when she is still only seventeen, but she is already head waitress and is looking to be an assistant manager when she turns eighteen in a few months time. She works all the hours god sends and she has definitely earned her success. God knows, she must get her work ethic from me rather than her father - the bloody slacker.

Speaking of Rick the Dick, he had the brass front to turn up on my doorstep after all! He'd made the mistake of ringing Chloe first though when he was on his way, and she promptly locked up the house and darted straight over to her nan's. Our next door neighbour said he had turned up in a taxi and spent a good ten minutes hollering through the letterbox and banging on the door, before she came out and gave him a piece of her mind. Undeterred, he made his way over to mum's house, but she soon gave him short shrift – taking great delight in telling him he had ceased being part of our family the day he abandoned his wife and daughter for some silly young airhead and then pointing him in the direction of the nearest Travel Lodge. Reluctant at the best of times to part with any money, he descended on his parents instead, who put up with about a week of his sponging and bullshit before telling him it was about time he stood on his own two feet for once in his life. The last update I had from Chloe was that he was now working somewhere in deepest darkest Scotland and was doing a merry dance with some rich widow. Best of luck to her – she would need it.

Chloe had finally decided to give her father a wide berth after proclaiming she was sick and tired of having to keep up the pretence of liking him, and declaring that she had better things to do with her spare time than spend it on the train to and from Inverness. She genuinely didn't seem to miss him and was so busy with work and her social life that she really didn't have time to slot a poor excuse for a father into her stupidly busy timetable.

Josh was now back on the scene. After a couple of unsavoury boyfriends, one of whom had tried to pressurise Chloe into having sex she had confessed one night (and who hadn't been seen within a mile radius of our house since David had visited him to have a "quiet word"), she had realised that the grass wasn't greener on the other side after all and had appreciated what a good lad Josh was. He too had experienced playing the field and hadn't liked it one bit. He had sent her the world's biggest bouquet of flowers on her birthday and, just like that, it was all back on again. I had to concede, they did make a lovely couple. She was developing into a stunning young woman and he was maturing nicely.

My house was on the market and under offer, but it was a weird one for me. On the one hand I was excited about what lay ahead for me and David, on the other hand, disposing of the house had stirred up a lot of mixed emotions for me. That building was full of memories, some good, some bad. I'd been so happy when Richard and I had first collected the keys and embarked on our married life there, and initially we did have some good times – but they were all tainted now with the knowledge that the man was a prick, through and through.

But I remembered bringing Chloe home and watching her sleep in that little Moses Basket at the end of our bed, and later moving her into her own room to sleep in her cot, the sides of which we later dropped down to provide her very first bed. She fell out of it several times and nearly gave me a heart attack, and once drew all over her newly decorated walls with a marker pen she had nicked out of my handbag, but the less said about that, the better.

There had been other great times – meals and gatherings and parties and nights when Kirsty and I had literally cried with laughter, taking the rise out of almost everyone we knew behind their backs, for our own amusement.

And of course, there had been more recent memories made there, of days and nights spent with David, rediscovering our love for each other – yes, we'd had what shall officially be known forever as "the hiccup" – but everything else had been wonderful…and it was just as well that those walls couldn't talk….

But now it was time to move on. David's share of his former home, the business and the joint bank accounts had actually resulted in a rather hefty, healthy bank balance, and after my years of struggling and just getting by, a quick call to the mortgage company had, to my surprise, confirmed that a current sale of my property, taking into account today's market conditions, would mean a profit for me of approximately sixty-three thousand pounds. Loaded!

We had been spending so much time down in Newquay again that it made sense to reconsider our options. Once I'd realised that Suzanne was long gone, and even if she came back, it wouldn't affect my relationship with David, I'd fallen in love with Newquay all over again. When the rain stopped and the sun shone, we'd make the most of it and sunbathe on Towan Beach, or we'd pack a picnic and visit the gardens of Trenance Park. I'd been welcomed into the heart of David's family, and although his parents' home was tiny in comparison to the house he himself had previously owned, they insisted that we cram into the little second bedroom, "roughing it" as they described it – something that had never happened with Suzanne, as his parents suspected that their clean but cluttered house was not somewhere she felt she could even take her shoes off and relax.

We socialised an awful lot with Jenny and Billy and their assortment of slightly peculiar but actually lovely friends and on a couple of occasions it felt like I was right back in the '80s again, when we decamped to the beach and partied into the small hours, dancing to the strains of Shalamar and Billy Ocean and other such classics from my teenage years.

When David was offered a great job at a company just outside of Newquay, overseeing a team of tradesmen and training new members of staff, it was an offer we just couldn't refuse. The pay was more than we could have anticipated, for rather less hours than he was used to putting in, so we had to give it a go. I didn't need asking twice if I wanted to jack my job in because I was desperate for a change in career! For the time being we could survive without my wages, and it may be that I would just need to do a few hours a week, maybe even seasonal work, to top up our funds.

Chloe had almost snatched my hand off when I'd suggested that she ask for a transfer within the company and join us in Newquay. Apparently she'd already made preliminary enquiries, "just in case"!

I was consumed with guilt though at the prospect of leaving mum behind. I knew she had my sister and brother and other family members and friends to make sure she was okay and not too lonely, but I still fretted over moving away from her. Until she sternly told me to stop being such a silly girl, to give my head a wobble, and that in any event she would be splitting her time now between her own home in Wigan and whatever place we bought in Newquay! She'd finally returned to the holiday destination we'd visited year after year with my dad and she had made peace with it, re-discovering her passion for the amazing scenery and the dramatic coastline.

House prices in Newquay were extortionate but we managed to find a three bedroomed house in need of some work. We were going to stay with David's parents until it was habitable, as there was apparently going to be an army of helpers and tradesmen in and out of there once we exchanged contracts and all I had to do was keep them in food and beer – although not too much beer until the clock ticked past five o'clock in the afternoon, David warned me.

And David…David, David, David. He had certainly come through on his promises so far. He had assured me that I would never have reason to doubt him again and it was looking as if he was going to be proved right. The man was rock solid – dependable, trustworthy and clean of conscience. And, god damn it, he was still so handsome! Once he'd moved back in with me, and his mind was a worry-free zone, he was eating healthily and substantially again, laughing like a drain and, let's just say, getting his fair share of physical exercise, if you know what I mean.

It was as if the years had just melted away and we were back to being silly teenagers again, just without the dubious 1980s fashion sense and slightly more worldly wise.

Don't get me wrong…it hasn't all been sunshine and roses – we'd already had our fair share of ups and downs but we'd weathered them all, together.

When Fudge passed away and David's dad had a major health scare in the same week, we were there to look after each other. When Chloe was having a tough time at work briefly due to some bullying tantics employed by an older member of staff, he stopped me from going kicking their head in and gave Chloe some sensible advice on how to deal with it. When some lowlife pinched a load of his tools out of his van, I helped to track down some of the stolen gear on-line and spent hours scouring ads looking for replacements for a decent price.

And when my beloved George passed away, unexpectedly, on Christmas Day 2016, he sat me down and gently broke the news to me and held me in his arms while I wept and screamed angrily about the unfairness of life and the loss of this lovely man. He also drove me all the way down to London to lay flowers outside of George's Highgate home; waiting patiently in the freezing cold for precisely three hours while I sobbed along with other fans, reading tributes that had been left there and taking endless photographs.

He didn't even flinch when I insisted on making the pilgrimage to George's Oxfordshire home on his birthday, to celebrate with hundreds of other fans. He quietly sat on the grass verge in the sunshine and listened to me singing along out of tune and whooping as two local policeman joined in with a particularly raucous version of 'Outside'. Billy said he was off his rocker but David insisted it was all in the name of love.

He accepted that me and George came as a package, and promised that wherever we lived, cardboard-cut-out-George could come with us. Chloe said I needed my bumps testing. David did of course respond by saying that he would gladly test my bumps, in private of course. She said he was a dirty old perv.

I have to say, when I pick the love of my life (George having always been unavailable), I pick a good one. When Billy nearly knocked my head off with that football on Towan Beach all those summers ago when I was just seventeen, and David came over to apologise to me, despite the fact that I gave him a load of abuse in return, my heart did somersaults, my mind was blown, my body was weak, and I knew in that very first moment that my life would never be the same again.

From the second he came over and spoke to me, he ceased to be 'Dave', whether he liked it or not.

He became 'David' – my man, my heart, my life, my everything.

The closest thing to heaven I have ever known.

Also by Antonia K. Lewis

I Called Him David

Visit

www.antoniaklewis.com

for exclusive news, blog and photographs!

You can also find Antonia on Facebook, Instagram and Twitter: **www.twitter.com/AntoniaKLewis2**

Printed in Germany
by Amazon Distribution
GmbH, Leipzig